Praise for

'A writer who has created a world of her own – a world claustrophobic and irrational which we enter each time with a sense of personal danger … Miss Highsmith is the poet of apprehension' GRAHAM GREENE

'Highsmith is a giant of the genre. The original, the best, the gloriously twisted Queen of Suspense' MARK BILLINGHAM

'One thinks of comparing Miss Highsmith only with herself; by any other standard of comparison, one must simply cheer' AUBERON WAUGH

'Highsmith was every bit as deviant and quirky as her mischievous heroes, and didn't seem to mind if everyone knew it' J. G. BALLARD, *DAILY TELEGRAPH*

'My suspicion is that when the dust has settled and when the chronicle of twentieth-century American literature comes to be written, history will place Highsmith at the top of the pyramid, as we should place Dostoevsky at the top of the Russian hierarchy of novelists' A. N. WILSON, *DAILY TELEGRAPH*

'One of the greatest modernist writers' GORE VIDAL

'One closes most of her books with a feeling that the world is more dangerous than one had ever imagined' JULIAN SYMONS, *NEW YORK TIMES BOOK REVIEW*

'For eliciting the menace that lurks in familiar surroundings, there's no one like Patricia Highsmith' *TIME*

'No one has created psychological suspense more densely and deliciously satisfying' *VOGUE*

'Highsmith should be considered an essential postwar writer who captured the neurotic apprehensions of her times. By her hypnotic art Patricia Highsmith puts the suspense story into a toweringly high place in the hierarchy of fiction' *THE TIMES*

'Highsmith writes the verbal equivalent of a drug – easy to consume, darkly euphoric, totally addictive ... Highsmith belongs in the moody company of Dostoevsky or Angela Carter' *TIME OUT*

'Her novels, with their mysterious non sequiturs, weird pairings and attractions and moments of stifled comedy, have an unearthly sheen all their own ... Highsmith was a genuine one-off, and her books will haunt you' *DAILY TELEGRAPH*

'To call Patricia Highsmith a thriller writer is true but not the whole truth: her books have stylistic texture, psychological depth, mesmeric readability' *SUNDAY TIMES*

'I can't think of anyone else who writes the kind of novel Highsmith does, and can't imagine anyone doing it with a fraction of her frightening talent' *SPECTATOR*

'Patricia Highsmith's novels are peerlessly disturbing ... bad dreams that keep us thrashing for the rest of the night' *NEW YORK TIMES BOOK REVIEW*

'An atmosphere of nameless dread, of unspeakable foreboding, permeates every page of Patricia Highsmith, and there's nothing quite like it' *BOSTON GLOBE*

'Mesmerising ... not to be recommended for the weak-minded and impressionable' *WASHINGTON POST*

VIRAGO
MODERN CLASSICS
607

© Ruth Bernhard

Patricia Highsmith (1921–1995) was born in Fort Worth, Texas, and moved to New York when she was six, where she attended the Julia Richman High School and Barnard College. In her senior year she edited the college magazine, having decided at the age of sixteen to become a writer. Her first novel, *Strangers on a Train*, was made into a classic film by Alfred Hitchcock in 1951. *The Talented Mr Ripley*, published in 1955, introduced the fascinating anti-hero Tom Ripley, and was made into an Oscar-winning film in 1999 by Anthony Minghella. Graham Greene called Patricia Highsmith 'the poet of apprehension', saying that she 'created a world of her own – a world claustrophobic and irrational which we enter each time with a sense of personal danger' and *The Times* named her no.1 in their list of the greatest ever crime writers. Patricia Highsmith died in Locarno, Switzerland, in February 1995. Her last novel, *Small g: A Summer Idyll*, was published posthumously, the same year.

DEEP WATER

Patricia Highsmith

Includes an interview with Gillian Flynn

virago

VIRAGO

This edition published in 2015 by Virago Press

5 7 9 10 8 6 4

First published in the USA by Harper & Brothers 1957
First published in Great Britain by William Heinemann London 1958

A CIP catalogue record for this book
is available from the British Library.

ISBN 978-0-34900-626-0

Typeset in Goudy Oldstyle by M Rules
Printed and bound in Great Britain by
Clays Ltd, Elcograf S.p.A.

Papers used by Virago are from well-managed forests
and other responsible sources.

Virago
An imprint of
Little, Brown Book Group
100 Victoria Embankment
London EC4Y 0DY

An Hachette UK Company
www.hachette.co.uk

www.virago.co.uk

To E. B. H. and Tina

'There is no better dodge than one's own character, because no one believes in it ... '

— *Pyotr Stepanovitch in Dostoevsky's*
THE POSSESSED

I

Vic didn't dance, but not for the reasons that most men who don't dance give to themselves. He didn't dance simply because his wife liked to dance. His rationalization of his attitude was a flimsy one and didn't fool him for a minute, though it crossed his mind every time he saw Melinda dancing: she was insufferably silly when she danced. She made dancing embarrassing.

He was aware that Melinda twirled into his line of vision and out again, but barely aware, he thought, and it was only his familiarity with every physical detail of her that had made him realize that it was she at all. Calmly he raised his glass of Scotch and water and sipped it.

He sat slouched, with a neutral expression on his face, on the upholstered bench that curved around the Mellers' newel post, staring at the changing pattern of the dancers and thinking that when he went home tonight he would take a look at his herb boxes in the garage and see if the foxgloves were up. He was growing several kinds of herbs now, repressing their growth by depriving them of half their normal sunlight and water with a view to intensifying their flavour. Every afternoon he set the boxes in the sun at one o'clock, when he came home for lunch, and put them back into the garage at three, when he returned to his printing plant.

Victor Van Allen was thirty-six years old, of a little less than medium height, inclined to a general firm rotundity rather than fat, and he had thick, crisp brown eyebrows that stood out over innocent blue eyes. His brown hair was straight, closely cut, and like his eyebrows, thick and tenacious. His mouth was middle-sized, firm, and usually drawn down at the right corner with a lopsided determination or with humour, depending on how one cared to take it. It was his mouth that made his face ambiguous – for one could read a bitterness in it, too – because his blue eyes, wide, intelligent, and unsurprisable, gave no clue as to what he was thinking or feeling.

In the last moments the noise had increased a decibel or so and the dancing had become more abandoned in response to the pulsing Latin music that had begun to play. The noise offended his ears, and still he sat, though he knew he could have wandered down the hall to his host's study and browsed among the books there if he had cared to. He had had enough to drink to set up a faint, rhythmic buzzing in his ears, not entirely unpleasant. Perhaps the thing to do at a party, or at any gathering where liquor was available, was to match your drinking with the augmenting noise. Shut the noise out with your own noise. You could set up a little din of merry voices right inside your head. It would ease a great many things. Be never quite sober, never quite drunk. *Dum non sobrius, tamen non ebrius.* A fine epitaph for him, but unfortunately not true, he thought. The plain, dull fact was that most of the time he preferred to be alert.

Involuntarily his eyes focused on the suddenly organizing pattern: a conga line. And involuntarily he found Melinda, smiling a gay catch-me-if-you-can smile over her shoulder, and the man over her shoulder – way over it and practically in her hair, in fact – was Joel Nash. Vic sighed and sipped his drink. For a man

2

who had been up dancing until three last night, and until five the night before, Mr Nash was doing very well.

Vic started, feeling a hand on his left sleeve, but it was only old Mrs Podnansky leaning towards him. He had almost forgotten she was there.

'I can't thank you enough, Vic. You really won't mind picking it up yourself?' She had asked him the same thing five or ten minutes ago.

'Of course not,' Vic said, smiling, standing up as she got up. 'I'll drop around tomorrow at about a quarter to one.'

Just then Melinda leaned towards him, across Mr Nash's arm, and said almost in Mrs Podnansky's face, though she looked at Vic, 'Fuddy-duddy! Why don't you dance?' and Vic saw Mrs Podnansky jump and recover with a smile before she moved away.

Mr Nash gave Vic a happy, slightly tipsy smile as he danced off with Melinda. And what kind of smile would you call that? Vic wondered. Comradely. That was the word. That was what Joel Nash had intended it to be. Vic deliberately took his eyes from Joel, though he had been on a certain train of thought that had to do with his face. It wasn't his manner – hypocritical, half-embarrassed, half-assed – that irritated him so much as his face. That boyish roundness of the cheeks and of the forehead, that prettily waving light-brown hair, those regular features that women who liked him would describe as not *too* regular. Most women would call him handsome, Vic supposed. Vic remembered Mr Nash looking up at him from the sofa as he handed him his empty glass for the sixth or eighth time last night, as if he were ashamed to be accepting another drink, ashamed to be staying fifteen minutes longer, and yet a certain brash insolence had predominated in his face. Up to now, Vic thought, Melinda's boy friends had at least had more brains or less insolence. Joel Nash wouldn't be in the neighbourhood for ever, though. He was a salesman for the Furness-Klein Chemical Company of Wesley,

3

Massachusetts, up for a few weeks of briefing on the company's new products, he had said. If he had been going to make a home in Wesley or Little Wesley, Vic had no doubt that he would take Ralph Gosden's place, regardless of how bored Melinda became with him or what a fluke he turned out to be in other respects, because Melinda was never able to resist what she thought was a handsome face. Joel would be more handsome than Ralph in Melinda's opinion.

Vic looked up and saw Horace Meller standing beside him. 'Hi there, Horace. Looking for a seat?'

'No, thanks.' Horace was a slight, greying man of middle height with a narrow sensitive face and a somewhat bushy black moustache. His mouth under the moustache wore the polite smile of a nervous host. Horace was always nervous, though the party was going as well as any host could have wished. 'What's happening at the plant, Vic?'

'Getting Xenophon ready,' Vic replied. In the din they could not talk very well. 'Why don't you drop around some evening?' Vic meant at the printing plant. He was always there until seven, and by himself after five, because Stephen and Carlyle went home at five.

'All right, I will,' Horace said. 'Is your drink all right?'

Vic nodded that it was.

'I'll be seeing you,' Horace said, moving off.

Vic felt a void as soon as he had left. An awkwardness. Something unsaid, and Vic knew what it was: Horace had tactfully refrained from mentioning Mr Joel Nash. Hadn't said Joel was nice, or welcome, or asked anything about him, or bothered with any of the banalities. Melinda had manoeuvred Joel's invitation to the party. Vic had heard her on the telephone with Mary Meller the day before yesterday: '... Well, not exactly a guest of ours, but we feel responsible for him because he doesn't know many people in town ... Oh, thanks, Mary! I didn't think

4

you'd mind having an extra man, and such a handsome one, too ...' As if anyone could pry Melinda away from him with a crowbar. One more week, Vic thought. Seven more nights exactly. Mr Nash was leaving on the first, a Sunday.

Joel Nash materialized, looming unsteadily in his broad-shouldered white jacket, bringing his glass. 'Good evening, Mr Van Allen,' Joel said with a mock formality and plopped himself down where Mrs Podnansky had been sitting. 'How're you tonight?'

'Oh, as usual,' Vic said, smiling.

'There's two things I wanted to say to you,' Joel said with sudden enthusiasm, as if he had at that very moment thought of them. 'One is I've been asked to stay a couple of weeks longer here – by my company – so I hope I can repay *both* of you for the abundant hospitality you've shown me in the last few weeks and –' Joel laughed in a boyish way, ducking his head.

Melinda had a genius for finding people like Joel Nash, Vic thought. Little marriages of true minds. 'And the second?'

'The second – Well, the second is, I want to say what a brick I think you are for being so nice about my seeing your wife. Not that I have seen her very much, you understand, lunch a couple of times and a drive in the country, but—'

'But what?' Vic prompted, feeling suddenly stone sober and disgusted with Nash's bland intoxication.

'Well, a lot of men would have knocked my block off for less – thinking it was more, of course. I can easily understand why you might be a little annoyed, but you're not. I can see that. I suppose I want to say that I'm grateful to you for not punching my nose. Not that there's been anything to punch it for, of course. You can ask Melinda, in case you're in any doubt.'

Just the person to ask, of course. Vic stared at him with a calm indifference. The proper reply, Vic thought, was nothing.

'At any rate, I wanted to say I think you're awfully sporting,' Nash added.

5

Joel Nash's third affected Anglicism grated on Vic in an unpleasant way. 'I appreciate your sentiments,' Vic said, with a small smile, 'but I don't waste my time punching people on the nose. If I really don't like somebody, I kill him.'

'Kill him?' Mr Nash smiled his merry smile.

'Yes. You remember Malcolm McRae, don't you?' Vic knew that he knew about Malcolm McRae, because Melinda had said that she had told Joel all about the 'McRae mystery', and that Joel had been very interested because he had seen McRae once or twice in New York on business matters.

'Yes,' Joel Nash said attentively.

Joel Nash's smile had grown smaller. It was now a mere protective device. Melinda had undoubtedly told Joel that Mal had had quite a crush on her. That always added spice to the story.

'You're kidding me,' Joel said.

In that instant, from his words and his face, Vic knew two things: that Joel Nash had already made love to his wife, and that his own dead-calm attitude in the presence of Melinda and Joel had made quite an impression. Vic had frightened him – not only now, but on certain evenings at the house. Vic had never shown a sign of conventional jealousy. People who do not behave in an orthodox manner, Vic thought, are by definition frightening. 'No, I'm not kidding,' Vic said with a sigh, taking a cigarette from his pack, then offering the pack to Joel.

Joel Nash shook his head.

'He got a bit forward, as they say – with Melinda. She may have told you. But it wasn't that so much as his entire personality that irked me. His cocksureness and his eternally passing out somewhere, so people'd had to put him up. And his revolting parsimony.' Vic fixed his cigarette in his holder and clamped it between his teeth.

'I don't believe you.'

'I think you do. Not that it matters.'

6

'You *really* killed Malcolm McRae?'

'Who else do you think did?' Vic waited, but there was no answer. 'Melinda told me you'd met him, or knew about him. Did you have any theories? I'd like to hear them. Theories interest me. More than fact sometimes.'

'I haven't any theories,' Joel said in a defensive tone.

Vic noticed a withdrawal, a fear, just in the way Mr Nash was sitting on the bench now. Vic leaned back, raised and lowered his shaggy brown eyebrows, and blew his smoke out straight in front of him.

There was a silence.

Mr Nash was turning over various remarks in his mind, Vic knew. Vic even knew the kind of remark he would make.

'Considering he was a friend of yours,' Joel began, just as Vic had known he would, 'I don't think it's very funny of you to joke about his death.'

'He wasn't a friend of mine.'

'Of your wife's.'

'A different matter, you'll admit.'

Mr Nash managed a nod. Then a sidewise smile. 'I still think it's a pretty poor joke.' He stood up.

'Sorry. Maybe I can do better next time. Oh, just a minute!' Joel Nash turned.

'Melinda doesn't know anything about this,' Vic said, still coolly leaning back against the newel post. 'I'd just as soon you didn't tell her.'

Joel smiled and waved a hand as he walked away. The hand was limp. Vic watched him walk to the other side of the living-room, near Horace and Phil Cowan, who were talking together, but Joel did not try to join them. He stood by himself and took a cigarette. Mr Nash would wake up in the morning still believing it was a joke, Vic thought, though he would be wondering a little, too, enough to ask a few people some questions as to what

Vic Van Allen's attitude towards Malcolm McRae had been. And various people – Horace Meller, for instance, and even Melinda – would tell him that Vic and Mal had never hit it off very well. And the Cowans or Horace or Mary Meller, if pressed, would admit that they had noticed something between Mal and Melinda, nothing more than a little flirting, of course, but ... '

Malcolm McRae had been an advertising executive, not a very important one but there had been an obnoxious air of superiority and patronage about him. He had been the type women call fascinating and men generally loathe. Tall and lean and immaculate, with a long narrow face in which nothing stood out in Vic's memory except a large wart on his right cheek like Abraham Lincoln's, though his eyes were supposed to have been fascinating, too, Vic remembered. And he had been murdered, for no known reason, in his Manhattan apartment by an assailant the police had up to now failed to find. That was why Vic's story had made such an impression on Joel.

Vic relaxed still more against the newel post and stretched his legs out in front of him, recalling with a peculiar relish now how Mal had stood behind Melinda on the golf course with his arms around her, showing her how to make a shot that she could have done better than he if she had wanted to. And that other time, around three in the morning, when Melinda had coyly retreated to her bed with a glass of milk and had asked Mal to come in to talk to her. Vic had stubbornly sat on in the living-room, pretending to read, determined to stay there no matter what time it got to be, so long as Mal was in her room. There was no comparison in their intellects, Mal's and Melinda's, and Mal would have been bored stiff if he had ever had her for half a day to himself. But there had been the little lure of sex. There was always Melinda's little come-on that went something like 'Oh, Vic? I love him, truly I do, but just not in that way. Oh, it's been like this for years. He doesn't care for me that way either, so ... ' with

8

the upturned, expectant, green-brown eyes. Mal had come out of Melinda's room after twenty minutes or so. Vic was sure there hadn't been anything between them, ever. But he remembered a certain satisfaction when he had heard that Mal had been killed last December. Or had it been January? And his first thought had been that Mal might have had it from a jealous husband.

For a few moments Vic imagined that Mal had come back to Melinda's room that night after he had gone to his room on the other side of the garage, that he had known about it, and that he had planned the murder meticulously, gone in to New York on some pretext, called on Mal with a sash weight under his coat (the murderer must have been a friend or an acquaintance, the papers had said, because Mal had evidently let him in quietly), and had battered Mal to death. Silently and efficiently, leaving no fingerprints – neither had the real murderer – then driving back to Little Wesley the same night, giving as an alibi, in case anybody had ever asked him for one, that he had been watching a movie in Grand Central at the time Mal had been murdered, a movie that he would actually have seen, of course, at some other time.

'Victor-r?' Mary Meller bent down towards him. 'What're you pondering?'

Vic slowly stood up, smiling. 'Not a thing. You're looking very peachy tonight.' He was referring to the colour of her dress.

'Thank you. Can't we go and sit down in some corner and you talk to me about something?' Mary asked him. 'I want to see you change your seat. You've been there all evening.'

'The piano bench?' Vic suggested, because it was the only spot in sight where two people could sit next to each other. The dancing, for the moment, had stopped. He let Mary take him by the wrist and draw him towards the piano bench. He felt that Mary didn't particularly want to talk to him, that she was trying to be a good hostess and chat with everybody, and that she had left him to the last because he was rather difficult at parties. Vic didn't care. *I have no pride*, he thought proudly. He often said it to Melinda because it irritated her.

'What were you talking to Mrs Podnansky so long about?' Mary asked him when they had sat down.

'Lawn mowers. Hers needs sharpening, and she's not satisfied with the job Clarke's did for her the last time.'

'So you offered to do it, I'll bet. I don't know what the widows of the community would do without you, Victor Van Allen! I wonder how you have *time* for all your good deeds!'

'Plenty of time,' Vic said, smiling with appreciation in spite of himself. 'I can find time for anything. It's a wonderful feeling.'

'Time to read all those books the rest of us keep postponing!' She laughed. 'Oh, Vic, I hate you!' She looked around at her merrymaking guests, then back at Vic. 'I hope your friend Mr Nash is having a good time tonight. Is he going to settle in Little Wesley or is he just here for a while?'

Mr Nash was no longer having such a good time, Vic saw. He was still standing by himself, brooding at a figure in the rolled-up carpet near his feet. 'No, he's just here for a week or so, I think,' Vic said in an offhand tone. 'Some kind of business trip.'

'So you don't know him very well.'

'No. We've just met him.' Vic hated to share the responsibility with Melinda. Melinda had met him one afternoon in the bar of the Lord Chesterfield Inn, where she went nearly every afternoon around five-thirty more or less for the express purpose of meeting people like Joel Nash.

'May I say, Vic darling, that I think you're extremely patient?'

Vic glanced at her and saw from her straining, slightly moistening eyes that she was feeling her drinks. 'Oh, I don't know.'

'You are. You're like somebody waiting very patiently and one day – you'll do something. Not explode exactly, but just – well, speak your mind.'

It was such a quiet finish that Vic smiled. Slowly he rubbed at an itch on the side of his hand with his thumb.

'I'd also like to say, since I've had three drinks and I may not have such an opportunity again, that I think you're pretty wonderful. You're *good*, Vic,' Mary said in a tone that meant he was good in a Biblical sense, a tone that betrayed a little embarrassment at having used such a word in such a sense, and Vic knew she was going to ruin it by laughing at herself in another few seconds. 'If I weren't married and you weren't, I think I'd propose to you right now!' Then came the laugh that was supposed to erase it all.

Why did women think, Vic wondered, even women who had married for love and had had a child and a fairly happy married life, that they would prefer a man who demanded nothing of them sexually? It was a kind of sentimental harking back to virginity, a silly, vain fantasy that had no factual validity whatsoever. They'd be the first ones to feel affronted if their husbands neglected them in that respect. 'Unfortunately, I am married,' Vic said.

'Unfortunately!' Mary scoffed. 'You adore her, and I know it! You worship the ground she walks on. And she loves you, too, Vic, and don't forget it!'

'I don't want you to think,' Vic said, almost interrupting her, 'that I'm so good as you put it. I have a little evil side, too. I just keep it well hidden.'

'You certainly do!' Mary said, laughing. She leaned towards him and he smelled her perfume which struck him as a combination of lilac and cinnamon. 'How's your drink, Vic?'

'This'll do for the moment, thanks.'

'You see? You're even good about drinking! – What bit your hand?'

'A bed bug.'

'A bed bug! Good lord! Where'd you get it?'

'At the Green Mountain Hotel.'

Mary's mouth opened incredulously; then she shrieked with laughter. '*What* were you doing there?'

'Oh, I put in an order weeks in advance. I said if any bed bugs turned up, I wanted them, and finally collected six. Cost me five dollars in tips. They're living in my garage now in a glass case with a piece of mattress inside for them to sleep on. Now and then I let one bite me, because I want them to go through their normal life cycle. I've got two batches of eggs now.'

'But why?' Mary demanded, giggling.

'Because I think a certain entomologist who wrote a piece for an entomologist journal is wrong about a certain point in their reproductive cycle,' Vic answered, smiling.

'What point?' asked Mary, fascinated.

'Oh, it's a small point about the period of incubation. I doubt if it has any value at all to anybody, though as a matter of fact insecticide manufacturers ought to—'

'Vi-ic?' Melinda's husky voice slurred. 'Do you mind?'

Vic looked up at her with a subtly insulting astonishment, and then got up from the bench and gestured graciously towards the piano. 'It's all yours.'

'You're going to play? Good!' Mary said in a delighted tone.

A quintet of men was ranging itself around the piano. Melinda swooped on to the bench, a sheaf of shining hair swinging down like a curtain and concealing her face from anyone standing on her right, as Vic was. Oh, well, Vic thought, who knew her face better than he did? And he didn't want to see it anyway, because it didn't improve when she drank. Vic strolled away. The whole sofa was free now. To his distaste, he heard Melinda's wildly trilling introduction to 'Slaughter on Tenth Avenue', which she played abominably. Her playing was florid, inaccurate, and one would think embarrassing, yet people listened, and after they listened they liked her neither more nor less for it. It seemed to be neither a liability nor an asset to her socially. When she floundered and gave up a song with a laugh and a childish, frustrated flutter of hands, her current admirers admired her just the same. She wasn't going to flounder on 'Slaughter', however, because if she did she could always switch to the 'Three Blind Mice' theme and recover herself. Vic sat down in a corner of the sofa. Everybody was around the piano except Mrs Podnansky, Evelyn Cowan, and Horace. Melinda's swinging attack on the main theme was evoking grunts of delight from her male listeners. Vic looked at Joel Nash's back, hunched over the piano, and closed his eyes. In a sense he closed his ears also, and thought of his bed bugs.

Finally, there was applause which rapidly died down as Melinda began 'Dancing in the Dark', one of her better numbers. Vic opened his eyes and saw Joel Nash staring at him in an absent, yet intense and rather frightened way. Vic closed his eyes again. His head was back as if he were listening, enraptured, to the music. Actually, he was thinking of what might be going on now in Joel Nash's liquor-fuddled mind. Vic saw his own rather pudgy figure on the sofa, his hands peacefully clasped on his abdomen, his round face smiling a relaxed smile that by now would have become enigmatic to Joel Nash. Nash would be thinking, maybe he *did*. Maybe that's why he's so nonchalant about Melinda and me. Maybe that's why he's so strange. He's a *murderer*.

Melinda played for about half an hour, until she had to repeat 'Dancing in the Dark' again. When she got up from the piano, people were still pressing her to play some more, Mary Meller and Joel loudest of all.

'We've got to be going home. It's late,' Melinda said. She often left immediately after a session at the piano. On a note of triumph. 'Vic?' She snapped a finger in his direction.

Vic got up obediently from the sofa. He saw Horace beckoning to him. Horace had heard, Vic supposed. Vic went over.

'What's this you told your friend, Mr Nash?' Horace asked, his dark eyes shining with amusement.

'My friend?'

Horace's narrow shoulders shook with his constrained laughter. 'I don't blame you a bit. I just hope he doesn't spread it around.'

'It was a joke. Didn't he take it as a joke?' Vic asked, pretending to be serious. He and Horace knew each other well. Horace had often told him to 'put his foot down about Melinda', and Horace was the only person Vic knew who had ever dared say that to him.

'Seems to me he took it pretty seriously,' Horace said.

'Well, let him. Let him spread it around.'

Horace laughed and slapped Vic's shoulder. 'Just don't get yourself in jail, old man!'

Melinda tottered slightly as they walked out to the car, and Vic took her elbow gently to steady her. She was almost as tall as he, and she always wore flat sandals or ballet slippers, but less for his sake, Vic thought, than because they were more comfortable and because her height in flat shoes better matched the height of the average man. Even though she was a bit unsteady, Vic could feel the Amazonian strength in her tall, firm body, the animal vitality that pulled him along with her. She was heading for the car with the undeterrable thrust of a horse getting back to stable.

'What'd you say to Joel tonight?' Melinda asked when they were in the car.

'Nothing.'

'You must have said something.'

'When?'

'Well, I *saw* you talking to him,' she persisted sleepily. 'What were you talking about?'

'Bed bugs, I think. Or was it Mary I was talking about bed bugs to?'

'Oh!' Melinda said impatiently, and snuggled her head against his shoulder as impersonally as if he had been a sofa pillow. 'Must've said something, because he acted different after he talked to you.'

'What did he say?'

'It's not what he said, it's the way he *a-a-acted*,' she drawled. Then she was asleep.

She lifted her head when he shut off the motor in the garage and, as if walking in her sleep, got out, said, 'G'night, dear,' and went into the house through the door at the side of the garage that opened into the living-room.

The garage was big enough for five cars, though they had only two. Vic had had it built so that he could use part of it as a work room, keep his tools and his boxes of plants, his snail aquaria, or whatever else he happened to be interested in or experimenting with that took space, all in apple-pie order, and still have enough room to walk around in. He slept in a room on the opposite side of the garage from the house, a room whose only door opened into the garage. Before he went to his door he bent over the herb boxes. The foxgloves were up – six or eight pale-green sprigs already forming their characteristic triad leaf clusters. Two bed bugs were crawling around on their piece of mattress, looking for flesh and blood, but he was not in the mood to offer his hand tonight, and the two dragged their flat bodies off slowly in search of cover from his flashlight beam.

2

Joel Nash came for a cocktail three days after the Mellers' party, but he didn't stay to have dinner with them, though Vic asked him and Melinda pressed him. He said he had an engagement, but anyone could have seen that he hadn't. He announced smilingly that he wasn't staying another two weeks after all, but was leaving the following Friday. He smiled more than ever that evening and was on a defensive tack of being facetious about everything. It was an indication to Vic of how seriously Mr Nash had taken him.

After he left, Melinda accused Vic again of having said something to offend him.

'What could I possibly have said?' Vic demanded innocently. 'Has it occurred to you that you might have said something to offend him? Or done something, or not done something?'

'I know I didn't,' Melinda said, sulking. Then she made herself another drink instead of asking Vic to make it, as she usually did.

She wouldn't mind the loss of Joel Nash very much, Vic thought, because he was so new and because he wouldn't have been around very long at best, being a travelling salesman. Ralph Gosden would be another matter. Vic had been wondering if

Ralph would scare as easily as Joel had, and had decided that it was worth a try. Ralph Gosden was a twenty-nine-year-old painter of fair ability in the portrait field and with a small income from a doting aunt. He had rented a house near Millettville, about twenty miles away, for one year, of which only six months were gone. For four months Ralph had been coming for dinner about twice a week – Ralph said their house was so nice, and their food was so good, and their phonograph was so good, and all in all nobody was quite so hospitable in Little Wesley or anywhere else as the Van Allens were – and Melinda had been going up to visit Ralph several afternoons a week, though she never quite admitted going there any afternoon. Finally, after two months of it, Melinda had presented her portrait painted by Ralph, apparently by way of accounting for the many afternoons and evenings when she had not been home at one o'clock, or at seven either, when Vic had come home. The portrait, a prettified, dashed-off horror, hung in Melinda's bedroom. Vic had forbidden it in the living-room.

Ralph's hypocrisy was nauseating to Vic. He was forever trying to discuss things that he thought Vic would be interested in, though Ralph himself was interested in nothing beyond what the average woman was interested in, and behind this façade of friendship Ralph tried to hide the fact that he was having an affair with Melinda. It was not that he objected to Melinda's having affairs with other men *per se*, Vic told himself whenever he looked at Ralph Gosden, it was that she picked such idiotic, spineless characters and that she let it leak out all over town by inviting her lovers to parties at their friends' houses and by being seen with them at the bar of the Lord Chesterfield, which was really the only bar in town. One of Vic's firmest principles was that everybody – therefore, a wife – should be allowed to do as she pleased, provided no one else was hurt and that she fulfilled her main responsibilities, which were to manage a household and to take care of her offspring, which Melinda did – from time to time. Thousands of married men had affairs with impunity, though Vic had to admit that most men did it more quietly. When Horace had tried to advise Vic about Melinda when he had asked him why he 'put up with such behaviour', Vic had countered by asking him if he expected him to act like an old-fashioned husband (or wife), spurning his spouse as unclean, demanding a divorce, wrecking a child's existence for nothing more than the petty gratification of his ego? Vic also implied to Horace or to whoever else dropped a hint about Melinda, that he considered her behaviour a temporary aberration and the less fuss made about it the better.

The fact that Melinda had been carrying on like this for more than three years gave Vic the reputation in Little Wesley of having a saintlike patience and forbearance, which in turn flattered Vic's ego. Vic knew that Horace and Phil Cowan and everybody else who knew the situation – which was nearly everybody – considered him odd for enduring it, but Vic didn't mind at all being considered odd. In fact, he was proud of it in a country in which most people aimed at being exactly like everybody else.

Melinda had been odd, too, or he never would have married her. Courting her and persuading her to marry him had been like breaking a wild horse, except that the process had had to be infinitely more subtle. She had been headstrong and spoilt, the kind who gets expelled from school time after time for plain insubordination. Melinda had been expelled from five schools, and when Vic met her at twenty-two, she had thought life was nothing but the pursuit of a good time – which she still thought, though at twenty-two she had had a certain iconoclasm and imagination in her rebellion that had attracted Vic because it was like his own. Now it seemed to him that she had lost every bit of that imagination and that her iconoclasm consisted in throwing costly vases against walls and breaking them. The only vase left in the house was a metal one, and its cloisonné had several dents. She hadn't wanted to have a child, then she had, then she hadn't, and finally after four years she had wanted one again and had produced one. The birth had not been so difficult as the average first child's, Vic had learned from the doctor, but Melinda had complained loudly before and after the ordeal, in spite of Vic's providing the best nursing for her and of his giving all his time to her for weeks, to the exclusion of his work. Vic had been overjoyed at having a child that was his and Melinda's, but Melinda had refused to give the child any but the minimum of attention or to show that she cared for it any more than she would have cared for a stray puppy that she was feeding in the house. Vic supposed that the conventionality of having a baby plus being a wife was more than her constitutional rebelliousness could bear. The child had implied responsibility, and Melinda balked at growing up. She had taken out her resentment by pretending that she didn't care for him in the same way any more, 'not in a romantic way,' as she put it. Vic had been very patient, but the truth was that she had begun to bore him a little, too. She was not interested in anything he was interested in, and in a casual way he was interested in a great many things – printing and bookbinding, bee culture, cheese making, carpentry, music and painting (good music and good painting), in star-gazing, for which he had a fine telescope, and in gardening.

When Beatrice was about two years old, Melinda began an affair with Larry Osbourne, a young and not very bright instructor at a riding academy not far from Little Wesley. She had been in a kind of sulking, puzzled state of mind for months before, though whenever Vic had tried to get her to talk about what was bothering her she had never had anything to say. After she began the liaison with Larry, she became gayer and happier and more pleasant to Vic, especially when she saw how calmly he took it. Vic pretended to take it more calmly than he did, though he asked Melinda if she wanted to divorce him. Melinda hadn't wanted to divorce him.

Vic invested $50 and two hours' time in talking the situation over with a psychiatrist in New York. The psychiatrist's opinion was that, since Melinda scorned the counsel of a psychiatrist for herself she was going to bring unhappiness to Vic and eventually a divorce, unless he was firm with her. It was against Vic's principles, as an adult, to be firm with another adult. Granted Melinda wasn't an adult, he still intended to go on treating her as one. The only new idea the psychiatrist put into his head was that Melinda, like many women who have a child, might be 'finished' with him as a man and as a husband, now that he had given her the child. It was rather funny to think of Melinda's being so primitively maternal as this, and Vic smiled whenever he remembered that statement of the psychiatrist's. Vic's explanation was that plain contrariness had motivated her in rejecting him: she knew he still loved her, so she chose to give him no satisfaction by showing that she loved him in return. Perhaps love was the wrong word. They were devoted to each other, dependent on each other, and if one was gone from the house, he or she was missed by the other, Vic thought. There wasn't a word for the way he felt about Melinda, for that combination of loathing and devotion. The rest of what the psychiatrist had told Vic about the 'intolerable situation' and of his heading for a divorce – all that only inspired Vic to prove him wrong. He would show the psychiatrist and the world that the situation was not intolerable and that there would be no divorce. Neither was he going to be miserable. The world was too full of interesting things.

During Melinda's five-month affair with Larry Osbourne, Vic moved from the bedroom into a room he had had especially built for himself, about two months after the affair began, on the other side of the garage. He moved as a kind of protest against the stupidity of her affair (that was about all he had ever criticized Larry for, his stupidity), but after a few weeks when he had his microscope and his books in the room with him and he discovered how easy it was to get up in the night without worrying about disturbing Melinda and look at the stars or watch his snails that were more active at night than in the daytime, Vic decided that he preferred the room to the bedroom. When Melinda gave up Larry – or, as Vic suspected, Larry gave her up – Vic did not move back into the bedroom, because Melinda showed no sign of wanting him back and because by then he didn't want to move back anyway. He was content with the arrangement, and Melinda seemed to be, too. She was not so cheerful as she had been when Larry was around, but within a few months she found another lover – Jo-Jo Harris, a rather hyperthyroidal young man who started a short-lived record shop in Wesley. Jo-Jo lasted from October to January. Melinda bought several hundred dollars' worth of records from him, but not enough to keep him in business.

Vic knew that some people thought Melinda stayed with him because of his money, and perhaps that did influence Melinda to some extent, but Vic considered it of no importance. Vic had always had an indifferent attitude towards money. He hadn't earned his income, his grandfather had. The fact that Vic's father and he had money was due only to an accident of birth, so why shouldn't Melinda, as his wife, have an equal right to it? Vic had an income of $40,000 a year, and had had it since his twenty-first birthday. Vic had heard it implied in Little Wesley that people tolerated Melinda only because they liked him so much, but Vic refused to believe this. Objectively, he could see that Melinda was likeable enough, provided one didn't demand conversation. She was generous, a good sport, and she was fun at parties. Everybody disapproved of her affairs, of course, but Little Wesley – the old residential parent town of the newer and more commercial town of Wesley, four miles away – was singularly free of prudery, as if everybody bent over backwards to avoid the stigma of New England puritanism, and not a soul, as yet, had ever snubbed Melinda on a moral count.

3

Ralph Gosden came for dinner on Saturday night, a week after
the Mellers' party, his old gay, confident self, even gayer than
usual because, having been away at his aunt's in New York for
about ten days, he perhaps felt that his welcome at the Van
Allens' was not so threadbare as it had been just before he left.
After dinner Ralph abandoned a discussion with Vic of H-bomb
shelters, of which he had seen an exhibition in New York and
evidently still knew nothing about, and Melinda put on a stack
of records. Ralph looked in fine fettle, good for four in the
morning at least, Vic thought, though this morning might be his
last at the Van Allen house. Ralph was one of the worst offend-
ers about staying late, because he could sleep the next morning
if he cared to, but Vic usually matched him, staying up until four
or five or even seven in the morning, simply because Ralph
would have preferred him to retire and leave him alone with
Melinda. Vic also could sleep late in the mornings if he wanted
to, and he had the edge over Ralph in endurance, both because
two or three in the morning was Vic's average hour of retiring
and because Vic never drank enough to make him particularly
sleepy.

Vic sat in his favourite armchair in the living-room, looking at the *New Wesleyan*, and now and then glancing over the top of the newspaper at Ralph and Melinda, who were dancing. Ralph was wearing a white dacron suit that he had bought in New York and was as pleased as a girl with the slim, trim figure it gave him. There was a new aggression in the way he clasped Melinda around the waist at the beginning of each dance, a foolhardy self-assurance that made Vic think of a male insect blithely dancing its way through its last moments of pleasure before sudden, horrible death. And the insane music Melinda had put on was so appropriate. The record was 'The Teddybears', one of her recent purchases. For some reason, the words lilted maddeningly through Vic's head every time he stood under his shower:

Beneath the *trees* where nobody *sees*,
They'll *hide* and *seek* as long as they *please*!
Today's the *day* the teddybears have their *pic-nic*!

'Ha! Ha! Ha!' from Mr Gosden, reaching for his drink on the cocktail table.

Home on the range, Vic thought, where never is heard an intelligent word.

'What's happened to my Cugat?' Melinda demanded. She was on her knees in front of the record shelves, making an unsystematic search. 'I can't find him *anywhere*.'

'I don't think it's in there,' Vic said, because Melinda had pulled a record out of his section. She looked at it dazedly for a moment, made a face, and put it back. Vic had a little section of the bottom shelf where he kept his own records, a few Bachs, some Segovia, some Gregorian chants and motets, and Churchill's speeches, and he discouraged Melinda from playing them because the mortality rate was so high for records that she handled. Not that she liked any of his records. He remembered playing the Gregorian chants once when she was dressing to go out with Ralph, though he knew she didn't like them. 'They don't put me in a mood for anything except *dying!*' she had blatted at him that night.

Ralph went into the kitchen to fix himself another drink, and Melinda said:

'*Darling*, do you intend to read the paper all night?'

She wanted him to go to bed. Vic smiled at her. 'I'm memorizing the editorial page poem for today. "Employees serve the public *and* They have to keep their *place*. But being humble in this *world* Is never a *disgrace*. And many times I ask myself—"'

'Oh, stop it!' Melinda said.

'It's by your friend Reginald Dunlap. You said he wasn't a bad poet, remember?'

'I'm not in the mood for poetry.'

'Reggie wasn't either when he wrote this.'

In retaliation for the slight to her friend, or perhaps just on a wild whim, Melinda turned the volume up so suddenly that Vic jumped. Then he deliberately relaxed and languidly turned the page of his newspaper as if oblivious of the din. Ralph started to turn the volume down, and Melinda stopped him, violently grabbing his wrist. Then she lifted his wrist and kissed it. They began to dance. Ralph had succumbed to Melinda's mood now and was dipping his steps with swishing movements of his hips, laughing his braying laugh that was lost in the booming chaos of sound. Vic did not look at Ralph, but he could feel Ralph's occasional glances, could feel his mingled amusement and belligerence – the belligerence slowly but surely, with each drink he took, replacing whatever decorum he might have had at the beginning of the evening. Melinda encouraged it, deliberately and systematically: Bait the old bear, hammer it in, kick him, she managed to convey to everyone by her own example, because he's not going to retaliate, he's not going to be dislodged from his armchair, and he's not going to react at all, so why not insult him?

Vic crossed the room and lazily plucked Lawrence's *The Seven Pillars of Wisdom* from the shelf and carried it back to his chair. Just then Trixie's pyjama-clad form appeared in the door-way.

'Mommie!' Trixie screamed, but Mommie neither heard nor saw her.

Vic got up and went to her. ''S matter, Trix?' he asked, stooping by her.

'It's too loud to *sleep!*' she yelled indignantly.

Melinda shouted something, then went to the phonograph and turned it down. 'Now what is it?' she asked Trixie.

'I can't sleep,' Trixie said.

'Tell her it's a most unjustifiable complaint,' Vic said to Melinda.

'Aw – right, we'll turn it down,' Melinda said.

Trixie glared with sleep-swollen eyes at her mother, then at Ralph. Vic patted her firm, narrow hips.

'Why don't you hop back in bed so you'll be wide awake for that picnic tomorrow?' Vic asked her.

The anticipation of the picnic brought a smile. Trixie looked at Ralph. 'Did you bring me a sewing kit from New York, Ralph?'

'I'm afraid I didn't, Trixie,' Ralph said in a sugary voice. 'But I bet I can get you one right here in Little Wesley.'

'You will not,' Melinda said. 'She wouldn't any more know what to do with a sewing kit than—'

'Than you would,' Vic finished for her.

'You're being rather rude tonight, Mr Van Allen,' Melinda said icily.

'Sorry.' Vic was being purposely rude tonight in preparation for the story he was going to tell Ralph. He wanted Ralph to think he had reached the end of his tether.

'Are you staying for breakfast, Ralph?' Trixie asked, swaying from side to side in Vic's arm.

Ralph forced a guffaw.

'I hope he is,' Vic said. 'We don't like our guests to go off on an empty stomach, do we, Trix?'

'No-o. Ralph's so funny at breakfast.'

'What does he do?' Vic asked.

'He juggers eggs.'

'Juggles, she means,' Ralph explained.

'I guess I ought to stay up for that,' Vic said. 'Come on, Trixie, back to bed. It's quiet now, so you'd better seize the moment. You know, *carpe diem* and *carpe noctem*, too.'

Trixie went with him readily. She loved him to put her to bed, hunt for the kangaroo she slept with and tuck it in with her, then kiss her good night on both cheeks and the nose. Vic knew that he spoiled her but, on the other hand, Trixie got very cold treatment from her mother, and he felt that he should try to compensate. He buried his nose in her small soft neck, then lifted his head, smiling.

'Can we have the picnic at the quarry, Daddy?'

'Uh-uh. The quarry's too dangerous.'

'*Why?*'

'Suppose there's a strong wind. We'll all get blown right down.'

'I wouldn't mind that! – Is Mommie going on the picnic?'

'I don't know,' Vic said. 'I hope so.'

'Is Ralph going?'

'I don't think so.'

'Do you like Ralph?'

By the light of the merry-go-round lamp on her bed-table he could see the brown flecks in her green eyes, like her mother's eyes. 'Um-hm. Do you?'

'Mm-m,' she said dubiously. 'I liked Jo-Jo better.'

It stung him a little that she still remembered Jo-Jo's name. 'I know why you liked him. He gave you a lot of Christmas presents. That's no reason to like anybody. Don't I give you a lot of presents, too?'

'Oh, I like you best, Daddy. Of course I like *you* best.'

It was too facile, Vic thought. She was getting awfully facile. Vic smiled, thinking how pleased Trixie would be if he told her he had killed Malcolm McRae. Trixie had never liked Mal because he had not liked her and, being a tightwad of the first water, he had never brought her a present of any kind. Trixie would whoop with joy if he told her he had killed Mal. His stock would go up 200 per cent. 'You'd better go to sleep,' Vic said, getting up from the bed. He kissed both cheeks, the tip of her nose, then the top of her head. Trixie's hair was the colour of her mother's now, but it would probably get a little darker, like his. It grew straight down from a partless crown and looked the way a six-year-old brat's hair ought to look, Vic thought, though Melinda complained because it was so difficult to curl. 'You asleep?' he whispered.

Trixie's lashes were down on her cheeks. He turned off the light and tiptoed to the door.

'*No!*' Trixie yelled, giggling.

'Well, you'd better get to sleep! I mean it now!'

Silence. The silence gratified him. He went out and closed the door.

Melinda had turned another lamp out and the living-room was much darker. She and Ralph were doing a slow, shuffling dance in the corner of the room. It was nearly four o'clock.

'Is your drink all right, Ralph?' Vic asked.

'What? Oh, yes, thanks. I've had about enough.'

It couldn't possibly mean that Mr Gosden was thinking of leaving, not at four in the morning. Melinda was dancing with her arms around Ralph's neck. Because she thought he had said something horribly rude to Joel Nash she was going to be extremely accommodating to Ralph tonight, Vic supposed. She was going to encourage him to stay and stay, and stay for breakfast, too, no doubt, even if Ralph turned white with fatigue, as he sometimes did. 'Stay, darling, please. I'm in the mood to stay up tonight,' and he'd stay, of course. They all did. Even the ones who had to go to an office the next day, and Mr Gosden didn't. And of course the later they stayed the more chance there was that Vic would go to his room and leave them alone. Often Vic had left Melinda and Ralph alone at six in the morning, reasoning that if they had spent all afternoon together, why not let them spend two and a half hours more together until he came in at eight-thirty to get his breakfast? It was another petty thing, perhaps, annoying Melinda's callers by sitting up all night in the living-room with them, but somehow he had never been able to be so obliging as to get out of his own house to please them, and besides he always read a couple of books, so his time was not wasted.

Tonight Vic was aware of a strong, primitive antagonism to Mr Gosden that he had never felt before. He thought of the bottles and bottles of bourbon that he had provided for Mr Gosden. He thought of the evenings that Mr Gosden had ruined for him. Vic stood up, put his book back on the shelf, then went quietly towards the door that opened into the garage. Behind him, Melinda and Ralph were now practically necking. His leaving without saying anything could be explained as (a) his not wanting to embarrass them when they were kissing each other; (b) that he was possibly coming back in a moment, or (c) that he was too annoyed with their behaviour to say good night to either of them. Explanation (b) was the correct one, but only Melinda would think of it, because Mr Gosden had never seen him leave and come back. He had done it several times with Jo-Jo.

Vic turned on the fluorescent light in the garage and walked slowly through, glancing at his neat herb boxes, at his aquaria full of land snails that were gliding through the moistened jungle of oat shoots and Bermuda grass in which they lived, glancing at his opened electric drill case on his work-table and automatically noting that every tool was present and in its proper place.

His own room was almost as severe and functional as the

garage – a plain three-quarter bed with a dark-green slip-cover on it, one straight chair and one leather desk chair, a huge flat-topped desk on which stood dictionaries and carpenters' manuals, ink bottles, pens and pencils, account books, and paid and unpaid bills, all arranged in an orderly manner. There were no pictures at all on his walls, only a plain calendar, donated by a local lumber company, over his desk. He had the ability to sleep for as long as he wished without the aid of anything or anyone to awaken him, and he looked at his wrist-watch and set himself to awaken in half an hour, at seventeen minutes to five. He lay down on the bed and methodically relaxed himself from head to toe.

Within about a minute he was asleep. He had a dream of being in church and of seeing the Mellers there. Horace Meller smiled and congratulated him for having murdered Malcolm McRae in defence of his marriage. The whole town of Little Wesley was in church, and everyone smiled at him. Vic woke up smiling at himself, at the absurdity of it. He never went to church, anyway. Whistling, he combed his hair, straightened his shirt under his pale-blue cashmere sweater, and strolled back through the garage.

Ralph and Melinda were in a corner of the sofa and had apparently been reclining, or half reclining, because they both straightened up at the sight of him. Ralph, pink-eyed now, looked him up and down with drunken disbelief and resentment.

Vic went to the bookshelf and bent over, scanning the titles.

'Still reading?' Melinda asked.

'Um-hm,' Vic said. 'No more music?'

'I was just about to leave,' Ralph said hoarsely, getting up. He looked exhausted, but he lighted a cigarette and threw the match viciously in the direction of the fireplace.

'I don't want you to leave.' Melinda reached for his hand, but Ralph swung away and took a step back, staggering a little.

''S awfully late,' Ralph said.

'Practically time for breakfast,' Vic said cheerfully. 'Can I interest anybody in some scrambled eggs?'

He got no answer. He chose the pocket-book *World Almanac*, a book he could always browse in with pleasure, and went to his armchair.

'I should think *you'd* be getting sleepy,' Melinda said, looking at him as resentfully as Ralph.

'No.' Vic blinked his eyes alertly. 'Had a little nap just now in my room.'

Ralph wilted visibly at this information and stared at Vic with a stunned expression as if he were about to throw up the sponge, though his eyes, shrunken and pink in his pale face, burned all the harder. He stared at Vic as if he could have killed him. Vic had seen the same look on Jo-Jo's face, and even on Larry Osbourne's lean, blank face, a look inspired by Vic's demoniacal good humour, by his standing clear-eyed and sober at five in the morning while they wilted on the sofa, wilted lower and lower in spite of their efforts to haul themselves upright every fifteen minutes or so. Ralph picked up his full glass and drank half of it at one draught. He'd stay to the bitter end now, Vic thought, as a matter of principle: it was nearly six in the morning, and what was the use of going home to sleep now, since tomorrow was ruined anyway? He might pass out, but he'd stay. He was too drunk to realize, Vic supposed, that he could have Melinda all the afternoon tomorrow if he wanted her.

Suddenly, as Vic watched him, Ralph staggered backwards, as if something invisible had pushed him, and sat down heavily on the sofa. His face was shiny with perspiration. Melinda pulled him towards her, her arm around his neck, and began to cool his temples with her fingers which she dampened against her glass. Ralph's body was limp and sprawled, though his mouth had set grimly and his eyes still bored into Vic as if he were trying to hang on to consciousness now by simply staring fixedly at one thing.

Vic smiled at Melinda. 'Maybe I'd better make those eggs. He looks as if he could use something.'

'He's fine!' Melinda said defiantly.

Whistling a Gregorian chant, Vic went into the kitchen and put a kettle of water on for coffee. He held up the bourbon bottle and saw that Ralph had finished about four-fifths of it. He went back into the living-room. 'How do you like your eggs, Ralph – besides juggled?'

'How do you like your eggs, darling?' Melinda asked him.

'I jus' like 'em – like 'em juggled fine,' Ralph mumbled.

'One order of juggled eggs,' Vic said. 'How about you, puss?'

'Don't call me "puss"!'

It was an old pet name of Vic's for her that he hadn't used in years. She was glaring at him from under her strong blonde eyebrows, and Vic had to admit she was not quite the little puss she had been at the time he married her, or even at the earlier part of this evening. Her lipstick was smeared, and the end of her long, upturned nose was shiny and red, as if some of her lipstick had got on it. 'How do you want your eggs?' he asked.

'Do' want any eggs.'

Vic scrambled four eggs with cream for himself and Melinda, since Ralph was in no condition to eat any, but he made only one piece of toast, because he knew Melinda would eat toast now. He didn't wait for the coffee, which was not quite dripped through, because he knew Melinda wouldn't drink coffee at this hour either. He and Mr Gosden could drink the coffee later. He brought the scrambled eggs, lightly salted and peppered, on two warm plates. Melinda again refused hers, but he sat beside her on the sofa and fed them to her in small amounts on a fork. Every time the fork approached, she opened her mouth obediently. Her eyes staring at him all the while, had the look of a wild animal who trusts the human food-bringer just barely enough to accept the food at arm's length, and then only if there is nothing in sight that resembles a trap and if every movement of the food-bringer is slow and gentle. Mr Gosden's red-blond head was now in her lap. He was snoring in an unaesthetic way with his mouth open. Melinda balked at the last bite, as Vic had known she would.

'Come on. Last bite,' Vic said.

She ate it.

'I suppose Mr Gosden had better stay here,' Vic said, because there was nothing else to say about Mr Gosden.

'I have every intention of 's shtaying here,' Melinda said.

'Well, let's stretch him out.'

Melinda got up to stretch him out herself, but his shoulders were too heavy for her in her condition. Vic put his hands under Ralph's arms and pulled him so that his head was just short of the sofa arm.

'Shoes?' Vic asked.

'Don't you touch 's shoes!' Melinda bent over Ralph's feet wobblingly and began to untie his shoe-laces.

Ralph's shoulders shook. Vic could hear the faint chatter of teeth.

'He's cold. I'd better get a blanket,' Vic said.

'I'll get the blanket.' Melinda staggered towards her bedroom but evidently forgot her purpose, because she detoured into the bathroom.

Vic removed the remaining shoe, then went into Melinda's bedroom to get the plaid lap rug that was always lying somewhere in the room. Now it was on the floor at the foot of the unmade bed. The lap rug had been one of Vic's presents to Melinda on her birthday about seven years ago. Seeing it reminded him of picnics, of a happy summer they had spent in Maine, of one winter evening when for some reason there had been no heat and they had lain under it on the floor in front of the fireplace. He stopped a moment, vaguely debating taking the green woollen blanket from her bed instead of the lap rug, then decided that was meaningless and he might as well take the lap rug. Melinda's room, as usual, was in a state of disorder that both repelled him and interested him, and he would have liked to stand there a few moments looking at it – he almost never went into Melinda's bedroom – but he did not permit himself even a complete glance around it. He went out and closed the door behind him. He heard the water running in the bathroom as he passed the door. He hoped she wasn't going to be sick.

Ralph was sitting up now with unfocusing eyes, his body shaking as if he had a chill.

'Would you care for some hot coffee?' Vic asked him.

Ralph said nothing. Vic draped the lap rug around his shaking shoulders, and Ralph lay back feebly on the sofa and tried to drag his feet up. Vic lifted both his feet and tucked the blanket under them.

'You're a good egg,' Ralph mumbled.

Vic smiled a little and sat down at the end of the sofa. He thought he heard Melinda being sick in the bathroom.

'Shoulda thrown me out a long time ago,' Ralph murmured. 'Anybody who doesn't know how much he can take—' He moved his legs as if to get off the sofa, and Vic casually leaned on his ankles.

'Think nothing of it,' Vic said soothingly.

'Ought to be sick – ought to die.' There were tears in Ralph's blue eyes that made them look even glassier. His thin eyebrows trembled. He seemed to be in some self-flagellating trance in which he might really have enjoyed being hurled out of the house by the seat of his pants and his collar.

Vic cleared his throat and smiled. 'Oh, I don't bother throwing people out of the house if they annoy me.' He leaned a little closer. 'If they annoy me in that way – with Melinda –' he nodded meaningly towards the bathroom – 'I kill them.'

'Yes,' Ralph said seriously, as if he understood. 'You should.

Because I do want to keep you and Melinda as friends. I like you both. I mean it.'

'I do kill people if I don't like them,' Vic said even more quietly, leaning towards Ralph and smiling.

Ralph smiled, too, fatuously.

'Like Malcolm McRae, for instance. I killed him.'

'Ma'colm?' Ralph asked puzzledly.

Vic knew he knew all about Mal. 'Yes. Melinda's told you about McRae. I killed him with a hammer in his apartment. You probably saw something in the papers last winter about it. He was getting too familiar with Melinda.'

Whether it was sinking very far in or not, Vic couldn't tell. Ralph's eyebrows drew slowly together. 'I remember ... You killed him?'

'Yes. He began flirting with Melinda. In public.' Vic tossed Melinda's cigarette lighter up and caught it, two, three, and four times. It was sinking in. Ralph was up on one elbow.

'Does Melinda know you killed him?'

'No. Nobody knows,' he whispered. 'And don't tell Melinda, will you?'

Ralph's frown deepened. It was a little too much for Ralph's brain to cope with, Vic thought, but Ralph had grasped the threat and the hostility. Ralph clenched his teeth and jerked his feet suddenly from under Vic's arm. He was leaving.

Vic handed him his shoes without a word. 'Like me to drive you home?'

'I can drive myself.' Ralph staggered around, trying to get his shoes on, and finally had to sit down to do it. Then he got up and stumbled towards the door.

Vic followed him and handed him his magenta-banded straw hat.

'G'night I had a very nice time,' Ralph said, running his words together.

'Glad you did. Don't forget. Don't say anything to Melinda about what I told you. Good night, Ralph.' Vic watched him crawl into his open convertible and zoom off, skidding the car's rear end off the road and righting it again as he went on down the lane. Vic didn't care if he drove the car into Bear Lake. The sun was coming up in a bright orange glow above the woods straight ahead.

Vic heard no sounds from the bathroom now, which meant that Melinda was probably sitting on the floor, waiting for another attack of nausea. She did that whenever she got sick, and it was impossible to persuade her to move from the floor until she was sure the attack was over. Finally, he got up from his chair, went to the bathroom, and called, 'Are you all right, honey?' and got a reasonably clear murmur that she was. He went into the kitchen and poured himself a cup of coffee. He loved coffee and it almost never kept him awake when he wanted to sleep.

Melinda came out of the bathroom in her robe, looking better than she had half an hour before. 'Where's Ralph?'

'He decided to go home. He said to say good night and that he had a very nice time.'

'Oh.' She looked disappointed.

'I tucked the blanket around him, and he felt better after a while,' Vic added.

Melinda came over and put her hands on his shoulders. 'I think you were very sweet to him tonight.'

'That's good. You said earlier you thought I was rude.'

'You're never rude.' She gave him a kiss on his cheek. 'G'night, Vic.'

He watched her walk to her room. He wondered what Ralph was going to say to Melinda tomorrow. Ralph would tell her, of course. He was that type. Melinda would probably telephone him in a few minutes, as she always did when he left, if she didn't fall asleep first. He didn't think Ralph would tell her over the telephone, though.

35

4

It was astonishing to Vic how quickly the story travelled, how interested everybody was in it – especially people who didn't know him well – and how nobody lifted a finger or a telephone to tell the police about it. There were, of course, the people who knew him and Melinda very well, or fairly well, knew why he had told the story, and found it simply amusing. Even people like old Mr Hansen, their grocer, found it amusing. But there were people who didn't know him or Melinda, didn't know anything about them except by hearsay, who had probably pulled long faces on being told the story, and who seemed to take the attitude that he deserved to be hauled in by the police, whether it was true or not. Vic deduced that from some of the looks he got when he walked down the main street of the town.

Within four days of telling the story to Ralph, people Vic had never seen or at least never noticed before were looking at him intently when he passed them in his car – an old, well-kept Oldsmobile that was an eye-catcher anyway in a community where most people had much newer cars – and pointing him out with whispers to other people. He seldom saw a smile among the strangers, but all he saw was smiles among his friends.

During those four days he saw nothing of Ralph Gosden. On the Sunday after the dawn departure, Ralph had called Melinda and insisted on seeing her, Melinda said, and she had left the house to meet him somewhere. Vic and Trixie had picnicked alone that day on the shore of Bear Lake, and Vic had chatted with the boat-keeper there and arranged for Trixie to rent a canoe for all summer. When he and Trixie had come back to the house, Melinda had been there and all hell had broken loose. Ralph had told her what he had said. Melinda had screamed at Vic, 'It's the most *stupid* – vulgar – idiotic thing I've ever heard of!' Vic took her vituperation calmly. He knew she was furious probably because Ralph had shown himself a coward. Vic felt that he could have written their conversation. Ralph: 'I *know* it isn't true, darling, but it's obvious he doesn't want me hanging around any more, so I thought—' Melinda: 'I don't care what he wants! All right, if you're too much of a coward to face up to him . . .' And Melinda would have realized, during their talk, that he must have said the same thing to Joel Nash.

'Does Ralph really think I killed McRae?' Vic asked.

'Of course he doesn't. He just thinks you're an ass. Or else out of your head.'

'But he doesn't think it's funny.' Vic shook his head regretfully. 'That's too bad.'

'What's funny about it?' Melinda was standing in the living-room, her hands on her hips and her moccasined feet wide apart.

'Well – I suppose you'd have to hear it the way I said it to find it funny.'

'Oh, I see. Did Joel find it funny?'

'Apparently he didn't. Seems to have scared him out of town.'

'That's what you wanted to do, wasn't it?'

'Well, yes, frankly.'

'And Ralph, too. You wanted to scare him, didn't you?'

'I found them both terrible bores and terribly beneath you – I think. So Ralph's scared, too?'

'He's not scared. Don't be silly. You don't think anyone would believe a story like that, do you?'

Vic put his hands behind his head and leaned back in the arm-chair. 'Joel Nash must have believed something. He certainly disappeared, didn't he? I don't think it was very bright of him, but then I never thought he was bright.'

'No. Nobody's bright but you.'

Vic smiled at her good-naturedly. 'What did Joel say to you?' he asked, and he saw from her shifting of her position, the way she flung herself down on the sofa, that Joel Nash had said nothing to her. 'What did Ralph say?'

'That he thought you were decidedly unfriendly and he thought—'

'Decidedly unfriendly. How unusual. I was decidedly bored, Melinda, decidedly tired of wining and dining bores several times a week and sitting up all night with them, decidedly tired of listening to drivel, and decidedly tired of their thinking that I didn't know or care what they were up to with you. It was decidedly dull.'

Melinda stared at him in surprise for a long moment, frowning, her mouth turned stubbornly down at the corners. Then suddenly she put her face down in her hands and let the tears come.

Vic came to her and put his hand on her shoulder. 'Honey, is it worth crying about? Are Joel Nash and Ralph worth crying about?'

She flung her head up. 'I'm not crying over them. I'm crying over the injustice.'

'*Sic*,' Vic murmured involuntarily.

'Who's sick?'

He sighed, really trying to think of something to say to comfort her. No use saying, '*I'm* still here, I love you.' She wouldn't want him now, perhaps never would. And he didn't want to be a dog in the manger. He wouldn't object to her having a man of some stature and self-respect, a man with some ideas in his head, as a lover, Vic thought. But he was afraid Melinda would never choose that kind or that that kind would never choose her. Vic could visualize a kind of charitable, fair-minded, civilized arrangement in which all three of them might be happy and benefit from contact with one another. Dostoevsky had known what he meant. Goethe might have understood, too.

'You know, just the other day in the paper,' Vic began conversationally, 'I read a piece about a *ménage à trois* in Milan. Of course I don't know what kind of people they were, but the husband and the lover, who were very good friends, were killed together in a motor-cycle accident, and the wife had them buried together with a niche in the same tomb for herself when she dies. Over the tomb she put the inscription: "They lived happily together". So you see, it can be. I just wish you'd choose a man – or even several men, if you like – who have some brains in their heads. Don't you think that's possible?'

'Yes,' she said tearfully, and he knew she wasn't even thinking about what he had said.

That was Sunday. Four days later, Melinda was still sulking, but he thought she would come out of it in a few days if he handled her properly. She was too energetic and too fond of having a good time to sulk for very long. He bought tickets for two musical comedies in New York, though he would rather have seen two other plays that were on. There would be time for the other plays later, he thought. There was all kinds of time now that Melinda wasn't busy or exhausted in the evenings. On the day he had gone to New York to buy the tickets, he had also paid a visit to the newspaper division of the Public Library and had re-read the McRae story, because he had forgotten many of the details. He learned that the elevator operator in McRae's apartment house was the only person who had seen the murderer, and he had described him very vaguely as being rather heavy set and not very tall. That fitted him, too, and Vic remarked this to Horace.

Horace smiled a little. He was a chemist in a medical analytical laboratory, a cautious man, accustomed to speaking in understatements. He thought Vic's story was fantastic and even a little dangerous, but he was for anything that would 'straighten Melinda out'. 'I've always said all Melinda needed to straighten herself out was a little firmness from you, Vic,' Horace said. 'She's been asking for it for years – just a little sign that you care what she does. Now don't lose the ground you've gained. I'd like to see you two happy again.'

Horace had seen them happy for three or four years, but it seemed so long ago, Vic was surprised that Horace even remembered. The ground that he had gained. Well, Melinda was staying home, and willy-nilly she had more time for Trixie and for him. But she was not yet happy about it. Vic took her for cocktails several times at the bar of the Lord Chesterfield Inn, thinking that since even Sam the barman knew about the McRae story, Melinda would not have liked to go there alone: she had so often sat in the Lord Chesterfield bar with Ralph or Larry or Jo-Jo. Vic had tried to interest Melinda in two designs he had brought with him one afternoon, both Blair Peabody's, for the cover of Xenophon's *Country Life and Economics*. Blair Peabody, a leather worker whose shop was in a barn in Connecticut, had done the tooling on all the leather-bound books that Vic had published. These two designs of Blair's were based on Greek architectural motifs, one somewhat more decorative and less masculine than the other, both beautiful in Vic's opinion, and he had thought Melinda would enjoy choosing between the two, but he had hardly been able to make her look at them for five seconds. For politeness' sake, which was really to insult him by its carelessness, she had expressed a preference for one over the other. Vic had been crushed and wordless for several moments. It surprised him sometimes to find how much Melinda could hurt him when she wanted to. That afternoon Melinda had been more interested in the pianist the Lord Chesterfield had engaged for the summer. There was a poster about him with a photograph in a corner of the bar. He was to arrive in about a week. Melinda said if he played in the Duchin style, like the one they had had last year, she would die.

The evenings in New York when they saw the musical comedies were more of a success. Both shows were on Saturday nights, and Trixie spent the first one at the Petersons', the parents of Trixie's best friend Jancy, and on the second, Mrs Peterson came over with Janey to keep Trixie company during the first part of the evening. Trixie could be relied on to fall soundly asleep by ten at least, and Mrs Peterson generally stayed on until midnight before she left the house. On both evenings after the theatre Vic and Melinda went to a supper club where there were dance orchestras, though Vic did not propose dancing because he felt Melinda would have refused him. For all her good humour on those evenings, Vic could feel her lurking resentment because he had cut her off from Joel and Ralph. The second of the evenings, when they got home at four in the morning, Melinda was in the kind of gay mood that sometimes inspired her to wade in the brook that went through the woods only a few yards from the house, or to drive over to the Cowans' and jump in their swimming pool, but she did those things only with people like Ralph or Jo-Jo. She didn't propose a wade in the brook when they got home, and Vic knew it was because *he* was there, her stodgy husband, and not one of the exuberant young men. He started to suggest the brook, but he didn't. He didn't really feel that silly, didn't want to cut his feet on the stones that they wouldn't be able to see in the dark, and he didn't think Melinda would appreciate such a proposal from him, anyway.

They sat on Melinda's bed, still completely dressed, looking through some Sunday papers Vic had bought in Manhattan, all the papers except the *Times*, which was delivered to them on Sunday mornings. Melinda was laughing at something she was reading in the *News*. She had slept on his shoulder during most of the ride home. Vic felt very wide awake and could have stayed up the rest of the night. Perhaps, he thought, his wide-awakeness was due to the unusual circumstances of his sitting on Melinda's bed – it had been years since he had sat on her bed – and, though he was interested in what he was reading about American defectors in China, another part of his mind tentatively examined the sensations that sitting on her bed produced in him. Intimacy, rapport, were not among them, he thought, or the anticipation of them. He felt a little uncomfortable. Yet he was aware of something plucking at him to ask her if she minded if he stayed in her room tonight. Just slept in her bed with his arms around her, or perhaps not even touching her – Melinda knew that he wouldn't do anything to annoy her. Then he thought of what she had said about the Cowans tonight on the drive to New York, that the Cowans had changed towards them because of his 'bad taste' in telling the McRae story, that the Mellers as well as the Cowans were cooler towards them. People were shunning them, Melinda insisted, though Vic, insisting that they weren't, pointed out incidents that proved people were not shunning them at all, and reminded her that the Cowans were leading a quiet life just now because Phil was working hard on his economics book, trying to finish it before he had to start teaching again in September. Vic wondered if he should risk asking her if he might stay in her room tonight, or would she seize it as another opportunity to show him how much she resented him by refusing him indignantly? Or, even if she didn't refuse indignantly, would it so surprise her that it would spoil the pleasant mood of the evening? Did he particularly *want* to stay, anyway? He didn't.

Melinda yawned. 'What're you reading so hard?'

'About defectors. If the Americans go over to the Reds, they call them "turncoats". If the Reds come over to us, they're "freedom-loving". Just depends from what side you're talking.' He smiled at her.

Melinda made no comment. He hadn't thought she would make a comment. He got up slowly from the bed. 'Good night, honey. Sleep well.' He bent and kissed her cheek. 'Did you enjoy the evening?'

'Umm-m, I did,' Melinda said with no more expression than a little girl might have used in replying to her grandfather after a day at the circus. 'Good night, Vic. Don't wake Trixie when you go by her room.'

Vic smiled to himself as he went out. Three weeks ago she wouldn't have thought about Trixie. She would have been thinking about calling Ralph as soon as he had left her room.

June was a delightful month, not too warm, not too dry, with twice or thrice weekly rains that came around six in the evening, lasted about half an hour, and brought the raspberries and strawberries in the woods behind the house to a fat, juicy perfection. Vic went out with Trixie and Janey Peterson on several Saturday afternoons and gathered enough to supply both families with berries for cold cereal, pies, and ice-cream for a week at a time. Trixie had decided not to go to camp this summer, because Janey wasn't going. She and Janey had registered at the Highland School four miles away from Little Wesley, a semi-private grade school which offered sports and arts and crafts classes five days a week from nine to four in summer. It was the first summer that Trixie had caught on to swimming, and she did so well that she won first prize in a swimming contest for her age group. Vic was glad Trixie hadn't wanted to go to camp this summer, because he liked to have her with him. He supposed he had the Petersons' comparative lack of money to thank for Trixie's being with him. Charles Peterson, an electrical engineer in a leather factory in Wesley, made less money than most of Little Wesley's inhabitants. Or, rather, he supported his family on what he earned, whereas many people in Little Wesley, like himself and Phil Cowan, for instance, had incomes with which to supplement their earnings. Melinda, to Vic's regret, looked down on the Petersons as a bit uncouth and couldn't see that they were no more uncouth than the MacPhersons, for example, and that perhaps what she objected to was their white clapboard house. Vic was glad it didn't bother Trixie.

In a distinguished British publisher's annual that came out in June, the Greenspur Press of Little Wesley, Massachusetts, was cited for 'typography, fine workmanship and general excellence', a tribute Vic valued more than any material success that could have come to him. It was Vic's boast that in the twenty-six books he had published, there were only two typographical errors. Xenophon's *Country Life and Economics* was his twenty-seventh book, and there were as yet no errors that either he or his meticulous printer, Stephen Hines, could find, though they had the added peril of the left side of the pages being in Greek. The likelihood of typographical errors in spite of rigorous proof reading was going to be the subject of an essay that he would write one day, Vic thought. There was something demoniacal and insuperable about typographical errors, as if they were part of the natural evil that permeated man's existence, as if they had a life of their own and were determined to manifest themselves no matter what, as surely as weeds in the best-tended gardens.

Far from noticing any coolness in their friends – which Melinda still insisted she did – Vic found their social relations much easier. The Mellers and the Cowans no longer issued an invitation tentatively, half-expecting that Melinda would make a date with Ralph or somebody else at the last minute, as she often had. Everybody treated them as a couple now, and as a couple supposedly happy and getting along. Vic had loathed, in the last years, being coddled by understanding hostesses, being pressed to take second helpings and big pieces of cake as if he had been a neglected child or some kind of cripple. Perhaps his marriage with Melinda had been something short of ideal, but there were certainly many worse marriages in the world – marriages with drunkenness, with poverty, with sickness or insanity, with mothers-in-law, with unfaithfulness but unfaithfulness that was not forgiven. Vic treated Melinda with as much respect and affection as he had at the beginning of their marriage, perhaps with even more now, because he realized she missed Ralph. He did not want her to feel bored or lonely, or to think that he was unconcerned if she did feel that way. He took her to two or three more shows in New York, to a couple of Tanglewood concerts, and on one week-end they drove up to Kennebunkport with Trixie to see a play that Judith Anderson was in, and they spent the night at a hotel. Nearly every evening Vic came home with a little present for Melinda – flowers, a bottle of perfume, or a scarf he had seen at the Bandana, the only chic women's shop in Wesley, or simply a magazine that she liked, like *Holiday*, which they didn't subscribe to because Melinda said it was expensive and that the house was already cluttered with magazines that came every month, though *Holiday* in Vic's opinion was better than many of the magazines whose subscription they continually renewed. Melinda's sense of economy was odd.

She had never wanted a maid, for instance, and yet she never did much to keep the house straight, either. If the bookshelves were ever dusted, Vic did it – about every four months. Occasionally Melinda would get started with the vacuum cleaner, and give up after one or two rooms. When people were due to come over, the living-room, kitchen, and bathroom were 'checked', Melinda's undefined term. But she could be relied on to keep a supply of steaks in the freezing compartment of the refrigerator, green vegetables and potatoes and plenty of oranges, and one of the things that Vic appreciated very much in her, she could be relied on eventually to come home for dinner with him regardless of what she did in the afternoon. Perhaps she considered she owed him this much, Vic didn't know, but she was as determined about it as she was determined sometimes to keep her appointments with her lovers. And about once a week she managed to cook one of his favourite dishes – frogs' legs provençale, or chile, or potato soup, or roast pheasant, which she had to get from Wesley. She also saw to it that he was never out of his pipe tobacco, which had to be ordered from New York and was hard to keep track of because Vic smoked his pipe sporadically, and sometimes the tobacco humidor was in the living-room and sometimes in the garage or his own room, which Melinda seldom went into. Vic thought that his friends, even Horace, did not always remember the nicer things about Melinda, and Vic often took the trouble to remind them.

On Saturday night of the 4 July week-end, Vic and Melinda went to the annual dance at the club, the biggest affair of the summer. All their friends were there, even the Petersons and the Wilsons, who didn't belong to the club but had been invited by members. Vic looked around for Ralph Gosden, expecting to see him, but Ralph was not there. Ralph had been seeing a good deal of the Wilsons, according to Evelyn Cowan, who had been advising June Wilson about her flower garden. Evelyn was an enthusiastic gardener. The Wilsons had been in Little Wesley only four months, and they lived in a modest house on the north side of town. Evelyn Cowan had told Vic, when they met one day in the drugstore, that Don Wilson was taking a very serious view of the story he had told Ralph about Malcolm McRae, and Vic felt sure that Ralph was helping to rub it in by making himself out a victim of Vic's jealousy, ill will, and general 'bad taste'. Ralph would of course have said that Melinda had been nothing but a dear friend of his and, since the Wilsons were rather out of the group who knew him and Melinda well, Vic supposed that they had swallowed it. People in Little Wesley had not been particularly friendly to the Wilsons since their arrival, and Vic thought it was Don's fault. He was humourless and standoffish at social gatherings, perhaps because he considered smiles and conviviality unintelligent or unbecoming in a writer. And he was such a hack – western stories, detective stories, love stories, some of which his wife collaborated on, though Vic had heard from somebody that her speciality was children's books. The Wilsons had no children.

Don Wilson and his wife stood against the wall, Don looking lank and unhappy, and his wife, who was small and blonde and usually animated, looking rather subdued. Vic supposed it was because they didn't know many people, and he had nodded and smiled a hello to them and was about to go and chat with them, but Don Wilson's unmistakably cold response stayed him. Perhaps Wilson was surprised to see him there at all, Vic thought, much less to see him greeted by all his old friends as if nothing had happened.

Vic circulated around the edge of the dance floor, chatting with the MacPhersons and the Cowans and with the inevitable Mrs Podnansky, whose two grandsons were here tonight. The younger grandson, Walter, had just got his law degree from Harvard. That evening Vic realized that there was something in what Melinda said about people shunning him – people he did not know at all. He saw people pointing him out to their dancing partners, then discussing him volubly, though always out of his earshot. Other total strangers turned away with self-conscious little smiles as he passed them, when at another time they might have introduced themselves and started talking. Strangers often started conversations with Vic about his printing plant. But Vic did not mind the shunning and the whispers. It made him feel strangely more comfortable and secure, in fact, than he usually felt at parties, perhaps because the whispering and pointing, at both him and Melinda, fairly guaranteed that Melinda would behave herself tonight. Melinda was having a good time, he could see that, though tonight she would probably tell him that she had not had a good time at all. She looked beautiful in

48

a new amber-coloured taffeta gown that had no belt and fitted her strong narrow waist and her hips as if it had been cut for her to the millimetre. By midnight she had danced with about fifteen partners, including a couple of youngish men Vic didn't know, either one of whom might have been Ralph Gosden's successor under ordinary circumstances, but Melinda was merely pleasant and gracious to them without being coy or hoydenish or *femme fatale* or pretending to have been swept off her feet by them – all of which tactics he had seen her use on other occasions. Neither did she drink too much. Vic was extremely proud of Melinda that evening. He had often been proud of the way she looked, but seldom, that he could remember, of the way she behaved.

As Melinda came towards him after a dance, he heard a woman say, 'That's his wife.'

'Oh, yes? She's lovely!'

Someone's laughter obliterated part of the conversation. Then:

'Nobody knows, you see! But some people think so . . . No, he certainly doesn't, does he?'

'Hi,' Melinda said to Vic. 'Aren't you tired of standing up?' Her large green-brown eyes looking slurringly at him, as she often looked at men, though usually with a smile. She was not smiling now.

'I haven't been standing up. I've been sitting with Mrs Podnansky part of the time.'

'She's your favourite party girl, isn't she?'

Vic laughed. 'Can I get you something to drink?'

'A quadruple Scotch.'

Before he could go off to get her anything, one of the young men who had danced with her before came up and said a solemn, 'May I?' to Vic.

'You may,' Vic said, with a smile. He didn't think the emphatic 'May I?' was a result of the McRae tale, though of course it might have been.

Vic glanced over at Don Wilson and saw that Don was watching him again. Vic got himself a third helping of lemon ice – liquor had no charm for him that evening – and seeing Mary Meller looking rather detached, he took another portion of ice for her. Mary accepted it with a warm, friendly smile.

'Evelyn and Phil want us to cool off with a dip over at their house after the dance is over. Can you and Melinda come?' Mary asked him.

'We didn't bring our suits,' Vic said, though that hadn't stopped them on other occasions when they had jumped into the Cowan pool naked. Melinda had, at least. Vic was a little shy about such things.

'Drop by your house for your suits – or not?' Mary said gaily. 'It's such a dark night, who cares?'

'I'll ask Melinda,' Vic said.

'She looks lovely tonight, doesn't she? Vic—' Mary touched his arm and he leaned a little closer. 'Vic, you're not feeling uncomfortable tonight, are you? I wanted you to know that all your real friends are still your friends, the same as ever. I don't know what you've heard tonight, but I hope nothing unpleasant.'

'Didn't hear a thing!' Vic assured her, smiling.

'I talked to Evelyn. She and Phil feel the same as we do. We know you just said it as a – as a joke, in spite of what people like the Wilsons are trying to say.'

'What're they trying to say?'

'It's not her, it's him. He thinks you're odd. Well, we're all odd, aren't we?' Mary said, with a gay laugh. 'He must be looking for another plot for a story. I think he's *very* odd!'

Vic knew Mary well enough to know that she was more concerned than she was pretending to be. 'What is he saying?' Vic asked.

'Oh, he's saying – that you don't react normally. I can imagine what Ralph Gosden's been saying. I mean the fuel he's added to the fire. Oh, Don Wilson's just saying that you ought to be watched and that you're very mysterious.' Mary whispered the last word, smiling. 'I told him we'd all had the opportunity of watching you for the past nine or ten years, and that you're one of the finest, sweetest, most unmysterious men I've ever known!'

'Mrs Meller, may I have this dance with you?' Vic asked. 'Do you think your husband would mind?'

'Why, Vic! I can't believe it!'

He took her ice plate and carried it with his own to the refreshment stall a few feet away, then returned and swept Mary out on to the floor to the music of a waltz. The waltz had always been his favourite dance. He waltzed very well. He saw Melinda notice him and stop short with surprise. Horace and Evelyn were looking at him, too. Vic shortened his steps so that he would not look silly, because a joyous exuberance had filled him as if a long-repressed desire had burst forth. He felt he could have flown with Mary, if it had not been for the other couples that cluttered the floor around him.

'Why, you're a wonderful dancer!' Mary said. 'Why've you been hiding it all these years?'

Vic did not try to answer.

Long after the dance was over Vic felt a tingling exhilaration as if he had achieved a triumph. When Melinda had finished a dance, he went over to her, made a little bow and said, 'May I, Melinda?'

She hid her surprise almost immediately by closing her eyes, turning her head away from him. 'Oh, darling, I'm tired,' she said.

On their way home, when Melinda asked, 'What inspired you to dance tonight?' he was able to pass it off, to forestall her kidding him with 'I thought I might as well baffle people by being inconsistent as well as odd. I'm supposed never to dance, you know.'

Melinda hadn't been in the mood for the Cowans' swimming pool, though she had declined their invitation very graciously.

'I thought you were charming tonight,' Vic said to her at home.

'I have to put myself out to counteract some of the damage you've done,' she replied. 'I worked hard tonight.'

Vic shrugged involuntarily, smiled a little, and said nothing. Melinda had had just as good a time as she'd had at other club dances when she had got too high, or flirted, or got sick, or created some other kind of disturbance that hadn't enhanced their popularity, either.

Lying in his bed that night Vic relived the moments on the dance floor with Mary Meller. Don Wilson's scowling face. The whispering people. He thought that a few people there tonight really believed that he had killed Malcolm McRae – the people who knew him least. That was what Mary had tried to tell him. If Mary hadn't known him so well, or thought she knew him so well, she might be one of the people who suspected him, he thought. She had as much as said it that night of the party. *You're like somebody waiting very patiently and one day – you'll do something.* He remembered the exact words, and how he had smiled at their mildness. Yes, all these years he had played a game of seeming calm and indifferent to whatever Melinda did. He had deliberately hidden everything he felt – and in those months of her first affair he had felt something, even if it was only shock, but he had succeeded in concealing it. That was what baffled people, he knew. He had seen it in their faces, even in Horace's. He didn't react with the normal jealousy, and something was going to give. That was the conclusion people came to. And that was what made his story so good: something had given, and he had murdered one of Melinda's lovers. That was more believable than that he had taken it for four years without saying or doing anything. To have burst out, finally, was merely human. People understood that. Nobody on earth could prove that he had murdered Malcolm McRae, he thought, but neither could anybody prove that he hadn't.

6

It was a little more than two weeks after the Fourth of July dance, when Vic was breakfasting with Trixie one morning, that he saw the item in the *New York Times*:

SLAYER OF NEW YORK ADVERTISING
MAN FOUND

8-Month-Old Mystery Slaying of
Malcolm McRae Solved

With a spoonful of grapefruit poised in mid-air, Vic pored over it. The police had picked up a man working as a clerk in a haberdashery shop in the State of Washington who had confessed to the crime, and there was 'no doubt' that he was the murderer, though they were still checking the facts. The man's name was Howard Olney. He was thirty-one and a brother of Phyllis Olney, an entertainer, who had once been 'on intimate terms' with McRae. Olney, said the paper, blamed McRae for separating himself and his sister as a professional team. They were night-club entertainers, specializing in magic tricks. Phyllis Olney had met McRae in Chicago and had broken her contract to come with him to New York a year and a half ago. Olney had run out of money, his sister had never sent him any though she had promised that she would (who'd ever been able to squeeze a nickel out of Mal?), and, according to Olney, McRae had abandoned his sister, leaving her destitute. Nearly a year later Olney had hitchhiked to New York for the express purpose of avenging himself and his sister by killing McRae. Psychiatrists who had examined Olney said he showed manic-depressive tendencies, which would probably be taken into account when his trial came up.

'*Daddy!*' Trixie had finally got his attention. 'I said I'm going to finish your belt today!'

Vic had the feeling she had yelled it at him three times. 'That's great. You mean the braided belt.'

'The *only* belt I'm making this summer,' Trixie said in a tone that showed her annoyance with him. She dumped some puffed wheat from the little package in front of her on to her corn flakes, stirred them together, then reached for the bottle of ketchup. Trixie was in a ketchup period. Ketchup had to be on everything from scrambled eggs to rice pudding.

'Well, I'm looking forward to it,' Vic said. 'I hope you made it big enough.'

'It's a whopper.'

'Good.' Vic stared at her brown, smooth little shoulders crossed by the denim overall straps, thought vaguely of telling her to take a sweater this morning, then returned to the paper in his hand.

The remoteness of the murderer's relationship to his victim and the fact that he left no clues [said the paper] made this a nearly 'perfect' crime. It was only after months of patient inquiry into every friend and acquaintance of the murdered man that the police were able to pick up the trail of Olney ...

Whether the story would be in the *New Wesleyan* this evening or not, Vic thought, many people in Little Wesley received the *Times* every morning. Everybody who was interested in the story was going to know about it by tonight.

'Aren't you going to have any bacon and eggs?' Trixie asked.

Trixie usually claimed one piece of his bacon. He didn't want any bacon and eggs now. He saw that she had a big pool of ketchup in her bowl and that the cereal was probably inedible, even for Trixie. He got up slowly, went into the kitchen, and mechanically lit the fire under a skillet. He put in two pieces of bacon. He felt faintly nauseous.

'Daddy? I've just got fi-yuv *min-n-nits*!' Trixie yelled to him in a minatory tone.

'Coming up, puss,' he called back.

'Hey! Since when do you call *me* puss?'

Vic didn't answer. He'd tell Melinda this morning, he thought, before she had a chance to hear it from anybody else.

He had barely set the bacon down in front of Trixie when he heard the low moan of the school bus coming up the road. Trixie scurried about, collecting her badminton racket and the big red workman's handkerchief she was crazy about and wore around her neck most of the time, holding a piece of bacon in the fingers of one hand. She turned at the door, popped the bacon into her mouth, and Vic heard the crunch of baby teeth on it. 'Bye, Daddy!' and she was gone.

Vic stared at the sofa in the living-room, remembering a time when Mal had passed out there and had had to spend the night – though Mal had revived enough to ask to be put into a guest room, Vic recalled. He thought of Ralph lying there, that last evening, his head in the same spot Mal's head had been. Ralph was going to be amused by the story, Vic thought. Ralph might be back before long.

Vic went into the kitchen, heated the coffee for a moment,

then poured a cup for Melinda, adding a scant teaspoon of sugar. He carried the coffee to her door and knocked.

'Umm-m?'

'It's me. I've got some coffee for you.'

'Com-me in-n,' she drawled, half with sleepiness, half with annoyance.

He went in. She lay on her back, her arms under her head. She wore pyjamas, she slept without a pillow, and there was always something peculiarly Spartan about her, to Vic, on the rare occasions when he went into her room to awaken her, and when he saw her lying in her bed alone. There would be the wind sweeping the room, billowing the curtains as he opened the door on the coldest winter mornings. There would be a blanket kicked off on to the floor, because even in a temperature nearly freezing Melinda could keep warm under practically nothing. There was a blanket kicked off on the floor now. Melinda lay under a sheet. Vic handed her the big cup of coffee. It was her own blue and white cup, with her name on it.

She winced at the first hot sip. 'Oh-h-h-ah-h,' she groaned, falling back on the bed, letting the cup tip dangerously in her hand.

Vic sat down on the hard little bench in front of her dressing-table. 'Read some news this morning,' he said.

'Yes? What?'

'They found the man who killed Mal.'

She raised herself up on one elbow, all her sleepiness gone. 'Did they? Who was it?'

Vic had the paper under his arm. He handed it to Melinda.

She read it avidly, with a twinkling amusement that kept Vic staring at her. 'Well, what do you know,' she said finally.

'I trust you're pleased,' Vic said, managing a pleasant tone.

She shot a look at him, hard and quick as a bullet. 'Aren't *you*?'

'I doubt if I'm as pleased as you,' Vic said.

She sprang out of bed and for a moment she stood beside him in white pyjamas, on bare feet with crimson nails, looking at herself in the mirror, pushing her hair back from her face. 'That's right, you're not. You couldn't be.' Then she ran into the bathroom, as agilely as Trixie might have run.

The telephone rang by Melinda's bed, and at once Vic suspected it was Horace. Horace subscribed to the *Times*, too. Vic went out, crossed the living-room to the hall phone and picked it up. 'Hello?'

'Hello, Vic. Did you see the paper this morning?' Horace had a smile in his voice, but a friendly smile, not a malicious one.

'Yes, I saw it.'

'Did you know the man?'

'No, I've never heard of him.'

'Well—' Horace waited for Vic to speak. 'This'll end all the talking, anyway.'

'I haven't heard much of this talking,' Vic said rather crisply.

'Oh-h – I have, Vic. It hasn't been entirely good.'

'Well, Melinda's very happy, of course.'

'You know my opinion on that, Vic.' Horace hesitated again, but now he was groping for words. 'I think you've – Well, I think she's come a long way in these last couple of months. I hope it keeps up.'

Vic listened to the shower running in the bathroom. Melinda was in the bathroom, hadn't picked up the telephone in her room, he knew, but still he found himself tongue-tied. He couldn't discuss his personal problems with Horace. 'Thanks, Horace,' he said finally.

Usually Vic was at the plant by a quarter past nine or nine-thirty, but he sat in the living-room now, at ten past nine, waiting for Melinda to finish dressing, waiting for her to say whatever else she was going to say to him this morning, waiting to find out where she was going. He could tell by the haste of her preparations that she had some objective. He heard her dial a number on her telephone, but her voice did not come through the closed door, and he would not have wished to hear what she was saying, anyway.

Vic couldn't see her going back to Ralph, really, after he'd shown himself such a coward. Joel was in New York, but that was not an impossible distance if Melinda was determined to see him. Vic took a cigarette from the box on the rosewood cocktail table. He had just made the table, had polished its very subtly concave top as carefully as if it had been a lens. He had made it to replace the old cocktail table which he had also made, that dated from Larry Osbourne and had become so stained with cigarette burns and alcohol, in spite of the protective waxes he had always kept on it, that he had had no desire to refinish it. He wondered how soon the rosewood table was going to be stained with rings from highball glasses and burns from neglected cigarettes. When he heard Melinda's door open he sat down on the sofa so that he would appear deep in his newspaper when she came in.

'Are you memorizing that thing?' she asked him.

'I was reading something else. There's a new book on mountain climbing I'd like to buy.'

'There's a nice safe sport for you. Why don't you try it?' She took a cigarette from the box and lit it. She had on a white shirt, her flaring brown corduroy skirt, her brown moccasins. She slapped her key case into one empty, restless hand. She looked nervous and wild, the way he had seen her look many times at the start of an affair. This was the kind of mood that always got her tickets for speeding.

'Where're you off to?' he asked.

'Oh, I – just made a lunch date with Evelyn. So I won't be home for lunch.'

Vic was not sure if she was lying or not. Her reply hadn't told him where she was going now. He stood up and stretched, and tugged his sweater down evenly over his trousers. 'How about cocktails this afternoon? Can you make it to the Chesterfield by about six?'

She lowered her brows, swung a leg around, pivoting on a toe, like an adolescent. 'I don't think so, Vic. You don't really like it. Thanks, anyway.'

'Sorry.' He smiled. 'Well, I'll be going.'

They went into the garage together and got into their cars. Vic took a couple of minutes to warm his car up, but Melinda in her pale-green convertible was gone down the lane in a matter of seconds.

7

Two or three days after the dénouement of the McRae case, Vic received a telephone call in his office from a Mr Cassell. Mr Cassell said he was an agent of the Binkley Real Estate Company of East Lyme and that Vic's name had been given as a reference in regard to Mr Charles De Lisle who wanted to rent one of their houses.

'Charles De Lisle?' Vic asked puzzledly. He had never heard of the man.

'I'm sorry to trouble you at your office, Mr Van Allen, but we weren't able to reach your wife at home. It's actually Mrs Victor Van Allen on my record here, but I thought you might be able to vouch for Mr De Lisle as well as she. Can you tell us what you know about him as to his reliability? You know – it's just so we can have something to quote to the landlord.'

Vic had suddenly recognized the name: it was the name of the pianist in the Lord Chesterfield bar. 'I don't exactly – I suppose he's all right. I'll speak to my wife at noon and ask her to call you this afternoon.'

'Very well, Mr Van Allen. We'd appreciate it if you would. Thanks very much, good-bye.'

'Good-bye.' Vic hung up.

Stephen was waiting for him with some new paper samples. They began to examine them together, holding them in front of a naked two-hundred-watt light bulb, scrutinizing their areas for consistency of thickness. The paper was for the next book of the Greenspur Press, a book of poems by a young instructor at Bard College named Brian Ryder. Stephen had better eyes than Vic for the delicate marbling that showed up under the bright light, but Vic trusted his own judgement more when it came to the general quality of paper and how it would take the ink. They looked at six grades of paper, eliminated four after a few minutes, and finally concurred about one of the two remaining grades.

'Shall I send the order off now?' Stephen asked.

'May as well. They took an age the last time.' Vic returned to his desk, where he was writing letters of rejection to three poets and one novelist who had sent him manuscripts in the previous month. Vic always wrote his rejection letters himself, and by hand, because he hated writing them and would not have wished the task on Stephen and because he considered a courteous, handwritten letter from the publisher himself the only civilized way of communicating to the people whose work he had to reject. Most of the manuscripts he received were good. Some were very good, and he would have liked to publish those, but he could not publish everything he liked, and to the authors of manuscripts he considered very good he gave thoughtful advice as to where they might send them next. Most of his letters went something like: '... As you probably know, the Greenspur Press is a small one. We have only two hand presses, and because of our slow methods of operation it is impossible for us to print more than four books per year at most ...' His tone was modest, in keeping with the spirit of the Greenspur Press, but Vic was exceedingly proud of his slow methods, proud of the fact that it usually took the Greenspur Press five days to set ten pages.

Vic was especially proud of Stephen Hines and grateful to Providence that he had found him. Stephen was thirty-two, a married man with one small child. He was a quiet fellow, even-tempered and endlessly patient with all the corrections and adjustments that printing entailed. He was as meticulous as Vic, and Vic never thought, in his first difficult two years, that anyone as painstaking as himself would ever come along. But Stephen presented himself one day, six years ago, and had asked him for a job. Stephen had been working for a small commercial printing firm in Brooklyn. He wanted to live in the country, he said. He thought he would like working for the Greenspur Press. Vic put him on at union wages at first, but after two weeks gave him a twenty per cent rise. Stephen had not wanted to take it. He loved the plant, loved the green, mountainous countryside – he was from Arizona, and his father's farm had blown away in a dust storm, he said – and at that time he had not been married. Five years ago he brought his girl Georgianne up from New York, and they were married, with Vic standing as best man. Georgianne was the right girl for him, quiet, modest, and as in love with the country as Stephen. They bought the guest house of a large estate between Little Wesley and Wesley, a house set deep in the woods on a road that Stephen had to clear with his own hands to make wide enough for a car. Vic had helped them finance the house, and now Stephen had paid back three-quarters of it. He was devoted to Vic, though he never made a display of his devotion. It showed mostly in his attitude of respect towards Vic. He had called Vic 'sir' until Vic, after a couple of months, made a joking remark about it. Now Vic was not quite 'Mr Van Allen' or 'Vic', and Stephen called him nothing, to his face.

The other member of the Greenspur Press staff was old Carlyle, a small, stooped man of about sixty whom Vic had rescued from dereliction on the streets of Wesley. Carlyle had been begging, begging a quarter for a drink. Vic had bought him the drink and started talking to him. Vic had offered him a job as handyman and floor-sweeper in his plant, and Carlyle had accepted. Now his drinking was confined to two times per year – at Christmas and on his birthday. He had no family. Vic paid him enough to live comfortably in a room that he rented from an elderly woman whose house was on the north side of Little Wesley. Carlyle's tasks, in the four years he had been with Vic, had been enlarged to include mail sorting, press greasing, helping Stephen to lock up the chases, and carrying and fetching packages to and from the railroad station in Wesley. He had become a more or less reliable driver of the light-weight Dodge truck that stood always at the back entrance of the plant. It was debatable if Carlyle earned his $60 a week salary, but the Greenspur Press did not financially earn its keep, either, Vic reasoned, and he felt that he was con-tributing a great deal towards making the last years of Carlyle's life happy by employing him when nobody else would. So long as the worst Carlyle did was run the Dodge off the edge of the culvert bridge at the end of the lane, get drunk twice a year, and chew tobacco – Carlyle was an inveterate tobacco chewer and main-tained a spittoon in the corner of the printing room which he emptied reasonably often – he could stay on until he died of old age.

The plant itself was a one-storey structure painted dark green so that it was almost camouflaged among the dense, overhanging trees that grew all around it. It had a weird shape, having origin-ally been a smallish barn of the kind used to store tools. This room was now the room that held the presses and the composing tables. Vic had built a smaller square room on to one end, which was his office, and another room at the other end, which was a storeroom for paper and types. To make the building moisture-proof Vic had covered the outside with roof insulation and then covered the whole with sheets of tin which he had then painted. A somewhat rutty road wound from the plant to a larger dirt road about two hundred yards away. The plant was a ten-minute drive from where Vic lived.

On the day that he received the call about Charles De Lisle, Melinda was not home at one o'clock. Vic ate a solitary lunch and read a book at the table. He felt curiously disturbed, as if somebody were looking at him from behind as he walked around in the empty house. He put on the Gregorian chants and turned them up loud so that he could hear them when he went out to put his herb boxes back into the garage just before three. There had been no note from Melinda in the house. Vic had even looked in her room for one, though Melinda had never left one there. She usually put a note in the middle of the living-room floor when she left one.

Was she with Charles De Lisle? The question had risen to the surface of his mind like a bubble, making a small, unpleasant explosion when the words had come. Why should he think that? He remembered Charles De Lisle's face, but very vaguely, as being on the swarthy side – narrow, dark, and he had heavily brilliantined hair. Vic remembered thinking that he looked like an Italian crook. He had seen him only once, he thought, one afternoon about three weeks ago when he had had a cocktail with Melinda in the Lord Chesterfield bar. Melinda hadn't made a single comment about his piano playing, Vic thought, which was unusual.

He put Charles De Lisle out of his mind. One thing he didn't want to be guilty of was suspicion before suspicion was necessary. Melinda was always innocent until she proved herself guilty.

Melinda was still not at home when Vic arrived at a quarter to seven that evening. Trixie had been home since four-thirty, and Vic asked her if she had heard from her mother.

'Nope,' Trixie said indifferently. She was lying on her stomach on the floor, reading the funny paper page of the *New Wesleyan*.

Trixie was used to her mother's being out at odd times. She had had it for the better part of her life.

'How about a game of Scrabble?' Vic asked her.

Trixie looked up at him, thinking it over. Her little oval, sun-kissed face reminded Vic suddenly of an acorn, a shiny, brand-new acorn just dropped from a tree, with a pointed tip that was Trixie's chin and a cap that was her straight bangs and the straight-down hair that had just been cut so that it reached the middle of her ears. 'All right!' Trixie said finally, and jumped up and got the Scrabble box from a book-shelf.

The phone rang and Vic answered it. It was Melinda.

'I'll be home around eight, Vic. Go ahead and eat if you want to, but I'm bringing somebody by for a drink – if you don't mind,' she added heavily, and he could tell she had had a few drinks already. 'Okay?'

'Okay,' he said. He knew whom she was bringing, too. 'Okay, I'll be seeing you.'

'Bye-bye.'

He hung up. 'Mommie won't be home for about an hour, shug,' Vic said. 'Are you getting hungry?'

'I'm not hungry,' Trixie said.

Trixie loved to eat with them. She would wait hours – though Vic's deadline for her was nine – so that she could have her dinner when they had theirs. Usually they ate at about eight-thirty. They wouldn't tonight, Vic thought. He forced himself to concentrate on the game. He and Trixie played with her making two moves to his one in order to even out the score a little. Trixie was already a better speller than her mother, Vic thought, though he did not think it diplomatic to tell Trixie so. Vic had taught her to read when she was three. They were well into their second game, Trixie had eaten a chocolate doughnut with ketchup, and it was growing very dark before he heard the sound of two cars coming up the driveway.

Trixie heard it, too, and cocked her head. 'Two people coming,' she said.

'Your mother's bringing a guest.'

'Who?'

'I don't know. She just said somebody. Your play, Trix.'

He heard Melinda's slurring, low-pitched voice, her step on the stone walk, then she opened the door.

'Hi!' Melinda called. 'Come on in, Charley. Vic, I'd like you to meet Charley De Lisle. Charley, my husband.' She gestured perfunctorily.

Vic had risen to his feet. 'How do you do?'

Charley mumbled something and nodded. He looked embarrassed. He was about thirty-five, slight and not very tall, with close-set and rather furtive eyes over which his dark eyebrows grew together.

'Charley's the pianist at the Lord Chesterfield,' Melinda said.

'Yes, I know. Well, how do you like our town?' Vic asked pleasantly.

'I like it fine,' Charley said.

'Sit down, Charley. Aren't you going to make us a drink, Vic? What'll you have?'

Charley mumbled that he supposed he'd have rye and water. Vic went off to the kitchen to make the drinks. He made Charley's drink and then two Scotch and waters for himself and Melinda. He poured an orange juice for Trixie. When he went back into the living-room Trixie was still standing in the middle of the floor, staring with a neutral, fixed curiosity at Charley De Lisle. Vic passed the drinks around on a tray.

'I had a call about you today, a telephone call,' Vic said to Charley.

Charley looked up at him, blank and surprised.

'A real estate agent wanted to know if I knew you. I'm afraid I couldn't give him much of a reference.' Vic's smile was friendly.

66

'Oh, lord, did they call *you*?' Melinda laughed. 'Sorry, Vic, *I'll* call them tomorrow,' she said boredly. 'But Charley's already got his home. He's moving in tomorrow. It's a wonderful cottage in the woods. Do you know that little house off fifteen about two miles south of East Lyme? I thought I once drove you up the road to show it to you. I've noticed it was vacant since spring, and I thought Charley would like it better than a hotel, because he's going to be here another six weeks, so I found the real estate agency that handles it – *finally* – and I got it for him. Charley adores it.' Melinda was picking out records to play.

'That sounds very nice,' Vic said. Melinda must have driven up the road to show it to somebody else, he thought. Two miles south of East Lyme made it just two miles closer to Little Wesley than he had thought it would be. Then he tried to neutralize his thoughts, tried very hard. He had no reason to feel hostile towards Mr De Lisle. Mr De Lisle looked as if he were afraid of his own shadow.

Melinda had chosen piano records, and she was playing them a bit loud. When a second record dropped down, she asked Charley if he knew who the pianist was. Charley knew.

Vic fixed another drink for himself and Melinda. Charley was only sipping at his. When he came back into the room, Melinda was saying to Trixie, 'Why don't you go and play in your room, darling? You're making an awful mess there.'

Trixie was absently building something with the Scrabble counters on the floor in front of the fireplace. Now she gave a sigh and slowly began to replace the counters in the box, at a rate that would keep her there twenty minutes.

'That drink isn't poisoned, you know,' Melinda said to Charley.

'I know.' He smiled. 'I have to watch out for the ulcer. Also I've got to work tonight.'

'I hope you'll stay for dinner, though. You don't have to work till eleven. You can get to Ballinger in six minutes from here.'

'Maybe by rocket,' Vic said, smiling. 'He'd better give himself twenty minutes if he wants to stay alive.'

'Charley works at the Hotel Lincoln in Ballinger from eleven to midnight,' Melinda announced to Vic. Her nose could have used some powder, but she looked very well with her dark-blonde hair loose and flowing back, the way the wind had left it, her smooth, slightly freckled face aglow with suntan and with animal good spirits now. She had not had enough to drink to begin wilting. Vic could see why men found her charming, even irresistible, when she looked this way. She leaned towards Charley, putting a hand on his sleeve. 'Charley – stay for dinner?' And without waiting for his answer, she jumped up. 'My gosh, I left the steak in the car! I've got the most beautiful steak, handpicked from Hansen's!' She ran out of the house.

Charley absolutely refused to stay for dinner, however. 'I've got to be going,' he said as soon as he had finished his first drink.

'Well, you're not going to leave without playing something!' Melinda said.

Charley got up docilely, as if he knew it was of no use to argue with Melinda, and sat down at the piano. 'Anything in particular?' he asked.

Melinda was propping up the piano top. 'Whatever you like.'

Charley played 'Old Buttermilk Sky'. Vic knew it was one of Melinda's favourites, and Charley must have known it, too, because he had winked at her as he struck the first notes.

'I wish I could play like that,' she said when he had finished. 'I play it, but not like that.'

'Show me,' Charley said, getting up from the bench.

She shook her head. 'Not now. Do you think you can teach me to play it like that?'

'If you play at all – sure,' Charley said bluntly. 'I'll be taking off.'

Vic got up. 'Very nice meeting you,' he said.

'Thanks. Same here.' Charley picked up his raincoat.

Melinda went out with him to his car. She stayed about five minutes. When she came in, neither of them said anything for a while.

Then Melinda said, 'Anything new with you today?'

'Nope,' Vic said. She would not have heard him if he had told her about anything that was new. 'I think it's high time we ate, don't you?'

Melinda was more than usually pleasant the rest of the evening. But the next day she was again not home at one o'clock, and again not home until nearly eight. Charley De Lisle was giving her piano lessons in the afternoons, she said.

8

Vic knew what was happening, and he tried to make Melinda admit it and stop it before it got all over town. He simply told her, in a quiet way, that he thought she was seeing too much of Charley De Lisle.

'You're imagining things,' she said. 'The first person I've been able to talk to in weeks without being treated like a pariah, and you hate it. You don't want me to get any fun out of life, that's all!'

She could say things like that to him as if she really meant them. She could actually stymie him and make him wonder if she really believed what she said. In an effort to be fair with her, he tried to see it the way she told it, tried to imagine that it was impossible that she could be attracted to a greasy, sick-looking night-club entertainer. But he couldn't see it that way. She had made the same denials in regard to Jo-Jo, and Jo-Jo had been equally repellent from Vic's point of view, and yet *that* had happened. Jo-Jo had been so amusing, a laugh a minute. He'd been so nice to Trixie. Now Charley De Lisle was such a wonderful piano player. He was showing her how to improve her playing. He came over a couple of afternoons a week now, after three when

Vic had left the house, and he gave Melinda a lesson until five when he had to go to work at the Lord Chesterfield. Trixie was generally home in the afternoons, so what was the harm in his coming over? But sometimes Melinda wasn't home for lunch, and sometimes they didn't play the piano in the afternoon, because an ash-tray that Vic had seen on the keyboard at two o'clock would be there when he got home at seven. Sometimes they were up at Charley De Lisle's house, where there wasn't a piano.

'Just what do you expect me to think about this?' Vic asked her.

'Nothing! I don't know what you're up in the air about!'

Useless to point out to her that she hadn't seen or talked about anybody else but Charley De Lisle for two weeks. Useless and embarrassing to tell her that even Trixie was aware of it, and was practically taking it for granted now. In the second week of Mr De Lisle, Vic had come home one evening when Melinda hadn't been in, and Trixie had said, very casually, 'I guess she's up at Charley's house. She wasn't home when I got home.' That had hurt him, even worse than the way Trixie had looked at Charley that first evening had hurt him. Vic remembered walking into the living-room with a couple of fresh drinks and seeing Trixie perched on the arm of the armchair, staring at Charley with a wide-eyed, apprehensive, yet completely helpless curiosity, as if she had known then that she was looking at the man who was going to take Ralph's place, that she was going to be seeing him very often from now on whether she liked him or not, whether he was nice to her or not. The memory of Trixie looking at Charley from the armchair haunted Vic. He felt that that was the first instant that his suspicion had become an absolute certainty. He felt that Trixie in her innocence had known intuitively what he had only suspected at that time.

Vic said in a light, joking tone, 'It's too bad I'm married to you, isn't it? I might have a chance with you if I were a total stranger

and met you out of the blue. I'd have money, not be too bad looking, with lots of interesting things to talk about—'

'Like what? Snails and bed bugs?' She was dressing to go out
with Charley that afternoon, fastening around her waist a belt
that Vic had given her, tying around her neck a purple and yellow
scarf that Vic had chosen carefully and bought for her.

'You used to think snails were interesting and that a lot of
other things were interesting, until your brain began to atrophy.'

'Thanks. I like my brain fine and you can have yours.'

It was Sunday. Vic had wanted to drive up to Bear Lake with
Melinda and Trixie and row around a little while – he and
Melinda in a rowboat and Trixie in her canoe. Week-ends were
the only time Trixie could go up to the lake, and she loved it. So
had Melinda enjoyed it, until two or three weeks ago. But she was
going out with Charley, and they were just going to drive around
in the country, Melinda had said, but she wasn't taking Trixie
with her.

'I may not be here when you get back,' Vic said.

'Oh? Where're you going?'

'I thought Trixie and I might go down to see Blair Peabody.'

'Oh,' she said, and he felt she hadn't even heard him. 'Well, so
long, Vic,' she said as she passed him in the hall. 'Have fun with
Blair.'

Vic stood in the living-room, listening to her car's motor fading
down the lane. He shouldn't have said that about her brain
atrophying, he thought. It wouldn't do any good to insult her. He
was sorry he had. Better to take it lightly and casually, as if he
didn't resent anything, as if there were nothing to resent, and she
might tire of Charley in another week or so. If he showed his dislike of Charley, that was sure to make her go after him, just out of
contrariness. He ought to reverse his tactics completely, be a good
egg and all that. From Melinda's point of view, Vic knew De Lisle
was neither handsome nor entertaining, except on the piano. But

he had to admit that being a good egg with Jo-Jo and with Ralph Gosden hadn't got him anywhere. And the thought of Melinda dragging Charley to parties at the Cowans' and the Mellers' – she hadn't done it yet, but it was coming, he knew – the shame of endorsing socially a guttersnipe like Charley De Lisle seemed more than he could bear. And everybody would know that Melinda had picked up the first man she could find after the McRae story had exploded. Everybody would know now that he was disgusted and helpless to combat it, however indifferent he pretended to be, because obviously he had made an effort to hold off Melinda's lovers by telling the story about McRae.

He tried to pull himself together. What was the alternative to treating Mr De Lisle in a courteous and friendly manner? Debasing himself by showing that Mr De Lisle was worth his irritation. Debasing himself by trying to derive satisfaction from stopping the affair. Those weren't his methods and never had been. No, the proper attitude was to be courteous and civilized, no matter what happened. He might lose that way, might be scoffed and laughed at, but he would certainly lose the other way, lose Melinda's respect and his self-respect, whether he stopped the affair or not.

He did not go to see Blair Peabody. Janey Peterson called up Trixie and asked to come over, and Trixie seemed just as happy to play around the house if Janey came over, so Vic decided to spend the afternoon reading about Tiberius.

Janey's father drove her over, and Vic chatted with him on the front lawn for a few minutes. He was a strongly built, fair-haired man with a pleasant air of frankness and modesty about him. He had a bag of fresh home-made doughnuts with him, and Janey and Trixie took a couple and dashed off, and Vic and Peterson stood there munching and talking about the hydrangea bushes on the front lawn that were now in full bloom. Peterson said his were new young plants and evidently too young to bloom this year, because they hadn't.

'Take a couple of ours,' Vic said. 'We've got more than we need.'

Peterson protested, but Vic went to the garage, got the pitch-fork and a couple of burlap bags, and dug up two of the bushes. There were four hydrangea bushes, scattered in no particular pattern on the lawn, and Vic happened to detest hydrangeas. At least he did that afternoon. Their big pastel pompoms of blossoms looked tawdry and insipid. He presented the two bushes, their roots wrapped in burlap, to Peterson with his greetings to Mrs Peterson.

'She'll be tickled pink with these,' Peterson said. 'It'll certainly improve the lawn. Give my regards to your wife, too. Is she here?'

'No. She's out visiting a friend,' Vic answered.

Peterson nodded.

Vic was not sure, but he thought Peterson had looked a little embarrassed when he asked about Melinda. Vic waved at him as his car pulled away, then turned back towards the house. The lawn looked as if two small bombs had hit it. He left it that way.

Melinda came in at a quarter to seven. Vic heard her car, and after a few moments went from his room through the garage into the living-room, ostensibly to get a few sections of the *Times*. He half expected to find De Lisle with her, but Melinda was alone.

'No doubt you've been imagining me in the depths of iniquity this afternoon,' she said, 'but we went to the trotting races. I won eight bucks. What do you think of that?'

'I didn't imagine anything,' Vic said, with a smile, and turned the radio on. There was a news commentator he wanted to hear at seven o'clock.

Janey Peterson stayed for dinner with them, and then Vic drove her home. He knew that Melinda would call Charley while he was out of the house. Charley had had a telephone installed almost immediately, because Melinda had used all the influence she had – or rather that the name Van Allen had – to get the company to put the phone in without the usual two or three weeks' delay. Vic wished she hadn't said that about the 'depths of iniquity'. He wished she weren't quite so crude. She hadn't always been so crude. That was the fault of the company she kept, of course. Why had she said anything at all if she hadn't done anything with De Lisle or didn't intend to? When a woman as attractive as Melinda handed it to them on a platter, why should a man like De Lisle resist? The morals to resist didn't come very often any more. That was for people like Henri III of France, after his wife the Princesse de Condé died. There was devotion, Henri sitting in his library the rest of his life, with his memories of the Princesse, creating designs of skulls and crossbones for Nicolas Ève to put on book covers and title pages for him. Henri would probably be called psychotic by modern psychiatrists.

Charley De Lisle came twice to the house for dinner during the following week, and one evening the three of them went to an outdoor concert at Tanglewood, though Charley had had to leave before it was over in order to be at the Hotel Lincoln by eleven. One of the evenings he dined with them was a Monday, when he didn't work and could stay later than eleven, and Vic obligingly said good night around ten o'clock, went to his own room, and did not come back. Charley and Melinda had been sitting at the piano, but the piano stopped, Vic noticed, as soon as he left. Vic finally went to bed and to sleep, though the sound of Charley's car leaving awakened him, and he looked at his wrist-watch and saw that it was a quarter to four.

The next morning Vic knocked on Melinda's door at about nine o'clock, carrying a cup of coffee for her. He had had a call from Stephen a few minutes before, saying that his wife was not feeling well and that he didn't want to leave her alone. Stephen had asked if Melinda could possibly come and spell him, because two other women he might have called on were out of town with their husbands on vacation. Melinda didn't answer his knock, and Vic pushed the door open gently. The room was empty. The beige cover on the bed looked unusually taut and smooth. Vic carried the coffee back to the kitchen and poured it down the sink.

Then he went on to the plant. He called Stephen and told him that Melinda had had an early appointment to go shopping with a friend in Wesley, but that she ought to be back by noon, and that he would call him again. Vic called home at eleven and at twelve. She was in at twelve, and he asked her, in a perfectly ordinary voice, how she was, and then told her about Georgianne. Georgianne was pregnant, six or seven months pregnant, Vic thought. Stephen had had a doctor for her, and they didn't think it was going to be a miscarriage, but Georgianne needed somebody with her.

'Sure, I'll be glad to go,' Melinda said. 'Tell Stephen I can be there in about half an hour.'

She sounded very willing to go, both to expiate her sins of last night, Vic supposed, and also because she really did like doing things for people, doing errands of mercy. It was one of the nice things about Melinda, perhaps one of the curious things, that she loved taking care of people who were sick, anybody who was sick, loved helping a stranger in distress – someone with a flat tyre, an uncashable cheque, or a nose bleed. It was the only direction in which she showed her maternal instinct, towards the stranger in distress.

Melinda's staying out all night was not going to be mentioned, Vic thought, but Charley De Lisle would be just a little different the next time Vic saw him, because De Lisle hadn't the aplomb to be quite the same. He'd be a little more servile and furtive. It was the fact that De Lisle would dare to face him at all that angered Vic.

The evening at Tanglewood had come two days later, and Vic was very calm and amiable that night, even paid for the refreshments in the intermission, though the Van Allen family had provided the tickets, too. Mr De Lisle seemed to be feeling very pleased with himself. A pleasant summer job in the delightfully cool Berkshires, a made-to-order mistress whom he didn't have to pay for – on the contrary, she paid for him, bought him liquor and took him food – and didn't have to be responsible for, because she was married. To top it all, the husband didn't mind! Mr De Lisle's world must have been a very rosy one indeed, Vic thought.

On Friday of that week Vic ran into Horace Meller in the drugstore and Horace insisted on their having a quick drink together before they went home. Horace wanted to go to the Lord Chesterfield bar. Vic proposed a little beer parlour known as Mac's two blocks away, but Horace remarked that it was two blocks away and they were right across the street from the Chesterfield, so Vic agreed to the Chesterfield, thinking it would look odd if he argued about it.

Mr De Lisle was at the piano when they went into the bar, but Vic did not look his way. There were people at four or five tables, but Melinda, Vic had noted with a quick glance as he came in, was not among them. They stood at the bar and ordered Scotch and soda.

'We missed you at the club last week,' Horace said. 'Mary and I putted around the first couple of holes all afternoon. We kept thinking you'd turn up.'

'I was reading,' Vic said.

'How's Melinda? I haven't seen her lately either.'

'Oh, she's fine. She's been doing some swimming with Trixie at the club. Just not on Sundays, I suppose.' She'd taken Trixie once to the club pool, after a lot of begging on Trixie's part.

Mr De Lisle stopped playing, and a few people applauded. Vic was aware of De Lisle standing up, bowing, and stepping off his platform, going through the door into the lobby beyond.

'I'm glad she's coming around,' Horace said. 'You know – I hope you'll forgive me for talking to you sometimes in the past –

about Melinda, I mean. I never meant to meddle. I hope you know that, Vic.'

'Of course I know, Horace!' Horace had leaned closer to him, and Vic looked into his serious brown eyes, framed by the bushy eyebrows and the little wrinkling pouches below. Horace was around fifty, Vic realized. He should know a lot more than he himself did, at thirty-six. Horace straightened up and Vic could see that he was embarrassed, that it had been a speech Horace had thought he ought to make, and Vic tried to think of the right thing to say now.

'I just wanted you to know – and Mary feels the same way – that we knew things would straighten out and we're awfully glad they have.'

Vic nodded and smiled. 'Thank you, Horace.' He felt a sudden, frightening depression, as if his soul, somewhere, had slid down a hill into darkness.

'At least I assume things are straightening out,' Horace said.

'Oh, yes, I think they are.'

'I thought Melinda looked awfully well the night we came over. The night of the club dance, too.'

The night the Mellers had come over had been only two nights after the dance, Vic remembered. There had been an evening since, when the Mellers had invited them to hear some new records Horace had bought, when Melinda had been too tired from an afternoon with Charley De Lisle to go. The Mellers hadn't seen Melinda and Charley together yet. It'd take them only two minutes, if they ever saw them together, to know what was happening. Melinda had been considerably more gracious to people during the time the town had been debating the McRae story. That was all Horace meant by her straightening out.

'You're very thoughtful tonight,' Horace said. 'What's the next book going to be?'

'Oh, a book of poems,' Vic said. 'By a young man called Brian Ryder. I think I showed you a couple one day in my office.'

'Yes, I remember! A little metaphysical for me, but—' Horace smiled. There was a silence, and then he said, 'I hear the Cowans are going to treat us to a big outdoor party soon. They want to celebrate Phil's book. He's just about to finish the second draft of it. Evelyn says she feels they've been cooped up and have had to neglect their friends, so she wants a big outdoor affair with lanterns – and I think costumes.' Horace chuckled. 'I suppose we'll all end up cooling our heads in the swimming pool.'

Mr De Lisle was now offering 'The Song from Moulin Rouge'. Light and gentle and sentimental. Melinda had been playing it lately, trying to imitate Charley's style. Have you met Charley De Lisle? Vic wanted to ask Horace. You will. Probably before the Cowans' party.

'What do you think of the new pianist?' Horace asked. 'Makes our old hostelry practically like New York.'

'Pretty good, isn't it?' Vic said.

'I'd rather have silence. Lesley's business must be good this year. I hear the rooms are all taken, and there's a pretty good crowd here today.' Horace had half turned and was watching De Lisle, who was in profile to them.

The man had a date with my wife this afternoon, Vic wanted to state in a firm voice. I don't want to look at him or hear him.

'Know his name?' Horace asked.

'No idea,' Vic said.

'He looks like an Italian.' Horace turned back to his drink.

He did look like an Italian of the worse type, though Vic didn't think he was, and it was an insult to the Italian race to assume that he was. He resembled no particular race, only an amalgamation of the worst elements of various Latin peoples. He looked as if he had spent all his life dodging blows that were probably aimed at him for good reason.

'Time for the other half?' Horace asked.

Vic woke up. 'I don't think I have, Horace. I told Melinda I'd be in about six-thirty tonight.'

'All right, you be there,' Horace said, smiling.

Vic insisted on paying the bar tab. Then they walked out into the fresh air together.

9

The Cowans' party was a costume party. People were to come as their favourite hero or heroine, fictional or factual. Melinda was having a hard time deciding who she should be. She wasn't quite satisfied with Mary Queen of Scots, or Greta Garbo, or Annie Oakley, or Cleopatra, and she thought somebody else might go as Scarlett O'Hara, though Vic said he doubted it. Melinda went through them all, imagining the costume for each in detail. She felt there should be some character more appropriate for her, if she could only think of her.

'Madame Bovary?' Vic suggested.

She finally decided on Cleopatra.

Charley De Lisle was going to play the piano at the Cowans' party. Melinda had arranged it. She told Vic with naïve triumph that she had persuaded Charley to do it for fifty dollars instead of the hundred he had wanted, and said that Evelyn Cowan hadn't thought that was a steep price at all.

Something in Vic stirred with revulsion. 'I assumed he was going as a guest.'

'Yes, but he wouldn't have played. He's very proud about his work. He says no artist should give his work away. In a room full of strangers, he wouldn't touch the piano, he says. It wouldn't be professional. I can see what he means.'

She could always see what De Lisle meant.

Vic had made no remarks about De Lisle lately, or the time Melinda spent out of the house. The situation had not changed, though De Lisle had not come for dinner any more, and Melinda had not stayed out all night a second time. Neither had they been to any social affair to which Melinda might have dragged Charley, so perhaps none of their friends suspected anything yet, Vic thought, though Evelyn Cowan might by now. And everybody would certainly know after the Cowan party, which was why Vic dreaded it. He longed not to go, to beg off somehow, and yet he knew his presence would have a slightly restraining influence on Melinda, and that logically it was better if he did go. There were many times when logic was of no comfort.

Xenophon was printing. Stephen stood at the press all day, banging a page out at fifteen-second intervals. Vic relieved him three and four times a day while he rested by changing his task. Stephen's wife Georgianne had given birth to a second son after her seventh month of pregnancy. She and the child were doing well, and Stephen appeared happier than he had ever been, and his happiness seemed to pervade the shop in the month of August. Vic set up the other press so that he could print along with Stephen. They could set only five pages at a time, as they had no more Greek type, but the twenty pages alone would have taken Stephen more than a month without Vic's help. They were printing a hundred copies. Vic could match Stephen in endurance at the press, and he loved to stand in silence, hour after hour, the only sounds the final impacts of their platens against paper, with the summer sun streaming through the open windows and falling on the freshly printed sheets. All was order and progress in the plant in the month of August. At six-thirty or seven every evening, Vic stepped out of that peaceful world into a chaos. Since he had started the printing plant he had always stepped out of it in the evenings into something less peaceful, but the two worlds had never contrasted so profoundly before. The contrast had never before given him a feeling that he was being torn apart.

Vic did not think about his costume for the Cowans' party until the day before it, and then he decided on Tiberius. The costume was simple, a toga made from one of the oatmeal-coloured draperies that had used to hang at the living-room windows, heelless house slippers with leather straps that crossed over the toes, two cheap but classic clips that he bought himself rather than use any of Melinda's, and that was that. He thought for decency's sake that he should wear a tee-shirt and some walking shorts underneath instead of merely underwear.

The party was on a Saturday night of a particularly warm weekend, but since it was never really warm in the Berkshires in the evenings, the lanterns set around the edge of the Cowans' lawn and around the swimming pool suggested festivity and not an unpleasant warmth. Vic and Melinda arrived early, at a quarter to nine, so that Melinda could be on hand to welcome Charley, who was coming at nine, and to introduce him to the Cowans. Only the Mellers were there as yet, sitting with the Cowans on the side terrace where there were more lanterns and a huge bowl of punch that stood on a low table surrounded by glasses.

'Hello, there!' Evelyn greeted them. 'Well, look at Cleopatra!'

'*Good* evening,' Melinda said, slinking up the terrace steps in her trailing green dress, puffing on her serpentine cigarette-holder which she carried on a forefinger. She had even put a henna rinse in her hair.

'And Cicero?' Horace said to Vic.

'It could be,' Vic admitted, 'but that's not what I intended.'

'Ah, Tiberius,' Horace said.

'Thank you, Horace.' He had mentioned to Horace that he was interested in Tiberius lately, and was reading all he could find

83

on him. 'And you?' Vic peered with amusement at Horace's waist-line that had been enlarged with a pillow. 'A Venetian Santa Claus, perhaps?'

Horace laughed. 'You're way off! I'll let you guess.'

But Vic was distracted from guessing because Evelyn was pressing a glass of punch upon him.

'It's the last you'll *have* to drink, if you don't like it, Vic, darling, but you've got to drink one tonight for luck!' Evelyn said.

Vic lifted his glass to Phil Cowan. 'Here's to *Buried Treasures*,' Vic said. 'May they be uncovered.'

Buried Treasures was the title of Phil's book. Phil bowed and thanked him.

The MacPhersons arrived, got up as a couple of Vikings, a costume that was singularly fitting for Mrs MacPherson's tall, sturdy figure and her broad, fat, faintly pink face. The MacPhersons were in their fifties, but they had been sporting enough to wear knee-high skirts and sandals with straps that criss-crossed up their respectively fat and skinny calves, and they looked extremely pleased by the roar of laughter they caused as they came on to the terrace.

Evelyn put some music on the phonograph, and Phil and Melinda started to dance in the living-room. Two more cars arrived. Two couples walked up the lawn, followed by Mr De Lisle in his white dinner jacket. He hung back from the advancing group, looking around for Melinda. Vic pretended not to have seen him. But Melinda, hearing the hubbub of greetings, came out on the terrace, saw Charley and rushed to him, taking him by the hand.

'You might at least have come as Chopin!' Melinda cried, a sentence she had probably made up days ago to say. 'I'd like you all to meet Charley De Lisle!' she announced to everybody. 'This is Mr and Mrs Cowan, our hosts, Mr and Mrs MacPherson –' She waited for De Lisle to mumble his 'How do you do?' – 'Mr and

Mrs Meller – the Wilsons, Don and June – Mrs Podnansky and Mr—'

'Kenny,' said the young man who was one of the young men Melinda had danced with at the Fourth of July dance at the club.

'Mr De Lisle is going to play for us this evening,' Melinda said.

There was a murmur of interest and a small patter of hands. Charley looked uncomfortable and nervous. Melinda got him a glass of punch, then took him into the house, pointing out the piano at the back of the living-room as if the house were her own. The Wilsons also looked a bit ill at ease, standing near the punch bowl. Wilson was probably too hot in his raincoat, tightly belted with its collar turned up, and he also wore a hat with its brim pulled down. Some detective story writer, Vic supposed. He had not taken much trouble with his costume, but he was rather shamefacedly carrying a pipe, and his scowl perhaps went with whatever character he was trying to portray. His slender blonde wife was barefoot and dressed in a sleazy something like a short nightgown of pale blue. Either Trilby or a share-cropper, Vic thought.

Vic felt awkward and bored from the start, and he was utterly sober at the end of his first glass of punch, though he had joined Melinda, at her insistence, in a stiff one before they left the house. It was one of those evenings when he was going to stay stone sober the whole night, even if he had several more drinks, and when every moment between twelve-thirty, when De Lisle would return from Ballinger, and five or whenever Melinda chose to go home, was going to drag, and was going to be excruciating as well because of having to listen to De Lisle's scintillating piano from twelve-thirty onwards.

Mr De Lisle was at the piano already, grinding it out, and Melinda was leaning over him, beaming like a mother showing off a prodigy. Vic could see them from the terrace through the tall picture windows of the house. He moved towards the terrace steps, passing the Wilsons, who were talking with Phil at the punch bowl.

'How are you?' Vic said to both the Wilsons, making himself smile. 'Glad to see you.'

The Wilsons acknowledged it timidly. Maybe their main trouble was shyness, Vic thought. At any rate, they were infinitely preferable socially to Charley De Lisle, who, Vic had just realized, had not even looked at him when Melinda had been introducing him on the terrace, though Vic had been looking at him. Which reminded Vic that both De Lisle *and* Melinda were retaliating for his not having spoken to De Lisle the day he was in the Chesterfield with Horace. Melinda had reprimanded Vic for it the next day. *I hear you were in the Chesterfield bar and you didn't even speak to Charley!* Vic lifted his head and took a deep breath of fresh air as he strolled out farther on the lawn. The air was sweet with the honeysuckle that grew on the Cowans' low stone wall at the edge of the lawn, but as he passed a gardenia bush, the gardenia became stronger. Vic turned and walked back towards the house. It was only nine-thirty. Another full hour before there would be a respite from De Lisle. Vic marched up the terrace steps towards the living-room door, braced to find anything going on inside.

But Melinda was dancing with Mr Kenny.

'Mr Van Allen,' said a woman's voice beside him. It was Mrs MacPherson. 'You're such a scholar. Can you tell me what people wear under their togas or do they wear anything?'

'Yes.' Vic smiled. 'I've heard they wore underwear.' No use telling her the Latin name for it, he thought. She'd think he was stodgy. He added, 'I understand that when orators orated and wanted to show the populace their honourable scars, they left off their underwear so they could lift up their togas and show the people whatever part of the body they wanted to.'

86

'Oh, what fun!' Mrs MacPherson squealed.

She was the daughter of a wealthy Chicago meat packer, Vic recalled. 'Yes. I don't suppose I'll be much fun tonight. I've got on walking shorts and a tee-shirt underneath.'

'Oh-ho!' she laughed. 'Horace told me you're going to publish the most beautiful book this summer.'

'Xenophon?'

'Yay-yuss! That was it!'

Then somehow Vic found himself on a sofa with her, talking about Stephen Hines, whom she knew slightly because they went to the same church, and about the MacPhersons' garage roof, which they didn't know whether to repair or to tear off and rebuild. George MacPherson – Mac – was a completely ineffectual fellow, Vic knew from other similar conversations with Jennie MacPherson. Vic had given them advice about enlarging their cellar a couple of years ago. Mac had retired, on his wife's money, and managed to do nothing at all at home – except drink, some people said. Vic discussed the roof problem thoroughly and at length, quoting prices and building companies' names. It was more interesting to Vic than most party conversations, and it made the time pass. He noticed that Melinda went over to Charley at exactly ten-thirty-two, put a hand on his shoulder and told him – Vic felt sure – that it was time he had to leave, and Charley nodded. He finished the song he was playing, stood up and wiped his shiny flat forehead amid the slight but enthusiastic applause.

'Charley's leaving, but he says he'll be back at twelve-thirty, and we'll carry on from there!' Melinda announced to all and sundry, waving an arm.

She went out with him on to the terrace, a fact which was noted by Horace, Vic saw. Then Horace looked over at Vic, gave him a casual nod and a smile, but Vic could read Horace's thoughts in his eyes. It crossed Vic's mind that perhaps many or all of the women, being quicker at such things, had already guessed that De Lisle was Melinda's new conquest and were refraining from showing that they had noticed it for politeness' sake. But of course not all the women were that polite. Vic didn't know. He found himself looking around at everybody in the room, examining each face. He got nowhere.

Evelyn was herding people into the living-room, in a circle, for the costume judging. There was to be no judge except the applause each contestant received.

Martha Washington (Mrs Peter Jauch) stepped forward first, being the First Lady, complete with ruffled cap, ruffled apron, candy box, and a cigarette holder sticking out of her mouth at a jaunty angle. She curtsied somewhat shakily. Then came Lady Macbeth, with a candlestick, accompanied by her husband, who was Hamlet, looking quite mad with a hand mirror.

Vic kept his eyes away from the terrace door, already reconciled to Melinda's having gone to Ballinger with De Lisle, but after five minutes or so she came in again, alone, and fixed a cigarette coolly into her holder in preparation for the judging.

Ernest Kay, a skinny, shy fellow who turned up at parties about once a year, got the loudest applause that had yet come with his Dr Livingstone costume – riding breeches with ancient puttees, pith helmet, a monocle for some reason, and an absurdly long, narrow-shouldered cotton riding jacket which hung almost to his knees. Vic, when his turn came, got a surprising amount of applause and loud cries of 'Take it off, Vic!' He unfastened one shoulder clip, revealed his walking shorts and tee-shirt with a complete turn and a bow, then refastened the toga with a flourish like a practised Roman. Melinda got applause and howls, and she held her act, dropping her ashes disdainfully into Phil Cowan's hair.

Little Martha Washington got the prize for women – a cellophane bag of goodies including a small box of candy, lipstick, and perfume, and she looked at the box of candy suspiciously and asked, 'What brand is *this?*'

Dr Livingstone won it for the men's costumes, a package wrapped in a great deal of tissue and in his nervousness at being watched by the whole party he dropped it, and there was more laughter. Finally, he held up a hip-moulded bottle of brandy. 'I presume this is Mr Stanley,' he murmured, and everybody laughed and applauded.

There was more music from the phonograph, more trays of drinks, and two maids put out a baked ham and a great many other things on the long table that stood against the windows. Vic went out on the terrace. People were playing some kind of game on the terrace, crawling on hands and knees blindfolded, carrying plastic glasses of water between their shoulder blades. The game was called 'Llama'. You raced a competitor blindfolded, to the end of the terrace, always moving hands and knees alternately as four-footed animals did, and without spilling the water, although much water was spilled. Vic could not think of anything he felt less in the mood to do, though he stood a long while watching, and he was still standing there when De Lisle returned at half-past twelve.

Melinda met De Lisle at the living-room doorway, took his arm and brushed her cheek quickly against his bluish cheek, and Charley smiled, looking more at ease than before. He even turned his head in Vic's direction, saw him, and gave a quick little smile that seemed to Vic to say, 'Just what're you going to do about it?' Vic felt a prickle of anger. He regretted his automatic smile in reply to De Lisle's smile. De Lisle looked like a criminal. He was the kind of person one really didn't want to turn one's back on in the house for fear he would steal something. Vic was of a mind to tell Evelyn or Phil that it might be a good idea to put away anything valuable that was portable, since it wasn't entirely unknown for hired entertainers to pocket a few things around a house, but he realized it would reflect on Melinda, who was obviously sponsoring De Lisle tonight, so he couldn't. He was hamstrung.

'Vic, come on!' Evelyn took his hand. 'You haven't played the game yet!'

Vic got down on his hands and knees, tucking his toga up in his shorts. His competitor was Horace – Galileo. The plastic glasses of water were set on their backs, then they were off. From the living-room came a four-hand arrangement of 'Melancholy Baby', an intricate arrangement that had taken some time to coordinate, an audible proof that Melinda and De Lisle had spent a great deal of time together.

Horace dropped his glass.

Vic had won. He was matched with Ernest Kay and defeated him. Then with Hamlet for the championship. Hamlet, Dick Hewlett, was a bigger man and could cover ground faster, but Vic's coordination was better. He could move left-hand-right-knee, left-knee-right-hand as fast as a little trotting dog. He made everybody shriek and roar with laughter. Don Wilson was standing in a corner of the terrace watching with a faint smile. A wreath was placed on Vic's head, then somebody dropped gardenias within the wreath. The over-sweet smell emanating from his head made him think of the sickening smell of Charley's brilliantine. As Vic was straightening out his toga, he caught sight, across half a dozen people, of Evelyn Cowan in the doorway nodding towards the piano and whispering something to her husband who leaned closer to her. Vic saw Evelyn's eyebrows go up and down with a kind of sad resignation, and Phil put his hand on his wife's shoulder and pressed it quickly. Vic moved towards the door almost against his will. The piano had stopped.

Melinda and De Lisle were simply sitting on the piano bench talking to each other. But Melinda's face had that warm animation that Vic for many years had not seen directed towards himself.

'Vic!' Phil said. 'Come and have something to eat!'

It was the host pressing him to eat again, because he was neglected and scorned by his wife. Have another piece of cake, Vic. 'I think I might, thanks,' Vic said cheerfully, and took a slice of ham on a plate, a dab of potato salad, a stalk of celery, though he had no appetite whatsoever.

'Did you bring your bathing suit?' Phil asked.

'Yes. So did Melinda. They're in the room where the coats are.' When Vic looked towards the piano again, Melinda and De Lisle were gone. Phil went on talking, and he talked too, trying to be pleasant and party-like, though he could feel Phil's awareness of Melinda and De Lisle's disappearance as acutely as his own aware-ness.

From the terrace, Vic heard Evelyn's voice say, 'Is anybody ready for a swim?'

And a couple of moments later, hardly any time later, a woman's voice which he didn't recognize called from the back of the hall, 'Say, the door's locked! – Is the door locked?'

And Phil, in the very act of moving towards the hall, checked himself and looked at Vic. 'There's plenty of time. We don't have to rush.'

'Oh, no,' Vic agreed, rubbing his upper lip. 'I suppose I've time for another drink.' But he didn't want another drink, and turning to find his plate, which he had left on the corner of the buffet table, he saw that his unfinished drink stood beside it.

Phil Cowan, walking away towards the terrace, said, 'Excuse me, Vic,' over his shoulder, and disappeared.

Was he going to consult his wife as to what to do about the coat room, or whatever room it was that was locked? Vic felt a tingle of fear – or disgust, or panic, what was it? – creeping up his bare legs under the toga. Then he heard a woman say in a pleas-ant, expressionless voice, so that he couldn't tell if it was addressed to Melinda herself or not, 'Oh, Melinda!' from the hall, and as if this were a signal to retreat, Vic went out on the terrace and strolled to the darker end of it. Don Wilson was still there, talking to a woman. The woman was Jennie MacPherson. Vic stood looking out across the lawn to the swimming pool. Some of the lanterns had gone out, but he could still see its lazy L shape, the wide-angled L and its rounded corners, by the light of two or three lanterns. There was no moon tonight. Two people splashed into the pool at the same time, in different arms of the L. The pool was really a boomerang shape, he thought.

'What're you doing here all by yourself?' Evelyn Cowan was suddenly beside him, blotting her shoulders with a towel. Her black bathing suit had a frilly skirt like a ballet costume.

'Oh, I'm enjoying myself,' Vic said.

'Aren't you going to take a swim?'

'I might, when Melinda does.'

Somebody called Evelyn from the pool just then, and she said, 'Well, hurry up!' to Vic, and ran down the terrace steps.

Melinda and De Lisle came out on the terrace, in swim suits, with two or three other people also in suits. One of the people was Horace, and seeing Vic, Horace detached himself and came over.

'Is Tiberius in retirement already?' Horace asked.

Tongue-tied, Vic watched Melinda in her green bathing suit waving good-bye to two couples who were leaving and crossing the lawn towards the cars in front of the house.

'Aren't you having a dip?' Horace asked.

'No, I don't think so,' Vic said. 'But I'll come down to the pool,' he added, for no reason that he knew of, because he didn't want to go down to the pool.

He and Horace walked down together in silence. Finally Horace said, 'Looks like the party's thinning out a little.'

Vic hung back out of the glow of the lanterns. De Lisle was standing on the edge of the pool with a can of beer in each hand, watching Melinda, who was swimming in a fast over-hand stroke down one arm of the L towards the end of the pool. De Lisle came around the edge of the pool to meet her. He had not been in yet, Vic saw from his dry blue shorts. De Lisle's body looked scrawny and pale, and here and there patches of black hair grew, not only on his sunken-in chest but high on his left shoulder blade. He stooped and handed a beer to Melinda as she hauled herself out, and she said in her loud, distinct voice, 'I've got a *foul* headache! This'll kill or cure!' She caught sight of Vic.

Vic turned away, strolled towards a gardenia bush with the intention of examining a blossom, though it was so dark he could hardly see the white flowers.

'Hi, there!' Melinda's voice called behind him. She tossed his rolled-up trunks at him, and Vic caught them. 'Aren't you coming in?'

From across the pool De Lisle was grinning in their direction. The lantern glow made his face cadaverous.

Melinda hit the water with a belly-whopping *splat*, which didn't seem to bother her, because she took a couple of easy strokes, then rolled over on her back. 'Oh, it's divine!' she shouted just as Vic had known she would, and he knew also that she had by now had so much to drink that she didn't know or care what she was saying. She was just as likely to come out with, 'Charley, I adore you!' as she had one night, when Jo-Jo was around, said 'Jo-Jo, I adore you!' and their friends who had heard it – the Cowans, Vic remembered – had discreetly ignored it.

There was the distant slam of a car door from the road.

Now De Lisle was gingerly descending the metal ladder at the far end of the pool. Vic took his trunks towards the remotest gardenia bush to change, because he was expected to go in, but he felt a revulsion about getting into the pool while Melinda and De Lisle were there, about even getting near the pool, because De Lisle had been in its water. The gardenia bush was thirty yards from the pool, in the darkest corner of the lawn. Vic was as careful to get the bush exactly between himself and the pool as he would have been if it had been broad daylight. He left his toga, his walking shorts and underwear and tee-shirt behind the bush, and stepped forth barefoot in his brown swimming trunks.

Horace had left, Vic saw, evidently gone back into the house. Melinda was just climbing up the ladder as Vic got to the pool.

'Cold?' Vic asked.

'No, it's not cold,' Melinda said. 'I've got a headache.' She whipped off her white rubber cap and shook her damp hair out.

De Lisle was hanging on to the gutter of the pool, not cutting a very athletic figure. 'Feels pretty cool to me,' he said.

'Have you got an aspirin, Evelyn?' Melinda asked.

'Oh, of course!' Evelyn was standing near by on the grass. 'But they're not in the bathroom – I don't think. I think they're in the bedroom. Come on with me. I'll just make a small detour to look at the coffee.'

'I smell that coffee way out here,' Phil said, getting up from the edge of the pool. 'Anybody want coffee?'

'Not just now, thanks,' Vic said. He was the only one who answered. Vic suddenly realized he was alone with Charley De Lisle.

'You're not coming in?' Charley said to Vic, pushing off from the edge of the pool, swimming in a vague side-stroke towards the shallow end.

The water looked black and uninviting. Not cold, just uninviting. He wanted to walk away, to leave De Lisle there alone, but he felt it would look like some kind of retreat, like a silly change of mind after he had gone to the trouble of putting on his swimming trunks. 'Oh, I suppose so,' Vic said, sliding immediately off the edge of the pool into deep water. He was a buoyant swimmer, a strong swimmer, but he was not in the mood for swimming now, and the sudden coldness of the water, the messy wetness of

94

his hair, shocked him unpleasantly, and started up a little dynamo of anger within him.

'Nice pool,' De Lisle said.

'Yes,' Vic replied as coolly as a snobbish club member might use to a non-member. Vic, treading water, looked at the terrace where two lanterns still burned. There was nobody on the terrace, Vic thought.

De Lisle was on his back, floating. One of his white arms came up and lashed the water awkwardly and a little frantically, though where he was would be barely over his head, Vic knew. Vic would have loved to grab him by the shoulders and hold him under, and even as he thought of it, Vic swam towards him. De Lisle was now making an overhead stroke to bring him to the edge of the pool, but Vic reached him in a second, grabbed his throat and pulled him backward. There was not even a bubble as De Lisle's head went under. Vic had him under the chin and by one shoulder now, and unconsciously he tugged him towards where the water was over Vic's head, though it was easy to keep his own head above the surface because of De Lisle's threshing efforts to rise under his hands. Vic made a scissor-like movement with his legs and caught both De Lisle's thighs between his calves. Vic's head went under as he tipped backwards, but his hands kept their grip and he pulled himself forward and rose again. De Lisle was still under.

It's a joke, Vic thought to himself. If he were to let him up now, it would be merely a joke, though perhaps a rough one, but just then De Lisle's efforts grew violent, and Vic concentrated his own effort, one hand on the back of De Lisle's neck now, his other hand holding De Lisle's wrist away from him under the water. De Lisle's free hand was ineffectual against Vic's grip on the back of his neck. One of De Lisle's feet broke the surface of the water, then disappeared.

Suddenly Vic was aware of the placidity of the water around

him, of the soundlessness all around him. It was as if his ears had gone dead. Vic relaxed his grip somewhat, though he still held De Lisle under. Vic looked around the lawn, at the house, the terrace. He saw no one, but he suddenly realized – almost objectively, with no sense of shock – that he hadn't made absolutely sure that there had been no one on the terrace or on the lawn before he pulled De Lisle under. He still held the faintly buoyant shoulders under, not really able to believe yet that he was dead or even completely unconscious.

It's a joke, Vic thought again. But now it was too late for it to be a joke, and even as that came to his mind like a piece of news he realized that he'd have to say that De Lisle must have got an attack of cramp while he was dressing himself on the lawn, and that he hadn't seen or heard anything of it. Vic tentatively released the shoulders. The back of De Lisle's head came up a little above the water, but his face stayed down.

Vic climbed out of the pool. He walked directly towards the gardenia bush and began to change his clothes. He heard voices and laughter from the kitchen at the end of the house. He hurried into his toga, flinging it around him with the movement he had practised at home, then started for the back door of the kitchen, which opened on the lawn.

They were all in the kitchen, Melinda, Evelyn and Phil, Horace and Mary, but only Evelyn greeted him as he went in.

'How about a sandwich and some coffee, Vic?' Evelyn asked him.

'I could use some coffee,' Vic said.

Phil was pouring a cup of coffee and Melinda was standing near him, groggily assembling a ham sandwich and murmuring something about her headache still being with her. As Vic stood leaning against the sink, the atmosphere seemed almost oppressively like the atmosphere of dozens of other ends-of-parties he had known – the hosts in the kitchen with the handful of people who had lingered on, the handful of people who were completely at ease, because they knew one another very well, and because everybody was in a relaxed and easy mood, due to the lateness of the hour and the liquor they had drunk. And at the same time Vic felt absolutely certain that everything that was said or done now was going to be discussed and re-discussed later, and argued about: Evelyn trying to resume a story she had evidently started before he came in about meeting somebody, an old friend, at the Goat-and-Candle, whose little boy had had a strange heart operation. Horace endeavouring to listen. And Phil now handing him a cup of coffee, saying, 'Here you are, Vic. Sugar?' And Evelyn interrupting, 'What about *me*?' meaning she wanted coffee, too. And Melinda saying, with her morning-after despair already upon her, 'My God, what did I do to deserve this *booming* headache?' to no one in particular, yet in such a booming voice that Evelyn got up and went to her. 'Honey, have you still got it? Why don't you try one of those wonderful yellow pills I've got? They'll do it, I know.'

Melinda walked half across the kitchen when Evelyn left the room to get the yellow pills, and Vic thought she was going to follow her, but she turned completely around again. 'Where's Charley?'

Vic said, 'He's still swimming.'

'*Swimming?*' Melinda said in an incredulous tone.

'Well, he was still in when I left him,' Vic said.

Melinda started to go out on the lawn, then stopped in the doorway, swung herself outward holding to the door-jamb, and yelled, 'Charley! Come on in!' She came back in herself without waiting for an answer.

Then very quickly Evelyn was back, Melinda swallowed the pill, and immediately went to the door again and called, '*Charley!*' then went out to get him.

And Vic saw Phil and Evelyn exchange a look and a smile,

because Melinda was so concerned tonight with Charley. Phil picked up a sandwich and took a bite.

Then they heard a scream. '*Vic!*' Melinda shrieked. '*Phil!*'

They ran out, Phil ahead, then Vic and Horace. Melinda was standing, helpless, on the edge of the pool.

'*He's drowned!*' Melinda said.

Phil took off his jacket and jumped in. Vic had a glimpse of Phil's grim, pale face as he turned towards them, dragging Charley. Vic took one arm, Horace the other, and they hauled Charley out.

'Do you –' Phil began, gasping, 'do you know anything about artificial respiration?'

'A little,' Vic said. He was already turning Charley face down, putting the right hand under his cheek, extending the other arm upwards. Melinda was in his way, feeling for Charley's heart, frenziedly feeling for a pulse in the wrist.

'I can't find his pulse!' Melinda said hysterically. 'Call Dr Franklin!'

'I'll call him!' Evelyn ran towards the house.

'That may not mean anything,' Phil said quickly. 'Go ahead.' He was feeling Charley's left wrist.

Vic was on his knees facing Charley, lifting the bony, thin-skinned rib-cage, letting it go, lifting from under the armpits. 'Does this look right, Horace?'

'It looks right,' Horace said tensely. He knelt beside Vic, watching Charley's face. 'You're supposed to keep the mouth open,' he said, reaching unhesitantly as a doctor into Charley's mouth, pulling the tongue forward.

'Do you think we should hold him up and drain the water out of him?' Phil asked.

'No, you don't do that,' Horace said. 'You don't waste time with that.'

Vic lifted the ribs higher. He had never tried to give artificial respiration before, but he had read about it very recently in *The*

World Almanac, one evening when Charley had been at the house, Vic happened to remember. But he remembered, too, that the book advised artificial respiration if the breathing had stopped and the heart was still beating, but Charley's heart was not beating. 'Do you think,' Vic said between strokes, 'we should turn him over and try to massage his heart?' and though he thought he was calm, he felt it was a stupid, excited question, and just the kind of question he might have been expected to ask.

'No,' Horace said.

'You're not doing it *right!*' Melinda shrieked on her knees beside Vic.

'Why? What's the matter?' Phil asked.

'Do you think I should get a blanket?' Mary's high-pitched voice asked.

'You're not doing it *right!*' Melinda began to cry, to moan between the jagged sobs.

'Let me take over when you get tired, Vic,' Phil said. He kept feeling for a pulse in the left wrist, but from his frightened face Vic knew that he had not felt a flutter.

Evelyn came running back. 'Dr Franklin's coming right away. He's calling the hospital and they're sending an ambulance.'

'Don't you think we should get a blanket for him?' Mary said again.

'All right, I'll get one,' Evelyn said and went off to the house again.

'What do you think happened?' Phil asked. 'Cramp?'

Nobody answered.

Melinda moaned, rocking from side to side, her eyes shut.

'I wonder if he hit his head? Was he diving, Vic?' Phil asked.

'No. He was paddling around' – Vic released the unelastic ribs – 'in the shallow part.'

'He seemed all right?' Mary asked.

'Yes,' Vic said.

Then Phil pushed Vic away. 'Let me take over.'

A siren wailed in a slow, mournful rise and fall, came closer, and wailed still lower and stopped. Phil went on intently with the lifting and dropping of the ribs and shoulders. A couple of white-clad interns ran across the lawn towards them, carrying an oxygen tank.

The light on the scene was ghastly – the dismal, blanching light of dawn. Nobody could come back to life in a light like this, Vic thought. It was a light for dying. Watching the interns bustling about, asking questions, recommencing the artificial respiration, Vic realized his own fatigue. He seemed to awaken from a trance. He realized for the first time that, if De Lisle were revived, he was doomed. That hadn't even crossed his mind while he had been giving him artificial respiration. He had simply done the best he could with the artificial respiration, he was sure of that, made the same movements he would have made if it had been Horace under his hands. He had gone through the proper motions, but he hadn't *wanted* De Lisle to come back to life. Then, for a moment, it seemed unreal that he had drowned De Lisle, seemed like something he had imagined rather than done. Vic began to watch De Lisle's face intently, as all the others did – all the others except Melinda, who still wailed and whimpered, still stared into space in front of her as if she were out of her mind.

An intern shook his head in discouragement.

Vic heard a door slam. Then Dr Franklin, a spry, serious little man with grey hair – the doctor who had seen Trixie into the world and who had set broken arms, treated acute indigestion, lanced boils, prescribed diets for, and tested the blood pressures of all of them – hurried across the lawn with his little black bag.

'You've been giving the artificial respiration since you called me?' he asked, feeling De Lisle's wrist, lifting one of his lids.

'Since before,' Evelyn said. 'Since a few minutes before.'

Dr Franklin, too, gave a displeased jerk of his head.

'You don't think there's any hope?' Evelyn asked.

Melinda moaned louder.

'Doesn't look like it,' Dr Franklin replied in a cheerless voice. He was preparing an injection.

'Oooooooh-hooo-oo-hooooo!' Melinda covered her face.

Dr Franklin, apparently used to emergency night calls and to what he found on them, paid absolutely no attention to her, though he would have, Vic thought, if it had been he who had drowned. Dr Franklin would have had time for a word to a wife. He stuck the needle into De Lisle's arm.

'We should know in a few minutes,' Dr Franklin said. 'Otherwise ...' He was holding De Lisle's left wrist.

Phil stood up, moved a few feet away, then Evelyn came over to him. Horace and Mary joined them, as if they were compelled to relieve their tension by putting a little distance between themselves and the dead man. Vic bent and took Melinda gently by the arm, but she shook him off. Vic joined the others.

Phil looked ashen, as if he were about to faint. 'I suppose we could all use some coffee,' he said, but nobody moved.

Everybody was glancing back at the cluster of interns and doctor, at the body half covered by the steamer rug.

'I'm afraid there's nothing we can do,' Dr Franklin said, standing up. 'We'll take him to the hospital.'

'He's *dead!*' Melinda screamed at them, and leaned back on her hands on the grass in a curiously relaxed position.

Then, as they put De Lisle on a stretcher, she jumped to her feet. She wanted to go to the hospital. Vic and Phil had to restrain her physically. One of her fists caught Vic in the ear. Her fight tore her dress in front, and Vic saw one of her breasts quite bare, trembling like a maenad's breast in her fury. Vic had her elbows now, behind her. He released her, suddenly ashamed, and she bolted forward and collided with Phil, gave a shriek of pain, and held her nose. They guided her towards the house.

When they got to the kitchen, Evelyn was coming towards them with a cup of coffee. 'There's a couple of phenobarbs in it,' she said in a low voice to Vic.

Melinda accepted the coffee with a kind of insane greediness and drank it off, although from its steaminess it must have been very hot. Her nose was bleeding, and her breast was still bare. Vic took off his toga and put it around her, held part of it against her nose, and she made a sudden wild swing at him and knocked some glasses and cups off the drain-board, then collapsed on a straight chair, dragging Vic, who had been trying to hold her, down with her. Vic's knee came down on a piece of glass. Then Melinda was suddenly quiet, her head back and her eyes staring up at the ceiling. The blood slid down her upper lip, and Vic blotted it with the toga until Evelyn came with some paper tissues and an ice cube for the back of her neck. Melinda gave no sign that she felt the ice cube against her hot skin.

Vic glanced behind him. Horace and Mary stood together near the stove, Phil was in the middle of the kitchen, looking dazed and frightened, and it crossed Vic's mind that Phil would look guiltier than anyone else in the room if anyone suspected that De Lisle had been murdered and that one of them must have done it.

'You don't suppose he wanted to kill himself, do you?' Phil asked Vic.

Melinda's head came up. 'Of course he didn't want to! Why should he want to with the whole *world* at his feet and every – every gift and talent a man could ask for!'

'What was he doing when you left the pool, Vic?' Phil asked.

'He was paddling around. Floating on his back, I think.'

'He didn't say anything about the water being cold?' Evelyn asked.

'No. I think he'd said earlier it was pretty chilly, but—'

'*You* did it,' Melinda said, looking at Vic. 'I bet you hit him on the head and held him under.'

'Oh, Melinda!' Evelyn said, coming towards her. 'Melinda, you're upset!'

'*I bet you hit him and drowned him!*' Melinda said in a louder voice, throwing Evelyn's hands from her. 'I'm going to call the hospital!' She jumped up.

Phil caught her arm, but her momentum swung her against the refrigerator. 'Melinda, don't do that! Not now!'

'*Vic killed him, I know he did!*' Melinda shrieked, loud enough for the whole neighbourhood to hear her, though there were no houses for a quarter of a mile around. 'He *killed* him! Let me go!' She swung at Vic as he approached her, swung short, and then Horace stepped in, trying to catch one flailing wrist. 'I'm going to ask them to look at his *head*!' Then suddenly with one of her arms held by Phil, the other by Horace, Melinda was rigidly still, her wild hennaed head lifted, her wet eyes closed.

'We'd better try to get her to bed here, Vic,' Evelyn said. 'What about Trixie? Will she be all right?'

'She's with the Petersons. She'll be all right,' Vic said.

Horace had released his hold on Melinda's arm. He came towards Evelyn with a tired smile on his lips. 'We'll take off, Evelyn – unless there's anything else we can do.'

'I don't guess there is, Horace. I think she could stand two more of these, don't you?' she asked him quietly, the phenobarbitals in her palm poised over another cup of coffee. 'They're only quarter grains.'

'Absolutely,' Horace said. He turned to Vic. 'Good night, Vic. Call us, will you? Don't let – don't let anything get you down.' He patted Vic's arm.

In spite of his low voice, Melinda heard, broke her trancelike rigidity and shouted at Horace. 'Get him down? He should be down! He should be at the bottom of that pool!'

'Melinda!'

'Melinda, stop it!' Phil said. 'Here, drink this!'

Melinda did not shout again, but it was nearly an hour before they got her to bed in the guest room upstairs.

Phil called St Joseph's Hospital in Wesley as soon as Melinda was quiet. They told him that Charles De Lisle was dead.

10

Vic drove home with Melinda about noon. She did not say a word to him in the car. She had hardly said a word since she had come downstairs at eleven o'clock. Her eyes were puffy and she seemed still groggy from the sleeping pills. She had not put on any lipstick, and her mouth looked thinner, set in a straight line as she stared through the windshield. Vic left her at the house, put on a pair of slacks and a clean shirt, then drove to the Petersons to pick up Trixie. He supposed he should tell the Petersons what had happened. They would think it unnatural of him if he didn't.

Vic said, when he was standing in the driveway with the two of them, out of earshot of the children, 'There was an accident last night at the Cowans'. A man drowned in their swimming pool.'

'*What!*' Katherine Peterson said, her eyes stretching.

'Who?' Peterson asked.

Vic told him. They had never seen De Lisle, but they had to know all the details, how old he was, whether he had had anything to eat before – Vic didn't know – and how long he had been in the water before anybody found him. Vic said he couldn't be sure, because De Lisle had been swimming around when he got out, perhaps seven minutes before. It was apparently an attack of cramp. The Petersons agreed that it sounded like an attack of cramp.

Then Vic drove Trixie back home. She was in her Sunday best, because she had just been to Sunday school with Janey Peterson. She was telling Vic about a plastic glider you shot with a rubber on a stick that some of the boys at the Sunday school had. Trixie wanted one, and Vic stopped at the newspaper store in town and bought one for her out of the front window, but he was thinking of something else. There were two things that kept repeating themselves in his mind – the matter of the Wilsons and what Phil Cowan had asked him this morning. Between the two, Phil's question bothered him more. Phil had simply asked in a puzzled way this morning, 'Is Melinda in *love* with De Lisle?' And Vic had replied, 'I don't know anything about it, Phil.' It was a question that would have occurred to anybody. Certainly Melinda was acting as if she were in love with De Lisle, and Vic had no doubt that people were going to remember and talk about the way she had behaved with Charley all evening, about the duet they had played on the piano, and about Melinda's history of liaisons. It was not guilt or fear of detection that bothered him, Vic felt, it was the sharp pang of shame that Phil's direct question had given him. The Wilson matter was vaguer. This morning Evelyn had said during their coffee and orange juice, 'It's a wonder the Wilsons didn't notice anything when they were going home. Don left the house just about the time it must have happened. Don't you remember, Phil?' (But Phil didn't remember.) Evelyn said that the Wilsons had left practically as soon as she and Melinda had come into the house to get the aspirin for Melinda's headache, and that Don had come back a minute later for something – she couldn't remember what – that his wife had forgotten. Vic's question was, if Wilson had gone by on the lawn and seen their struggle in the pool, would he have gone on to his car without saying anything? That wasn't very likely. It was only that Wilson was such an odd, secretive character that the possibility even crossed Vic's mind.

Melinda was drinking a Scotch and water when Vic got home with Trixie. She did not even say hello to Trixie, and Trixie, though she had seen her mother dishevelled and out of sorts in the mornings before, knew that something worse than usual had happened. But after a long stare Trixie went into her room to change her clothes without asking any questions.

Vic went into the kitchen and scrambled an egg with cream for Melinda. He put a little curry powder in it, because she sometimes liked that on bad mornings. He brought it to her and sat down on the couch beside her. 'How about a bite of egg?' he asked.

No response. She took another sip of her drink.

'It's got a little curry in it.' He held some ready on a fork for her.

'You go to hell,' she murmured.

Trixie came back in overalls, with her glider. 'What's the matter?' she asked Vic.

'Charley's dead, that's what's the matter! He's drowned!' Melinda yelled, getting up from the sofa. 'And your father killed him!'

Trixie's mouth fell open. She stared at Vic. '*Did* you, Daddy?'

'No, Trixie,' Vic said.

'But he's *dead*?' Trixie demanded.

Vic frowned at Melinda. 'Did you have to say that?' he asked her. His heart beat fast with anger. 'Did you have to say what you did?'

'You should always tell a child the truth,' Melinda retorted.

'He's dead, Daddy?' Trixie asked again.

'Yes, he drowned.'

Trixie looked round-eyed at the news, but not in the least sorry, Vic thought. 'Did he hit his head?'

'I don't know,' Vic said.

'*No*, he didn't hit his head,' Melinda said.

Trixie stared from one to the other of them for a moment. Then she went out the front door, in a quiet way, to play.

Melinda went to the kitchen to replenish her drink – Vic heard her kick the bottom pantry door shut – then she came back and crossed the room and went into her own room.

After a minute Vic got up and put the scrambled egg slowly down the sink with hot water. He thought he felt very much like Trixie. Something, he realized, must be holding back his reactions of guilt or horror at what he had done. It was very strange. Lying sleepless on the Cowans' sofa, he had waited for fear to come, for panic, for guilt and regret, at least. He had found himself thinking of a pleasant day in his childhood when he had won a prize in geography class for making the best model of an Eskimo village, using half eggshells for igloos and spun glass for snow. Without consciously realizing it, he had felt absolutely secure. Secure from detection. Or was it that he believed he wouldn't be afraid if he were detected? He had such slow reactions to everything. Physical danger. Emotional blows. Sometimes his reactions were weeks late, so that he had a hard time attaching them to their causes.

The telephone rang. Vic went into the hall to get it.

'Hello?' Vic said.

'Hello, Vic. This is Evelyn. I hope I didn't wake you from a nap?'

'Certainly not.'

'How's Melinda?'

'Well – not so well. She's having a drink in her room.'

'I'm sorry, Vic – about last night.'

Vic didn't quite know what she meant. 'We're all sorry.'

'Dr Franklin called us. They're going to have a coroner's inquest tomorrow in Ballinger at two-thirty and we're all supposed to be there. I suppose somebody'll notify you, anyway. It's in the court-house.'

'All right. Thanks, Evelyn. I'll remember.'

'Vic – have you had any phone calls – about this?'

'No.'

'We have. I – Phil didn't think I should say anything to you, Vic, but I think it's better if you do know. One or two people – well, let's say one – said that they thought it was just possible that you had something to do with Charley's drowning. I don't mean they said it outright, but they implied it. You can imagine what *I* said. But I thought I should tell you that I do think there's going to be some whispering, Vic. It's too bad a lot of people noticed Charley and Melinda acting – you know, as if they had quite a crush on each other. But a lot did, Vic.'

'Yes, I know,' Vic said a little wearily. 'Who was it who talked to you?'

'I don't think I should say. It isn't fair, and it really doesn't matter, you know that.'

'Was it Don Wilson?'

A slight hesitation. 'Yes. You know, we don't know him very well, and he certainly doesn't know you. It'd be bad enough from someone who knows you, but he has no right whatsoever.'

Vic had hoped it was Don Wilson. He had hoped that was all Don Wilson had to say. 'Let's let it go. He's got a bad chip on his shoulder.'

'Yes. Something's wrong. I can't say that I like him. I never did. We had them to the party just to be friendly, you know.'

'Yes. Well, thank you for telling me, Evelyn. Is anybody else saying anything—'

'No. Certainly not like that, but—' The soft, earnest voice stopped and Vic waited again, patiently. 'As I said, Vic, several people commented on the way Melinda behaved with him, asked me if I thought anything had been going on. I told them no.'

Vic squeezed the telephone in embarrassment. He knew very well that Evelyn knew better.

'You know, Melinda's always getting these enthusiasms for people. Especially a pianist. I can understand it.'

'Yes,' Vic said, marvelling at the human capacity for self-deception. It had become so much a habit for their friends to ignore, to wink at Melinda's behaviour they could almost believe now that there was nothing to wink at. 'How is Phil?' Vic asked.

'He's still pretty shaken up. It's the first accident we've ever had in our pool, you know. And such a horrible one. I think Phil feels somehow personally responsible. It wouldn't take anything to make him fill the pool in, but I think that's a little unreasonable.'

'Of course,' Vic said. 'Well, thank you very much for calling me, Evelyn. We should all feel a little better after the inquest tomorrow. It'll help settle everything. We'll see each other at two-thirty in Ballinger, I suppose.'

'Yes. If there's anything we can do today to help you, Vic – I mean with Melinda – don't hesitate to call us.'

'Right, Evelyn. Thanks. Bye-bye.'

'Good-bye, Vic.'

He had said that about the inquest's helping to settle every-thing with an absolute, unthinking confidence in his own safety, he realized. His friends would be there – Phil Cowan and Horace Meller and their wives. He trusted their confidence in him. But for a moment he questioned himself about Horace: Horace had been unusually quiet after they had dragged Charley out of the pool, and also in the kitchen. Vic tried to recall his expression – intense, shocked, and at the last he had looked haggard, but Vic did not think he had seen any shadow of doubt in his face. No, he could rely on Horace. Melinda might accuse him in front of the coroner tomorrow, but Vic really didn't think she would. It took a kind of courage that he didn't think Melinda had. Underneath all her wildness she was rather a coward and a conformist. She would know that all their friends would turn against her if she accused him, and Vic did not think she would want that. She might fly into a tantrum, of course, and accuse him, but if she did, everybody would know it was a tantrum and know why. If anybody examined her character, that was about the end of Melinda. He did not think Melinda would want to subject herself to a scrutiny of her private life.

Vic came back from the plant a little before one on Monday, in time for a quick lunch and the drive to Ballinger before two-thirty. Melinda had spent the morning out – probably with Mary or Evelyn, Vic thought – because he had called her from ten o'clock onwards to tell her about the inquest at two-thirty. She refused to eat any lunch, but she did not take a drink until just before they left the house at two. For all her sleep, there were circles under her eyes, and her face looked pale and a little puffy – appropriate for the mourning mistress of a dead lover, Vic thought. She did not reply to anything he asked her or said to her, so Vic gave it up.

The inquest took place in the red brick court-house on the main square of Ballinger. There were several straight chairs and two desks in the room, at one of which sat a male secretary who took down in shorthand everything that was said. The coroner's name was Walsh. He was a handsome, serious man of about fifty, grey-haired and erect. Everybody was present and punctual, the Mellers, the Cowans, himself and Melinda, and Dr Franklin, who sat with folded arms. There were first the factual circumstances to be narrated and confirmed, and then everyone was asked if in his or her opinion the death was caused by accidental circumstances.

'Yes,' Phil Cowan replied firmly.

'Yes,' Evelyn said.

'I believe so,' said Horace, as firmly as Phil.

'I believe so,' Mary echoed.

'Yes,' Vic said.

Then it was Melinda's turn. She had been staring at the floor. She looked up frightenedly at the coroner. 'I don't know.'

Coroner Walsh gave her a second look. 'Do you believe anything or anyone other than accidental circumstances was responsible for Mr De Lisle's death?'

'I don't know,' Melinda said expressionlessly.

'Have you any reason for thinking that any person is responsible for Mr De Lisle's death?' he asked.

'I know that my husband didn't like him,' Melinda said, her head bowed.

Coroner Walsh frowned. 'Do you mean that your husband had a quarrel with Mr De Lisle?'

Melinda hesitated.

Vic saw Phil frown with annoyance and shift in his chair. Dr Franklin looked merely sternly disapproving. Evelyn Cowan looked as if she wanted to get up and shake Melinda by the shoulders and give her a piece of her mind.

'No, they hadn't quarrelled,' Melinda said. 'But I think my husband didn't like him just because I liked him.'

'Did you see your husband,' Coroner Walsh began patiently, 'make any move at all against Mr De Lisle?'

Another hesitation. 'No,' Melinda said, still staring with a curious shyness at the floor, though her naturally loud, clear voice had made the 'No' sound very positive.

Now the coroner turned to Dr Franklin. 'Doctor, in your opinion was Mr De Lisle's death due to accidental circumstances?'

'I have no reason to think otherwise,' Dr Franklin replied.

Dr Franklin liked him, Vic knew. They had become very well acquainted when Trixie was born. Dr Franklin hadn't the time or the temperament to be very sociable, but he always had a smile and a few words for Vic when they encountered each other in town.

'You noticed no marks on the body that might indicate a struggle of any kind,' the coroner said rather than asked. An atmosphere of general disapproval of Melinda was thickening in the room.

'There were very faint red marks around his shoulders,' Dr Franklin said in a somewhat weary tone, 'but these could have been made in pulling him out of the pool. Or perhaps during the artificial respiration which Mr Van Allen administered.'

Coroner Walsh nodded deeply in confirmation. 'I saw the marks. Your opinion seems to be the same as mine. And as far as I could discover there were no bruises on his head.'

'No,' said Dr Franklin.

'And the contents of his stomach? Was there anything which might have caused cramp, any indication of cramp in your opinion?'

'No, I can't say that there was. There was the smallest bit of food in the stomach, such as a small sandwich that might have been taken at a party. Nothing that should have caused cramp. But cramp is not always caused by food in the stomach.'

'Any alcohol?' said the coroner.

'Not more than four-tenths of a millimetre of alcohol. That is, per one cubic centimetre of whole blood.'

'Nothing that should have given him any trouble,' said the coroner.

'Certainly not.'

'Yet it is your opinion that Mr De Lisle's death was due to accidental circumstances?'

'Yes,' said Dr Franklin. 'That is my belief. The specific cause of death was drowning.'

'Could Mr De Lisle swim?' the coroner asked the whole room.

Nobody answered for a moment. Vic knew he couldn't swim well. Then Horace and Melinda simultaneously began:

'From what I saw of him in the—'

'He could certainly swim enough to keep his head above the water!' Melinda had found her tongue and her volume.

'Mr Meller,' said the coroner.

'From what I saw of him in the pool, he was not a good swimmer,' Horace said cautiously. 'This may or may not have any bearing on what happened, but I saw him clinging to the edge of the pool as if he were afraid to let go, and as Mr Van Allen said before – confirmed by Mr Cowan – Mr De Lisle had said he found the water pretty cool.' Horace gave Melinda a glance, not a kindly glance.

'None of you heard any outcry?' the coroner asked for the second time.

There was a chorus of 'No'.

'Mrs Van Allen?' the coroner asked.

Melinda was twisting her white gloves in her lap, staring at the coroner: 'No – but we couldn't have heard anything with all the noise we were making in the kitchen.'

'There wasn't so much noise,' Phil said, frowning. 'We'd turned the music off. I think we could have heard a shout if there'd been one.'

Melinda turned to Phil. 'You don't hear a shout if somebody's pulled under the water suddenly and held there!'

'*Melinda!*' Mary Meller said, horrified.

Vic watched the next few seconds with a strange detachment. Melinda half standing up now, shouting her opinion at the coroner – and Vic felt a certain admiration for her courage and her honesty that he hadn't known she possessed as he saw her frowning profile, her clenched hands – Mary Meller rising and taking a few hesitant steps towards Melinda before Horace gently drew her back to her seat. Phil's long, handsome face scowling, and Dr Franklin with folded arms, still maintaining his cool disdain of Melinda Van Allen that had begun, Vic knew, with her unreasoning demands and complaints of his treatment of her at the time of Trixie's birth. Melinda was repeating:

114

'Yes, I think my husband had something to do with it! I think he *did* it!'

Coroner Walsh's expression was a combination of annoyance and bewilderment. For a moment he seemed speechless. 'Have you anything at all – any proof to substantiate your belief, Mrs Van Allen?' His face had reddened.

'Circumstantial evidence. My husband was alone in the pool with him, wasn't he? My husband is a better swimmer than Charley. He's also very strong in his hands!'

Mary stood up, her small face looking even smaller and somehow concentrated in the pursed, tearful mouth, and started to leave the room.

'I must ask you, Mrs Meller,' the coroner said, 'not to leave – if you please. The law says all persons concerned must be present to the end of the inquest.' He smiled and bowed her back to her seat.

Horace had made no move to stop her. He looked as if he would have been glad to leave himself.

The coroner turned back to Melinda. 'You said your husband didn't like Mr De Lisle because you liked him. Were you perhaps in love with Mr De Lisle?'

'No, but I was very fond of him.'

'And do you think your husband was jealous of Mr De Lisle?'

'Yes.'

Coroner Walsh turned to Vic. 'Were you jealous of Mr De Lisle?'

'No, I was not,' Vic said.

Coroner Walsh turned to the Cowans and the Mellers and asked in a patiently reasoning tone, 'Did any of you ever notice anything in Mr Van Allen's conduct that would lead you to believe that he was jealous of Mr De Lisle?'

'No,' said Phil and Horace, practically in unison.

'No,' Evelyn said.

'Certainly not,' from Mary.

'How many years have you known Mr Van Allen, Mr Cowan?'

Phil looked at Evelyn. 'About eight years?'

'Nine or ten,' Evelyn said. 'We met the Van Allens as soon as they moved here.'

'I see. And Mr Meller?'

'I think it's ten years,' Horace said firmly.

'Then you know him well, you consider?'

'Very well,' said Horace.

'You would both vouch for his character?'

'Absolutely,' Phil put in before Horace could speak. 'And so would anybody else who knows him.'

'I consider him my finest friend,' Horace said.

The coroner nodded, then looked at Melinda as if he might be going to ask her a question or ask a question about her, but Vic could see that he didn't want to prolong it; and didn't want to probe any further into Melinda's relationship to De Lisle either. There was a friendly warmth in the coroner's eyes as he looked at Vic. 'Mr Van Allen, I believe you're the owner of the Greenspur Press in Little Wesley, aren't you?'

'Yes,' Vic said.

'A very fine press. I've heard of it,' he said, smiling, as if it were a foregone conclusion that every literate person in that section of Massachusetts had heard of the Greenspur Press. 'Have you anything more to add, Mrs Van Allen?'

'I've told you what I *think*,' Melinda said, spitting out the last word in her old-style.

'Since this is a court of law, we must have evidence,' the coroner said, with a slight smile. 'Unless anyone has evidence to offer that this death was not due to accidental circumstances, I hereby declare this inquest closed.' He waited. Nobody spoke. 'I declare this inquest closed with a verdict of death due to accidental circumstances.' He smiled. 'Thank you all for appearing here. Good afternoon.'

Phil got up and wiped his forehead with a handkerchief. Melinda walked to the door, holding a paper tissue to her nose. Down on the sidewalk, Dr Franklin took his leave first, saying a solemn 'Good afternoon' to all of them, hesitating a moment as he looked at Melinda, as if he were about to add something, but he said only 'Good afternoon, Mrs Van Allen,' and walked away to his car.

Melinda stood beside the car, still with the tissue to her nose, like a bereaved widow.

'Keep your chin up, Vic,' Phil said, patting his shoulder, and then he turned to go to his car as if to stop himself from saying more.

Evelyn Cowan laid her hand on Vic's sleeve. 'I'm sorry, Vic. Call us soon, will you? Tonight, if you want to. Bye-bye, Melinda!'

Vic saw that Mary wanted to say something to Melinda and that Horace was trying to discourage her from it. Then Horace came over to Vic, smiling, his narrow head lifted as if to impart courage to Vic by his own attitude, to show by his smile that Vic was still his friend, his finest friend.

'I'm sure she's not going to keep on like this, Vic,' Horace said in a low tone, just out of Melinda's hearing. 'So don't let it throw you. We'll all stand by you – always.'

'Thanks, Horace,' Vic said. Behind Horace he saw Mary's thin, sensitive lips working as she looked at Melinda. Then, as Horace took his wife's arm, she smiled at Vic and blew him a kiss as she walked away.

Vic held the car door open for Melinda and she got in. Then Vic got in behind the wheel. It was his car, his antiquated Oldsmobile. Vic circled the main square – a necessity because of the traffic regulations – then took the southbound street that led into the highway to Little Wesley.

'I'm not going to come around,' Melinda said, 'so don't think I am.'

Vic sighed. 'Honey, you can't go on weeping for somebody you hardly knew.'

'*You killed him!*' Melinda said vehemently. 'The Mellers and the Cowans don't know you as well as I, do they?'

Vic made no reply. What she said did not alarm him in the least – and he had felt no alarm during the inquest either, even at the question about the red marks on Charley's skin – but he was aware of a sense of annoyance with Melinda now, a sense of shame that was in itself reassuring because of its familiarity. Everybody knew why Melinda had accused him, why she had shed tears at the inquest, why she had grown hysterical at the Cowans' the night it had happened. The Cowans knew what her relationship with De Lisle had been. De Lisle had been just another sneaking paramour, but one who had happened to die right in their home. The Cowans and the Mellers must know, too, that he had had years of such scenes, years of tears over broken dates with cads and scoundrels, more tears when they went away, and that he had gone through it all uncomplaining, patient, behaving always as if nothing at all were happening – just as he had behaved at the inquest.

For a few moments, as Melinda snuffled into a fresh tissue, Vic felt something in him hardening against her. She had got what she deserved, and she was powerless to do anything against him. If she went to the police again, who would believe her? How could she prove it? She could divorce him, that was all. But Vic did not think that she would. He might refuse to give her alimony – and he had ample grounds to refuse – and he could also win the child with ease, not that Melinda would probably care. He did not think she would relish the prospect of having no money, of going back to her parents' dreary, boring household in Queens.

Melinda got out of the car when he stopped in front of the garage and went on into the house. Vic carried his herb boxes back into the garage. It was a quarter to four. He looked up at the sky and saw that there was going to be a slight rainfall around six.

He went into the garage again and carried out, one by one, his three aquaria of land snails, each of which was covered with a framed piece of copper screen to admit rain and to prevent the snails from crawling out. The snails loved the rain. He bent over one aquarium, watching the snails he called Edgar and Hortense as they slowly approached each other, lifted their heads, kissed, and glided on. They would probably mate this afternoon, in the light rain that filtered through the screen. They mated about once every week, and they were genuinely in love, Vic thought, because Edgar had eyes for no other snail but Hortense and Hortense never responded to the attempt of another snail to kiss her. Three-quarters of the thousand-odd snails he had were their progeny. They were quite considerate of each other as to which had the burden of egg-laying – a twenty-four-hour procedure at least – and it was only Vic's opinion that Hortense laid more often than Edgar, which was why he had given her the feminine name. That was true love, Vic thought, even if they were only Gastropoda. He remembered the sentence in one of Henri Fabre's books about snails crossing garden walls to find their mates, and though Vic had never verified it by his own experiment, he felt that it must be so.

Vic's guilt did not materialize. Perhaps it was because there were so many other things to think about and to take care of. Melinda was telling all their friends that she thought Vic had killed Charley, which could have been put down as the result of her shock after Charley's death, except that it went on for three weeks and she became more eloquent about it. And in the house she sulked and snarled at him. She seemed to be brewing some retaliation against him, and Vic did not know what form it would take. Between wondering what Melinda was going to do next and trying to minimize her behaviour to her friends, which he did in the most gallant and sympathetic manner, Vic had quite enough to occupy him in his hours away from the printing plant.

Horace came to see Vic at the plant about three days after the coroner's inquest. For the first few minutes Horace looked over the loose sheets of Greek type that were the day's work, looked at the design that Vic had chosen – not the one Melinda had so carelessly selected – for the cover of the book, but Horace got to the point of his visit before five minutes had passed.

'Vic, I'm a little worried,' he said firmly. 'You know what I'm worried about, don't you?'

Stephen and Carlyle had gone home. They were alone in the press room.

'Yes,' Vic said.

'She's been twice to see Evelyn, you know. Once to see Mary.'

'Oh,' Vic said, without surprise. 'I think she told me she'd been to Evelyn's.'

'Well, you know what she's saying?' Horace looked embarrassed. 'She told Mary she'd said the same thing to you at home.' He paused, but Vic did not speak. 'I'm not so much interested in that – except that it's a horrible thing to get around town – but what's going to happen to Melinda?'

'I suppose she'll quiet down,' Vic said in a patient tone. He slid one thigh on to the corner of a composing table. A robin's 'Cheep? – Cheep?' came clearly through the closed window behind Horace. He could see the robin on the sill, the little male robin. It was dusk. He wondered if the robin wanted something to eat or if there was some kind of trouble. Last spring the robin lived with his wife in a nest they had built in a low stone wall just outside the back door.

'Well, will she? What're you thinking?' Horace asked.

'Frankly, I was thinking about that robin,' Vic said, sliding off the table and walking to the back door. He looked at the still unfinished bread crumbs and diced fat that Carlyle had dropped below the tree that morning. Vic came back. 'Maybe he was just saying good night,' Vic said, 'but last spring we had to chase a snake away from their nest.'

Horace smiled, a little impatiently. 'I never know whether you're pretending unconcern or you're really unconcerned, Vic.'

'I suppose I'm concerned,' Vic said, 'but don't forget I've had it a good many years.'

'Yes, I know. And I don't want to meddle, Vic. But can you imagine Evelyn or Mary,' Horace said, raising his voice suddenly, 'going around to you and their other friends saying that their husband is a murderer?'

'No. But I always knew Melinda was different.'

Horace laughed, a despairing laugh. 'What're you going to do about it, Vic? Is she going to divorce you?'

'She hasn't said anything about it. Did she say anything to Mary about it?'

Horace looked at him a moment, almost with surprise. 'No, not that I know of.'

There was a long pause. Horace walked about in the space between two tables, his hands in his jacket pockets, as if he were thoughtfully measuring the floor with his steps. Vic, standing up now, took a deep breath. His belt felt loose, and he tightened it one hole. He had been eating less lately, deliberately, and it had begun to show in his waistline.

'Well – what do you answer her when she accuses you?' Horace demanded.

'Nothing!' Vic said. 'What can I? What can anybody say?'

The blank surprise came over Horace's face again. 'I could answer quite a lot. I could tell her, if I were you, that I'd put up with all I could stand, for years, and that this goes beyond – beyond putting up with. I can't believe that she means it, Vic,' he said earnestly. 'If she did, she wouldn't be living under the same roof with you!'

She wasn't really, Vic thought. Horace's fervour embarrassed him. 'I don't know what to make of it, Horace, I really don't.'

'Has it ever occurred to you that she might really be – a bit off, Vic? I'm no psychiatrist but I've had a chance to watch her over the years. This goes beyond self-indulgence or the fact that she's spoilt!'

Vic caught the note of hostility in Horace's voice and something rose in him automatically, rose to defend Melinda. It was the first time Horace had expressed his dislike of Melinda. 'I don't think it's going to go on, Horace.'

'But this is something that can't be undone later,' Horace protested. 'Nobody's going to forget this, Vic. And I think the whole town knows by now that she's accusing you. What kind of a woman is she? I don't see why you put up with it!'

'But I've put up with so much,' Vic replied with a sigh. 'I suppose it gets to be a habit.'

'A habit to torture yourself?' Horace looked at his friend with a tortured concern.

'It's not that bad. I can take it, Horace. So don't worry. Please.' Vic patted Horace's shoulder.

Horace let his breath out in a dissatisfied way. 'But I do worry.'

Vic smiled a little, went to the back door and locked it. 'I'd like to ask you to come to the house for a drink—'

'Thanks,' Horace interrupted in a negative tone.

'All right,' Vic said, smiling, but he again felt the creeping embarrassment, the shame, because Horace had turned against Melinda.

'Thanks, not now, Vic. Why don't you come over to see us? I know Mary'd like to see you.'

'Not tonight, I think. I'll take a rain check. Be sure to give Mary my regards, though. How's the pear tree looking?'

'Oh, better. Much better,' Horace said.

'Good.' Vic had given them some of his own fungicide concoction to spray on their pear tree because its leaves had started to develop red-brown spots.

They strolled out to their cars, talking about the likelihood of rain that evening. There was a hint of autumn in the air.

'We would like to see you soon, Vic,' Horace said before he got into his car.

'You will,' Vic answered, smiling. 'My love to Mary!' He waved cheerfully and got into his car.

Melinda was in the living-room when Vic got home, sitting on the sofa with a magazine.

'Good evening,' Vic said, smiling.

She glanced up at him sullenly.

'Can I fix you a drink?' he asked.

'Thanks, I'll do it.'

Vic had washed up and put on a clean shirt in his own room before coming into the house. He sat down in his favourite arm-chair with the newspaper. It was strange, and rather pleasant, to feel no desire for a drink at seven o'clock. He had not had a drink in three days. It made him feel secure and self-sufficient somehow. He was aware of a placidity that seemed to surround him, to show itself in his facial expression, while within he felt a steely hard-ness, a not entirely unpleasant tenseness whose components he did not really know. Hatred? Resentment? Fear? Guilt? Or was it simply pride and satisfaction? It was like a core in him. Another question was, had it always been in him or was it something new?

Melinda came in with her drink. 'Trixie's bringing home stories now,' she announced.

'Where is Trixie?'

'She went to a party at the Petersons'. Janey's birthday. She should come home with some fine stories tonight.'

'Am I supposed to go and get her or is Peterson driving her back?'

'He said he'd deliver her at about seven-thirty,' Melinda replied, collapsing on the sofa so hard that her highball almost spilled.

Her movement blew a roll of grey dust into view under the sofa. Vic looked at it with amusement.

'I believe I'll do some vacuuming before dinner,' he announced pleasantly.

Melinda's incongruously brooding, sullen face made him smile all the more. He got the vacuum from the hall closet and plugged it into the wall by the phonograph. He whistled as he worked, enjoying the swift disappearance of the dust rolls under the sofa, of the square of fine dust that he had found when he moved the arm-chair. He enjoyed, too, the strain of his muscles as he performed the humble, domestic chore of vacuuming his living-room. He drew his stomach in, did deep knee bends to reach under the bookcase, stretched up tall to get to the top of the curtains with the brush appliance. He liked exercise when he did something useful with it. He'd tackle the windows tomorrow, he thought. They'd needed washing for months. He was still vacuuming when Charles Peterson arrived with Trixie.

'Hello!' Vic called out to him in the car. 'Won't you come in for a minute?'

Peterson looked as if he didn't want to come in. Behind his shy smile, Vic sensed his unease. But he was coming in. 'How're you this evening?' he asked as he approached the door.

Trixie had run past Vic into the living-room, clattering a noise-maker that she had acquired at the party.

'We're fine,' Vic said. 'Can I offer you a beer? Some iced tea? A drink?' It was a fine picture that he and Melinda made, and Vic knew it: he in his shirt sleeves, vacuuming the living-room, and Melinda on the sofa with a highball, not even looking particularly tidy in her cotton blouse and skirt and her sandals and no stockings.

Peterson looked around a little awkwardly, then smiled. 'How're you, Mrs Van Allen?' he asked, a little fearfully, Vic thought.

'Very well, thank you,' Melinda said, with a contortion of her mouth that was supposed to pass for a smile.

'These kids' parties ...' Peterson said, with a laugh. 'They really take more out of you than grown-ups' parties.' He had a New England drawl in his *a*'s.

'You can say that again,' Vic said. 'How old is Janey? Seven?'

'Six,' Peterson said.

'Six! She's tall for her age.'

'Yes, she is.'

'Won't you sit down?'

'No, I'll be going on, thanks.' Peterson's eyes were drifting everywhere, as if he could read in a corner of the room, in the disarray of magazines on the cocktail table, the real explanation of the Van Allen scandal.

'Well, Trix looks as if she had a good time. Probably the noisiest one there.' Vic winked at her.

'I was not!' Trixie yelled, still talking at the top of her voice as she probably had at the party to make herself heard above twenty other screaming six-year-olds. 'I've got something to *tell* – you,' she said to Vic, on a note calculated to pique his curiosity.

'Me? Good!' Vic whispered enthusiastically. Then he turned to Peterson, who was making his way to the door. 'How're the hydrangeas doing?'

Peterson's face lit with a smile. 'Oh, they're fine. A little droopy for a while, but they've picked up fine now.' He turned around. 'Good night, Mrs Van Allen. It's nice to see you.'

Vic smiled. 'Good night, Charley.' He knew Peterson's friends called him Charley, and that it would please him if Vic called him that rather than 'Mr Peterson'.

'Good night,' Peterson said. 'See you again.'

It struck Vic that Peterson's smile was more genuine than when he had arrived.

'My goodness,' Vic said as he came back into the room. 'Couldn't you say good night to the man?'

Melinda only looked at him slurringly.

'Not very good for your public relations.' He put his hands on his knees and leaned towards Trixie. 'And couldn't you say good night and thank you?'

'I said all that at Janey's house,' Trixie replied. She looked quickly at her mother, then beckoned to Vic to come into the kitchen with her.

Melinda was watching them.

Vic went with Trixie. Trixie pulled his head down to her and whispered roaringly in his ear, 'Did you really kill Charley De Lisle?'

'No!' Vic whispered, smiling.

'Because Janey says you did.' Trixie's eyes were shining with eagerness, with a pride and excitement ready to be released in a yell or a hug if Vic should just say that he had killed Charley.

'You're a *wild* one!' Vic whispered.

'Janey said the Wilsons came over to see her mother and dad, and the Wilsons think you did it.'

'Do they?' Vic whispered.

'But you didn't?'

'No, I didn't,' Vic whispered. 'I didn't, I didn't.'

Melinda came into the kitchen. She looked at Trixie – the bored but intense look that held not a jot of anything that could be called maternal. Trixie didn't react to it at all. She was used to it. 'Go to your room, Trixie,' Melinda said.

Trixie looked to her father.

'All right, honey. Go,' Vic said, tickling Trixie under the chin. 'You don't have to talk to her like a flunkey, do you?' he said to Melinda.

Trixie went off with her head up, pretending affront, but she would forget it in a matter of seconds, Vic knew.

'Well,' Vic said, smiling, 'what's up?'

'I thought you ought to know that the whole town's wise to you.'

'Wise to me. What do you mean? They all know I killed Charley, I suppose.'

'They're all talking about it. You ought to hear the Wilsons.'

'I feel as if I have heard the Wilsons. I don't care to hear them.' Vic opened the refrigerator. 'What've we got for dinner?'

'There's going to be – there's going to be a public uproar about you,' Melinda said threateningly.

'Led by you. Led by my wife.' Vic was getting some lamb chops out of the freezing compartment.

'Do you think nothing's going to happen? You're wrong!'

'I suppose Don Wilson saw me drowning De Lisle in the swimming pool. Why doesn't he speak up about it? What's the use of all this murmuring behind people's backs?' He got out some frozen peas. Peas, a big salad of lettuce and tomato, and the chops. He didn't want a potato, and he knew if he didn't put potatoes on, Melinda wouldn't.

'Do you want to bet I don't do something?' Melinda asked.

He glanced at her, noticing again the circles under her eyes, the painful strain of her eyebrows. 'Darling, I wish you wouldn't keep on like this. It's useless. Do something. Do something constructive, but don't worry around the house all day – torturing yourself,' he added forcefully, borrowing a phrase from Horace. 'I don't want to see you with circles under your eyes.'

'Go to hell,' she murmured, and went back into the living-room.

It was a simple phrase, 'Go to hell,' certainly unoriginal and more or less vague, but it always disturbed Vic when he heard it from Melinda, because it could mean so many things – not always that she was at a loss for anything else to say, though sometimes it meant that, too. He knew that evening that she was planning something. Collusion with Don Wilson? But of what kind? How? If Don Wilson had really seen anything the night of the Cowans' party he'd have said so before now. Melinda wouldn't be keeping quiet anything of importance that he had told her.

Vic went back and finished his vacuuming with a zest. Melinda was a challenge, and he rather relished it.

He fixed the entire dinner, including apple sauce with an egg-white beaten into it for dessert. Trixie had fallen asleep in her room, and Vic did not awaken her, assuming that she had probably eaten more than enough at the Petersons'. Vic was very cheerful and talkative during the meal. But Melinda was thoughtful, she really did not attend to everything he said, and her inattention was not deliberate.

About ten days later, at the beginning of the month of September when the bank statement came in, Vic noticed that over a hundred dollars more than usual had been withdrawn, by Melinda, of course. Some of her cheques made out to 'cash' were among the cancelled drafts – one for $125 – but there was no cheque with any addressee that would give him a clue as to what she had used the money for. He tried to remember if she had bought any clothes, anything for the house. She hadn't, that he knew of. Ordinarily he would not have noticed an excess of a hundred dollars in their monthly budget, but because he was so wary now of Melinda's actions he supposed he had examined the bank statement with more than the usual care. The $125 cheque was dated 20 August, more than a week after De Lisle's funeral in New York (which Melinda had gone to New York for), and Vic did not think it could have been for flowers or for anything to do with the funeral.

Vic thought it possible that she had hired a private detective, so he began to look around for a new face in Little Wesley, a new face that might betray a particular interest in him.

12

September was a quiet month, as far as social events went. People were busy getting a cellar floor repaired, cleaning out drainpipes, checking their heating systems in preparation for the winter, and corralling the workmen to do all this, which sometimes took a week. Vic was called to Wesley by the MacPhersons to pass judgement on an oil stove that they intended to buy. And Mrs Podnansky had a dead squirrel in her well. She didn't use the well for anything except décor, and it was not that the water had to be clean, but the floating squirrel upset her. Vic got it out with one of his old butterfly nets attached to a rake handle. Mrs Podnansky, who had been angling for it with a bucket on a rope for days before she called him, she said, was all aflutter with gratitude. Her nervous, rather sweet face lighted up and she had looked for a few moments on the brink of making him a little speech – a little speech about her confidence in him and her affection for him in spite of the talk around the town, Vic supposed – but all she finally said, in a mischievous tone, was:

'I've a bottle of something awfully good in the kitchen. Calvados. My son gave it to me. Wouldn't you like to sample it?'

And Vic was unpleasantly reminded of the extra pieces of cake that pitying hostesses used to force upon him. He smiled and said, 'Thanks very much, my dear. I'm on the water wagon these days.'

The butterfly net, which Vic had not held in his hand for years, reminded him of the pleasure he had used to find in pursuing butterflies around the brook behind the house. He thought he should do some more of it.

Twice Vic passed Don Wilson in town, once on the sidewalk and once when Vic was driving and Wilson was on foot. Both times Wilson gave him a sneaking smile, a faint nod, and what might have been described as a long look, and both times Vic had called out 'Hi! How are you?' with a beaming smile. Vic knew that Melinda had been over to see the Wilsons several times. Perhaps Ralph Gosden had been there, too. Vic might have proposed asking the Wilsons to the house, except that they rather bored him, and besides he could feel that Melinda considered them her friends now, not his, and did not want to share them with him.

Then one afternoon June Wilson came to the printing plant. She came in shyly, apologized for coming unannounced, and asked Vic if he had the time to show her around the place. Vic said of course he had.

Stephen was standing at the press. He knew the Wilsons, and he greeted June with a surprised smile. Stephen did not stop his work. Vic took note of the way each had spoken to the other, looking for any coolness on Stephen's part, but he couldn't have said that he saw any. Stephen was a very polite young man, however. Vic showed June a chase of Greek type, which he was going to make impressions of on tissue paper that afternoon and correct, showed her the store room, introduced her to Carlyle, and then they watched Stephen for a few minutes, until June evidently thought the proper length of time had passed, because she suggested that they go into his office. Once in there, June lighted a cigarette quickly, and said in a straightforward way:

'I came here to tell you something.'

'What?' Vic asked.

'To tell you that I don't approve of what my husband is doing, and that I don't think the way he does. And I—' Her thin hands worked with the leather cigarette-case, tremblingly stuck the flap back into place to close it. 'I'm very embarrassed by the way he's acting.'

'What do you mean?'

She looked at him, her blue eyes wide and young and earnest. The sunlight through the window behind her burned like a golden fire in her short, curly hair. She was too slight and under-nourished-looking to be pretty, in Vic's opinion, and he was not sure how intelligent she was. 'You must know what I mean,' she said. 'It's terrible!'

'Yes, I've heard what he thinks – or what he's been saying. I can't say that it bothers me very much.' He smiled at her.

'No, of course. I understand that. But it bothers me because – because it's unjust, and we haven't been in this town very long, and it's going to make people hate us.'

'I don't hate you,' Vic said, still smiling.

'I don't know why you don't. Well, people are beginning to hate Don. I can't blame them. He's talking to people who're your friends – some of them. At least they know you well – most of them. When Don says what he does, people just – well, either they drop us then and there or they label Don as rude or cracked or something like that.' She hesitated. Her hands were trembling again on the cigarette-case. 'I wanted to apologize to you – for my husband – and to tell you that I don't share his ideas at all on this matter,' she said positively. 'I'm very sorry and I'm also ashamed.'

'Oh!' Vic said scoffingly. 'There's no harm done. Except to your husband probably. I'm sorry, too, but' – he looked at her, smiling – 'I think it's very nice of you to come here to tell me this. I appreciate it. I don't suppose there's anything I can do to help you?'

She shook her head. 'I suppose we'll weather it.'

'Who's we?'

'Don and I.'

Vic walked behind his desk, his hands in his pockets, looking down at the floor, pleasantly conscious of the fact that his front was absolutely straight now that there was no bulge at all below his braided belt. In fact, Trixie had had to take the belt back to school and shorten it by about four inches. 'I wonder if you and Don'd like to come over for a drink some evening?'

June Wilson looked surprised. 'Why, yes. I'm sure we would.' Then she frowned. 'Do you really mean that?'

'Of course I mean it!' Vic said, laughing. 'How about tomorrow evening, Friday? At about seven?'

She was so pleased she was blushing. 'I think that'll be fine. Well I'd better go. It's been awfully nice seeing you.'

'I've enjoyed it, too.' Vic walked out with her to the car, and made her a bow as she left.

That evening, when he came home, Melinda said, 'So I hear you've asked the Wilsons over for a drink.'

'Yes. You don't mind, do you?'

'Don Wilson doesn't like you, you know.'

'So I hear,' he said boredly. 'I thought we might do something to correct that. They seem quite nice.' And then Vic went out to get the power mower from the garage. Mowing the sprawling, informal lawn that bounded three sides of the house was his project that evening for the time between seven and dinner that had used to be the cocktail hour.

The Wilsons came at a casual twenty-past seven on Friday evening. Don made his greeting to Melinda in the same tone that he used to Vic, but his wife was not so secretive. She had a big smile for Vic. June took Vic's armchair, and Don chose the middle of the sofa where he sat slouched with his long legs crossed and out in front of him, a pose of exaggerated nonchalance. His expression was one of contemptuous amusement plus a look of having just noticed a bad smell. Also contemptuous, Vic supposed, were his unpressed trousers and his not very fresh shirt. His tweed jacket had leather elbow patches.

Vic fixed old-fashioneds – strong and with plenty of fresh fruit in them – and brought them in on a tray. Melinda and June were having a conversation about flowers that was boring Melinda terribly, Vic saw. He served the drinks all around, pushed the bowl of popcorn into the centre of the cocktail table, then sat down in a chair and said to Don, 'Well, what's new?'

Don sat up a little. The contemptuous smile was still there.

'Don's working in his head,' his wife volunteered. 'He'll probably be very quiet tonight, but don't mind.'

Vic nodded politely and sipped his drink.

'Nothing much new,' Don said in his growly baritone voice. He was looking at Vic now as the women went on talking.

Vic slowly filled his pipe, aware that he was being studied by Don Wilson. It was amazing how June Wilson could go on and on about nothing. Now it was dog shows, whether Little Wesley ever had a dog show. Vic saw Melinda take a big gulp of her drink. Melinda had no talent for small talk with another woman. Don Wilson was looking the living-room over thoroughly, Vic noticed, and he supposed that an inspection of the bookcase would come soon.

'Well, how're you liking the town?' Vic asked Don.

'Oh, very well,' Don said, his dark eyes glancing at Vic and away again.

'I hear you know the Hineses.'

'Yes. Very nice people,' Don said.

Vic sighed. He fixed a second round of drinks as soon as possible. Then he asked Don, 'Have you seen Ralph Gosden lately?'

'Yes. Last week, I think,' Don said.

'How is he? I haven't seen him in quite a while.'

'Oh, I think he's fine,' Don said, a bit of a challenge in his tone now.

Vic felt sorriest for June Wilson. The second drink was doing very little to relax her. She was still making a great effort with Melinda, really going through a kind of fluttering agony, all in the name of social intercourse. Vic decided that the only way Don Wilson might loosen up was if he got him alone, because his wife had probably told him to be on his best behaviour tonight, so Vic proposed a tour of the estate.

Don dragged himself up by sections, still wearing the insulting smile. *I'm* not afraid to take a turn around the grounds with a murderer, he might have been saying.

Vic took him into the garage first. He pointed out his snails, and talked about their eggs and their babies with a malevolent fervour when he saw that Don was mildly disgusted by them. He talked volubly about their rate of reproduction and about prodding them in races he staged for his own amusement, making them go over razor blades stood on edge, though he had never tried racing them in his life. Then he told Don about his bed bug experiment and the letter he had written to the entomological journal, which they had printed, and the letter of thanks they had written to him in return.

'I'm sorry I can't show you the bed bugs, but I got rid of them after the experiment was over,' Vic said.

Don Wilson stared politely at Vic's power saw, then at his herbs, then at the neat rows of hammers and saws that hung on a panel of the back wall of the garage, murderous instruments all, then at a small bookcase that Vic was in the process of building for Trixie's room. Don's face was betraying a certain surprise.

'Let me get you another drink!' Vic said suddenly, taking Don's glass from his hand. 'Wait here. I'll be right back. You've got to see our brook!'

Vic was back in a few minutes with a fresh drink for Don. Then they started out for the brook behind the house. 'This is where I sleep,' Vic said as they passed his wing on the other side of the garage, though he was sure Don had heard about his separate quarters. Don stared thoughtfully at the curtainless windows.

Vic discoursed for at least ten minutes on the glacial origin of a rise of ground behind the brook and of certain stones which he picked up from the brook's bed. Then he launched into the arboreal life around them. He was careful to keep his enthusiasm on the brink of hysteria, of aberration. Don could hardly have got a word in edgewise if he had wanted to.

Finally Vic stopped and said with a smile, 'Well, I don't know if all this interests you or not.'

'You must be a very happy man,' Don said with sarcasm.

'I can't complain. Life's been very good to me,' Vic replied. He added, 'I was lucky enough to be born with an income, which helps, of course.'

Don nodded, his long jaw set. It was obvious that he hated people with incomes. Don took a swallow from his glass. 'I wanted to ask you something tonight.'

'What?'

'What do you think killed Charley De Lisle?'

'*What* do I think? I don't know. I suppose it was cramp. Or else he really did get into water that was over his head.'

Don's dark-brown eyes bored into him, or tried to. 'Is that all?'

'What do you think?' Vic asked, teetering on a loose rock in the bank. He was on lower ground than Don, who towered now some five feet above Vic. Don was hesitating. No courage, Vic decided, not really any guts there.

'I thought you might have done it,' Don said in a casual tone.

Vic laughed a little. 'Guess again.'

Don said nothing, only continued to stare at him.

'Some people thought I killed Malcolm McRae, too, I hear,' Vic said.

'I didn't.'

'Good for you.'

'But I thought it was a very peculiar story to be spreading around,' Don added, mouthing the word 'peculiar'.

'It's funny that so many people attached importance to it. I think Ralph Gosden was scared out of his wits. Wasn't he?'

'It's a funny thing for you to get so much pleasure out of,' Don said unsmilingly.

Vic climbed the bank slowly, feeling very bored with Don Wilson. 'You seem to share an opinion with my wife that I killed Mr De Lisle,' Vic said.

'Yes.'

'Do you consider yourself psychic? Can you see what isn't there? Or do you just have a writer's imagination?' Vic asked in a pleasant tone.

'Could you take a lie detector test that you didn't kill him?' Don was becoming angry. The three strong drinks had begun to thicken his speech.

'I'd certainly be willing to,' Vic said tensely. Whether his sudden tension was due to boredom or hostility he didn't really know. He thought it was probably both.

'You're a very odd man, Mr Van Allen,' Don Wilson said.

'You're a very rude one,' Vic replied. They were standing on even ground now. Vic saw Don's bony hand tighten around his empty glass and he would not have been surprised if Don had suddenly hurled it into his face. Vic smiled with a deliberate blandness at him.

'Mr Van Allen, I don't care what you think of me. I don't care if I never see you again.'

Vic gave a laugh. 'That feeling is mutual.'

'But I think I will see you again.'

'You can't really avoid it unless you move.' Vic waited. Don said nothing, only stared at him. 'Shall we join the ladies?' Vic began to walk towards the house, and Don followed him.

Vic was sorry he had let himself speak sharply to Don – it wasn't really in character – but, on the other hand, one ought to be sensible occasionally, he supposed. It was sensible to let Don see that he could react with anger, normal anger, if he were sufficiently provoked. And as it was now, Vic could sense a subtle backing down in Don Wilson. For all Don's aggression, the evening was not going to him.

'How about you people staying for dinner?' Vic said affably to June Wilson as he and Don came into the living-room.

'Well – I think that's up to your wife,' June said. 'But I think—'

'Oh, I'll be glad to do the cooking,' Vic said. 'I think we've got a steak or two in there.'

Melinda, sulking on the sofa, gave him no backing up, however, and Vic knew that dinner was out.

'I think we should be going home,' June said. 'I'm getting a little high.' She laughed, managed quite a happy laugh. 'Melinda told me you made this table, Vic. I think it's *lovely*.'

'Thank you,' Vic said, smiling.

'Sit down, Don,' Melinda said, patting the sofa behind her. 'Have another drink.'

But Don did not sit down. He did not even reply.

'Say, where's Trixie?' Vic asked. 'Didn't you say she went to a five o'clock movie, honey?'

Melinda sat up, a startled expression coming through the sullenness. 'Oh, my *God*, I was supposed to pick her up in Wesley!' she said with unmaternal annoyance. 'What the hell time is it?'

June Wilson tittered. 'These modern mothers!' she said, putting her curly head back. She was nursing her last half inch of drink, and looked as if she would have been glad to stay there sipping and chatting all evening.

'It's eight-twenty-five,' Vic said. 'What time were you supposed to pick her up?'

'Seven-thirty,' Melinda groaned, still not getting up from the sofa.

Vic noticed that Wilson was looking at her with gloomy surprise and disapproval. 'Who's she with? Janey?' Vic asked.

'No-o. The Carter kids from Wesley. She's probably with them. She's probably all right or they'd have called us.' Melinda ran her fingers through her hair and reached for her drink.

'I'll give them a ring in a couple of minutes,' Vic said calmly, though his concern made quite a contrast to Melinda's indifference, and he could see that the Wilsons had taken notice of it.

The Wilsons were looking at each other. There was a silence of a whole minute or so. Then June stood up and said:

'We really must go. I can see you people have things to do. Thanks for the lovely drinks. I hope you'll come to our house next time.'

'Thanks, Melinda,' Don Wilson said, bending over the sofa. He and Melinda shook hands, and Melinda used his hand to pull herself up from the sofa.

'Thanks for coming,' Melinda said. 'I hope next time you come the house won't be in such an upset.'

'Why, I didn't notice any upset,' June said, smiling.

'Oh, it's one damned thing after another,' Melinda said.

The Wilsons trickled out of the door, with backward glances from June and promises to telephone very soon. Vic was glad that June considered the cocktail visit a success, but she wouldn't, of course, after her husband had told her their conversation. Probably Don wouldn't tell her that conversation. He'd just tell her that he thought Vic Van Allen was cracked, judging from the snails in the garage and from his insane enthusiasm for glaciers.

'Doesn't he ever talk?' Vic asked.

'Who?' Melinda had got herself another drink, straight on the rocks.

'Don Wilson. I couldn't get a word out of him.'

'No?'

'No. Shouldn't I call up the Carters? What's his first name?'

'I don't know. They live in Marlboro Heights.'

Vic made the call. Trixie was fine and wanted to spend the night. Vic talked to her and made her promise to go to bed by nine o'clock, though he didn't think she would stick to it.

'She's fine,' Vic said to Melinda. 'Mrs Carter said they'd drive her over sometime tomorrow morning.'

'What're you so merry about?' Melinda asked.

'Why shouldn't I be? Wasn't it a pleasant evening?'

'June Wilson bores me stiff.'

'Don bores me. We should've switched around. Say, it isn't very late. Why don't we drive over to Wesley and have dinner at the Golden Pheasant? Wouldn't you like that?' He knew she would, and knew she would hate admitting that she would, hate going with him instead of with some imaginary man, whom she was probably even then imagining.

'I'd rather stay home,' Melinda said.

'No, you wouldn't,' Vic said kindly. 'Go and put on your blouse with the gold thread. I think the skirt is fine.'

She was wearing a green velvet skirt, but as if to show her insolence towards him or perhaps June Wilson, she had topped the skirt with her old brown sweater, sleeves pushed up, and nothing around her neck. Comparable to Don's old trousers, Vic thought. He sighed, waiting for her inevitable turning away to go to her room, to put on the new blouse with the gold thread, just as he had suggested. Melinda swayed a little, her greenish eyes staring at him, and then she turned away, pulling her sweater over her head before she was even out of the room.

Why did he really do it, Vic asked himself, when he would have preferred staying home with a book? Or working on Trixie's bookcase? Patiently, with unflagging good humour, he tried to draw her out at the restaurant, tried to get a smile from her by describing twelve methods of summoning a waiter. Melinda only stared off into space – though she was staring around at other people, Vic knew. Melinda derived a great deal of pleasure from watching other people. Or was she looking to see if her detective was here? Not very likely, since he had proposed the Golden Pheasant and he didn't think the detective, if any, would trouble to follow their car at night. A detective would be hired to worm what he could out of their friends, he supposed. So far, no stranger had turned up in their set. Vic thought the Mellers or the Cowans would have mentioned a curious stranger if they had been questioned by one. No, Melinda was only staring at other people. She had a faculty which he really admired of being able to dream, to live vicariously for a while, in other people. He might have said something about this to her, but he was afraid that tonight she would take it as an insult. Or she would say, 'What else can I do with the life I've got?' So he talked of something else, of the possibility of going to Canada before the weather got cold. They might make some arrangement for Trixie to stay with the Petersons for ten days, Vic said.

'Oh, I don't think I'd care for that,' Melinda said, with a cool smile.

'This summer's gone by without a real vacation for either of us,' he said.

'Let it go by. I'm sick of it.'

'The winter's going to be even more boring – without a break somewhere,' he said.

'Oh, I don't think it's going to be boring,' she said.

He smiled. 'Is that a threat?'

'Take it the way you like.'

'Are you going to put arsenic in my food?'

'I don't think arsenic could kill you.'

It was a charming evening. Before they went home Vic stopped at Wesley's biggest drugstore to look over the book rack. He bought a couple of Penguin books, one on insects, the other on the installation of stained glass in church windows. Melinda went into a phone booth and made a very long call to someone. Vic could hear the murmur of her voice, but he made no effort to hear what she was saying.

13

Trixie entered the Highland School on 7 September and was put into the third grade because she could read so well. Vic was very proud of her. The school called him and Melinda in to discuss the matter of putting her into the third grade: she would need some extra help in arithmetic, geography, and probably also penmanship, and the school wanted to know if they could count on her parents to tutor her a bit at home. Vic said that he would be happy to tutor her and that he had plenty of time for it. Even Melinda gave an affirmative answer. So it was settled. As a surprise present and a reward, Vic gave Trixie the bookcase he had made, and filled its upper two shelves with new books for her, putting her old favourites in the two lower shelves. He was to tutor her two hours on Saturday and two hours on Sunday, come hell or high water, he told her, and she seemed to be fairly impressed. The tutoring began at the end of her first week in school. Half an hour of arithmetic, half an hour of penmanship on the living-room cocktail table, then a fifteen-minute break and an hour of geography, which was not quite such a mental strain on Trixie because Vic could make geography very funny.

Vic very much enjoyed tutoring Trixie. He had been looking

forward to it for years, to helping her first with arithmetic and algebra and geometry, then perhaps trig and calculus. It had always seemed the essence of parenthood and domesticity, the older generation passing down the wisdom of the race to the off-spring, as birds taught their young to fly. And yet the tutoring brought into focus certain uncomfortable facts, made him realize more acutely that he was leading two lives and that the friend-ships he now enjoyed with Horace and Phil, for instance, existed because they did not know the truth about him. He felt more guilt about that than he had felt for killing De Lisle.

He thought about such things as he watched Trixie's plump, uncomfortable hand trying to make a row of *b*'s, or *q*'s or *g*'s. 'Aye bee see dee ee eff *gee-ee*, aitch eye jay kay ellemeno *pee-ee*,' Trixie chanted periodically to rest from the penmanship labours, because she had known the alphabet for years. Vic tried to answer the question he had not been able to answer for the past four or five years: where were things going with Melinda and where did he want them to go? He wanted her to himself, but she was not attractive to him as a woman; that he realized, too. Neither was she repellent. He simply felt that he could get along without her, or any other woman, physically, for the rest of his life. And had he known that before he killed De Lisle? He couldn't answer that, he couldn't remember. De Lisle's murder was like a caesura in his experience, and it was strangely hard to remember, emotionally, before that time. He remembered a knot, a dark, hard knot of repressions and resentments in himself, and it was as if his mur-dering De Lisle had untied the knot. He was more relaxed now and, to be perfectly honest, happier. He couldn't see himself as a criminal, a psychopath. It was, indeed, much as he had foreseen the evening he had made the shocking statement to Joel Nash. He had indulged in a fantasy that night of having killed McRae him-self, assuming that McRae had provoked him sufficiently, and Vic remembered that he had started to feel better immediately. A discharge of repressed hatred, perhaps that was a better metaphor than the untying of a knot. But just what had pushed him across the line from fantasy to fact that night in the Cowans' swimming pool? And would it happen again under the right circumstances? He hoped not. Obviously, it was better to let off steam here and there rather than let it build up to explosive proportions. He smiled at the simple logic of it. He could imagine many things, but he could not imagine himself very angry, as most people became angry, raising their voices and banging their fists on tables. But perhaps he should set himself to try.

'Get some corners on those *r*'s,' Vic said to Trixie. 'You're making a string of croquet wickets.'

Trixie giggled, her concentration running out. 'Let's play croquet!'

'After you get through the *r*'s.'

Phil and Horace could never exactly condone his murder of De Lisle, Vic thought, so he was doomed to hypocrisy. But he could not keep himself from taking some comfort in the thought that Phil or Horace or any other man might have killed him, too, under similar circumstances. They simply wouldn't have done it in a swimming pool, probably. They might have chosen De Lisle's house, one afternoon when their wife was there. And perhaps they, too, might have felt better afterwards – perhaps. The whole house reflected Vic's happier state of mind. He had repainted the garage in a cheerful yellow, set out a little maple tree in one of the hydrangea holes and filled in the other hole and seeded it. The living-room looked as if happy people lived in it now, even if happy people didn't. He thought he had lost at least fifteen pounds – he had an aversion to weighing himself – and he hardly ever took a drink any more. He whistled more often. Or did he whistle just to annoy Melinda, just because she generally asked him to stop?

Melinda drove up in her car while Vic and Trixie were playing a rather unorthodox game of croquet on the lawn. There was a man with her, a man Vic had never seen before. Vic calmly bent over and finished his shot – a fifteen-foot shot over convex ground that bumped Trixie's ball lightly and left his sitting where hers had been, directly in front of the wicket. Trixie let out a wail and jumped up and down and stamped, letting off steam as if she had a big stake in the game, though Trixie's sole objective in croquet seemed to be to knock the ball as far as possible. Vic turned towards the driveway as Melinda and the man approached. He was a tall, broad-shouldered blond man of about thirty-two, in tweed jacket and slacks. His serious face smiled a little as he neared Vic.

'Vic, this is Mr Carpenter,' Melinda said. 'Mr Carpenter, my husband.'

'How do you do?' Vic said, extending his hand.

'How do you do?' Mr Carpenter said, with a firm grip. 'Your wife's just been showing me around the town. I'm looking for a place to live.'

'Oh. To rent or to buy?' Vic asked.

'To rent,' he replied.

'Mr Carpenter's a psychotherapist,' Melinda said. 'He's going to be working at Kennington for a few months. I found him asking questions in the drugstore, so I thought I'd give him a tour of the town. None of the real estate places are open on Sunday around here.'

That gave Vic his first suspicion. Melinda was explaining a little too carefully. Mr Carpenter's eyes were lingering on him with just a little too much interest, even for a psychotherapist. 'Did you tell him about the Derby place?' Vic asked.

'Showed it to him,' Melinda said. 'That's a little too barnlike. He wants more of something like Charley had, maybe in the woods, but comfortable.'

'Well, it's a good time of the year to be looking. Summer

people giving up their houses. What about Charley's place?' Vic asked, going her one better. 'Wouldn't that be free now?'

Mr Carpenter was looking at Melinda, and there was nothing about his expression that would have betrayed that he had ever heard of Charley.

'Y-yes,' Melinda said thoughtfully. 'We might ask about that. The owners should be in today, too.' She glanced towards the house, as if the telephone had crossed her mind.

But she wasn't going to telephone the owners just now, Vic knew, and probably not tomorrow either. 'Wouldn't you care to come in, Mr Carpenter?' Vic asked. 'Or are you in a hurry?'

Mr Carpenter indicated with a smile and a little bow that he would be happy to come in. They all walked towards the house, Trixie trailing them and staring at the newcomer.

'What do you think of Kennington?' Vic asked as they went into the house. Kennington was a psychiatric institute outside of Wesley, with about a hundred in- and out-patients. It was famous for its small, distinguished staff and for its homelike atmosphere. The long, low white building sat on a green hill and looked like a well-kept country home.

'Well, I only got there yesterday,' Mr Carpenter said pleasantly. 'The people are very nice. I expected that. I'm sure I'll enjoy my work.'

Vic did not think he should ask him exactly what he would be doing. That would show too much curiosity.

'Would you care for a drink?' Melinda asked. 'Or some coffee?'

'Oh, no, thank you. I'll just have a cigarette. Then I ought to be getting back to my car.'

'Oh, yes. He left his car in front of the drugstore, unlocked,' Melinda said, smiling. 'He's afraid somebody's going to steal it.'

'Not much of that around here,' Vic said genially.

'Certainly isn't like New York,' Mr Carpenter agreed, looking around the room as he spoke.

Vic was looking at his loose tweed jacket, wondering if the bulge under his arm could be a gun in a shoulder holster, or if it was a bulge at all. It might have been just a fold in the cloth. His heavy features wore a half-bored expression now that was deliberate, Vic felt. There was a certain veneer of the scholar about him, but only a veneer. He had the face of a man of action. Vic filled his pipe. He had a great taste for his pipe lately.

'Where're you staying now?' Vic asked.

'At the Ardmore in Wesley,' Mr Carpenter replied.

'Oh, you'll love it here once you get settled,' Melinda put in with animation. She was sitting on the edge of the sofa, smoking a cigarette. 'The mornings are so cool and fresh around here. It's really a pleasure to get in a car and drive along some of these roads at seven or eight in the morning.'

Vic couldn't think of a single morning when Melinda had been up and out at seven or eight.

'I expect I'll like it,' Mr Carpenter said. 'I'm sure getting myself settled won't be much of a problem.'

'My wife has a real genius for getting people settled,' Vic said, with an affectionate smile at Melinda. 'She really knows the houses and the countryside up here. Let her help you.' Vic smiled directly at Mr Carpenter.

He nodded slowly at Vic, looking as if he were thinking of something else.

'Trixie, go in the other room,' Melinda said nervously to Trixie, who was sitting in the middle of the floor staring at all of them.

'Well, she might be introduced first,' Vic said, getting up. He pulled Trixie gently to her feet by both hands. 'Trixie, this is Mr Carpenter. My daughter, Beatrice,' Vic said.

'How do you do?' said Mr Carpenter, smiling but not getting up.

'How do you do?' Trixie said. 'Daddy, can't I stay?'

'Not now, hon. Do as your mother says. You'll probably see Mr

Carpenter again. Run out and play and we'll finish our game in a little while.' Vic opened the front door for her and she ran out.

Mr Carpenter was eyeing him sharply when Vic turned around.

Vic smiled. 'Might as well let the child get some air on a day like this – Oh, look.' He picked up Trixie's copybook from the cocktail table. 'Don't you think that's a pretty handsome page? Look at it compared to last week.' He opened the book at an earlier page to show Melinda.

Melinda tried to pretend interest, tried quite well. 'It looks fine,' she said.

'I'm teaching my daughter calligraphy,' Vic explained to Mr Carpenter. 'She's just started in school and they put her in a class beyond her age group.' Vic turned over the pages of Trixie's copybook with a fond smile.

Then Mr Carpenter asked how old Trixie was, asked a question about the weather around Little Wesley, and then stood up. 'I must be going. I'm afraid you'll have to drive me back,' he added to Melinda.

'Oh, I don't mind a bit! We might go by that – that place we were talking about in the woods.'

'Charley's place,' Vic supplied.

'Yes,' Melinda said.

'Well, you must come back again,' Vic said to Mr Carpenter. 'I hope you enjoy your stay. Kennington's a fine place. We're very proud of it.'

'Thank you,' Mr Carpenter said.

Vic watched them until Melinda drove off, and then he turned back to the croquet game. Trixie had banged the balls all over the lawn. 'Now, where were we?' he asked.

As he played, and gave Trixie pointers that were usually not followed, Vic thought about Mr Carpenter. It would be much more fun not to let Melinda know he suspected anything, Vic thought. Then there was the possibility that he could be wrong, that Mr Carpenter was a psychotherapist and nothing else. But would a psychotherapist get into a car with a strange woman and be driven around in search of a house to rent? Well, that was barely possible, too, he supposed. But Mr Carpenter was not Melinda's type for a boy friend, that was one thing he felt sure of. He had an unmistakable air of being serious about something, whatever it might be, the look of a man who didn't let himself be distracted. Still, he was quite handsome. A detective agency might well have chosen him for a job like this. For the second time Vic tried to remember if he had seen Mr Carpenter anywhere on the streets of Little Wesley or Wesley. He didn't think he had.

Melinda was back in a very short time, not long enough for her to have gone by Charley's house. She went into the house without saying anything to him. When Vic had finished the game with Trixie, he went into the house, too. Melinda was washing her hair in the bathroom basin. The bathroom door was open.

Vic took *The World Almanac* down from the bookcase and sat down with it. He read about the antidotes for arsenic poisoning. She came out of the bathroom, went into her own room, and Vic called:

'Did you get Mr Carpenter back all right?'

'Um-hm.'

'Show him Charley's place?'

'Nope.'

'He seems a nice fellow.'

Melinda came in in her robe, barefoot, a towel around her head. 'Um-hm, I think he is. He's got a lot of brains. The kind of man you'd like to talk to, I should think.' There was the old nagging challenge in her tone.

Vic smiled. 'Well, let's see more of him – if he's got any time for us.'

On Monday, Vic called the Kennington Institute from his

office. Yes, they had a Mr Carpenter there. Mr Harold Carpenter. He was not always at the Institute, the woman on the telephone said, but she could take a message. 'Is this in regard to a house?' she asked.

'Yes, but I'll try again,' Vic said. 'I haven't found anything yet for him, but I wanted to keep in touch. Thank you.' He hung up before she could finish her question of what real estate company he represented.

14

They were playing it very carefully, Mr Carpenter and Melinda,
Vic thought, if Mr Carpenter was a detective. Even after a week
Vic wasn't quite sure, and he had seen Mr Carpenter two or three
more times. Once he had come to the house for cocktails and
once Melinda had asked him to drop in at the Mellers', who had
given a cocktail party with about eight guests. Here Mr Carpenter
met the Cowans and the MacPhersons but not the Wilsons,
because the Mellers – like the Cowans – had crossed the Wilsons
off their list. Horace talked for a while with Mr Carpenter at the
party, and later that evening Vic asked Horace what they had
talked about. Horace said they had talked about brain injuries,
and asked where they had met him. Vic told Horace what
Melinda had told him about their meeting. In fact, there was only
one thing interesting about the evening at the Mellers'. Vic
noticed that Melinda paid more than necessary attention to
Harold Carpenter. Vic thought it was deliberate, and for the
benefit of their friends as well as of himself. He smiled at both of
them, with a benign good humour. What did they expect to do?
Provoke him to another murderous attack? Was this the first
small, calculated step?

After about ten days Harold Carpenter began to come to the house quite often. He had taken Charley De Lisle's former house after all – which had not really surprised Vic, because the house made a good conversation piece: Harold could ask all kinds of questions about the deceased Charley, ask not only Vic but all of Vic's friends as well. 'Where are you staying?' was a question nearly everybody would put to a newcomer like Carpenter, and then Carpenter was launched. Vic supposed that within three weeks Carpenter had heard at least ten people's versions of the evening Charley had drowned. He must have done it very subtly, too, because neither Horace nor Phil came to him to tell him that he had been interrogated by Carpenter.

'Have you met Don Wilson?' Vic asked Carpenter one Saturday afternoon when he had dropped in to borrow Vic's hedge shears.

'No,' Carpenter replied a little wonderingly.

Melinda was within hearing.

'I suppose you'll get around to it,' Vic said, smiling. 'My wife sees the Wilsons quite often. You might enjoy him, I don't know.' Vic had no doubt that Carpenter had met Don. Don had probably picked Carpenter out for the job, gone to New York to do it for Melinda, because any trip she made to New York would have been noticed by Vic, she went so seldom. And an assignment like this would have needed personal contact. Harold Carpenter was a good private eye. Nothing rattled him. Vic said:

'When did you start your psychiatric training?' Carpenter had told him that he was in his last year at Columbia, and that he needed only his thesis plus some examination for his doctorate.

'Start? Oh, not until I was twenty-three. I lost some time by having to go to Korea.'

'And when did you stop?'

Carpenter did not bat an eye. 'Stop? What do you mean?'

'I meant stop your classes to start your field research for the thesis.'

'Oh, well, at the beginning of the summer, you might say. I went to some summer classes.' He smiled. 'In psychiatry, there's never a limit to how many courses you can take – or should take, to be a good doctor.'

It was all rather vague to Vic. 'And schizophrenia interests you most?'

'Well – I suppose so. It's the commonest affliction, as you know.'

Vic smiled. Melinda had gone into the kitchen to freshen her drink. Neither Vic nor Carpenter was drinking. 'I was wondering if you thought my wife had any schizophrenic tendencies.'

Carpenter frowned and smiled at the same time, showing his square white teeth in his generous, full-lipped mouth. 'I don't think so at all. Do you?'

'I don't really know. Not being an authority on the subject,' Vic said, and awaited something further from Carpenter.

'She has a lot of charm,' Carpenter said. 'A kind of undisciplined charm.'

'You mean the charm of no discipline.'

'Yes,' he said, smiling. 'I mean she has more charm than she thinks she has.'

'That's quite a lot.'

Carpenter laughed and looked at Melinda as she came back into the room.

It crossed Vic's mind then that Carpenter was the only person who had ever been to their house who had not, in some way, betrayed surprise on finding that he lived in another wing of the house. Carpenter had slipped up there. One or the other of them, however, was going to be very surprised before long. Which of them was it going to be? Vic smiled at Carpenter in a friendly way, as a good sportsman might at an opponent.

Carpenter stayed perhaps half an hour on the afternoon that he came to borrow the shears. He had a curious, half-absent way of looking around at everything, of staring at Trixie – as if there were anything odd about that specimen of rampant normality – of looking around in the garage, or the kitchen, or wherever he happened to be in the house. It was not entirely an absent look. Harold Carpenter was not an absent man. But he was around a little too much, considering their house was out of the way between Kennington and his own house, Charley's old house. That was another sign that pointed in the direction of his being a detective, or a psychiatrist hired, part time, to look him over.

And then on 4 October, when the bank statement came in, there was $200, at least $200, withdrawn that Vic couldn't account for. It was curious to think that they might be in Carpenter's pockets, that the $10 bill that Carpenter had used to buy a bottle of champagne on the evening of Melinda's birthday might have come directly from the Van Allen account. Vic had run into Carpenter on Commerce Street, the main street of Wesley, as he was coming out of a jewellery store where he had picked up his main present for Melinda. Carpenter had a couple of large books under his arm. He often had a large book of some sort under his arm.

'Are you busy tonight?' Vic had asked.

Carpenter hadn't been busy, and Vic had asked him if he would care to come out to the house for dinner. It was Melinda's birthday, and Vic imagined that Carpenter knew it. They were having a small dinner party, only the Mellers were coming, and he was sure Melinda would be glad to see him, Vic said. Carpenter looked politely hesitant, wanted to call Melinda first, but Vic said no, let it be a surprise for her. So Carpenter had accepted and had bought the champagne when Vic had told him that it was Melinda's birthday.

Vic and Melinda would have asked the Cowans, but Phil was away all week in Vermont, teaching, and Evelyn was feeling under the weather with a cold virus, she said. It was Vic who had proposed the dinner party, and he had had some trouble in persuading Melinda to give it. Melinda felt that their old friends were down on her lately, which was more or less true, but he pointed out that they were inviting her to their houses nevertheless and that if she wanted to improve matters she would have to invite them now and then, too. Vic had always had a hard time persuading Melinda to do any entertaining. Not that he felt they had to worry about what they owed their friends in the way of invitations – not in a town as informal as Little Wesley – but Vic thought that once or twice a year they might give a big cocktail party or an evening party, as the Cowans and the Mellers did at least three times a year. But the thought of even two people coming for dinner, or twenty coming for cocktails, put Melinda in a dither. She would worry that the liquor would run out, or that the ice-cream would melt before it could be served, or she would suddenly realize that the house needed a thorough cleaning, or that the kitchen needed new curtains, and she would fret so that Vic would finally suggest they abandon the idea of a party. Even with two people, old friends like the Mellers, a buried inferiority would come to the surface, and she would be as nervous and unsure of herself as a young bride who was being hostess for the first time to her husband's boss. Vic found it somehow very appealing, found Melinda appealingly young and helpless on these occasions, and he would do all he could to reassure her and give her confidence – even though for the preceding month he might have been annoyed by her single men friends whom she had invited for dinner twice in the week, and who never made her nervous in the least.

Vic had not thought Carpenter's presence would make her nervous – it might help, if anything, he thought – and he had invited him simply out of friendliness and good will. And Melinda's face did brighten when Vic walked in with him at seven-thirty. The Mellers were not due until eight. Carpenter presented his champagne, and Melinda thanked him and put it in the refrigerator to keep cold until they would open it after dinner. Melinda was pacing the house, sipping a highball, checking on the progress of the duck every five minutes, and checking with her eyes the cocktail table on which clean ash-trays, muddlers, and a big bowl containing a sour cream and shredded shrimp mixture stood in unaccustomed orderliness. And she was entirely dressed now in a dark-green linen sleeveless dress, gold sandals with wings on them, and a necklace of white coral pieces that suggested feral teeth about the size of tigers' fangs. Above the necklace her face looked absolutely terrified.

Vic left Carpenter and Melinda alone for a few minutes while he changed his shirt and put on a dark suit, then he returned and took Melinda's present from his jacket pocket and gave it to her.

Melinda opened it after a nervous, apologetic glance at Carpenter. Then her expression changed. 'Oh, Vic! What a watch!'

'If you don't like it, they'll take it back and you can change it for something else,' Vic said, knowing she would like it.

Carpenter was watching both of them with a pleasant face.

Melinda put the watch on. It was a dress watch of gold set with little diamonds. Melinda had ruined her old watch by going into the Cowans' pool with it one night, two or three years ago, and she had been wanting a dress watch ever since.

'Oh, Vic, it's just beautiful,' Melinda said, her voice softer than Vic had heard it in many, many months.

'And this,' Vic said, drawing something in an envelope from his other pocket. 'It's not really a present.'

'Oh, my pearls!'

'I just had them restrung,' Vic said. Melinda had broken them about a month ago, throwing them at him in an argument.

'Thank you, Vic. That's very nice of you,' Melinda said subduedly, with a glance at Carpenter as if she feared he might have been able to guess why the pearls had needed restringing.

Carpenter looked as if he were guessing, Vic thought. He might have been even more amused if he had known that while Vic was crawling around on the floor picking up the scattered pearls Melinda had kicked him.

The Mellers arrived with a rotary broiler for Melinda, the kind that worked by electricity in the kitchen. The Mellers knew they had an outdoor broiler that used charcoal. Mary Mellers gave Melinda a kiss on the cheek, and so did Horace. Vic had seen Mary when she had been warmer towards Melinda, but still it was a fine performance for Carpenter, he thought. Carpenter seemed to be keeping his eyes open especially for the social relations that night, how the Mellers behaved to him and how they behaved to Melinda. There was no mistaking the fact that the Mellers were friendlier towards him than towards Melinda.

During the cocktails Melinda kept getting up to go to the kitchen, and Mary asked if she could help in any way, but both Vic and Melinda declined her help.

'Don't think about it,' Vic said. 'Stay here and enjoy your drinks. I'm butling tonight.' He went into the kitchen to take care of the crucial problem of getting the duck from oven to platter. They lost the apple out of the duck's posterior, but Vic caught the ball of fire in mid-air and deposited it, smiling, on top of the stove.

'Oh, Christ,' Melinda muttered, ineffectually waving the carving knife and the honing stick. 'What *else* can happen?'

'We can burn the wild rice,' Vic said, checking in the oven. It didn't seem to be burning. He picked up the apple on a large spoon and started to put it back in the duck.

'I'm not even sure it belongs there – in a duck,' Melinda groaned.

'I don't think it does. Let's leave it out.'

'There's such a gap there,' Melinda said miserably.

'Don't think about it. We'll put some wild rice around it.'

Together they organized the duck, the wild rice, the peas, the hot rolls, the watercress salad. But the salad dressing wasn't made. Melinda always liked Vic to make the dressing, and besides, he had seven varieties of homegrown herbs in little labelled boxes to go in. He used the herbs in varying combinations.

'Don't worry about anything,' Vic said. 'I'll put everything back in the oven, and the dressing'll be made in a flash!' He slid the silver platter with the duck back into the oven, left Melinda to put the other dishes on top of the oven, then made the salad, crushing the garlic and salt together in the bowl while he added vinegar; then he put in the herbs – one, two, three different kinds – with his left hand while he stirred constantly with his right. 'Nice of you to have the watercress all washed,' he said over his shoulder.

Melinda didn't say anything.

'I hope Harold isn't expecting to begin with snails,' Vic said.

'Why should he?'

'He said he liked them. To eat, I mean.' Vic laughed.

'Did you tell him it'd be like eating your own flesh and blood?'

'No. I didn't. Well, the salad's ready. Would you like to go and alert the guests?'

Horace and Carpenter were deep in a conversation and were the last to come to the table. Horace looked troubled, Vic saw. Melinda was in a state of petrified anxiety as to whether everything tasted all right or was hot enough, and hardly got a word out for the first quarter of an hour. Everything did taste all right, and the dinner went along well enough. It was not quite as a dinner among old friends should have been, but that may have been partly due to Carpenter's presence. Vic noticed that Horace did not attempt to talk to Carpenter at the table. From Carpenter's sculpturesque, immobile pleasant features, Vic could learn nothing. Except that it was interesting that he and Melinda said so little to each other. It suggested to Vic that they had been together earlier in the day. Carpenter spent most of the dinner listening.

They had their coffee in the living-room. Horace strolled to a front window and stood looking out. Vic was watching him when he turned around finally, and Horace made him a sign to come over. Vic went. Horace opened the front door and they walked out on the lawn.

'He's not at Columbia University, that fellow in there,' Horace began immediately. 'He doesn't know anybody at Columbia. He seems to know one name – the head of the Psychology Department, but he's never heard of anybody else there.' Horace was frowning.

'I didn't think he would,' Vic said quietly.

'I don't mean he didn't *try* to sound as if he knew what was going on at Columbia, but I know enough about the Psychology Department there to know he's faking the whole thing. Is he one of Kennington's out-patients, did you say?'

Vic put his head back and laughed loudly into the empty night air. 'No, Horace. I said he was doing research there towards a thesis.'

'Oh. Is it true?'

'Well – I don't really know if it's true, considering what you've just told me.'

Horace lit a cigarette impatiently, but refrained from throwing the match on the lawn. 'I don't like him. What's he up to?'

'Search me,' said Vic, pulling up a few grass blades, holding them up against the pallid circle of the moon. It occurred to him that he should try some offset printing with grass blades, leaves, maybe a razor-cut cross section of a clover blossom. It would be very effective in Brian Ryder's book of poems, Vic thought. So many of his poems had allusions to plants and flowers.

'Vic—'

'What?'

'What's he up to? Don't tell me you haven't thought about it. Is he interested in Melinda?'

Vic hesitated. 'I don't think so,' he said indifferently. Might as well tell the truth when one could.

'He's trying something with this school business, that's certain. He didn't even make any excuses, such as having been at another school most of the time so he didn't know Columbia well. He stuck to Columbia – floundering. But floundering very slickly, if you know what I mean.'

'You've got me, Horace. I don't know what he's up to.'

'And staying in De Lisle's house. Didn't Melinda arrange that?'

'She recommended the house to him,' Vic conceded.

Horace thought for a moment. 'It'd be interesting to know if he knows Don Wilson.'

'Why?'

'Because I think he might. He might be a friend of Don's.'

'What do you mean? Hauled up here as a kind of spy?'

'Exactly.'

Vic knew Horace had gone that far. He wanted to see if Horace had thought he might be a detective. 'I don't think he's met Don. At least, the last time I asked Melinda she didn't think they knew each other.'

'Maybe they do know each other and that's why they're keeping apart.'

Vic chuckled, 'You're about as imaginative as Wilson.'

'All right, maybe I'm all wrong. I think he knows *something* about psychology. But he's not all he says he is. I'd just like to know his motives. How long is he going to be up here?'

'I gather about another month. He's making a pilot test of schizophrenic treatment over at Kennington.'

'I'd be interested to know just what kind of pilot test,' Horace said cynically. 'I know Fred Dreyfuss over there. I can easily find out.'

Vic made a sound indicating that he didn't consider it of much importance.

'How is Melinda these days?' Horace asked.

'Fine, I suppose,' Vic replied, feeling himself stiffen in the old automatic defence of Melinda before the world, though he knew that Horace wanted to know if she was still accusing him of killing Charley. If Horace wanted to know how Melinda was, he had seen her all evening.

'Well, she hasn't come to see Mary again,' Horace said, with a trace of defiance. 'You know, I don't think Evelyn'll ever get over that – from Melinda.'

'I'm sorry,' Vic said.

Horace patted Vic on the shoulder. 'I had a hard time with Mary. It's for your sake she agreed to come here tonight, Vic.'

'I wish everybody would try to forget it. I suppose that's too much to expect. Maybe in time.'

Horace made no reply.

They went back into the living-room. Melinda, her tension hardly decreased by alcohol, nervously proposed opening the champagne that Carpenter had brought, but Mary protested that she should save it, so the champagne was not opened. Nobody wanted an after-dinner highball. The Mellers got up to leave at a quarter-past ten, an hour earlier than they might have left, Vic thought, if Mary had been completely comfortable with Melinda and if Carpenter had not been there. Carpenter left when the Mellers did, thanking Melinda and Vic profusely. He drove off in his own car, a dark-blue two-door Plymouth, which he had modestly told Vic he had recently picked up secondhand.

'Don't you think he's loafing on the job?' Vic asked Melinda as they were standing at the front door.

'What job?' she asked quickly.

Vic smiled a little, and he could feel that it was not a very nice smile. 'Maybe you can tell me.'

'What do you mean?' Then retreating hopelessly, 'Who?'

'Mr Carpenter.'

'Oh. I suppose he – Well, I get the idea he's at Kennington most of the time.'

'Oh,' Vic said, subtly mocking. 'I just thought he was managing to spend an awful lot of time around us.'

Melinda went to the cocktail table and began to collect the cups and saucers. Vic got the tray from the kitchen to make things go faster. There were a million things to put away in the kitchen. Vic donned an apron and took off his wrist-watch in preparation for washing the dishes. He said nothing else that night that would indicate to Melinda that he thought Carpenter was a private detective. Melinda was bright enough to know that he would have picked up the slightest clue Carpenter offered, but she was not bright enough to know that Carpenter had already offered a few.

'Happy birthday, darling,' Vic said, taking a package with the red-and-white striped paper of the Bandana shop from the lower part of a cupboard.

'Another present?' Melinda said, her face relaxing, almost smiling with surprise.

'I hope it fits.'

Melinda opened the package, took out the white angora sweater, and held it up. 'Oh, Vic, just what I wanted! How did you know?'

'I live in the same house with you, don't I?' Then, for no particular reason, he went up to her and kissed her on the cheek. She did not draw back. She simply might not have felt it. 'Many happy returns.'

'Thank you, Vic.' She looked at him oddly for a moment, one eyebrow trembling, the tense line of her mouth hovering between a smile and grimness, as uncertain as her own mind.

Vic looked back at her, aware that he hadn't the least idea what she was going to do or say next, and aware with a sudden self-disgust that his own expression – his blandly lifted brows, his staring, unsurprisable eyes, his mouth that conveyed nothing except the fact that it was closed – was false and despicable. His face was a mask, and at least Melinda's was not, not at this moment. Vic tried to smile. Even that did not feel sincere.

Then Melinda looked somewhere else, moved, and it was gone.

In his bed that night Vic thought about the conversation with Horace. He felt that he had said exactly the right thing: if it transpired that Carpenter was a detective, Vic could say that he realized it all along, that it didn't bother him, and it would be a particularly gallant attitude to display in regard to Melinda, his wife, who had hired the detective against him. If Carpenter was not a detective, he had not shown stupidity in assuming that he was. Vic had not noticed a bulge under his jacket again, not after that first meeting. But there was still the two or three hundred out of their bank account, unexplained. Evidently Melinda was paying for him slowly.

As Vic slipped into sleep, the antagonism rose slowly in him against Melinda, almost involuntarily, wraithlike, groping like a wrestler for a hold. It rose in him as something habitual might force its way to the surface – the habit of falling asleep while lying on his back, for instance, as he was now – and before he was completely asleep he realized all this and let it glide smoothly over the surface of his mind, like any ordinary, not very vigorous thought that one thinks just before falling asleep. It was as if she wore a label, 'My Enemy', in his mind, and his enemy she was, beyond the reach of reason or imagination of change. The wraithlike antagonism in his mind found an imaginary grip and tightened, and he turned a little in bed and was asleep.

15

From the birthday party onward it was as if Harold Carpenter had decided to make an abrupt change of tactics. He began to see more of Melinda and less of the two of them together. This happened in a matter of three or four days after the party. Melinda spent two of those four afternoons with Harold, and took pains to tell Vic so. Vic showed not the least interest. He did, however, say:

'I don't care how much you see him outside of the house. I don't want you to ask him here again.'

Melinda stared at him, shocked. 'What's the matter?'

'I don't like the guy,' Vic said bluntly, looking back at the evening paper.

'Since when don't you like him? I thought you thought he was very interesting.'

'He is – *very*,' Vic said. He listened to Melinda's silence for a few moments. She was standing by the sofa, shifting restlessly from foot to foot now. And she was in one of her few pairs of high-heeled shoes, because Mr Carpenter was tall.

'And since when do you say who's coming to the house and who isn't?' Melinda asked in a still-controlled voice, feeling him out.

'Since now. I don't happen to like him. I'm very sorry. I don't feel like discussing it. Can't you see him at his house or out somewhere? He's not going to be here much longer anyway, is he?'

'No. I don't think he is. Maybe two weeks.'

Vic smiled at his paper, then turned the smile at her. Two weeks more on his payroll, he thought. He was tempted to let Melinda know now that he knew Mr Carpenter was on his payroll, but a perverseness kept him from it. 'Well, we'll all miss him, won't we?'

'I don't say *we'll* miss him,' Melinda said.

'Perhaps there'll be another along soon,' he said, and he felt her bristle.

She lighted a cigarette and threw her lighter down on a seat cushion of the sofa. 'You're in a lovely mood tonight, aren't you? Hospitable, gracious – courteous. All the things you boast about being.'

'I've never boasted about being those things.' He glanced at her. She looked frightened. 'All right, Melinda, I'm sorry. I have nothing at all against Mr Carpenter. He's very pleasant. He's a very nice young man.'

'You sound as if you don't mean that.'

'Do I? I'm sorry.' He was striking a curious note between sentimental concern and overt hostility. He found himself smiling. 'Let's forget about it, shall we? What's for dinner?'

'I want to know that I can ask him to the house, if I care to, without your being rude.'

Vic swallowed. It wasn't Melinda, he thought, and it wasn't Mr Carpenter himself, it was the principle of the thing. Again he felt the uncontrollable smile of habit. 'Of course you can bring him to the house, honey. I'm sorry I lost my temper.' He waited. 'When would you like to have him again? Were you thinking of asking him for dinner soon?'

'You don't have to overdo it!' Melinda was playing nervously with a string in her hand, yanking it taut again and again around one finger.

Let the string go, Vic told himself, though it annoyed him unreasonably. 'What's for dinner, honey? Would you like me to fix it?'

She started towards the kitchen suddenly. 'I'll go and fix it,' she said.

There was a condition in his head which suggested the image of dark tree-tops beaten violently in all directions by the wind. When he anticipated his actions, he imagined knocking ash-trays off tables as he reached for them, crushing snails' shells as he picked them up, because of a lack of control, but these things never happened. He watched his hands and they moved smoothly and precisely, as they always had, smallish, plump, innocuous hands, clean as a doctor's hands, except when he got ink on them at the printing plant from handling this and that in the press room. The snails still loved his hands, crawling slowly but unhesitatingly on to the forefinger that he extended to them, even when they were not lured by a scrap of lettuce held within their short vision.

He finally realized what the image of the beaten tree-tops was. It was a very distinct memory that he had of a storm coming up over a mountain in Austria. He had been about ten years old. His father had been alive, and he and his mother and father had been on one of their yearly trips to Europe. His father had been a consulting engineer in gyrostatics, a man with an ample private income, though he had gone through the pretence of working all his life, of being a man whose main interests were the practical ones of earning a living which he did not need and of pursuing a career whose progress could not have been of vital importance to him. Vic remembered very well: His father had finished a period of two or three weeks' work in Paris, and their going to Munich and Salzburg had been part of a holiday before they came home.

They had gone to an absolutely fairy-tale-like hotel on the St Wolfgangsee, Vic thought, or had it been the Fuschlsee? And it had been winter – no snow on the ground yet, but they had been expecting it any moment, and then the storm had come up over the mountains outside their window. Vic remembered the deep-set windows, and the fact that, for all the thickness of the walls of the hotel, he had been cold, and that there had been nothing they could do about it because, whatever the heating facilities of the hotel had been, they hadn't been adequate. His father, an extremely polite man, burdened by his sense of financial superiority to almost everyone else, would have suffered a much colder temperature in the room before he would have complained. *Richesse oblige.* The storm had come, advancing over the mountains, which themselves had looked ominously close and black, like an insuperable dark giant of unknown dimensions. And the trees silhouetted on the mountain tops had bent this way and that, as if tortured by the crazy, brooding wind or as if trying to uproot themselves to flee from it. His father had said in a voice that betrayed his own excitement, 'There's snow in that cloud,' though the cloud had been nearly black, so black that their hotel room had become as dark as if it were evening. And when the black cloud had decided to roll down the mountain towards them, making a roaring chaos of the trees, Vic had fled from the window and cringed on the other side of the room. Vic remembered the astonishment, the disappointment on his father's face as he pulled him to his feet. Vic had been able to stand up but he could not force himself back to the window, though his father had wanted him to go. But it had really been the lashing trees that frightened him, not the storm itself.

Now he thought of the trees quite often when he heard of Melinda being out with Carpenter in the afternoon – though, as a matter of fact, he thought she often told him she was out with Carpenter, driving him out to Bear Lake, visiting with him in his house, or having cocktails with him at the Chesterfield bar, when she had been doing something else. He found this especially revolting. Outwardly, however, he reacted not at all to it. No more edged remarks, no frowns of annoyance. He asked Melinda perhaps twice more if she didn't want to ask Harold to the house, once when they were having the Mellers again and once when they had a standing six-rib roast. Melinda invited him neither time. And Vic thought, was this the technique? Trying to make him think their relationship had become so personal that they did not want to share their company with anybody else? That cold fish, Mr Carpenter. He had control, perhaps, but he was the worst actor in the world. Whom did he think he was fooling? He hadn't even succeeded in getting the town to talk more against Victor Van Allen. And the thought that *he* might be paying for all this was, to say the least, irksome.

Vic kept his temper until he saw Ralph Gosden and Don Wilson walking along the street together one day. It was about one o'clock, and Vic had driven through town on his way home to lunch in order to pick up a pair of Trixie's shoes that he had left at the shoemaker's to be repaired. When he came out of the shoemaker's, Wilson and Ralph were on the same sidewalk, walking towards him, and he saw them both flinch, he thought, at the sight of him, and at the flinching his anger flared.

'Hello, there,' Vic said, with a little smile as he approached them. 'I'd like to ask you something.'

They stopped. 'What?' Ralph asked, with a cocky smile, though his thin skin paled.

'I think you both know Mr Harold Carpenter,' Vic said.

Ralph was flustered, but Wilson finally mumbled that he had met him.

'I bet you have,' Vic said. 'Did you hire him?'

'Hire him? What do you mean?' Wilson's black eyebrows came down.

'You must know what I mean. He's not anything he says he is. I concluded that he was a detective, probably picked out by you, Wilson. Didn't you go to New York and choose him—?' Vic choked off the last phrase he might have said, 'for my wife'.

'I don't know what you're talking about,' Wilson said, scowling.

But Vic could tell from Ralph's scared eyes that he had hit the truth, or somewhere very near it. 'I think you know what I'm talking about. He's a detective and you know it, don't you? Don't you, Wilson?' Vic advanced a little and Wilson stepped back. Vic could have struck him, with pleasure.

Wilson glanced around him to see if anyone was watching them. 'He may be. I don't know the man very well.'

'Who picked him out? Didn't you? Or did you, Ralph?' he said, looking at Ralph. 'On second thoughts, you wouldn't have the courage. You just stand around and watch, don't you, Ralph?'

'Are you out of your head?' Ralph managed to say.

'What agency did you get him from, Wilson?' Vic asked, still leaning forward intently.

'What's the matter? Is he seeing too much of your wife?' Ralph chirped in. 'Why don't you kill him if you don't like him?'

'Shut up,' Wilson said to Ralph. Wilson seemed to be trembling.

'What agency?' Vic asked. 'There's no use stalling, I *know* he's a detective.' And if Carpenter wasn't, Vic thought, if he was all wrong then they could just consider him mad. That was fine. 'Neither of you talking? Well, I can get it out of Melinda. I didn't want to have to ask her, but she'll tell me soon enough. She doesn't think I know anything yet.' Vic looked at Wilson contemptuously. 'I'll make it known around here when I find out, Wilson. You might decide it's more comfortable if you move.'

'Oh, stop being God, Vic!' Ralph said, suddenly finding a little terrified courage. 'Do you think you own this town? And justice, too?'

'There're names for people like you, Ralph. Do you want me to call you a few of them?' Vic asked, his neck flushing with anger.

Ralph shut his mouth.

'I think you know my opinion of you,' Wilson said. 'I told it to you right to your face.'

'You're a brave man, Wilson. Why haven't you the courage to tell me where you found Carpenter? I'd like to discontinue his services, since I'm paying for them.' Vic waited, watching the emotions churning in Wilson's scowling face. 'No courage, Wilson?'

'Yes, I've got the courage. It's the Confidential Detective Service in Manhattan,' Wilson said.

'Confidential!' Vic put his head back and laughed. 'Ha-ha! Ho-ho-ho-o! Confidential!'

Wilson and Ralph exchanged nervous looks.

'Thanks,' Vic said. 'I'll call them up this afternoon. Tell me, did you pick him out, Wilson?'

Wilson said nothing. He backed away as if to leave, as if he had had enough.

'Didn't you pick him out, Wilson?' Vic called after them.

Wilson glanced back, but he did not speak. He didn't have to.

Vic had a quiet lunch alone – Melinda was not in – read some of the book about stained-glass windows, then went to the Manhattan classified directory and looked up the Confidential Detective Service under the heading 'Detective Service'. Confidential, he thought again, smiling.

A man's voice with a rather tough New York accent answered the telephone.

'Hello,' Vic said. 'I'm calling in regard to your employee Harold Carpenter, or the man who's going by that name on his present job.'

'Oh? Yes, I know who you're talkin' about.' The man sounded courteous enough, in spite of his ugly accent.

'We don't wish his services any longer,' Vic said.

'Oh. Awright. What's the trouble?'

'Trouble?'

'I mean, is there any trouble or complaints?'

'Oh, no. Except that the man he's supposed to be getting information about knows he's a detective and isn't letting anything out.'

'I see. Are you Mr – Mr Donald Wilson of Little Wesley, Massachusetts?'

'No, I am not.'

'Who are you?'

'I'm the man he's supposed to be watching.'

Silence for a moment. 'You are Victor Van Allen?'

'Correct,' Vic said. 'So – either send a fresh man up or give it up. I suggest you give it up, because I'm paying the bill, and if this nonsense keeps on I'm just going to refuse to pay it. And I don't think the money'll come from anywhere else.' Another silence. 'Do you understand?'

'Yes, Mr Van Allen.'

'Good. If there're any further bills, you may send them to me direct, if you care to. I suppose you have my address?'

'Yes, Mr Van Allen.'

'Righto. That's all. Thank you. Oh, just a minute!'

'Yes?'

'Send Mr Carpenter a wire discontinuing this assignment, will you, right away? I'll be willing to pay for that.'

'All right, Mr Van Allen.'

They hung up.

Melinda came in at seven-fifteen that evening, after cocktailing with Harold, she said.

'Did Harold get his telegram?' Vic asked.

'What telegram?'

'The telegram from the Confidential Detective Service taking him off the job.'

Melinda's mouth opened, but her face showed more anger than surprise. 'What do you know about it?' she asked aggressively.

'Wilson spilled the beans,' Vic said. 'What's the matter with Wilson, anyway? Why doesn't he stick to his typewriter?'

Trixie was listening, goggle-eyed, sitting on the living-room floor.

'*When* did he?' Melinda demanded.

'This noon. I ran into him and Ralph on the street. A more terrified, silly-looking pair I've never seen.'

'What did he tell you?' Melinda asked, consternation on her face.

'I simply asked him,' Vic began patiently, 'if Mr Carpenter was a detective. *Wasn't* he? I asked them both. And when Wilson said yes, which didn't take much pressure because he seemed to be scared out of his wits, I asked him what agency he worked for. And he told me, and I called them up and asked them to relieve Mr Carpenter of his assignment. I'm tired of paying the bills.'

Melinda threw her pocket-book at the sofa and took off her coat. 'I see,' she said. 'Was it the bills that—' She stopped.

He felt almost sorry for her in her defeat. 'No, my dear. Horace told me several days ago that Carpenter knows nothing about Columbia University. Horace does, you see, and right in the Psychology Department. I don't know whether he's made an arrangement of some kind with Kennington or not to let him pursue his research there. It doesn't interest me.'

Melinda stalked into the kitchen. She was going to get drunk tonight, Vic knew. And whatever she had drunk with Carpenter had probably laid a very solid foundation for it. And for a monumental hangover tomorrow. Vic sighed and continued his paper.

'Want a drink?' Melinda called from the kitchen.

'No, thanks.'

'You're so healthy these days,' she said as she came in with her own drink. 'The picture of health and physical fitness. Well, it may interest you to know that Mr Carpenter is a psychiatrist. He may not have graduated from anywhere,' she said, on a defensive note, 'but he knows a few things.'

Vic said with slow, measured disgust, 'I don't expect to see him again.' After a moment or so, when Melinda had said nothing, Vic asked, 'Why? Has he been psychoanalysing you?'

'No.'

'That's too bad. He might have enlightened me about you. I admit I don't understand you.'

'I understand *you*,' she snapped.

'Then why get a psychologist up here to look at me? What is he, anyway, a psychologist or a detective?'

'He's both,' she said angrily. She was walking about, sipping a dark-beige highball.

'Um-hm. And what does he have to say about me?'

'He says you're a borderline case of schizophrenia.'

'Oh,' Vic said. 'Tell him I said he was a borderline. Nothing more. He's something betwixt and between, something you step over and forget.'

Melinda snorted. 'He seems to be able to get you worked up—'

'Daddy, what's schizomenia mean?' Trixie asked, still rapt, her arms around her knees.

'It's an enlightening conversation for the child,' Melinda said mincingly.

'She's heard worse.' Vic cleared his throat. 'Schizophrenia, hon, means a split personality. It is a mental disease characterized by a loss of contact with one's environment and by dissolution of the personality. There. Understand? And it looks like your old daddy's got it.'

'A-a-aw,' Trixie said, laughing as if he were kidding her. 'How do you know?'

'Because Mr Carpenter says I have.'

'How does Mr Carpenter know you have?' Trixie asked, grinning, loving it. It was like the nonsense stories Vic told her about imaginary animals, and she would ask him could they fly, could they read, could they cook, could they sew, could they dress themselves, and sometimes they could and sometimes they couldn't.

'Because Mr Carpenter is a psychologist,' Vic replied.

'What's a psychologist?' Trixie asked.

'Oh, Christ, Vic, stop it!' Melinda said, whirling around from the other side of the room to face him.

'We shall continue this conversation at some other time,' Vic said, smiling at his daughter.

Melinda did get very drunk that night. She made two telephone calls that Vic managed not to listen to by going into the kitchen where it was impossible to hear a voice from Melinda's bedroom. Vic had fixed the dinner, which Melinda ate little of, and she was totteringly drunk by nine o'clock, Trixie's bedtime. By then Vic had defined several more psychological terms. It was difficult to explain to Trixie what consciousness was, but he told her that when people had had too much to drink and fell asleep on the sofa they were suffering from the loss of it.

16

The next day Melinda was still sleeping when Vic came home for lunch. He knew she had been up very late the night before, because he had seen the glow of her bedroom light on the back lawn when he turned out his own light at two-thirty. When he came home at seven that evening, she had still not taken the edge off her hangover, though she said she had slept until three. Vic had two things to tell her, one pleasant and one perhaps not so pleasant, so he told her the first one before dinner, when her hangover seemed to be at its worst, hoping it might make her feel better.

'You can be sure,' he said, 'that I'm not going to mention this detective episode to Horace or Phil or anybody else. So if Wilson and Ralph can keep their mouths shut, and they have every reason to, nobody needs know about it. Does anybody else know about it?' he asked with concern, as if he were on her side.

'No,' she groaned, completely vulnerable in her hour of suffering.

'I thought it might make you feel better if I told you that,' Vic said.

'Thanks,' she said indifferently.

His shoulders moved in an involuntary shrug. But she was not looking at him. 'By the way, I had a letter from Brian Ryder today. He's going to come up the third week in November. I told him he could stay with us. It'll be for two nights, three at the most. We've got a lot of work to do in the office, so we won't be here much.' After a moment, when she had made no sign that she had heard, as if the words had penetrated about as little as they would have penetrated the ears of a person asleep, he added, feeling rather odd and as if he were talking to himself, 'I'm sure from his letters he's a very civilized young man. He's only twenty-four.'

'I don't suppose you'd fix me another drink?' she said, extending her empty glass towards him, though she still stared at the floor.

She ate a good dinner that evening. She could always eat with a hangover, and besides it was one of her theories that the more you ate with a hangover the better you felt. 'Nail it down,' was her remedy. After dinner she felt well enough to take a look at the evening paper. Vic put Trixie to bed, then came back and sat down in the armchair.

'Melinda, I have a question to ask you,' he began.

'What?' She looked at him over the paper.

'Would you like a divorce from me? If I gave you a very good income to live on?'

She stared at him for perhaps five seconds. 'No,' she said firmly, and rather angrily.

'But what's this all coming to?' he asked, opening his hands, and feeling suddenly the soul of logic. 'You hate me. You treat me as an enemy. You get a detective after me—'

'Because you killed Charley. You know it as sure as you're sitting there.'

'Darling, I just didn't. Now come to your senses.'

'Everybody *knows* you did it!'

'Who?'

'Don Wilson knows it. Harold thinks so. Ralph knows it.'

'Why don't they prove it?' he asked gently.

'Give them time. They'll prove it. Or *I* will,' she said, sitting forward on the sofa, reaching abruptly for her pack of cigarettes on the cocktail table.

'How, I'd like to know. There's such a thing as framing a man, of course.' He said musingly, 'I suppose it's a little late. Say, why doesn't Don Wilson or Carpenter subject me to a lie detector? Not that they have any legal power to, however.'

'Harold said you wouldn't even react to it,' she said. 'He thinks you're cracked.'

'And the crack shall make you free.'

'Don't be funny, Vic.'

'Sorry. I wasn't trying to be funny. To get back to what I asked you before, I'll give you anything but Trixie, if you want to divorce me. Think of what it means. You'll have money to do what you want with, money to see the people you want to see. You'll be absolutely free of responsibility, free of responsibility for a child and for a husband. Think of the fun you could have.'

She was chewing her underlip as if his words tortured her – perhaps with temptation. 'I'm not finished with you yet. I'd like to destroy you. I'd like to smash you.'

He opened his hands again, lightly: 'It's been done. There's always arsenic in the soup. But my taste buds are pretty good. Then there's—'

'I didn't mean kill you. You're so – *nuts*, I don't suppose you'd mind *that* very much. I'd like to smash your lousy ego!'

'Haven't you? Darling, what more could you do than what you've been doing? What do you think I'm living on?'

'Ego.'

A laugh bubbled up in him, and then he was serious again. 'No, not ego. Just the pieces of myself that I can put together again and hold together – by force of will. Will power, if you like,

178

that's what I live on, but not ego. How could I possibly have any?' he finished desperately, enjoying the discussion immensely and also enjoying the sound of his own voice, which seemed to be objective, like his own voice on a tape-recording machine being played back to him. He was also aware of the Thespian tone he had assumed, making his words a combination of distilled passion and utter hamminess. He went on in rich, full tones, with an earnest gesture of one hand, 'You know that I love you, you know that I would give you anything that you wished or that I could give you.' He paused for a moment, thinking that he had also given her the other half of the bed in there, his half, but that he really couldn't say it for fear of making himself laugh, or making her laugh. 'This is my last offer. I don't know what more I can do.'

'I've told you,' she said slowly, 'I haven't finished with you yet. Why don't you divorce me? It'd be a lot safer for you. You certainly consider you've got grounds, don't you?' she said sarcastically, as if the grounds were illusory or as if he would have been a cad to use them.

'I never said I wanted to divorce you, did I? I'd feel – as if I were shirking my responsibility if I did. Besides, it isn't appropriate for a man to divorce his wife. She should divorce him. But what I've been getting at – this quarrelling—'

'You haven't heard the end of it.'

'That's what I mean. Must you reply to me in a belligerent tone?' His own tone was still sweet.

'You're right. I ought to save it for the final attack,' she said just as belligerently.

Vic sighed. 'Well I take it the *status quo* is still the *status quo ante*. When are you going to have Ralph and Wilson to the house? Bring them on. I can take them.'

She stared at him, her green-brown eyes as cold and steady as a toad's.

'Have you nothing more to say?' he asked.

'I've said it.'

'Then I think I shall retire.' He stood up and smiled at her. 'Good night. Pleasant dreams,' he said, taking his pipe from the little table beside his armchair. Then he walked into the other world of the garage and his room.

17

Don Wilson and his wife moved to Wesley in less than two weeks after Vic's encounter with him on the street. Once more Melinda gave her services as a house-finder, though in this case it was an apartment in Wesley. Vic saw it as a disorderly withdrawal. Wilson had been routed at the first brush. He had retreated for better cover, but now it was going to be difficult for him to keep that scowling eye on his enemy.

'What happened? Did people make it so unpleasant for him that he had to leave town?' Vic asked Melinda, knowing very well that was what had happened. Somehow, Vic supposed through Ralph, the story of the detective had leaked out. Ralph had perhaps fired a poorly aimed shot, telling people that Victor Van Allen had been tailed by a detective for five weeks just because he was so damned suspect, and Ralph's idea had probably been to arouse public opinion against Victor Van Allen if he could. But Vic's reputation had held. The repercussion was curious, as if a glass cannon ball had hit a stone wall and shattered into fragments, some of which had been picked up by the townspeople – pieces of a story out of which they could not make a whole. Who hired the detective, for instance? Some said Wilson himself –

except that he hardly looked as if he had the money to do it. Others simply assumed the detective – if indeed he had existed, if the whole thing was not a made-up story – had been part of the police force and that some kind of routine investigation had been conducted very quietly at this time, a few weeks after the De Lisle incident. Horace knew the story better than any, but even he did not venture to say now, or venture to ask Vic, whether Melinda had hired the detective or not. Vic knew he suspected it, but it was as if this fact, if it was a fact, was simply too shameful to talk about, and would have been too painful for Vic to turn his mind to, and to answer 'Yes' to, if Horace had asked him. Horace simply wore a pained expression these days.

Vic felt more cheerful and benign than ever. More and more Melinda was sullenly drunk. On one of her many dashes to Wesley to see Don Wilson she was arrested for speeding and also accused of drunken driving. She called Vic at his office from the police station in Wesley, and Vic hurried over. She was not very drunk, he saw, not drunk at all comparatively speaking, but the highway officer must have caught a whiff, or he deduced drunkenness from her probably foolhardy counter-attack when he had stopped her. In the station Melinda was boldly asking for an alcoholic content test to be made of her breath. But there was no apparatus in the station for such a test.

'Well, you can see she's not drunk,' Vic said to the police captain. 'I grant you she may have been speeding. I've known that to happen. I think you'd better handle the speeding part, Melinda, since I don't know what happened.'

Vic brought to bear all the tact at his command, knowing that if Melinda had her licence suspended for six months, all hell would break loose in the household. Melinda incarcerated would be most unpleasant. The police captain gave a lecture on the seriousness of driving while intoxicated, which Vic listened to with respect, knowing that a happy ending was coming. But Melinda broke in with, 'I certainly haven't been guilty of drunken driving before, and I insist I'm not drunk now!' Her conviction had some effect on the captain, and so, of course, did the fact that he was Victor Van Allen, an esteemed resident of Little Wesley and the founder of the Greenspur Press. Or at least Vic thought that the middle-aged captain looked intelligent enough to have heard of the Greenspur Press and to know his name, as a piece of local information, in connection with it. Melinda was let off with a $15 fine, which Vic paid out of his pocket. Melinda continued her dash to the Wilsons' in Wesley.

'Tell me, what's Don Wilson up to?' Vic asked her that evening.

'What do you mean what's he up to?'

'What're you both up to? You do so much consulting.'

'I like him. We have quite a lot to talk about. He's got some very interesting theories.'

'Oh. I never knew theories interested you.'

'Oh, they're more than theories,' Melinda said.

'What, for instance?'

She ignored the question. She was on her knees, cleaning out the bottom of her closet, dragging out shoes and forgotten stockings, shoe trees, a little dusty cloth doll of Trixie's.

'I think we ought to get a dog,' Vic said suddenly. 'It'd be nice for Trix. We've put it off long enough.'

'Just what our household needs,' Melinda said.

'I'll talk to Trixie about it and ask her what kind of a dog she'd like.' Melinda didn't want a dog. Vic knew. They had had long discussions about it, Vic pro and Melinda con, and he had always given in to her. He didn't care whether she argued about it now or not. 'By the way, how's June Wilson?' Vic asked.

'All right. Why?'

'I like her. Such a nice straightforward girl. How on earth did she marry him?'

'She's a dreary little girl. Maybe he couldn't see what he was marrying.'

'She came to see me about two months ago, you know, especially to tell me that she thought her husband was doing the wrong thing. She put it delicately, I remember. She just said she didn't think along her husband's lines, and she wanted me to know it. It's too bad Wilson's wished an ostracism on her, isn't it? What does she do while you two talk?'

Melinda wasn't biting that night.

Vic looked at her bent back for a few moments, watched her hands feverishly dusting shoes and lining them up, an outlet more constructive than usual for her frustrated energy. Vic knew what the atmosphere at the Wilsons' must be. It was the only place Melinda could still go without being treated with a certain coolness. And Wilson must be getting a little bored with her, must see in her an indirect cause of his retreat from Little Wesley and his present disfavour in the community, but he would feel obliged to be cordial to her. June would leave them alone, after giving Melinda a cool greeting, but since Melinda in general despised women, this wouldn't bother her at all. Vic supposed that Ralph was there sometimes. And perhaps Melinda went to see Ralph at his house sometimes when she said she was going to see the Wilsons. That was, if Ralph had the courage to let her come to his house. Vic smiled to himself as he looked down at Melinda's long, strong back and at her busy hands, wondering about the atmosphere at Ralph's house when they were alone together. He imagined Ralph too scared to touch her, and Melinda contemptuous of him for that, but she would be drawn to see him again and again because Ralph formed part of the little anti-Vic league. They'd chatter on about him, repeating themselves, whining, like a couple of old women.

Vic knocked on Trixie's door. 'Mademoiselle?' he called.

'Yep?'

He opened the door. Trixie was sitting on her bed, filling

colours in a picture book with crayons. He smiled at her. She looked so self-sufficient, so contented, all by herself. He was proud of her. She was her father's daughter. 'Well, Trix, what do you think about getting a dog?' he asked.

'A dog? A real dog?'

'I don't mean a stuffed one.'

'Oh, *boy*!' She wriggled forward, off the edge of the bed, then jumped up and down, screaming. 'A dog, a dog! Yippee!' She began socking Vic in the stomach with her fists.

He put his hands under her arms and lifted her up in the air. 'What kind would you like?'

'A big dog.'

'But what kind?'

'A – collie.'

'Hm. Can't you think of something more interesting?'

'A – German police!'

He swung her down and set her on her feet. 'They're so utilitarian. What about a boxer? I think I passed a place the other day on the East Lyme road that had a sign out about boxer puppies. You want a puppy, don't you?'

'Yes,' Trixie said, still hopping up and down, in a mood to want anything.

'Well, let's try there tomorrow afternoon. I'll pick you up at school at three o'clock. Okay?'

'Okay!' she said, the breath jerking out of her with her hopping. 'What does a boxer look like?'

'Don't tell me you don't know what a boxer looks like! They're brown with a black muzzle, about so high – I think you'll like a boxer.'

'Goody!'

'I hope that jumping tires you out, because you've got to go to bed. Get your clothes off.' He started towards the door.

'Run my bath!'

'Didn't you have a bath before dinner?'

'I want another bath.'

He started to remonstrate, then said, 'Okay,' and went across the hall into the bathroom and started the tub for her. Her bath mania in the last couple of days was inspired by the toy diver he had given her, which lay now on the end of the tub. He tossed the diver in and squeezed the bulb to keep him afloat. He was a little man some ten inches high dressed in a rubber diving suit and helmet with a tube coming out of his back. Vic watched the figure bobbing around on the surface for a couple of minutes, and when the water was fairly deep he let the bulb expand, and the man obediently sank, sending bubbles up over his head, until his weighted feet were standing on the bottom. Vic smiled, enjoying himself. He squeezed the bulb and brought him up again, then sank him again. It was a delightful toy. Vic had often thought that if he were not so attracted to printing he would have become an inventor of toys. It was the pleasantest occupation he could think of.

Trixie came in, took off her red-and-white striped robe, and stepped trustfully into the tub without even testing the temperature of the water.

'Mademoiselle, the bath is yours,' he said, going to the door.

'Daddy, when Charley drowned in the swimming pool, did he stand on his feet on the bottom, too?'

'I don't know, honey, I wasn't there.'

'Sure you were there!' she said, her blonde eyebrows scowling suddenly.

'Well, I couldn't see under the water,' Vic replied.

'Didn't you push him down feet first?'

'Well, I – I don't think I even *touched* the man!' Vic said, half joking and half serious.

'Sure you did! Janey says you did and so does Eddie and Duncan and – and Gracie and Petey and everybody I know!'

'Good lord, really? Why, that's terrible!'

Trixie giggled. 'You're kidding me!'

'No, I'm not kidding you,' Vic said seriously, realizing that he had often kidded her in this manner, however. 'Now, how do your little friends know this?'

'They heard it.'

'From whom?'

'From – their mothers and daddies.'

'Who? All of them?'

'Yes,' Trixie said, looking at him the way she did on those rare occasions when she told lies, because she didn't believe what she was saying and wasn't at all sure that he would.

'I don't believe it,' Vic said. '*Some* of them. Then you kids pass it all around.' You shouldn't do that, he wanted to say, but he knew that Trixie wouldn't obey, and he didn't want to sound, either to her or to himself, frightened enough to admonish her about the story.

'They all ask me to tell them how you did it,' Trixie said.

Vic leaned over and turned off the water, which was nearly up to Trixie's shoulders. 'But I didn't do it, darling. If I'd done it I'd be put in prison. Don't you know that? Don't you know that killing somebody is punishable by death?' He spoke in a whisper, both to impress her and because Melinda might have been able to hear them from the hall, now that the water was turned off.

Trixie stared at him with serious eyes for a moment, then her eyes slurred off, very like Melinda's, in the direction of her sunken diver. She didn't want to believe that he hadn't done it. In that little blonde head was no moral standard whatsoever, at least not about a matter as big as murder. She wouldn't so much as steal a piece of chalk from school, Vic knew, but murder was something else. She saw it or heard of it in the comic books every day, saw it on television at Janey's house, and it was something exciting and even heroic when the good cowboys did it in Westerns. She wanted him to be a hero, a good guy, somebody who wasn't afraid.

And he had just cut himself down by several inches, he realized.

Trixie lifted her head. 'I still think you drowned him. You're just telling me you didn't,' she said.

The next afternoon, Vic and Trixie bought a male boxer puppy for $75 from the kennel on the East Lyme road. The puppy had just had his ears clipped, and they were fastened together with a bandage and a piece of adhesive tape that stood up a little above his head. His pedigree name was Roger-of-the-Woods. It pleased Vic very much that Trixie had singled Roger out from the other pups mainly because of the lugubrious expression on his small, monkeylike face, and because of his bandage. At the kennel, he had bumped his ears against something twice, yelped, and his face had looked sadder than ever. Trixie rode home with the puppy in her lap and her arm around his neck, happier than Vic had ever seen her at any Christmas.

Melinda stared at the dog and might have made an unpleasant remark if she had not seen that Trixie was so delighted with him. Vic found a big cardboard box in the kitchen that would do for a bed, cut it down to ten inches deep and cut a door in one side for the puppy to walk through. Then he put a couple of Trixie's baby coverlets in the bottom and set the box in Trixie's room.

Vic had bought packages of dog biscuits and baby cereal and cans of a certain kind of dog food prescribed by the kennel man. The puppy had a good appetite, and after he had eaten that evening he wagged his tail and his expression seemed a little more cheerful. He also played with a rubber ball that Trixie rolled around on the floor for him.

'The house is beginning to take on some life,' Vic remarked to Melinda, but there was no answer.

18

Vic and Melinda went to another dance at the club in November, the 'Leaf Night' dance that yearly celebrated autumn in Little Wesley. Vic had not wanted to go when the club's invitation had arrived, but this attitude had lasted hardly more than fifteen seconds. It was the right thing to do to go, and Vic did usually try to do the right thing in the community. His first negative reaction to the club announcement had been caused by two or three factors, he thought: one was that the relationship between him and Melinda had been so much better at the time of the Fourth of July dance and he did not want to contrast the present with that happier period four months ago. Secondly, he was deep in the perusal of a manuscript in Italian – or rather a Sicilian dialect – which he was devoting all his evenings to and from which he did not wish to be distracted. Thirdly, there was the problem of persuading Melinda to go. She didn't want to go, though she wanted him to go. She wanted to be the crushed, dispirited wife who sat at home and wept, perhaps. Mainly she wanted to show herself – by not showing herself – as an enemy of her husband and not his helpmeet. But with only a couple of matters pointed out to her, Vic got her to go. A fourth minor annoyance, but one that he really couldn't complain about, was that he had to have his evening suit taken in at the waist of both trousers and jacket.

The big round ballroom of the club was decorated with autumn leaves of all kinds and colours, the chandeliers studded richly with pine cones, and here and there in the reddish-brown and yellow leaves hung a baby pumpkin. Once he was there, commencing his usual solitary patrol of the sidelines, Vic began to enjoy himself. He supposed he had momentarily, at home, doubted his own aplomb. He really hadn't known how much to believe of what Trixie had told him. Now he found it very interesting to stroll by or to stand near the same groups of people that he had seen in July. There was Mrs Podnansky, warmer and friendlier than ever. The MacPhersons – surely no change in them: Mac looked pink-eyed drunk at ten o'clock, though he was going to hold it well all evening probably; and as for his wife, if she betrayed any suspicion of Vic by the long curious look she gave him as she greeted him, it seemed to be cancelled out by her remark that he had certainly trimmed down.

'Did you go on a diet?' she asked, with admiration. 'I wish you'd tell me about it.'

And just for the fun of it, Vic stood with them awhile, telling them about a diet that he made up as he talked. Hamburger and grapefruit, nothing else. The hamburger could be varied with onions or not. But nothing else. 'The idea is to get so tired of hamburger and grapefruit that you don't even eat those,' Vic said, smiling. 'That finally happens.'

Mrs MacPherson was very interested indeed, though Vic knew as surely as he was standing there that she would never lose an inch from her sturdy waistline. And if she happened to mention the diet to Melinda, and Melinda knew nothing about it, that was as usual for Melinda, who, everybody knew, neither cared nor was aware of what her husband did or ate.

Everybody was cordial, and Vic felt that his own manner was

after all just about as cheerful as it had been in July. He asked Mary Meller to dance with him not once but twice. Then he danced with Evelyn Cowan. He did not ask Melinda to dance because he did not want to dance with her. He was concerned, however, with whether she had a fairly good time or not. He did not want her to be miserable. The Mellers were kind enough to talk with her for a while, he noticed, and then she danced with a man Vic had never seen before. Vic supposed she would get along, even though most of their friends – including the MacPhersons, he saw – certainly were not smiling upon her tonight. Vic had a drink with Horace at the long curved bar at the side of the room, and he told Horace about the Italian manuscript he had received. It was the diary of a semi-illiterate grandmother, who had come to America with her husband, from Sicily, at the age of twenty-six. Vic thought of cleaning up the manuscript just enough to make it intelligible, cutting it somewhat, and printing it. It covered the Coolidge administration in a most fantastic way, and the whole text, which related mostly to the upbringing of three boys and two girls, was interpolated with extremely funny comments on politics and current sports heroes such as Primo Carnera. One of her sons joined the police force, another went back to Italy, a third became a bookie for the illegal numbers games, one of the daughters went through college and married, and the other married and went with her engineer husband to live in South America. The woman's impressions of South America, from her home in Carmine Street, Manhattan, were alternately funny and hair-raising. Vic made Horace laugh loudly.

'Isn't this a new departure for you?' Horace asked.

Then Vic looked and saw Melinda standing with Ralph Gosden and the man she had danced with a couple of times this evening. 'Yes,' Vic said. 'But it's time I had one. The married daughter in South America sent me the manuscript. It's an absolute fluke, you see. She said she read about the Greenspur

Press in some South American publication and learned that I printed things in other languages besides English, so she was sending me her mother's diary, she said, in case I might be interested. It was a charming letter. Very modest and very hopeful at the same time. I'm thinking of printing the book half in Italian and half in English, as I did Xenophon. So few people would be able to understand this dialect.'

'How do you manage to read it? Do you know Italian that well?' Horace asked.

'No, but I can read it reasonably well with a dictionary, and I happen to have a dictionary of Italian dialects at home. Picked it up in New York secondhand years ago, God knows why, but now it comes in handy. I can make out nearly everything. The woman's handwriting is very clear, thank God.'

Horace shook his head. 'The man of many parts.'

Looking towards Melinda, Vic caught the eye of the heavy-set man she had been dancing with, who was just then staring at him. Even from far across the room Vic saw that the man's stare was naïvely curious. Perhaps Melinda had just been pointing him out to the man. Ralph was standing and talking to Melinda, his hands crossed in front of him, his limber body making a slight arc. Insubstantiality personified. Mr Gosden was not looking his way. Surely most of the people in the room knew that Ralph had been Melinda's lover, Vic thought. Now Ralph was laughing. He was behaving quite bravely tonight. Then Vic saw the stocky man spread his arms in an invitation to Melinda to dance, and they moved gracefully on to the floor. And Ralph Gosden watched them, or perhaps watched only Melinda, with his old fatuous smile. Vic saw that Horace had followed his eyes and he looked down at his drink again.

'Is that Ralph Gosden?' Horace asked.

'Yes. Dear old Ralph,' Vic said.

Horace began to talk about the lobotomized brain of an

epileptic that had come into his laboratory for analysis, about the irregularity of the lesions because during the operation, which had been under a local anaesthetic, the patient had moved. Horace was particularly interested in brain injury, brain surgery, and brain diseases, and so was Vic. It had always been their favourite subject of discussion. They were still talking about the behaviour report of the frontal lobotomy case, when Melinda walked up with the man she had been dancing with.

'Vic,' she said, 'I'd like you to meet Mr Anthony Cameron. Mr Cameron, my husband.'

Mr Cameron stuck out a big hand. 'How do you do?'

'How do you do?' Vic said, shaking his hand.

'And Mr Meller?'

Horace and Mr Cameron also exchanged a 'How do you do?'

'Mr Cameron's a contractor. He's up here to look for some land to build a house on. I thought you might like to talk to him,' Melinda said, with a faint singsong in her delivery that told Vic this was not the main reason she had introduced Mr Cameron to them.

Mr Cameron had staring, pale-blue eyes whose smallness contrasted with the bulk of the rest of him. He was not very tall and his head looked square and huge, as if it were made of something other than the usual flesh and bone. When he paused to listen to someone else speak, his mouth hung a little open. Horace was telling him about the pocket of land with a hill on it between northern Little Wesley and the bulge of the midtown section. The hill had a view of Bear Lake, Horace said.

'I've looked at it and it's not high enough,' Mr Cameron said, smiling at Melinda afterwards as if he had uttered a *bon mot*.

'There's not much high land around here unless you actually take to the mountains,' Vic said.

'Well, we may do that!' Mr Cameron rubbed his heavy hands together. His wavy, dark-brown hair looked greasy and as if it smelled unpleasantly sweet.

Then they got into the fishing possibilities of the region. Mr Cameron said he was a great fisherman and boasted of always coming home with a full creel. Vic discovered he had never heard of a quite commonplace fly for brook fishing. Still, he demonstrated his technique with a couple of full swings of his arms. Horace was beginning to eye him with distaste.

'Can I offer you a drink?' Vic asked.

'No, no, thanks. Never touch it!' Mr Cameron said in the loud voice of the outdoor man, beaming. He had small regular teeth, each one like the other. 'Well, this is a great party tonight, isn't it?' He looked at Melinda. 'Want to dance again?'

'Delighted,' Melinda said, lifting her arms.

'So long, Mr Van Allen, Mr Meller,' Cameron said as he danced away. 'Nice to meet you.'

'So long,' Vic said. Then he exchanged a look with Horace, but each of them was a little too polite to smile or make any comment.

He and Horace talked about something else.

Ralph Gosden did not dance with Melinda all the evening, and Mr Cameron claimed most of Melinda's dances. Melinda became rather high around two in the morning and began dancing more or less by herself, waving the very long, bright-green scarf that in the earlier part of the evening she had worn around her shoulders as a stole. Her dress was of pink satin – really an old dress, and he thought she had chosen it for this evening with a kind of martyrdom in mind – and with the green scarf it suggested the colours of a dainty, virginal apple blossom, though her face above the dress looked neither dainty nor virginal. Her hair had a wild charm, Vic supposed, streaked with lighter blonde strands from the summer sun, and waving loose as she moved. It would appeal to a man like Cameron, and so would her strong, supple body and her face that had lost much of its make-up now and was just a slightly drunken, down-to-earth, happy-looking face. At least Mr Cameron would think it happy. Vic could see the defiance in her dancing, in the wildly waving scarf which twice circled another couple around the necks. It was a defiance of everybody in the room. First, she had wanted to show herself to the community as a martyr, and in no time at all she had reversed to a pretence of devil-may-care revelry, equally determined to show everybody that she was having a better time than anybody else. Vic sighed, pondering the oscillations of Melinda's mind.

The next afternoon, while Vic was in the garage cleaning his snail aquaria, Mr Cameron walked up in shirt sleeves.

'Anybody home?' Mr Cameron asked cheerfully.

Vic was a bit startled, not having heard a car arrive. 'Well, I am,' he said. 'My wife's still asleep, I think.'

'Oh,' said Mr Cameron. 'Well, I was just passing by your road, and your wife said any time I was in the neighbourhood to drop in. So here I am!'

Vic didn't know what to say for a moment.

'What've you got there?'

'Snails,' Vic said, wondering if Melinda were possibly awake to take the man off his hands. 'Just a minute. I'll see if my wife's up.' Vic went into the house from the garage.

Melinda's door was still closed.

'Melinda?' he called. Then he knocked firmly. When there was still no answer, he opened the door. 'Melinda.'

She was lying on her side with her back to him. She slowly straightened and turned, with one stretching movement, like an animal.

'You've a gentleman caller,' Vic said.

She jerked her head up from the pillow. 'Who?'

'Mr Cameron, I believe it is? I wish you'd come out and take care of him. Or ask him in. He's outside.'

Melinda frowned, reaching for her slippers. 'Why don't you ask him in?'

'I don't *want* to ask him in,' Vic said, and Melinda glanced at him, surprised but unconcerned. He went out to Mr Cameron, who was bouncing on his heels in the middle of the driveway, whistling, and said, 'My wife'll be out in a minute or so. Would you like to wait in the living-room?'

'Oh, no. I'll take the air. Is that where you live?' he asked, nodding towards the projecting wing off the far side of the garage.

'Yes,' Vic said, pulling the corners of his mouth into a smile. He went back to his snail cleaning. It was an unattractive aspect of snail raising, cleaning their mess off the glass sides of the tank with a razor blade, and he loathed it when Mr Cameron strolled over to watch him, still whistling. To Vic's surprise, he was whistling part of a Mozart concerto.

'Where'd you get all those?' he asked.

'Oh – most of them were born here. Hatched.'

'How do they breed? In the water?'

'No, they lay eggs. In the ground.' Vic was washing the inside of a tank with a rag and soap and water. Delicately, he detached a young snail that had crawled up on the part of the glass he was washing, and set it down on the earth inside the tank.

'Look like they'd be good to eat,' Mr Cameron remarked.

'Oh, they are. Delicious.'

'Reminds me of New Orleans. Ever been to New Orleans?'

'Yes,' Vic said, with finality. He began on another tank, first detaching with his hands or the razor blade the snails of all sizes that were sleeping on the sides of the glass. He looked over at Mr Cameron and said, 'I wish you wouldn't take the screen off, if you don't mind. They crawl out very easily.'

Mr Cameron straightened up and slid the screen top back with a carelessness that made Vic wince, because he felt sure that a baby snail or two must have been crushed. Mr Cameron probably hadn't even seen the tiny baby snails. His eyes didn't focus that small. He was coming towards Vic in an aimless way with

196

his affable little smile when Melinda opened the door from the hall, and he turned to her.

'Hello, Tony! Good afternoon! How nice of you to stop by!'

'Hope you folks don't mind,' he said, walking slowly towards her. 'I was just cycling around, thought I'd drop in.'

'Drop in here and have a drink!' Melinda said gaily, opening the door wider.

'I'll have a beer, if you got it.'

Mr Cameron stayed for brunch at about four o'clock, and then for dinner at nine, both of which meals Vic prepared almost single-handed. He drank nine cans of beer. At six o'clock, when Vic had returned to the living-room from his own room to get some of the Sunday paper, Cameron had been sitting with Melinda on the sofa, bellowing out a story about how he acquired his name.

'What's your real name?' Melinda asked.

'Oh, it's Polish. You wouldn't even be able to pronounce it!' Mr Cameron told her with a roar of laughter.

He was like a phonograph turned on too loudly. Vic had sat for a while in the living-room with them. He had put on a clean shirt and freshly pressed slacks, in hopes that Cameron might think they had an engagement for the evening, but Cameron evidently considered the change of clothing in his honour and that his visit was just beginning. The strange thing was that Melinda seemed to be enjoying it, though she had grown a little tight in the course of curing a hangover by sipping Bloody Marys all day. Mr Cameron switched from describing a dynamiting process, with violent gestures, to enumerating the demands some clients made on him to provide a view plus shelter from the wind, plus a place for a swimming pool and a tennis court and a lawn, all on three acres of ground.

'Oh, they ask me for everything except a graveyard for when they die!' Mr Cameron finished, guffawing. It was a typical finish of his stories. Mr Cameron was outdoing himself. He was like a small boy trying to impress a girl by flourishing a knife or by setting a kerosene-soaked cat on fire.

Vic sat with his cheek in his hand, waiting.

The Petersons brought Trixie and the puppy back from their house, where Trixie had been all afternoon, but the Petersons refused to come in when they saw that they had company.

'*Please* come in,' Vic pleaded, but in vain. The Petersons were shy people. It was then that Vic slammed the front door shut in his anger, and said, taking a wild chance that Cameron would leave on it, 'Well, I suppose it'll soon be time for dinner.'

Mr Cameron did not say 'Good!' but something very much like it.

During what might have been called the cocktail hour, when the Idaho potatoes were baking and the biggest steak Vic had been able to find in the deep freezer was thawing on the drainboard, Mr Cameron suddenly stood up and announced that he had a treat for them. 'I'll be right back. I just want to get something from my bike!'

'What's he getting?' asked Vic, who had just come in from the kitchen.

'I don't know.'

'I wish you wouldn't laugh so hard at his damned stories. It's a bit late now to mention it, I suppose.'

'And maybe I enjoy his stories,' Melinda replied in an ominously calm voice. 'I think he's very interesting, and a very *real guy*.'

Vic could say nothing, because Mr Cameron was back, with a clarinet in his hand.

'Here it is,' he said, tossing to the floor the opaque plastic bag it had evidently been in. 'I always take it with me when I bike around. I like to stop in the woods and play it awhile. Did you say you had the Mozart Clarinet Concerto in A?'

'Oh, yes, Vic, look for it, will you?'

Vic went to the record cabinet and looked for it. They had had it for years. It was a seventy-eight.

'Let's try the second movement!' Mr Cameron said, lifting the horn to his lips and beginning to tootle. His fingers looked like splayed bunches of bananas on the chromium keys.

Vic looked for the second movement, found it, and put it on the machine. Mr Cameron began at once, playing the theme along with the orchestra, coming down on the notes hard but accurately. In a pause, he smiled triumphantly and looked at Melinda.

'I shouldn't come in so soon, but I like the music,' he said. 'How's this?'

Benny Goodman was coming in now, and so was Mr Cameron. Mr Cameron was louder. He closed his little eyes, and swayed like an elephantine Pan. He did the runs in the variations quite well. There was not a single mistake. There was just no quality.

'I think you're *marvellous!*' Melinda cried.

Mr Cameron took a moment out to grin at her. 'I only had three lessons in my life,' he said quickly and corked his mouth again with the instrument.

There followed the slow movement of the Third Brandenburg, the second movement of Mozart's Twenty-third Piano Concerto, and the second movement of Beethoven's Fifth Symphony. After the Brandenburg, Vic left Melinda to find the records for him, because he had to cook the steak and make the salad. During the dinner Mr Cameron talked of the pleasures of bicycling and of how he combined work and pleasure by cycling around on nearly all his jobs. He was friendly and open to Vic, glancing at him every few moments to include him in his audience, with a condescension that showed that he considered Vic just a household companion of Melinda's, just an old uncle or a bachelor brother. He was still performing for Melinda.

Trixie sat at the table staring at him with a certain puzzlement that Vic could easily understand. She had stared at him while he played his clarinet, making no comment and not attempting to talk to him – which was next to impossible because Mr Cameron hardly shut up for a moment. Decibels of vocal cords, laughter, or the clarinet burst from him constantly. He emanated noise.

'I've had it,' Vic murmured to Melinda after the dinner, as they were carrying the dishes back to the kitchen. 'Can you manage the rest of the dishes? I'm going into my room where it's quiet.'

'Please do,' Melinda said a trifle fuzzily.

Vic went into the living-room to say good night to Mr Cameron, who was walking about restlessly, hands in his pockets, talking in a cheerful, roaring tone to the boxer puppy, since there was no one else around to talk to.

'Good night, Mr Cameron,' Vic said, with a little smile. 'If you'll excuse me – I have some work to do.'

'Oh, sure,' he said sympathetically. 'I understand. Say, that certainly was a good dinner. I enjoyed it!'

'I'm glad you did.'

Vic plunged into the Sicilian grandmother's diary again, consulting his Italian dialect dictionary almost constantly. He succeeded in keeping out the duet of Melinda on the piano and Mr Cameron on the clarinet while he was reading but when he stopped reading it intruded again. Melinda was making mistakes and pounding on the keys afterwards to correct them. Mr Cameron's happy guffaws came clearly through Vic's partly opened window.

19

Melinda suddenly developed a taste for contracting. She began to spend her days with Mr Cameron, driving him about wherever he cared to go, and calling on their friends with him and asking them to advise him. In the evening, during dinner, she talked all the time now, talked about the ground rise, drainage, the view and the water table of some land east of Little Wesley that Mr Cameron had selected for his client. The client was coming up on Saturday to look at the land, and Tony had to have a complete description of the physical nature of the property for him to read when he got here.

'Don't you think water tables are fascinating?' Melinda asked. 'Tony explained to me how you can tell a false table from a real one. One kind of hill from the other, I mean. Some people think when there's a slight rise of ground there's a water table under it.'

Vic frowned a little. 'Do you mean simply water maybe? Or water supply? There's a water table everywhere.'

Melinda scowled across the table at him. 'What do you mean there's a water table everywhere? There's a water table where there's water!'

'Well, then there's water everywhere,' Vic said. 'The definition of water table is the upper limit of the ground that is saturated with water. Every kind of ground has its water table. There's a water table in the Sahara Desert, it just happens to be pretty low. I don't know what Tony's been telling you, but that's the way it is.'

Melinda said nothing for a while, quite a long while. When she spoke again it was about the white stone that Tony was now trying to locate.

'Tell him to try around Vermont,' Vic said.

'*That's* an idea! They've got beautiful stone up there! Remember that—'

'It isn't the marble of Paros, but it might do,' Vic said crisply, buttering a radish.

Then it was the drainage system. Tony had a wonderful idea for the drainage that would make an artificial brook through the property. Vic never quite understood where all the water would come from in the first place, but he was not impressed by Tony's idea, which Melinda thought original because Tony had evidently told her it was original.

'The Romans were doing that two thousand years ago,' Vic said. 'They did it in Avignon.'

'Where's Avignon, Daddy?' Trixie asked.

Vic suddenly realized that Trixie had missed her Sunday tutoring on account of Mr Cameron. 'Avignon is in southern France. It used to be the residence of the popes, oh – five hundred years ago, I guess. You'll have to go there some day. And they have a song "*Sur le pont d'Avignon – l'on y danse, l'on y danse – sur le pont d'Avignon – l'on y danse tout en rond . . .*"' He got her to sing it with him. They went on and on while they set the dessert on the table, on and on while Melinda frowned as if the singing were giving her a headache. Trixie never got tired of something like this, and they sang and sang through the dishwashing, and Vic taught her the second verse, and they sang that until Melinda burst out:

'Oh, for God's sake, Vic, *stop* it!'

When Vic next saw Horace, on Saturday morning in the hardware store in Little Wesley, Horace brought up Mr Cameron. They were walking out of the store together towards their cars in the parking lot next to the supermarket. Horace said:

'Well, I understand Ferris is going to buy the land over near the Cowans' place.' Ferris was the name of the wealthy New Yorker who was Cameron's client.

'Yes. How'd you know?'

'Phil told me. He said Melinda stopped by one day with the contractor. I understand she's been helping him out.'

'It gives her something to do,' Vic said quickly, and in an uninterested tone.

Horace nodded, and if he had been going to say anything else about Melinda and Cameron, he didn't say it. When they reached their cars, Horace said, 'Mary and I are going to try our luck with a spare-rib barbecue tomorrow night. The MacPhersons were coming over, but they can't make it. Why don't you and Melinda come by around five o'clock?'

Vic would have enjoyed it ordinarily, sitting around the Mellers' lawn, watching the sun go down, and sniffing the charcoal aroma of the roasting spare ribs. Now the first thing that came to his mind was that Melinda might not be free. It was the first time he had let himself realize it, that she was spending nearly every afternoon, had spent half this morning and was still out somewhere with Tony Cameron. 'Thanks Horace. Can I let you know? As far as I know, we can.'

'Fine,' Horace said, smiling. 'I hope you can. It's going to be winter soon. No more outdoor barbecues.'

Vic went home, the back of his car full of groceries for the week-end – Melinda wasn't doing much marketing lately – and with a new bit for his auger. He had broken a bit the other day when he had been angry, or rather when he had been thinking maddening thoughts. His thoughts had been playing around Tony and Melinda: what were their friends going to say about this? When were they going to start talking? Had Cameron and Melinda had an affair yet? They had had enough time and opportunity to, and Cameron's unchanged manner towards him would be quite in character with Cameron. Cameron the pachyderm. At moments Vic could smile at the situation. Cameron was so uncomplex. There was something even appealingly naïve and innocent about his big square face, and something very juvenile and open in the way he assumed it was perfectly all right if he went off with another man's wife and kept her for eight hours at a stretch. Vic knew, of course, that Melinda was encouraging him in this direction with her usual line, 'Oh, yes, I love Vic, but—' Not that Melinda necessarily wanted Cameron as a lover – Vic found that impossible to believe – but she wanted a romantic atmosphere to surround them when they were together, wanted to keep the road clear.

Melinda was not in when he got home. Trixie was away at the movies. Roger greeted him at the door, his stubby tail wagging, and Vic let him out on the the lawn, watched him absently as he sat down and made a puddle. Well, Vic thought, Mr Cameron was here for only another two weeks. His work on the Ferris house would be finished the end of November. Cameron himself had said that.

Melinda came in at six-thirty, with Cameron. Cameron had acquired a glowing pink sunburn. When he smiled his face seemed to blaze with joy and self-satisfaction.

'Brought my own beer this time!' Cameron said, swinging up a carton of half-quart cans.

'Good! Fine!' Vic said in the tone he might have used to a child. Then to Melinda, 'Can I talk to you for a minute?'

She came into the kitchen with him.

'We're invited to the Mellers' tomorrow at five for a barbecue. Would you like to go?'

Her face, flushed and excited from her outing with Cameron, brightened still more. 'Sure! Love to!'

'Okay, I'll tell Horace,' Vic said, relieved. He smiled, too.

'I suppose I can bring Tony if I want to, can't I?'

Vic turned back to her. He had been going to the telephone. 'No, I don't think you can bring Tony.'

'Why not?'

'Because I don't think he's the Mellers' cup of tea.'

'Oh, la-dee-da!' Melinda tossed her head. 'Since when do you say what's the Mellers' cup of tea?'

'I happen to know.'

'I'll ask them myself,' Melinda said, starting off for the phone.

Vic caught her arm and jerked her back. He closed the swinging kitchen door behind him. 'Oh, no, you won't. The Mellers don't care for him and that's that. They've asked us.'

'I'll take him along whether they like it or not!'

'I don't think you will, Melinda,' he said quietly, though he heard his voice shake with anger.

'How're you going to stop me?'

Vic closed his lips, ashamed of his own anger, and baffled by Melinda's abrupt fury. 'All right. Let's let it go,' he said.

Melinda looked at him a moment, then apparently taking his words as a concession of victory for herself, the corner of her mouth went up, and she walked past Vic out of the kitchen.

'Tony, don't you need a beer opener?' she asked, and Vic remembered that she had picked one up while she had been talking to him, that she had been holding it in her hand.

Vic did not go to the Mellers' barbecue the next day. He had left it up to Melinda to accept the invitation and he did not know what she had told them, but at the last minute he told her he was not going. Cameron arrived, not on his bicycle but in his *café au lait*-coloured Plymouth station wagon, in which he carried his bicycle around when he travelled, Vic supposed. Both

Cameron and Melinda looked long-faced when he said he was not going.

'What's the matter?' asked Cameron. He was in a freshly pressed summer suit and white shoes, out to make a good impression on the Mellers.

'Nothing. I just have some things I'd like to do. You two go ahead.'

'What're the Mellers going to think?' Melinda asked a little blankly.

'I don't know. You'll have to wait and see,' Vic said, with a disarming chuckle.

Mr Cameron's expression did not change. 'Sure wish you'd change your mind.'

Vic walked away from them on the lawn. 'You two go on. Have a good time and give the Mellers my regards.' Melinda's hands were fidgeting with her car keys, Vic saw. He went into his room.

A moment later the two cars left.

Vic reminded himself that Cameron probably wasn't having anything to do with Melinda – physically speaking. He really believed that. But it didn't help. And as he sat there in his room after they had left, trying to compose himself so that he could read, he almost regretted that he had been so childish as to refuse to go to the Mellers'. He could still go, he thought. But that seemed more childish now. No, he would not go. But he knew it would mean another painful or awkward conversation with Horace.

Melinda did not come home until one in the morning. Vic was in his room, reading in bed, and he did not go into the house to see her. He didn't want to see her, anyway. She was probably drunk. The time of her coming home, ten-past one, made Vic think that she had been sitting with Cameron in some bar in the latter part of the evening, because all the bars closed punctually at one.

Horace called on him at twenty to seven the next evening, when Vic was at the plant. Vic had predicted that he would get a visit from Horace today, and he had predicted the expression on Horace's face.

'What happened to you yesterday?' Horace asked. 'We called you at home. You didn't answer.'

Vic felt himself flush with shame as if he had been caught out in a serious lie. He had heard the telephone ring last evening and he had not answered it. 'I took a little walk after Melinda left. I wasn't in the house.'

'Well, we certainly missed you.'

'Oh, I wanted to think over some things. You know. I thought Mr Cameron could handle my share of the barbecue.'

'That he did!'

'Was it good?'

'Oh, it was fine. Mr Cameron entertained us with his clarinet.'

'Yes, I've heard him, too,' Vic said.

'You don't care for him, I gather. Neither do I.'

Vic felt another stab of shame, but he kept his face calm and pleasant. 'What do you mean?'

'Shall I say it straight, Vic? I don't like Cameron and I don't like the way he acts around Melinda. And I don't like the way you're just taking a back seat again, waiting for things to blow over.'

'Well, don't they usually?' Vic asked, smiling, but he felt trapped and uncomfortable.

'You weren't there last night. Melinda got pretty tight and said several things – such as that she thought Cameron was the answer to her prayer. Cameron acts as if he—'

There was a gentle rap on the door.

'Come in,' Vic said.

Stephen Hines opened the door. 'Oh, hello, Mr Meller. How are you?'

'Fine, thank you, and you?'

'Fine, too. Carlyle took the truck,' Stephen continued to Vic. 'He's going to call at the post office tomorrow morning and see if that new roller's come.'

'All right. There's no hurry on that,' Vic said, mechanically reckoning that it would be three weeks before they used the new roller on Ryder's poems. Vic had deliberately allowed an ink roller to rust in order to get a texture effect when he printed directly on to the paper with it.

'Is there anything else?' Stephen asked.

'I don't think so, Stephen.'

'Good night, then. See you tomorrow.'

'Good night,' Vic said. Then he turned to Horace. 'By the way, Xenophon's back from the bindery! Would you like to see one of them?'

'I would, Vic – but I think what we're talking about is more important, don't you?'

'Go ahead, Horace.'

'Well – I got the impression Cameron's thinking of taking Melinda away and she acts as if she's quite willing to go.'

'Taking her away?' Vic asked with astonishment, some of which was genuine.

'His next job is in Mexico, and he has two aeroplane tickets to Mexico City – or so he said, and I don't think he was drunk – except with his own power. But Melinda was talking about going to the ends of the earth with him. Why don't you tell him where to head in, Vic?'

'It's news to me. I hadn't heard any of that.'

'Well, you should have. You're partly to blame, Vic. What real effort have you made to get back with Melinda on any kind of basis after the De Lisle affair?'

Vic's mind teetered on the two meanings of the word 'affair' before he could shape his answer. 'I have tried,' he said simply.

'As far as I know, you're still living in your own part of the house,' Horace said, hiding his embarrassment in an aggressive tone. 'You're young, Vic. Thirty-six, aren't you? Melinda's still younger. What sort of marriage *do* you expect to have with her? You'll wake up some morning and find her gone!'

'I don't care to manage her,' Vic said. 'I never did. She's a free human being.'

Horace looked at him, puzzling. 'You're just giving up? Because I think you may lose to Cameron.'

Vic was silent for several seconds. He was not thinking of what to answer. Partly he was feeling his embarrassment at the conversation, tasting it on his tongue, partly he was panicky lest Horace alter his opinion of him in any way, lower his estimation of him. 'All right, Horace. I'll have a little talk with her about Mr Cameron.'

'I think it'll take more than talking. Either you change your whole attitude – or else.'

Vic smiled. 'Aren't you exaggerating?'

'I don't think so, Vic.' Horace lighted a cigarette. 'Vic, why're you so damned aloof? What's the purpose?'

'I'm not aloof. Will you go for a drink at the local?' He started gathering the few things he wanted to take home.

'Your whole attitude's wrong, Vic. If it ever had a chance of being right – and maybe it did once – it's wrong now.'

'Those are the strongest words I've ever heard you use, Horace.'

'I mean them.'

Vic looked at Horace, feeling a little off balance. 'Shall we go for that drink?'

Horace shook his head. 'I'll be going. I didn't mean to blow my top, but I think I'm really glad I did. Maybe you'll take this one seriously – Cameron, I mean. Good night, Vic.' Horace went out and closed the door.

A strange sensation, like fear, came over Vic as soon as he was alone. He finished gathering his papers, went out, and locked the door behind him. Horace's car was just disappearing down the lane. Vic got into his own car. A cool tingle went up his spine into the back of his neck. Then he swallowed and relaxed his hands on the wheel. He knew what the trouble was. He had not allowed himself really to think about Cameron, except to think that Cameron would be gone in another couple of weeks. He had not allowed himself to put his brain to the problem that Cameron created. And Horace had pointed that out. It was as if Horace had pointed a finger at a fire burning right at his feet, a fire he had chosen to ignore. (On the other hand, he considered he had a right to ignore it if he wanted to. If a fire were at his feet, the only person who would be hurt would be himself. What had upset him most, he thought, was that Horace had forced him for a moment into a conformist's attitude, a conformist's vision of things.) But perhaps Horace was right in saying that he hadn't realized some important facts. He hadn't, for instance, admitted to himself that Melinda might really like Cameron, that Cameron might be Melinda's type precisely. That bluntness, that primitiveness, that really outdid her own! And that pachydermal naïveté! Cameron was the kind who would 'take her away', wait for a divorce, and then marry her properly. And he was, indeed, Melinda's type precisely. It was an overwhelming revelation to him.

Trixie was alone in the house when Vic got home. The boxer puppy came loping to greet him, jumping into the air and wriggling at the same time in a movement that always reminded Vic of a leaping trout.

'Was your mother here when you got home?' he asked.

'Nope. I guess she's out with Tony,' Trixie said, and went on reading the comic page in the evening paper.

Vic fixed himself a drink. As he carried it to his armchair, he noticed the new blue-and-white box of Nelson Thirty-three pipe tobacco on the little table beside the chair. It must have come today, and Melinda had unwrapped it and put it there. She must have ordered it about two weeks ago, Vic thought, must have ordered it on one of the days that she had spent with Tony.

20

Brian Ryder arrived by train in Wesley the following Saturday. He was a pleasant, intense young man with the energy of a young Tarzan and the physique that went with it. The first thing he wanted to do was walk around the town, even before he and Vic had an opportunity to discuss his poems. The walk took him nearly two hours in the afternoon, and he returned with damp hair, his face shining. He had found Bear Lake and taken a dip in it. The temperature was about forty degrees. Bear Lake was nearly eight miles away. Vic asked him how he had made it so fast.

'Oh, I took a jog along the road, going there,' he replied. 'I like to run. And on the way back I caught a ride with a fellow. He said he knew you.'

'Oh? Who?' Vic asked.

'His name was Peterson.'

'Oh, yes.'

'He seems to think a lot of you.'

Vic made no reply. Melinda was sitting on the sofa in the living-room, pasting photographs in her album. She had not said anything to Brian after Vic had introduced them, but she kept staring at him with overt curiosity that reminded Vic of the way

Trixie always stared at a new man whom Melinda had brought home. Now Brian looked at her in his naïve, direct way, as if he expected her to contribute something to the conversation or simply to show a little friendliness before he and Vic went off to work, but she said nothing and she didn't smile, even when Brian caught her eyes.

'Shall we go into my room and talk?' Vic asked. 'I've got your manuscript in there.'

That evening, Melinda brought Cameron home for dinner. Cameron said with a guffaw:

'I'd have taken your wife out to dinner, Vic, but she insisted on coming home to you.'

The unbelievable crassness of it left Vic speechless. Brian had heard him. From then on Vic noticed that Brian spent quite a lot of the evening simply watching Cameron and Melinda with a serious, speculative expression on his face. And they put on quite a show. Cameron kept going in and out of the kitchen, helping Melinda put things on the table as if he lived there. Their conversation with each other was about what they had done that afternoon and about building materials and the price of cement. Vic attempted to talk to Brian about poets and poetry, but their voices were no match for Cameron's. Vic kept a little smile on his face to hide his irritation from Brian. He was not sure that he succeeded. Brian was a very observant young man.

After dinner Cameron said, 'Well, Vic, Melinda tells me you two've got a little talking to do, so – I thought I'd take her out maybe for a little dance at the Barmaid.'

'That sounds nice,' Vic said pleasantly. 'I think they've got draught beer there, haven't they?'

'They sure have!' Cameron replied, patting his solid, well-fed belly. For all he ate and drank, he was not fat. He had the hard, hipless bulk of a gorilla.

Brian looked Melinda up and down appreciatively when she

came out of her room in high-heeled, low-cut pumps and a short bright-red jacket over her dress. She had taken more pains than usual with her face, and her blonde hair was neatly brushed.

'Expect me when you see me,' she said gaily as she went out the door.

The gorilla followed her, grinning expansively.

Vic plunged into conversation with Brian so that Brian would not have the chance to ask him any questions, but in the young man's face Vic could see his mind hanging on to the questions tenaciously. Brian would not forget to ask them later. Vic reproached himself for not having had a talk with Melinda days ago. Horace had been right. He should have said *something* to her. But would it really have done any good? Had it done any good when he spoke to her about De Lisle?

'Your wife's a *very* attractive woman,' Brian said slowly in a lull in their conversation.

'Do you think so?' Vic asked, smiling. And then he suddenly remembered Brian's surprised 'Do you sleep here?' on seeing his room beyond the garage, like the thoughtless, brutal question of a child. It had pained Vic unreasonably. He could not get it out of his mind.

They sat up talking of books and poets until past midnight, when Brian politely suggested that Vic might be wanting to go to bed. Vic knew that Brian wanted to get at the anthology of German metaphysical poets that Vic had taken down from a shelf for him, so Vic excused himself. But in his own room, Vic stayed up reading until Melinda came home at two o'clock. Brian's light was still on. Vic hoped that Brian wouldn't see her drunk. Vic had no idea whether she was drunk or not. He turned out his own light at about two-thirty. Shortly afterwards, very faintly, he heard Melinda's slow, happy, drunken laugh through his partly opened window. He wondered what Brian had found to talk to her about.

The next morning Melinda said, 'I think your little friend is terribly cute.'

'He's a terribly good poet,' Vic said.

Brian was away on his morning walk. He would probably come back with bird feathers, as he had yesterday. This morning, when Vic had looked into his room, he had found the bed made and a blue feather, a pebble, a mushroom, and a dried leaf laid out in a neat horizontal row in the middle of the writing-table, as if Brian had sat there pondering them.

'He said he thought you were very attractive, too,' Vic said, though he did not know why he bothered repeating it to her. Melinda's opinion of herself was high enough.

'Since we're exchanging messages, you can tell him I think he's the most attractive young man I've seen since I left high school.'

Vic suppressed a comment that sprang to his mind. 'You're seeing Tony this afternoon?'

'No, I thought I might see Brian.'

'Brian's busy.'

'Not all the afternoon. He asked me to go for a row on Bear Lake.'

'Oh, I see.'

'But Tony's coming over this evening. We're going to play some records. I bought five new records yesterday in Wesley.'

'I don't want him here tonight,' Vic said quietly.

'Oh?' Her eyebrows went up. 'And why not?'

'Because I want to talk to Brian, and I don't want the music coming in the window, even if I talk to him in my room.'

'I see. And where do you want us to go?'

'I don't care where you go.' He lit a cigarette and stared down at the folded *Times* on the cocktail table.

'And what're you going to do if I bring him here, anyway?'

'I'm going to ask him to leave.'

'Isn't this as much my house as yours?'

There were so many replies to this that he could make none of them. He drew on his cigarette.

'Well?' she said, slurring her eyes up at him.

Useless to point out that because of Brian she might behave better. Useless. It was all useless.

'I told you, I'll ask him to leave if you bring him. He'll leave all right.'

Vic smiled a little.

'If you do, I'll divorce you.'

'You don't think I mean it, do you? I will, though, I think I'm ready to take you up on your alimony offer. Remember?'

'I remember.'

'Well – any time.' She was standing up now, her hands on her hips, her long body relaxed and her head lowered as it always was when she fought, like the head of an animal in combat.

'And what brought this on?' Vic asked, knowing very well what had brought it on. He felt the cool terror again along his spine. Melinda was not answering him. 'Mr Cameron?'

'I think he's a lot nicer than you are. We get along fine.'

'There's more to life than getting along,' Vic said quickly.

'It helps!'

They stared at each other.

'You believe me, don't you?' Melinda said. 'All right, Vic, I want the divorce. You asked me if I wanted it a couple of months ago. Remember?'

'I remember.'

'Well, does the offer still hold?'

'I never go back on my word.'

'Shall I start the proceedings?'

'That's customary. You can accuse me of adultery.'

She took a cigarette from the cocktail table and lighted it with an air of nonchalance. Then she turned and walked into her own room. A moment later she was back again. 'How much alimony?'

'I said a generous allowance. It'll be generous.'

'How much?'

He forced himself to think. 'Fifteen thousand a year? You won't have to support Trix on it.' He could see her calculating. Fifteen thousand a year would mean he couldn't print so many books a year, that he'd have to let Stephen go, or dock his salary, which Stephen would probably agree to. For a whim of hers, Stephen and his family would have to go on short rations.

'That sounds all right,' she said finally.

'And Cameron isn't exactly a pauper.'

'He's a wonderful, *real* man,' she replied, as if he had called him something derogatory. 'Well, I suppose we're settled. I'll start whatever I have to do on Monday.' With a nod of conclusion, she went back into her room.

Brian came in a few minutes later, and he and Vic went into Vic's room to continue their selection of sixty poems from the hundred and twenty of Brian's manuscript. Brian had categorized them into three piles, his favourites, second favourites, and the remainder. They were mostly on nature, with metaphysical and ethical overtones, or themes, which gave them a flavour like that of Horace's odes and epodes – though Brian had said, rather apologetically, that he had never cared for Horace and couldn't remember a single poem of his. Brian preferred Catullus. There were some passionate love poems, more or less ecstatic and unphysical love poems but as exquisite as Donne's. His poems about the city, New York, were not so sure as the others, but Vic persuaded him to include one or two in the book for variety's sake. Brian was very persuasive that morning, in a kind of ecstatic good spirits himself, and Vic more than once had the feeling Brian wasn't listening to what he said. But when Vic suggested a jacket colour of red-brown, Brian woke up and disagreed. He wanted pale blue, a specific pale blue. He had a small piece of a bird's eggshell he had found that morning that was precisely the colour he wanted. Colours were very important to him, he said. Vic put the shell fragment carefully away in his desk drawer. Then Vic described the ornamental colophons that he had thought of for the end of certain of the poems – a feather, grass blades, a spider's web, a basket-worm's cocoon, and this Brian enthusiastically approved of. Vic had experimented in offset printing of all these objects and had got splendid results.

Brian stood up restlessly and asked, 'Is Melinda here?'

'I think she's in her room,' Vic said.

'I told her we'd go for a row this afternoon.'

They weren't quite finished choosing the poems, but Vic saw that Brian's mind was no longer on it. There would be time after the row and before dinner, he supposed. 'Go ahead,' Vic said, feeling weak suddenly.

Brian went.

Cameron arrived at seven o'clock that evening and installed himself in the living-room with the smiling joviality of a man who expects a good dinner. Brian was helping Melinda in the kitchen. She was preparing a small sucking-pig, which Vic vaguely remembered that she had said Brian had insisted on buying when he saw it in a butcher's shop in Wesley that afternoon. The whole afternoon had been vague to Vic. He did not know how the hours had passed, could not remember what he had done, except that at some point he had used a hammer for something and had struck his left thumb, which throbbed now when he pressed it against his forefinger. He found himself talking to Cameron, who never shut up, without thinking about anything he was saying. He forced himself to concentrate for a moment on what Cameron was saying and heard '– never was much in the kitchen myself. You know, you've either got a knack for it or you haven't!' Vic shut it off again like a radio programme he did not want to listen to. Something about Brian's being in the kitchen disturbed him. Why wasn't Brian in the living-room, talking to him about things that they were interested in? Cameron would have had to shut up. Then he remembered that he had laid down an ultimatum this morning in regard to Cameron's coming tonight, and that Melinda had promised to start divorce proceedings on Monday morning, tomorrow, and that Cameron was here tonight, anyway, looking especially complacent. Had Melinda already told him about the divorce proceedings?

Cameron heaved himself up from the sofa and announced that he was going to take a look in the kitchen.

In a few minutes he came out again, grinning. 'Say, Vic, how about me getting two or three dozen of your snails? I know a plain butter and garlic sauce that you can't beat anywhere! A child could make it and it tastes as good as New Orleans!' He slammed his palms together and rubbed them. 'Do you want to get 'em or shall I? Melinda said I ought to ask you first.'

'The snails are not for eating,' Vic said.

Cameron's face fell a little. 'Oh. Well – what the hell are they for?' he asked, laughing. 'Melinda said—'

'I don't use them for anything. They are useless,' Vic said, spitting the words out with a particular bitterness.

Melinda came out of the kitchen. 'What's the matter with having a few snails? Brian wants some and Tony says he can fix them. Let's have a real gala dinner!' She made a sweep with the cooking spoon, turned around almost into Cameron's arms and patted his cheek.

Vic glanced at Brian, who had followed Melinda out of the kitchen. 'I just told Tony the snails aren't for eating,' Vic said.

'Go out and get some, Tony,' Melinda said. She was on the way to being drunk.

Tony made a start and stopped, staring at Vic.

'The snails are not for eating,' Vic said.

'Look – I didn't say I *wanted* the snails,' Brian began awkwardly, not quite addressing either Melinda or Vic. 'I mean, *I* didn't say that.'

'They ought to taste good, they're so well fed. Steak and carrots and Boston lettuce. Go out and get some, Tony!' And then Melinda nearly fell in the swinging door as she pushed it to go back into the kitchen.

Tony was staring at him like a stupid animal, like a dog that wasn't quite sure of the signal, his thick body poised to move. 'How about it, Vic? You won't even miss three dozen.'

Vic had clenched his hands into fists and he knew that Brian had noticed his hands, and still he kept them clenched. 'You can't eat snails right away, you know,' he said in a suddenly light, almost smiling tone. 'You have to starve them for two days so that they're clean. Mine have all been eating. I suppose you know that.'

'Oh,' Cameron said, shifting his weight back evenly on his big feet. 'Well, that's too bad.'

'Yes, it is,' said Vic. He glanced at Brian.

Brian was watching him tensely, his hands behind him against the sideboard of the glass cabinet, his blue shirt pulled taut across his strong, rounded chest. He had a wary, surprised look in his eyes that Vic had not seen before.

Vic looked at Cameron, smiling. 'I'm sorry. Maybe next time I can remember to take a few snails out for you and keep them a couple of days without food.'

'Fine,' Cameron said uncertainly. He rubbed his hands again, smiled, and flexed his shoulders. And then he fled into the kitchen.

Brian smiled. 'I certainly didn't mean to start anything about the snails. It was Melinda's idea. I said it was all right with me if you were in the habit of eating them. I could tell they were pets of yours.'

Vic paid him the compliment of saying nothing in reply, took his arm, and drew him towards the living-room. But they had not even sat down when Melinda called 'Brian!' from the kitchen.

They had never had such a meal, even at any Christmas. Melinda had apparently tried to cook everything in the kitchen – three kinds of vegetables, sweet potatoes and mashed potatoes, three kinds of dessert standing on the sideboard, two dozen rolls, besides the sucking-pig in the centre of the table, precariously laid on two shallow cookie sheets and a big pie-pan between so that there would be no dripping on the tablecloth, though there was some dripping at either end because the pie-pan made the cookie sheets slant downward. Vic found the smiling pig very disturbing and the abundance of food rather disgusting, though their two guests and Trixie, who had come back from somewhere at seven-thirty, seemed to take it as a big indoor picnic and enjoyed themselves noisily. At the table Vic realized what it was about Brian that made him uncomfortable: Brian was displaying some of the forwardness of Cameron towards Melinda. Vic knew that Brian thought her attractive, but the way he smiled at her, the way he helped her take her apron off, suggested that, consciously or unconsciously, he had taken his cue from Cameron that Melinda was fair game for anybody and so meant to enjoy a part of her himself. Vic realized that Brian would also have had to take his cue from his own tolerance of Cameron, and Vic, very definitely, felt that he had lost face with Brian Ryder. He imagined, from the snail altercation onward that Sunday evening, that Brian treated him with less respect.

The evening petered out miserably. Melinda got too drunk to want to go out with Cameron, who invited her out, and she sat on the sofa more or less mumbling jokes, mumbling the inanities of a drunk, which Brian listened to – out of politeness or curiosity, Vic didn't know – forcing a laugh out of himself now and then. Cameron sat spraddle-kneed in Vic's armchair, leaning forward with a beer can in his hand, in some fog of simple-minded beatitude that evidently made him immune to boredom or to the sensations of plain fatigue that might have inspired him to say good night. There were long silences. For the first time in months, Vic had about five strong drinks. The sordidness of the scene affected him as much as any mental pain he had ever borne, yet he could not bring himself to call Brian away with him to his room, which would have looked like a total rout for him. Vic had made a torturous effort to talk to Cameron about building stone, about water tables, about his next assignment in Mexico, but Cameron's slightly bloodshot pale-blue eyes had been drawn again and again to Melinda on the sofa, and for once his voice had kept shutting off. Cameron stayed until two-twenty in the morning. Brian, who had been in a half-recumbent position in the other corner of the sofa from Melinda, day-dreaming or pondering or savouring or whatever poets did, hauled himself up just after Cameron stood up, and bade him a surprisingly cordial good night.

Looking at his watch, Brian said that he hadn't realized it was so late and that he should have said good night earlier. 'We have a few more things to talk about before I catch my train at eleven, haven't we, Mr Van Allen?'

'I think we have – a few.'

'Then I'll let my morning walk go by tomorrow so we'll have some time.' He bowed, a little shyly. 'Good night, Melinda. That was an unforgettable banquet. You're very kind to go to all that trouble. Thank you.'

'Your idea,' Melinda said. 'Your little piggy-wiggy.'

Brian laughed. 'Good night, sir,' he said to Vic, and went off to his room.

The 'sir' and the 'Mr Van Allen' and the 'Melinda' went around in Vic's head stupidly for a few seconds. Then he said, 'A delightful evening.'

'Wasn't it? You should have liked it. It was quiet.'

'Yes. What happened to the new records?'

A glimmer of recollection came to her glazed eyes. 'I forgot them. Damn it.' She started to get up.

Vic let her walk half across the room before he could bring himself to try to stop her, taking her lightly by one arm above the elbow. 'Wait till tomorrow. Brian won't be able to sleep.'

'L'go of me!' she said irritably.

He let her go. She stood swaying in the middle of the floor, looking at him challengingly.

'I was surprised not to hear anything from Cameron tonight,' Vic said. 'Don't you think he ought to make me a statement of his intentions?'

'I asked him not to.'

'Oh.' He lit a cigarette.

'Everything is settled, everything is fine. And I'm fine.'

'You're drunk.'

'Tony doesn't mind if I'm drunk. Tony understands why I get drunk. He understands me.'

'Tony's just a wonderfully understanding man.'

'Yes,' she said positively. 'And we're going to be very very happy together.'

'Congratulations.'

'And Tony already has two tickets for—' She paused to think. 'Mexico City! His next job is down there.'

'Oh. And you're going with him.'

'That's all you can say. "Oh."' She spun on her heel, as she often did when she was happily drunk, and she lost her balance, but Vic caught her. He immediately let her go.

'I can't tell you what a pleasure the evening was for me, too,' he said, making a little bow as Brian had done. 'Good night.'

'Good night,' she said, imitating him.

21

By ten-thirty the next morning Vic and Brian and Trixie and the puppy were on the road to Wesley in Vic's car to meet Brian's eleven o'clock train. Trixie's school was competing in a glee club contest of Massachusetts grade schools, and she hadn't to be at school until a quarter to eleven to board a bus that was taking the Highland School glee club to Ballinger. Trixie was part of a glee club of fifty that was going to render 'The Swan' in the competition. Vic had had time that morning to listen to her practise once more – though she had got impatient midway and stopped. Her voice was shrill and accurate, though a little wavery on the high notes. Vic dropped her off at the school gates, and promised to be in Ballinger by twelve sharp to hear her chorus.

'Isn't Melinda going?' Brian asked.

'No. I don't think so,' Vic said. Melinda hadn't the least interest in Trixie's glee club. She had been sleeping this morning when they left the house, so Brian had not had an opportunity to say good-bye to her.

'She's a *most remarkable* woman,' Brian said, pronouncing the words slowly and firmly, 'but I don't think she knows her own mind.'

'No?'

'No. It's a pity. She's got such vitality.'

Vic had no reply. He did not know precisely what Brian was thinking in regard to Melinda and he really didn't care. He felt extremely nervous and irritable that morning, felt the kind of nervousness that comes from a fear of being late for something, and he kept looking at his watch as if they were going to arrive in Wesley in plenty of time.

'I've *certainly* had a good time up here,' Brian said. 'And I want to thank you for taking such trouble about the – the format. There's not another publisher in the world who'd take the trouble you would about it.'

'I enjoy it,' Vic said.

At the station, they had five minutes or so before Brian's train arrived. Brian pulled a piece of paper out of his pocket.

'I wrote a poem last night,' he said. 'I wrote it all at once in about five minutes, so it's probably not one of my best, but I'd like you to see it.' He held it out abruptly to Vic.

Vic read:

What has been done cannot be undone.
The ultimate effort made before the ultimatum was given,
The positive and overflowing gesture made,
And the love lost like a flower floating
Down the stream, just beyond, just too fast
For the hand to recapture.
I cannot make the stream turn back,
For there I am, too, floating,
Just behind the fleeing flower.

Vic smiled. 'For five minutes, I don't think it's bad at all.' He handed it back to Brian.

'Oh, you can keep that. I have another copy. I thought you might show it to Melinda.'

Vic nodded. 'All right.' He had known Brian was going to say that. He had known from the first line that the poem had been inspired by Melinda, and that the poet's objectivity to his own work had allowed Brian not only to show the poem to him but to ask him to deliver it.

In the remaining minutes they walked slowly up and down the platform, Vic keeping an eye on Brian's small suitcase for him, because Brian was not watching it at all. Brian stretched himself tall as he walked, his hands in his pockets and his eyes looking into the distance everywhere with the eager, planless, undoubting optimism of youth, just as he had looked when he had arrived in Little Wesley, Vic remembered. Vic wondered if he had given much of a thought to what Cameron might mean in his and Melinda's life, or whether his meeting with Melinda had been sufficient unto itself – like one of those brief infatuations Goethe had so often had with chambermaids and barmaids and people's cooks, which had always struck Vic as *infra dignitatem* and somehow ludicrous, though they had netted Goethe a poem or even two. Biology was really the major miracle of existence. That this dedicated young man with a heart like a clean pane of glass had, at any rate for a few hours, fallen under the spell of Melinda. How glad he was that Brian was not staying up here! So glad, that he began to smile.

The train was coming in.

Brian whipped his hand out of his pocket suddenly. 'I'd like to give you this.'

'What?' Vic said, not really seeing anything in the boy's bony fist.

'It's something that belonged to my father. I've got three pairs of them. I value them very much, but I intended – if I liked you – to give you a pair. I hope you'll take them. I do like you, and you're the first person to publish – to publish my first book.' He stopped as if he were choked off. His fist was still extended.

Vic put out his hand, and Brian dropped something wrapped

in wrinkled tissue paper into it. Vic opened it and saw two blood-stone cuff-links set in gold.

'My father always encouraged me to write poetry,' Brian said. 'I didn't tell you much about him. He died of tuberculosis of the throat. That's why he took so much trouble to make me like the out-of-doors.' Brian glanced at the train that was stopping. 'You will take them, won't you?'

Vic started to protest, but he knew Brian would be displeased. 'Yes, I'll take them. Thank you, Brian. I feel very honoured.'

Brian smiled and nodded, not knowing what to say now. He climbed the train steps with his suitcase, and stopped to wave back at Vic, wordless, as if they were miles apart.

'I'll send you the galleys the day they're done!' Vic called. He put the cuff-links into his jacket pocket and walked back to his car, starting to wonder if Melinda was up yet, to wonder if she had an appointment to meet Cameron in Ballinger, or wherever she was going to start the divorce business. Melinda would not actually go into a lawyer's office with Cameron, but she would probably have him wait outside for her. Vic knew her well. She would wake up with a hangover today, full of nervous, remorseful, destructive energy, and she would start the thing rolling. Vic could imagine the face of the lawyer to whom she would speak, in Ballinger or wherever. It would be somewhere near – she might even do it in Wesley after a bolstering visit to the Wilsons – and the lawyer would undoubtedly know of Victor Van Allen. Little Wesley's number one cuckold. Vic lifted his head and began to hum. For some reason, he hummed 'My Old Kentucky Home'.

Driving through the main part of Wesley, he looked around for Don Wilson, and for June Wilson. He saw Cameron. Cameron was coming out of a cigar store, yelling back and smiling at some-body and stuffing something into a trousers pocket. Vic saw him when he was about half a block in front of him on the right side of the street, and not really knowing what he was about, Vic stopped his car in the middle of the block at just the place where Cameron was about to cross the street.

'Hello, there!' Vic called cheerfully. 'Need a lift?'

'Well! Hi!' Cameron grinned. 'No, my car's right across the street.'

Vic glanced over. Melinda was not in the car.

'If you've got a few minutes – get in and let's have a little chat,' Vic said.

Cameron's smile collapsed suddenly, and then as if he thought he ought to pull himself together and face it like a man, he gave the belt of his trousers a hitch and smiled and said, 'Sure.' He opened the car door and got in.

'Fine day, isn't it?' Vic said genially, moving the car off.

'Fine, fine.'

'How's the work going?'

'Oh, great. Mr Ferris isn't too pleased with the speed, but—' Cameron laughed, and laid his big hands on his knees.

'I suppose you're used to that from clients.'

The conversation went on like that for several more exchanges. It was the kind of conversation that Cameron enjoyed, the only kind, Vic supposed. Vic had decided not to mention Melinda, not even in the most casual way. He had decided to take Mr Cameron to the quarry. It had come into his mind all at once, just after he had said, 'If you've got a few minutes . . .' There was lots of time, lots of time still to be in Ballinger for Trixie's performance with the chorus. Vic was suddenly calm and collected.

They talked of the growth of Wesley in the last few years. The dull aspect of this conversation was that it hadn't particularly grown in the last few years.

'Where're we going?' Cameron asked.

'I thought we might drive out to that quarry I was telling you about last night. The old East Lyme quarry – which is not a pun. It'll only take about two minutes from here.'

'Oh, yeah. The one you said they abandoned?'

'Yes. The owner died, and nobody else came along before all the machinery rusted. It's quite something to see. An enterprising man could still do something with it if he could put up the money to buy it. There's nothing wrong with the rock there.' Vic had never heard himself sound calmer.

Vic turned off the East Lyme road into a dirt road, and then at a certain place, invisible until one was upon it, he turned into a rutty, single-lane road so nearly overgrown with young trees and bushes that he could hear them brush the sides of his car as they moved through.

'This is one place you don't want to meet somebody else head on,' Vic said, and Cameron laughed as if it were terribly funny. 'That was a great evening last night,' Vic went on. 'You've got to come again soon.'

'You're the damnedest hospitable people I ever met,' Cameron said, shaking his head and laughing with boorish self-consciousness.

'Here we are,' Vic said. 'You've got to get out to see it properly.'

Vic had stopped the car in a small area between the edge of the woods and the abyss of the quarry. They got out, and Roger hopped out with them. The quarry spread before them and below them, an impressive excavation of some quarter of a mile in length and somewhat half that in depth. At the very bottom of it lay a lake of water, shallower on their left where fragments of rock had slid down the nearly white rock cliff into the water, but deep to their right where the neat excavations of the engineers had removed the limestone in right-angled blocks, like giant steps, and where the water lapped only a few feet over some blocks and became black with depth just beyond. Here and there on the perimeter of the quarry stood stiff, rusted cranes at various angles as if the workmen had simply stopped one day at quitting time and not come back.

'Sa-a-ay!' Cameron said, putting his hands on his hips and

surveying it. 'That's pretty colossal! I had no idea it was this big.'

'Yep,' Vic said, moving off towards the right a little, and closer to the edge. The puppy followed him. 'Plenty of stone left, don't you think?'

'Sure looks like it!' Cameron was going closer to the edge himself now.

The place where they were standing was where Vic and Melinda and Trixie had come in the past to picnic, and Vic told Cameron so, but he did not add that they had stopped coming because it was too nerve-racking to keep watching to see that Trixie did not go too near the edge.

'It's a good place for swimming, too, down there,' Vic said. 'You can get down to the water by a little path.' He strolled away from the edge.'

'Say, I bet Ferris would've liked this colour,' Cameron said. 'He's complaining because the stone we've got's too white.'

Vic picked up a jagged, off-white rock about the size of his head as if to examine it. Then he drew his arm back and threw it, aiming at Cameron's head, just as Cameron turned towards him.

Cameron had time to duck a fraction, and the rock glanced off the top of his head, but it staggered him back a little, nearer the edge. Cameron glowered at him like a bewildered bull, and Vic – in what seemed to take him a whole minute – picked up another rock twice the size of the other, and running with it a step or two, launched it at Cameron. It caught Cameron in the thighs, and there was a quick flail of arms, a bellowing half scream, half roar, whose pitch changed as Cameron dropped downwards. Vic went to the edge, in time to see Cameron bounce off the steep slope very near the bottom of the cliff and roll noiselessly on to the stone flat. There was no sound then, except for the dwindling trickle of little stones that were following Cameron's path downwards. Then the puppy gave an excited yip, and turning, Vic saw

Roger with his forelegs down and his rear end up, ready to play with him.

Vic glanced around the rim of the quarry, at every edge of trees, then down at the shallow end of the lake, where sometimes he had seen a pair of small boys or a wandering man. There was no one around now. He went to his car for a rope. He thought there was a rope in the trunk compartment.

There wasn't, and he realized that it had been months since the rope had been there and that he had used it for something that Trixie had wanted. He debated a coil of heavy twine versus one of his snow chains, and took a snow chain.

Then he hurried along the edge of the quarry towards the path he knew. The path was steep and sometimes he slid a yard almost straight down, catching on to a tough little bush to slow himself, but he was not really hurrying, he felt, and he took the time to look back to see if Roger was making it all right. Once Roger hesitated and whimpered at a steep spot, and Vic reached back and put a hand under his chest and lifted him down.

Cameron was lying on his back with one arm over his head, a position he might have assumed while sleeping. His big square face was obscured by blood, and there were wide patches of blood on his shirt under the unbuttoned tweed jacket. Vic looked around for a suitable rock. There were rocks galore to choose from. He chose one shaped rather like a flattened horse's head, and carried it to the edge of the limestone flat on which Cameron lay. It would take several stones, Vic thought, so he selected four more slab-like ones. Then he dragged Cameron's body, gingerly to avoid being stained by his blood, to the edge of the stone where the water lapped. Roger was cavorting about Cameron, sniffing at the blood spots and barking as if he expected Cameron to get up and play with him, and Vic automatically snapped his fingers to call him off.

Vic laid the chain out on the stone, and rolled Cameron's body on to it. Then on a sudden inspiration, he unbuckled Cameron's alligator belt, opened his trousers, and pushed an elongated stone part way into his trousers, fastened them again and fastened the belt and buttoned the jacket. He laid two of the heavier stones against Cameron's ribs, and brought the two ends of the chain up over them. The chain was like a flexible ladder, some twelve inches wide, and he had a choice of where to lock the fastener. It was a dog-leash type of fastener, and it went over any length of the chain. He drew the chain as tightly as possible over the rocks and fastened it obliquely to a link. Then he took a look into the water, found the darkest point just off the corner of the flat on which he stood, and rolled the heavy body off. He was painfully conscious of the sharp, jutting corner of rock going into Cameron's spine as he rolled off, and it seemed to him that Cameron arched his back against the dig of the stone.

Cameron went down with a hollow, bubbling sound into the greenish-black water, and out of the corner of his left eye, as Vic watched the place where Cameron had sunk – though after two seconds there was nothing but swirling bubbles to see – Vic was aware of a pale step of limestone about three feet under the water, its side flush with one side of the rock on which he stood. It looked like the long, severe line of a tomb. God knew what kind of gigantic steps had been cut below the water. The place where he had rolled Cameron off was about forty feet deep, Vic remembered hearing someone say once when he had stood here with Melinda and Trixie. But directly below, he saw as soon as the water stilled, was another step – a still ghastlier morgue slab – perhaps fifteen or twenty feet down. He could not see anything resting on it, and he hoped Cameron had glided off.

Roger was barking gaily. He slid his forefeet to the edge of the stone, stuck his muzzle into the water, then drew back again, shaking his head and wagging his tail. He looked at Vic, grinning as much as a boxer could grin, and wagging his stub of a tail as if to say, 'Well done!'

Vic stooped and washed his hands in the water. Then he walked back to where Cameron had lain, saw blood on the rocks, and started to scuff over them with his shoe, dragging little jagged pebbles and limestone dust over the spots until at least they could not have been seen from the top of the cliff. But it seemed to him that to go on about his business was more important than to cover up his trail at this particular time, so he whistled to Roger and they set off up the path again.

Back at his car, Vic wiped his shoes carefully of dust, took a look at them for scratches and blood, and then checked the sides of his car. His car had been through many overgrown lanes, including this one, however, in the summer months of fullest foliage, and the fenders and sides had many scratches, if anyone cared to examine the car for scratches. There was no new deep scratch from this trip today.

'Hop in, Roger!' Vic said, and Roger, who loved cars, hopped obediently into the front seat and stood up looking out of the open side window. Vic drove back slowly through the narrow road, honking providently at the sharpest corner in case another car had been approaching, but there was no car, and he would not have been in the least alarmed if there had been, he thought. It probably would have been someone he knew or had a nodding acquaintance with, and they would have offered politely to back out of each other's way, and Vic would have ended by backing, and he would have smiled and passed the time of day and gone on.

Vic drove to Ballinger, to the square, vine-covered high school building where a half dozen school buses stood parked at the side of the gravel driveway. Parents were still arriving in cars and on foot, but they were hurrying as if they were late. It was five minutes to twelve. Vic parked behind one of the buses and went into the side entrance of the building, where the other parents were going, producing the white card that Trixie had given him nearly a week ago. Admit two, said the card.

'Hi, there, Vic!'

Vic turned around and saw Charles Peterson and his wife. 'Hello! Is Janey singing?'

'No. She's got the whooping cough,' Charles said. 'We're here to see a couple of her friends who're in it and make her a report.'

'Janey's sick because she can't sing today,' Katherine Peterson said. 'I certainly hope Trixie doesn't come down with the whooping cough. She spent two afternoons with Janey in the last five days.'

'Trixie's had it,' Vic said. 'Have you tried Adamson's Elixir? It tastes like raspberry syrup and Janey'll love it.'

'No, we haven't,' Charles Peterson said.

'Comes in an old-fashioned bottle. You can get it at the little drugstore on Church Street. The main drugstore won't have it. We had to ration it out to Trix or she'd have drunk the whole bottle at once. And it really helps the whooping cough.'

'Adamson's Elixir. We'll remember that,' Charles said.

Vic waved to them, and moved a little away, so that he could seat himself somewhere alone in the auditorium. He greeted two or three more mothers of friends of Trixie's whom he knew very slightly, but he managed to sit next to people whom he did not know. He preferred to be alone while he listened to the chorus that Trixie was in, but it was not because of what he had just done at the quarry, he thought. He would always have preferred to be alone at such a thing. The auditorium had elongated panelled windows on either side, a balcony above, and a huge stage that dwarfed the massed figures of the children, none of whom was more than ten years old. He listened appreciatively to a chorus singing the lullaby from *Hansel and Gretel*, and then to a rollicking camp-fire song whose words were about marshmallows, woods and trees, sunsets and midnight swims. Then a sweet, melodic lullaby of Schubert, and then the Highland School singing Saint-Saëns's 'The Swan'.

Over the wa – ter the – snow – white swan . . .

They were little boys and little girls together, and though the boys seemed shriller, the girls were louder and more enthusiastic. They glided smoothly into the repeated chorus which he had heard Trixie humming around the house for weeks. And then, as the final lines dwindled away, symbolizing the disappearing swan, it seemed to Vic that he could hear Trixie's voice alone from the crowded stage. Trixie was in the first row, standing every now and then on tiptoe, her face with its open mouth upturned.

The swan – like mist has gone – with the light – the light . . .

It seemed to him that she was singing in joyous celebration of Cameron's disappearance, instead of the swan's. As well she might, he thought.

22

When Vic came home that day from his office Melinda was on the telephone in her room. She hung up almost as soon as he had closed the door, and came into the living-room with a frowning, irritated expression on her face.

'Hello,' Vic said to her. 'How're you today?'

'Fine,' Melinda said. She had a cigarette in one hand and a drink in the other.

Trixie came out of her room. 'Hi, Daddy! Did you hear me?'

'I certainly did! You were fine. I could hear you over everybody else!' He swung her up into the air.

'But we didn't win first prize!' she yelled, kicking and giggling.

Vic dodged her sturdy little brown shoes and set her down. 'You won second. What's the matter with that?'

'It isn't first!'

'You have a point. Well, I thought you were fine. It sounded beautiful.'

'I'm pretty glad it's over,' Trixie said, closing her eyes and languidly wiping her forehead, a gesture she had learned from her mother.

'Why?'

'I'm pretty sick of that song.'

'I'll bet you are.'

Melinda sighed heavily, impatient as usual with their conversation. 'Trixie, *why* don't you go into your room?'

Trixie looked at her, feigning more affront than she really felt, Vic thought, then went skipping off down the hall to her room. It was always a surprise to Vic that Trixie obeyed Melinda, and it was always a reassurance that Trixie's extroverted psyche was practically indestructible.

'Well, I got Brian off at eleven,' Vic said. He reached into the inside pocket of his jacket and brought out Brian's poem. 'He asked me to give you this. It's a poem he wrote last night.'

Melinda took it with a sour, absent expression, frowned at it for a moment, then dropped it on the cocktail table. She strolled towards a window with her glass in her hand. She had on high heels, a narrow black skirt, a fresh white cotton blouse, and she looked as if she had dressed to go out to meet someone, though she had rolled the sleeves of the blouse up part way, untidily, in some moment of impatience.

'Did you have your car greased yet?' Vic asked.

'No.'

'Would you like me to take it tomorrow? It should've been done about ten days ago.'

'No, I don't want you to take it.'

'Well – did you start the divorce proceedings today?' Vic asked.

She waited a long while, then said, 'No, I did not.'

'Is Cameron coming over tonight?'

'He might.'

Vic nodded, though there was no one to see him, because Melinda's back was turned. 'At what time? For dinner?'

'I don't happen to know!'

The telephone rang and Melinda dashed for it in her room.

'Hello? Who? ... Oh ... No, he's not, but I'm expecting to hear from him. Shall I have him call you? ... I see ... Yes ... Well, I wish I knew, too. He was supposed to call me this afternoon ... Listen! If you do hear from him, please have him call *me*. Will you? ... Thanks. Good-bye, Mr Ferris.'

Melinda came back into the living-room, got her glass from the window-sill, and took it into the kitchen to refill it. Vic sat down with the evening paper. He could have used a drink, but it was a small point of discipline to him this evening to forgo a drink. Melinda came back with her fresh drink and sat down on the sofa. Ten minutes or so passed in silence. Vic had made up his mind not to say anything more about Cameron, or to say anything about the telephone call from Ferris, or about any other telephone call that might come.

And then the telephone rang again, and Melinda ran into her bedroom. 'Hello?' she said hopefully. 'Oh, hi ... *No*, have you heard? ... Oh ... *Gosh!*' she exploded with such surprise that Vic tensed the least bit. 'That's funny ... That's not like him at all ... I know, Don, and I'm terribly sorry, but I've been waiting for *him*. I called June earlier, you know, around six ... No, nothing, I didn't do a damned thing all day – except wait ... Yes,' with a sigh.

Vic could imagine the conversation. Don had probably asked Melinda and Cameron for cocktails, a celebratory cocktail hour after they had started the divorce papers. The last 'Yes' would be in answer to the question whether Vic was here. Vic had heard the same 'Yes' many times before.

'I'm sorry, Don ... Give Ralph my regards ...'

There would be a little cloud over the enemy camp tonight.

When Melinda came in, Vic broke his resolution, and asked, 'Did Cameron run out?'

'He probably had to work late somewhere.'

'He's probably run out,' Vic said.

'On *what?*'

'On you.'

'My eye he has.'

'It's a great strain on a man. You don't seem to realize it. I don't think Cameron can take it.'

'What's a strain?'

'What Cameron was trying to do. He's probably used one of those tickets to Mexico City,' Vic said, and saw Melinda stop her pacing and look at him, and he could read in her face as easily as if it were printed there that she was thinking it remotely possible that he had done that. Then she said:

'Since you seem to be interested, he left his car in Wesley unlocked with the window open and papers and stuff on the seat. So I doubt if he's gone to Mexico.'

'Oh. Well, I'm not very interested. I just think he's run out and I doubt very much if you'll hear from him again.'

Roger came and sat down at Vic's feet, smiling up at him as if they had a very funny private joke. Vic reached down and scratched his head.

'Roger been fed?' he asked.

'I don't happen to know.'

'You been fed, Roger?' he asked, then got up and went down the hall and knocked on Trixie's door.

'Come in?'

Trixie was propped up comfortable against her pillows, reading a book.

'Did you feed Roger?'

'Uh-huh. At five o'clock.'

'Uh-huh. Thank you. You didn't give him too much again, did you?'

'He wasn't sick,' Trixie said coolly, arching her eyebrows.

'Well, that's fine. And how about you? Aren't you getting hungry?'

'I want to eat with you and Mommie!' she said, beginning to frown, already protesting the possibility that she might have to eat earlier and alone.

'Well, I'm not sure Mommie's going to eat here. She might be having dinner with Tony somewhere.'

'Good. Then we'll eat together.'

Vic smiled. 'All right. Do you want to come in and help me fix dinner?'

He and Trixie fixed dinner for three, and set the table for three, though Melinda refused to sit down with them. Melinda had not done any marketing, so Vic had opened one of the cans of whole chicken that had been sitting on the shelf for a forgotten length of time. He had also opened a bottle of Niersteiner Domthal from the back of the liquor closet and poured some for Trixie and himself into stemmed glasses over a couple of ice cubes. He had made mashed sweet potatoes topped with toasted marshmallows, because Trixie loved them. Vic and Trixie had a long discussion about wines, how they were made and why they were different colours, and Trixie got tipsy enough to insist on classifying root beer as a wine, really her favourite, she said, so Vic let her call it a wine without correcting her.

'What're you doing, getting the child drunk?' Melinda asked, passing by them with her fourth or fifth drink.

'Oh, a glass and a half,' Vic said. 'She'll sleep better. You should consider it a blessing.'

Melinda disappeared into the living-room, but Vic could feel her frustration building up in the atmosphere of the house. He would not have been surprised to hear the crash of a hurled lamp, or the splashing sound of a magazine flung against the wall, or simply the sound of the front door being wrenched open, followed by the cool draught that would sweep through the house when she left the door open to stroll out on the lawn, or perhaps to get into her car to go God knew where. Then Trixie got the giggles and nearly choked trying to tell him about a boy in school who could carry his books in the seat of his pants.

Vic heard Melinda making a telephone call, and at that particular moment Vic wanted a cigarette, so he went into the living-room to get it, and heard enough of what Melinda was saying to know that she was calling Cameron's hotel in Wesley to ask if they had received any message from him. They hadn't. Vic went back to serve Trixie her favourite dessert – plain sugared whipped cream, which Vic had whipped with his own hands, spiralled into a little bowl and crowned with a maraschino cherry.

He had some more wine with his cigarette and went on chatting amiably with Trixie, though she was nearly falling asleep in her chair.

'What're you two celebrating?' Melinda asked, leaning in the doorway between the living-room and the dining alcove.

'Life,' Vic said. 'Wine.' He lifted the glass.

Melinda straightened up slowly. She had bitten her lipstick off, and she had that vagueness of outline that was not so much that her make-up was slipping as that her mind was becoming fuddled. Vic stared at her, wondering if the fuzziness emanated from her eyes, which were always the first indication to him of how much she had drunk. But her eyes stared directly at him now. 'What did you say to Tony?' she asked.

'I didn't see Tony today,' Vic said.

'No?'

'No.'

'*Tony pony!*' Trixie yelled, giggling.

Melinda lifted her glass and took a big swallow, making a face afterwards. 'What did you tell him?' she demanded.

'Nothing, Melinda.'

'Didn't you see him in Wesley?'

Vic wondered if Don had happened to see them. 'No,' he said.

'What're you so happy about tonight?'

'Because Tony isn't there!' Trixie squealed.

'Shut up, Trixie! What did you do to him?' Melinda asked, advancing on Vic.

'Do to him? I haven't seen him.'

'Where were you all afternoon?'

'I was at the office,' Vic said.

Melinda went into the kitchen for another drink.

Trixie drowsed in her chair. Vic moved his chair closer to hers, to catch her if she toppled.

Melinda came back with a kind of frozen, drunken horror on her face as if she had just seen something terrible in the kitchen, and Vic was about to ask her what had happened, when she said, 'Did you kill him? Did you kill him, too?'

'Melinda, don't be absurd.'

'Tony wouldn't be afraid to call me. Tony wouldn't forget. Tony's not afraid of anything, not even you!'

'I didn't think he was afraid of me,' Vic said. 'That's obvious.'

'That's why I know he didn't forget!' Melinda said, beginning to sound breathless. 'That's why I know something's happened to him! And I'm going to tell *everybody* – right now!' She set her glass down hard on the table, and at that instant there was a deep, sleepy roll of thunder, and Vic immediately thought that the rain tonight – and he had noticed that it looked like rain since about four o'clock – would wash away the tread marks of his tyres, if any, on the dirt road, and a very good rain would help to wash away the bloodstains on the white rocks.

Melinda was in her room, getting her coat, he supposed. He was not in the least afraid of what she might say to anyone, but he was afraid that something might happen to her if she drove her car in this state. Vic was getting up to go to her room when he saw Trixie lean sideways, and with a swoop of his left arm he caught her and softened the bob of her heavy head. He settled her head on his shoulder and walked to Melinda's room.

'I don't think you should drive in this condition, Melinda,' he said.

'I've driven in worse. Do you know if the Mellers are in?'

He gave an involuntary laugh. The Mellers were farther out of the way than the Cowans or the MacPhersons, who were in the direction of Wesley and Ralph and the Wilsons, and so she had asked him the question to save herself a trip. He looked at her as she bent over her dressing-table, gathering lipstick and keys, swaying in her cream-coloured topcoat, and he suddenly felt that he didn't care what happened to her tonight, because she was going out to denounce him again and it would serve her right to smash herself into a tree or to get stuck in a ditch on a fast turn. Then he thought of the hairpin turn on the hillside halfway between their house and the Mellers'. There was a cliff there, and the road would be slippery tonight. He thought of Cameron's body at the end of its fall, bouncing noiselessly off the final slope and rolling to a dead stillness. 'Where do you want to go?' he asked. 'I'll drive you.'

'Thanks!' She whirled around and her eyes struggled to find him. She frowned and blinked. 'Thanks a lot!' she shouted, the words incongruously sharp and clear.

Vic was sliding his hand nervously up and down Trixie's soft, overalled thigh. Suddenly he turned and carried Trixie to her room, laid her down gently on her bed, and came back to Melinda's room just in time to collide with her as she was rushing out of the door. The impact staggered them both back, and then Vic lost his head, or perhaps his temper, and the next thing he realized was that he was on top of Melinda on the bed, trying to hold her arms, pinning one arm down but failing to catch the other.

'You're in no condition to drive!' he shouted.

Melinda's knee was against his chest, and suddenly it pushed him with an amazing force and he was catapulted backwards, nearly somersaulted backwards, and he heard an explosive crack in his ears. Then there was some kind of lull, during which he was aware that he was smiling foolishly, and he saw the weave of her grey rug very distinctly for a moment beside his shoe, and realized that he was trying to get himself from one knee on to his feet. He staggered a little and noticed on the grey rug nearly a dozen red dots, heard the upward whine of Melinda's car starting outside, which was peculiarly nauseating, and then he felt his warm blood sliding down the back of his collar.

He stood up and headed mechanically for the bathroom. The whiteness of his face frightened him so that he stopped looking at it. He felt the wet back of his head, feeling for the wound. It was like a wide, smiling mouth in his hair, and he knew it would need stitches. He debated pouring a whisky before he telephoned for a doctor, versus possibly fainting before he could get the whisky and make the call, stupidly spent about a minute debating, and then went directly to Melinda's telephone.

He dialled the operator, and asked her to dial Dr Franklin, then on second thoughts Dr Sewell, another Little Wesley doctor, because he didn't want Dr Franklin to see another domestic crisis involving the Van Allens. Vic had never spoken before to Dr Sewell, so he introduced himself first.

'Hello, Dr Sewell. This is Victor Van Allen on Pendleton Road ... Yes. I'm very fine. How are you?' The pale peach-coloured wall in front of Vic was disintegrating, but he kept his voice very steady. 'I wondered if you could possibly come out to the house tonight and bring some equipment to do a few stitches?'

23

Vic had sometimes wondered what would happen if he, or Horace Meller, someone with fairly regular habits, were suddenly and inexplicably to disappear. He had wondered how soon anybody would become alarmed and just how logically the investigation would be conducted. He was going to have an opportunity to find out in the case of Cameron.

The morning after he had cut his head, while he was breakfasting with Trixie, the telephone rang and he answered it, but hearing a murmur from Melinda and then a voice say, 'Good morning, Mrs Van Allen. This is Bernard Ferris,' he hung up. A few minutes later, Melinda stormed through the dining-room on the way to the kitchen for her orange juice.

'That was Tony's client,' she said to Vic. 'He says Tony's company's going to make a *thorough* investigation.'

Vic said nothing. He felt a trifle weak from loss of blood, he thought, or it may have been the sleeping pill the doctor had given him last night that made his head a little fuzzy. He had slept so soundly he had not even heard Melinda come in.

'What's the matter?' Trixie asked Vic. She was still round-eyed with surprise at seeing the bandage on his head, though Vic had made light of it and told her that he bumped it in the kitchen.

'Tony seems to be missing,' Vic said.

'They don't know where he is?'

'Nope. It looks like they don't.'

Trixie started to smile. 'You mean he's hiding somewhere?'

'Probably,' Vic said.

'Why?' Trixie asked.

'I don't know. Can't imagine.'

From Melinda's haste around the house that morning, Vic supposed that she had an appointment with somebody, perhaps Mr Ferris. He supposed Cameron's company would send a detective up, today or tomorrow. Vic went off to work at the usual time. Stephen and Carlyle and the garbage collector who removed scraps from the printing plant asked Vic about his head, because he was sporting a fat, disc-shaped bandage in the very spot where monks usually have their heads shaved, and Vic told them all that he had risen up under a metal cabinet door in the kitchen and given himself an awful dig.

Around five o'clock in the afternoon Melinda arrived with a detective who introduced himself as Pete Havermal from the Star Investigation Bureau in New York. The detective said that a Mr Grant Houston of Wesley had seen Cameron getting into a car which Vic was driving on the main street of Wesley at some time between eleven and twelve yesterday morning.

'Yes,' Vic said. 'That's correct. I ran into Tony after I'd dropped a friend off at the—'

'What do you mean, you ran into him?' the detective interrupted rudely.

'I mean that I saw him, coming out of a tobacco store, I think, crossing the street almost in front of my car, and I stopped and said hello to him. I asked him if I could give him a lift anywhere.'

'Why didn't you tell me that last night?' Melinda asked in a loud voice. 'He told me he hadn't seen Tony all day!' she informed the detective.

'He said his car was right there,' Vic went on, 'but he wanted to talk to me about something, so he got in.'

'Uh-huh. And where did you go?' asked Havermal.

'Well – nowhere. We wouldn't have moved at all if we could've stayed there. But I wasn't parked.'

'Where did you go?' the detective repeated, beginning to make notes in a tablet. He was a pudgy yet tough-looking man, pig-eyed, businesslike, somewhere in his early forties. He looked as if he could get rough, if he had to.

'I think we circled a couple of blocks – to the southeastward, to be exact.' Vic turned to Carlyle, who was standing by the door to the press room, listening spellbound, with his spittoon in his hands. 'This isn't important, Carlyle. You can go,' Vic said.

Carlyle limped back into the press room with the spittoon.

'You went around a couple of blocks,' said the detective. 'For how long?'

'Oh, possibly fifteen minutes or so.'

'And then what?'

'Then I dropped Mr Cameron back at his car.'

'Oh, really,' Melinda said.

'Did he get into the car?' the detective asked.

Vic pretended to try to remember. 'I can't say, because I don't think I watched him.'

'And what time was this?'

'I'd say eleven-thirty.'

'And then what did you do?'

'I drove to Ballinger to hear my daughter sing in a school contest.'

'Uh-huh. What time was that?'

'Just before twelve. The contest started at twelve.'

'Were you there, Mrs Van Allen?'

'No,' Melinda said.

'See anybody you knew at the school contest?' asked the detective, squinting at him out of one pig eye.

'No ... Oh, yes, the Petersons. We chatted a little bit.'

'Petersons,' Havermal said, writing. 'And what time was that?'

Vic was tired of it. He gave a laugh. 'I just don't know – exactly. Maybe the Petersons would know.'

'Um-m. And what did Cameron want to talk to you about?'

Vic again pretended to try to think. 'He asked me – Oh, yes, whether I thought there was going to be more building around Ballinger or around Wesley in the next few years. I told him I honestly couldn't say. There hadn't been much lately.'

'What else did he talk about?'

'You're wasting your time!' Melinda put in to Havermal.

'I don't know. He seemed a little nervous to me, a little ill at ease. He said something about starting his own contracting business around here because he liked the country. He wasn't very definite.'

Melinda snorted with disbelief. 'I never heard him say anything about starting a business up here.'

'How did he seem nervous?' Havermal asked. 'Did he tell you why he was nervous or mention anything he was going to do that day?'

'I'll tell you one thing he was going to do, Mr Havermal,' Vic began, deliberately letting his anger show. 'He was going to meet my wife, who was going to start divorce proceedings against me for the purpose of marrying Mr Cameron. They had aeroplane tickets for Mexico City. You look as if you hadn't heard that. Didn't my wife tell you? Or did she just tell you that I killed Mr Cameron?'

It was easy to see from the detective's expression that Melinda hadn't told him anything about a divorce. Havermal looked from one to the other of them. 'Is that true, Mrs Van Allen?'

'Yes, that's true,' she said, sullenly emphatic.

'I don't think there's any need to ask me or anybody else why Mr Cameron was ill at ease with me,' Vic went on. 'The wonder is that he could have asked my opinion about his business plans or got in my car at all.'

'Or that you would have asked to give him a lift,' the detective said.

Vic sighed. 'I try to be polite – most of the time. Mr Cameron has been a frequent guest at our house, you know. Perhaps my wife told you that. If you want to know why I denied having seen Cameron Monday, it was because I was sick of him, and because he'd stood my wife up on a date they'd had that evening, and she was upset and on the way to being drunk. I didn't want to discuss Cameron with her. I think you can understand.'

Havermal looked at Melinda. 'You say you've known Cameron about a month?'

'About,' Melinda said.

'And you intended to marry him?' Havermal was looking at her as if he had begun to doubt her sanity.

'Yes,' she said, hanging her head like a guilty schoolgirl for a moment, then jerking it up again.

'How long ago did you decide to marry him?' the detective asked.

'Just a few days ago,' Vic volunteered.

The detective looked at Vic sharply. 'I guess you didn't like Cameron.'

'I did not,' Vic said.

'Cameron, you know, disappeared some time before one o'clock yesterday. He had a lunch appointment he didn't keep,' Havermal said.

'No, I didn't know,' Vic said, as if he didn't care either.

'Yeah. He did.'

Vic took a cigarette from a pack on his desk. 'Well, he was a very strange fellow,' he remarked, deliberately using the past tense. 'Always trying to be friendly, always trying to keep on the good side of me, God knows why. Isn't that true, Melinda?' he asked ingenuously.

She was scowling at him. 'You had time to – to do something to him between eleven-fifteen and twelve.'

'On Commerce Street in the middle of Wesley?' Vic asked.

'You had time to go somewhere else. Nobody saw you drop him back at his car,' she said.

'How do you know? Have you asked everybody in Wesley?' Vic continued to the detective, 'I couldn't do anything to Cameron that he didn't want me to do. He was twice as big as I am.'

The detective was keeping a thoughtful silence.

'He gave me the impression of being scared yesterday,' Vic said, 'perhaps scared of what he'd started with my wife. I think he may have run out on the whole thing.'

'You didn't maybe tell him to run out, Mr Van Allen?' asked Havermal.

'No, indeed. I didn't even mention my wife.'

'Tony doesn't scare, anyway,' Melinda said proudly.

Havermal still looked astounded. 'Did you see Cameron at any time again yesterday?'

'No,' Vic said. 'I spent the afternoon here.'

'How did you hurt your head?' Havermal asked unsympathetically.

'Oh, I bumped it on a cabinet in the kitchen.' Vic looked at Melinda and smiled a little.

'Oh.' He stared at Vic for a minute with professional inscrutability. The narrow gash of his mouth might have been smiling, or smirking, or expressing contempt. One couldn't tell. 'Okay, Mr Van Allen. I guess that's all for the moment. I'll be back again.'

'Any time.' Vic walked with the detective and Melinda to the door.

No doubt the detective was off to ask Melinda some questions about her relationship with Cameron. It would certainly put a different light on the story. Vic sighed and smiled, wondering what would happen next.

There was a small photograph of Cameron – square-faced, unsmiling, a little startled-looking, suggesting his expression just before he had gone over the edge of the quarry – in the evening edition of the *New Wesleyan*. It was captioned 'Have You Seen This Man?' 'Friends' of Cameron had reported his disappearance late the previous evening. His company, Pugliese-Markum Contractors, Inc., of New York, was making a thorough search for him and had sent an investigator to Wesley. 'It is feared, in view of the physical nature of his work, that some accident may have befallen him,' the paper ventured.

Horace called Vic a little after seven and asked him if he knew where Cameron might be or what might have happened to him. Vic said that he didn't and after that Horace did not seem much interested in the story. He asked Vic if he and Melinda could come over for dinner, because a friend of theirs who was in Maine had just sent a barrel of lobsters packed in ice. Vic declined with thanks, and said that dinner was already under way at the house. Vic had got the dinner under way, but Melinda was not at home. He supposed she was with the detective or the Wilsons and might not call or be back at all.

Less than an hour later, as Vic and Trixie were finishing their meal together, a car drove up outside. It was Horace, angry. Vic knew what had happened.

'Can we go in your room, Vic? Or somewhere? I don't want—' He glanced at Trixie.

Vic went over to Trixie, put his arm around her, and kissed her cheek. 'Would you excuse me, Trix? Got some business to talk over. Drink your milk, and if you have any more of that cake, make it a small piece. Understand?'

They crossed the garage and went into Vic's room. Vic offered Horace his one comfortable chair, but Horace did not want to sit down. Vic sat on his bed.

'We've just had a visit from the detective – as you've probably guessed,' Horace said.

'Oh. Was Melinda with him?'

'No. She spared us that. Well, she's accusing you again!' Horace burst out. 'I came very near throwing Mr Havermeyer, or whoever he is, out of the house. I did throw him out finally, but not before I'd said a few things to him. And so did Mary.'

'His name's Havermal. It's not his fault. It's just his job.'

'Oh, no. This fellow's the kind who'd inspire anybody to punch his nose. Of course, it doesn't help to have him sitting in your living-room asking you if you don't think your best friend could have got angry enough to kill somebody. Or at least shanghai him out of town. I told him Vic Van Allen wouldn't have bothered. I said perhaps Mr Cameron saw a blonde he thought he'd like better than Melinda and went off with her to another town!'

Vic smiled.

'What's this about you being the last person who saw him?'

'I don't know. Was I? I saw him at about eleven-thirty yesterday.'

Horace shrugged his narrow shoulders. 'They can't seem to find anybody who saw him after twelve. And to think, Vic, I had to listen to that juvenile business about Melinda getting a divorce in order to marry him! I told Havermal he'd better not spread that around. I told him I knew Melinda as well as I knew you – almost – and I know she makes wild threats when she gets angry.'

'I'm not sure it was just a threat, Horace. Melinda seemed pretty set on a divorce a few days ago.'

'What? Well, the fact remains, she didn't start one. I know

because I asked. I asked Havermal what he'd found to substantiate the divorce idea. He hadn't found anything.'

Vic kept silent.

Finally, Horace sat down. 'Well, Vic – just what happened
when you picked up Cameron and drove him around?'

Vic felt his eyes widen in a protective stare. 'Nothing. Melinda
wasn't mentioned. He was making conversation. It was the first
time I'd seen him act a little unsure of himself. You see, Horace,'
Vic continued, pushing his luck with Horace just as he had
pushed it with Havermal, 'that's what makes me think Melinda
was telling me the truth when she said she was going to get a
divorce. Matter of fact, she was supposed to start the divorce yesterday. She may not have had an appointment with a lawyer, but
she was going to start it yesterday, she told me. Then she mentioned Cameron's having two tickets for Mexico City, and she
was going with him. No wonder Cameron wasn't comfortable
with me. He didn't have to get in my car, of course, but you know
the way he is. He acts first and thinks later, if at all. It crossed my
mind that he might have had a date with Melinda at some
lawyer's office yesterday afternoon. He'd be just crass enough to
go up there and sit with her while they got the papers started.'

Horace shook his head in disgust.

'But, as I said to the roving detective, Cameron might also
have run out on the whole thing. He'd have to run out on his job,
too. At least on this assignment. He couldn't have faced Melinda
in Little Wesley after running out.'

'No. I see what you mean,' Horace said thoughtfully. 'That's
probably just what he's done.'

Vic got up and opened a cabinet in the bottom of his desk. 'I
think you could use a drink, couldn't you?' He always knew when
Horace could use a drink. 'I'll go over and get some ice.'

'No, thanks. No ice for me. I'll take this for medicinal pur-
poses – and it always seems more medicinal without ice.'

Vic got a glass from the top of his desk, washed it in his tiny bathroom, and took his own tooth glass for himself. He poured three fingers for each of them. Horace sipped his appreciatively.

'I need this,' Horace said. 'I seem to take these things harder than you do.'

'You seem to,' Vic said, smiling.

'And you're in for another. It's like after the De Lisle business.'

'A big year for the detective agencies,' Vic said, and saw Horace look at him. Horace had still not asked him outright if Carpenter had been a detective.

'It's funny that Cameron's company doesn't look for him in New York, or Miami, or wherever a fellow like Cameron would go,' Horace said. 'Or Mexico City. Well – maybe they are looking.'

Vic deliberately changed the subject, slightly, by talking about the likelihood of finding a man who had chosen, say, to go to Australia to hide himself. The chances would be practically nil that he would be found, if he could get round the immigration authorities and enter Australia. They went on into the subject of individual blood chemistry. Horace said they could now identify an individual from a bit of his dried blood found on something perhaps months after his disappearance. Vic had also heard about that.

'But suppose you haven't the person?' Vic asked, and Horace laughed.

Vic thought of Cameron's blood on the white rocks of the quarry, and of Cameron some forty feet below in the water. If they found the blood, they would logically look for the body in the water, but perhaps there would be no blood left in the body, and no skin left on the fingertips. But Cameron might be identifiable. Vic wished he could go and take another look at the blood spots, do what he could to obliterate them, but he didn't dare go to the quarry for fear he might be seen. It seemed the only careless, stupid thing he had ever done in his life – to leave a trace where he had not wanted to leave a trace, to have failed to do properly something of such importance.

By the time Horace got up to leave he was laughing. But it was not quite like Horace's usual laughter. He said with an effort at cheerfulness, 'Well, we've weathered a lot, haven't we, Vic? They'll find Cameron somewhere. The police must have been alerted in all the big towns. They always are.'

Vic thanked him for his visit, and then he was gone. Vic stood in the garage, listening to his car going into the distance and thinking that Horace had not asked him where Melinda was or when she was coming back, knowing that Vic probably wouldn't have known and that questions would have embarrassed him. Vic went over to his snail aquaria.

Hortense and Edgar were making love, Edgar reaching down from a little rock to kiss Hortense on the mouth. Hortense was reared on the end of her foot, swaying a little under his caress like a slow dancer enchanted by music. Vic watched for perhaps five minutes, thinking of absolutely nothing, not even of the snails, until he saw the cup-shaped excrescences start to appear on the right side of both the snails' heads. How they did adore each other, and how perfect they were together! The glutinous cups grew larger and touched, rim to rim. Their mouths drew apart.

Vic looked at his watch. Five minutes to ten. It struck him as a strangely depressing time of the evening. The house was utterly silent. He wondered if Trixie was asleep? He cleared his throat and the small, rational sound was as noisy as a foot over gravel.

The snails made no sound. Hortense was shooting her dart first. She missed. Or was that part of the game? After a few moments, Edgar tried, missed, drew back and struck again, hitting the right spot so that the dart went in, which inspired Hortense to try again, too. She had a harder time, aiming upwards, but she made it after three deliberate and patient tries. Then as if shocked into a profounder trance, their heads went back a little, their tentacles drew almost in, and Vic knew that if they had had lidded eyes they would have been closed. The snails were motionless now. He stared at them until he saw the first signs that the rims of their cups were going to separate. Then he walked up and down the garage floor for a minute, suffering an unaccustomed sense of restlessness. His mind turned to Melinda, and he went to the snails again to keep himself from thinking of her.

A quarter to eleven. Was she at the Wilsons'? Were all the jaws working at once? Was the detective there, or would he have gone to bed after his hard day? Would anyone possibly think of the quarry?

Vic bent over the snails, looking at them now through a hand magnifying lens. They were connected only by the two darts. They would stay like this for at least another hour, he knew. Tonight he hadn't their patience. He went into his room to read.

24

Hortense spent twenty-four hours laying her eggs about five days later, and Detective Havermal was still prowling the community, doing a far more thorough and out-in-the-open job than Carpenter had done on the De Lisle case. Havermal visited the Cowans, the MacPhersons, the Stephen Hineses, the Petersons, old Carlyle, Hansen the grocer, Ed Clarke the hardware store proprietor (Vic was highly respected at Clarke's Hardware and probably spent more money there than any other of Ed's customers), Sam at the Lord Chesterfield bar, Wrigley, the newsdealer who delivered papers to the Van Allens, and Pete Lazzari and George Anderson, the two garbage men who collected from the printing plant and the Van Allen house, respectively. Havermal visited them with his purpose more or less obvious, Vic gathered – to make Vic responsible for Cameron's disappearance – and he asked direct questions. The general attitude of the interrogated, Vic learned, was one of extreme caution in making any statements to Havermal and also one of resentment. It was unfortunate for Havermal that his personality was so antagonizing. Even the garbage collectors, simple men, grasped the import of Havermal's insinuations, and reacted negatively.

Said Pete Lazzari to Vic, 'I ain't interested in what Mrs Van Allen does, I sez. I know she drinks some, that's all. You're tryin' to nail a guy for murder. *That's* pretty interestin'. I known Mr Van Allen six years, I sez, and you won't find a nicer guy in town. I heard of punks like you, I sez to him. You know where you belong? I sez. On my truck along with the rest of the muck!' Pete Lazzari was all torso and no legs, and could toss loaded ash-cans of garbage twelve feet into the air over the rim of his truck like nothing.

On his second visit to the Mellers', Horace turned him away at the door. Stephen Hines gave him a lecture on the English principle of law that a man is innocent until he is proved guilty, and on its deterioration in America because of unlettered, base-minded persons like Havermal.

Melinda informed Vic that the air-lines had been checked and that Tony had not taken any plane. But Cameron had bought two tickets. Havermal had found that out, and also the fact that they were under the names of Mr and Mrs Anthony Cameron.

'He might have turned his ticket in and bought another ticket under another name,' Vic said.

'No, he couldn't,' Melinda said triumphantly. 'You have to have a Tourist Card to get into Mexico, and they look at the card before the plane leaves New York. Tony told me.'

Vic smiled. 'Remember the story the Cowans told us when they went to Mexico a couple of years ago? Evelyn had lost her birth certificate and they hadn't time to get one for her, so they just told the clerk at the Mexican Consulate their names, and he wrote out Tourist Cards for them without asking for any identification at all. That Tourist Card business is just a way of mulcting three dollars, or whatever it is, from every tourist who enters Mexico. Otherwise they'd let you in on an ordinary passport just as any other country does.'

Melinda had no retort to that. She seemed restless and troubled, and there was an air of defeat about her as Havermal's stay in Little Wesley dragged on to a week. Havermal had exhausted everything there was to try. He had cruised the countryside around Wesley, Melinda said, in a radius of the distance a car could travel and still get to Ballinger in about thirty-five minutes. Vic did not know whether he had discovered the quarry or not – he must have used a map of the district, but Vic knew that some maps did not show the quarry – and this time Vic did not push his luck by asking Melinda if he had. It had rained heavily twice since Havermal had been in Little Wesley. There were rust stains on some of the flat rocks around the quarry where pieces of equipment had lain or were still lying. It would probably be hard to decide which stains were from blood and which from rust. It was incredible, Vic thought, that Havermal had not looked at the quarry by now, but perhaps he hadn't. He seemed to be spending a good half of his time cruising the roads, as Melinda said, and perhaps beating the underbrush for a body.

Havermal made one more call on Vic at the printing plant. He had nothing more concrete to throw at Vic than some critical statements that Don Wilson had made. 'Don Wilson thinks he's got your number. He thinks you killed De Lisle, too. It's pretty funny when a guy with a strong motive in both cases happens to be the last guy two *dead* guys are seen with,' said Havermal.

'You mean you've found Cameron's body?' asked Vic, wide-eyed, but really Havermal didn't even inspire him to get any fun out of the interview.

'Yeah, we found the body,' Havermal said, watching Vic so pointedly that Vic knew it wasn't so, but he followed through with an ingenuous:

'*Where?* Why didn't you say so?'

Insolently, Havermal made no answer, and after a few seconds went on to something else. When Don Wilson came up again, Vic said with a gentle smile:

'Don Wilson had better watch out. I could certainly sue him

for libel, and I don't think he could afford it. His wife's very sweet, don't you think?'

'And dumb,' Havermal commented.

'Well,' Vic said, still affable, 'I don't think you'll get much out of the people up here if you go around insulting them.'

'Thanks,' Havermal said in the tone of a honking goose.

'I'd like to thank you for one thing before you leave Little Wesley,' Vic said, 'and that is for showing me how solid the community is in – well, liking me. Not that I've even striven for the approval of the community or particularly craved it, but it's awfully nice to know it's there.'

Havermal left not long after that, without even a parting shot at him. Vic picked up the two cigarette butts that Havermal had ground out on the floor and dropped them in his waste-basket. Then he went back into the printing room. He was in the middle of arranging a dried skeleton of an oak leaf and a flattened basket-worm's cocoon in a graceful composition to serve as a colophon beneath one of Brian Ryder's poems.

Vic had another demonstration of community loyalty that evening. Hal Pfeiffer, editor of Wesley's *New Wesleyan*, called him to say that a detective named Havermal had been into his office to give a slanderous account of an investigation he had been making in regard to the Cameron case and the part in it 'possibly' played by Victor Van Allen and his wife, had offered his story ostensibly as local news, and Mr Pfeiffer had given him short shrift and had shown him the door.

'I've never met you, Mr Van Allen, but I've heard about you,' said Mr Pfeiffer over the telephone. 'I thought I'd tell you about this in case you were possibly worried about any such thing as this happening. The *New Wesleyan* doesn't want anything to do with characters like Havermal.'

Vic reported that to Melinda.

There was even a story from Vic's cleaners. When Vic went in to pick up some clothes that were ready, Fred Warner, the manager, leaned over the counter and whispered that 'that detective' had been in to have a look at any of Victor Van Allen's clothes that had been brought in lately. The detective had found a pair of trousers with blood on them, but Mrs Van Allen had been with him, and she had explained, Warner said, that the trousers were stained with Vic's own blood, because he had cut his head one evening.

'The bloodstains were all on the back part of the pants,' Warner said, chuckling, 'on the top part. Easy to see it was a couple of drips from a head accident, but you should've seen how disappointed that detective was! He's a real bloodhound – just not a very good one, eh, Mr Van Allen?'

And then Havermal suddenly left.

The whole town seemed to give a sigh of relief, Vic thought. People on the streets seemed to smile more, to smile at each other, as if to say that their solidarity had defeated one more detested outsider. Parties broke out. Even the Petersons invited Vic and Melinda to a party at which Vic met several people he had not met before, people who treated him with a great deal of respect. At this party – composed of people whom Melinda would ordinarily have tried to look down on – it first came to Vic's notice that Melinda was changing. She was not particularly warm or charming as she had been at parties after the De Lisle incident, but she smiled, even at him, she made no grimaces over the punch which he knew she loathed, and she did not insult anybody, as far as Vic knew. It set off some disjointed speculations in Vic's mind. She wasn't behaving herself to offset a bad public opinion of him now, because there wasn't any need of it. Was she simply tired of pretending to be sullen, worn out from emanating hatred? Hatred was a tiring emotion, but Melinda had nothing else to do with herself. Was she possibly pleased because he was rather a guest of honour at the Petersons' party? But she had never been pleased by anything like that before. Vic even wondered if she were in a conspiracy with Havermal to get him off guard and then spring some evidence that they hadn't yet told him about. But no, he had an overwhelming conviction that Havermal had shot his last bolt in Little Wesley and missed. There was nothing gloating about Melinda these days. She was just a bit sweeter, softer. Thinking back, Vic could recall even a few smiles from her at home. And she hadn't been to see Don Wilson for a week, Vic thought.

'How's Don Wilson?' Vic asked after they came home from the Petersons' party. 'You haven't mentioned him lately.'

'Did I ever mention him?' Melinda asked, but her voice was not belligerent.

'No. I guess you didn't,' Vic said. 'Well, how is he? Business all right?'

'Oh, he's stewing over something,' Melinda said in a curiously preoccupied tone that made Vic look at her. She was looking at him from the living-room sofa where she had sat down to remove her shoes. She was smiling a little. And she wasn't at all drunk. 'Why'd you ask?'

'Because I hadn't heard anything from him lately.'

'I guess you heard enough at one point. Havermal told me he told you what he'd said.'

'That wasn't the first time. I didn't mind.'

'Well – he didn't get anywhere, did he?'

Vic looked at her, bewildered, though he kept his calm, pleasant expression like a mask. 'He certainly didn't. Didn't you want him to get somewhere?'

'I suppose I wanted to know the truth.' She lighted a cigarette with her familiar arrogance, flinging the match at the fireplace and falling far short. 'Don seemed to have some good theories. I guess they were just theories.' She looked at him with a trace of self-consciousness, as if she didn't expect him to believe she meant it.

He didn't believe she meant it. She was playing some kind of game. Slowly he filled his pipe, letting several moments pass during which she might have gone on. He was not going to go on, but neither was he going to walk out to his room immediately, which was what he wanted to do.

'Well, you certainly were a hit tonight,' she said finally.

'David against the Goliaths. And little David won. Didn't I?' he asked with his ambiguous smile that he knew was still ambiguous to Melinda.

She was staring at him and visibly pondering her next move. It was a physical one. She slapped her hands together, got up, and said, 'What do you say we have an honest drink after all that pink lemonade? God, was it awful!' She started for the kitchen.

'Not for me, Melinda. It's a little late.'

'Two o'clock? What's come over you?'

'Sleepiness,' he said, smiling as he walked towards her. He kissed her cheek. She might have been a statue, but her immobility was probably more surprise than indifference, he thought. 'G'night, honey. I suppose Trixie's spending all day tomorrow at the Petersons', isn't she?' Trixie had gone to the Petersons' with Vic and Melinda, and around ten o'clock she had gone up to Janey's bedroom to sleep.

'I suppose.'

'Well, good night.' As he went out of the door into the garage, she was still standing there as if undecided whether to fix herself a drink alone or not.

The next surprise Vic got came from Horace, who told him that Melinda had been over to see Mary and had 'broken down' and said she was sorry for ever having said anything against Vic, that she regretted having shown herself such a fool and such a disloyal wife, and she wondered if she could ever live it down.

'She said "a fool in so many ways",' Horace amended, trying to remember it all verbatim for Vic. 'Mary even called me up at the lab to tell me about it.'

'Really,' Vic said, for the second time. 'I've noticed a change in her lately, but I never thought she'd come out with a repentance – and to Mary.'

'Well—' Horace seemed ashamed of his jubilant reaction. 'Mary said she couldn't have been nicer yesterday. I tried to call you last night to see if we could get together, but you were out.'

'Melinda and I took Trixie to a movie she wanted to see,' Vic replied.

Horace smiled as if he were pleased to hear that he and Melinda had gone to a movie together.

'I suppose things are looking up. You know, in just about two days, Horace, I'm going to have copies of the Ryder book and I'd like you to see it. You remember I told you I was using real feathers and leaves and insects to print from.'

'Of course, I remember! I thought I'd buy a copy to give to Mary as a Christmas present, if it was ready in time.'

'Oh, it'll be ready. I'll give you a copy for her. Apart from the feathers, the poems are pretty good, too.'

'I'll buy it. How's the Greenspur Press ever going to take in a nickel giving everything away?'

'As you like, Horace.'

'Well, Vic—'

They were standing on the corner of Main and Trumbull Streets, where they had run into each other. It was seven, dusk had come, and there was a chill mountain wind pouring on them from the east, an autumnal wind that made one – if one was in the right mood for it – feel vigorous and optimistic.

'Well, I'm glad Melinda talked to Mary,' Horace said. 'It made Mary feel a lot better. She wants so much to like you both, Vic.'

'I know.'

'She can't feel quite the same about Melinda yet – but I'm sure it'll come.'

'I hope so. Good to see you, Horace!'

They lifted a hand to each other and started for their cars.

Vic whistled on the way home. He didn't know how long Melinda's beatitude would last, but it was nice to go home and find dinner started, the living-room straightened, to get a pleasant hello and a smile.

25

The third of December was Vic's birthday. Vic hadn't thought of his birthday until 29 November, when he was calculating the day an order of sepia inks should arrive, and then he put his birthday out of his mind again, because he had heard no mention of it around the house. Two or three birthdays of his, in the past few years, had gone unnoticed except by Stephen and Carlyle, who always remembered and gave him a present, either singly or together. On 3 December, Stephen gave him a large and costly book of eighteenth-century English engravings, and Carlyle a bottle of brandy, which Vic opened at once and sampled with him.

Then when Vic walked from the garage into the living-room that evening, Melinda and Trixie and the Mellers greeted him with a roaring 'Happy Birthday!' The table was aglow with candles, and there was a big pink-and-white cake on it with little pink candles to the number, Vic supposed, of thirty-seven. He pocketed the sleeping snail that he had just found on the garage door-jamb as he came in. There was a heap of presents at one end of the sofa.

'My goodness!' Vic said. 'How'd you people get here? Fly?'

'I picked them up so you wouldn't see the car when you came in,' Melinda told him. She was wearing a very feminine and fetching black dress with black lace at the shoulders.

'And you'll have to deliver us,' Horace said. 'That means I can drink all I want to tonight. We've already started, I'm afraid, but we'll brim the glasses again and drink your health.'

They all sang a chorus of 'Happy Birthday, Dear Vic' to him with lifted glasses, and Roger barked all through it. Even Roger was sporting a red ribbon tied to the back of his collar. Then came the presents. Melinda handed him three tied-together boxes from Brooks Brothers, each of which contained a sweater – one a mustard-coloured coat sweater, one blue and red, which was an Italian import, and the third a white tennis sweater with a red stripe. Vic adored good sweaters. He was touched to the point of feeling a lump in his throat that Melinda had given him three. Horace gave him an electric razor, with the remark that he had been trying to convert him for years from his straight-edged razor and that he thought the only way was to put an electric razor in his hands. Then from Trixie an ebony brush and a comb, and from Roger a woollen tie. Mary gave him a latest edition of a carpenter and wood-worker's manual, a book Vic was never without, though he hadn't bought this edition.

'I wonder if I should give him his other present now or after dinner?' Melinda asked the Mellers anxiously.

The Mellers said to give it to him now, and Melinda went to her room and came back with a large box wrapped in gold paper. She set it down on the floor.

'I wasn't sure how it works, so I had it at the back of my closet in the dark,' she said.

Horace laughed. He and Mary obviously knew what it was and watched him expectantly as he unwrapped it and opened the corrugated box inside.

It was a Geiger counter complete with headphone, probe, and

shoulder strap. There were even ore samples. Vic was speechless, delighted. He went to Melinda and put his arm around her.

'Melinda – thanks,' he said, and pressed his lips against her cheek.

When he glanced at the Mellers, they were regarding him and Melinda with satisfied smiles, and Vic felt at once self-conscious and a little silly. Out of character, perhaps that was it. Because Melinda was out of character. She was acting, just as he had used to act, deliberately displaying an emotion or an attitude that was unlike the emotion or attitude he felt within himself. He and Melinda had essentially exchanged attitudes, Vic felt, since now he believed that his behaviour was truer to what he really felt than he had allowed it to be in years, and that Melinda was pretending her good will.

During the dinner – squabs, mashed potatoes, braised endives, and watercress salad – he tried to relax and really not to think, because he was groping in his mind for clues, for leads, as a man in a dark room that he has not been in before might grope for a light pull, knowing the light pull exists yet having no idea where. He was hoping that the aimless play of his brain might brush against the reason for Melinda's goodness. After De Lisle's death her decorum had been for the public, but this was for him. She was thoughtful and polite to him when there was nobody around to see her. But of course the public reaction to the second murder – it startled him a little that he called it 'murder' in his thoughts now – had been different, too. There had been a great deal more suspicion of him in regard to De Lisle than to Cameron. He had had it lucky that Havermal had been such an unpopular fellow. Havermal's story of the romance and intended elopement of Melinda and Cameron, therefore, had been considered highly suspect or greatly exaggerated by the majority of people who had heard it. Vic had been impressed by the fact that Trixie had not come home with a single canard against him. The only thing she had brought home to tell him was that one of her classmates had said that her parents had said that people liked to pick on people who were different from other people. Trixie had not really grasped what she was saying, and Vic had had to think to make sense of her words himself, but it seemed to be the old story of the conforming majority against the nonconformer, in this case his nonconformance being his income, he supposed, his nonprofitable publishing business, his tolerance of his wife's affairs, his televisionless household, and perhaps even his super-annuated car. Vic had given Trixie a talk then on persecuted minorities and individuals, with examples from history. Trixie was going to be a conformist *par excellence* after her childhood, Vic was sure, but he liked to think that he might have opened a small door in her mind about nonconformers. He had made the story of Galileo as interesting as he could.

When the time came to drive the Mellers home, Melinda wanted to go, too. That had not happened in years.

No one could have said the evening was not a success. The closest to it, Vic thought, had been the first birthday Melinda had celebrated in Little Wesley about nine years ago, when they had also invited the Mellers. But as he started out of the door into the garage with his sweaters and his Geiger counter he was struck by the contrast of his isolation now with his closeness to Melinda then, and he stopped, turned around, and went back into the living-room.

Melinda was in her bedroom, starting to remove her dress.

'I wasn't sure I thanked you enough,' Vic said. 'It's the nicest birthday I can remember.'

'I think you thanked me,' she said, smiling. 'Do you mind unfastening this? I can't reach the middle part.'

He put everything down on her bed and unhooked the rest of the hooks and eyes that went down the middle of her back. 'Who hooked you up?'

'Trixie. She's asleep now. Would you like a nightcap?'

A faint chill went up his spine. 'No, thanks. I thought I'd go over and try my counter on that crazy conglomerate rock in my room.'

'What rock?'

'I guess you haven't seen it. It's been there for months, though. In the corner by the filing cabinet.' She looked as if she were about to say, 'I want to go with you and look at it, too,' and he hoped she wouldn't.

She didn't. She looked from him down to the floor, then turned and began to pull her dress over her head.

'So I'll say good night,' Vic said, walking to the door.

'Good night, Vic. And happy birthday.'

He tried the counter, following the directions in the instruction book. After a moment he heard a click, then another, then a longer pause, and three more. The rocks in the conglomeration were of varying ages, of course. He put the set away, feeling tired and a little troubled. As soon as he lay down in bed, he thought of the way Melinda had asked him if he wanted a nightcap – tentatively, as if she didn't know him. Or was that it? He felt an echo of the same unpleasant chill. It was fear, and why did he have it? Just what had he to be afraid of if he had had a nightcap with her in her room, sat on her bed, perhaps even slept in her bed? His mind shied away from further imaginings, and returned to the fear he had felt. He didn't know why Melinda was being so friendly. That was part of it. He supposed it was the main part. He decided to proceed with even more caution – not be cold or unreceptive, just proceed with caution. Too often he had swallowed her bait and found himself wriggling on a hook. All he wanted was peace in the household, he reminded himself. Once there was real peace, a peace that could be trusted – Well, he could go on from there when he came to that.

The following evening, with really no forethought about it, Vic had a nightcap with Melinda in her room. She had not asked him into her room, he had simply brought her highball in to her and sat down, on a chair. But once there, he was uncomfortable, and began talking to her about getting some new curtains for her room.

'Oh, I don't care,' Melinda said. 'Curtains're awfully expensive, and after all who sees them?'

'That's right, who sees them? – Well, you.'

'I never look at them.' She was sitting in front of her dressing-table, brushing her hair. 'You know, Vic, I'm glad I didn't go away with Tony. I like you better,' she said matter-of-factly. 'You don't mind, do you?'

'No-o.'

'Well, do you?' She smiled at him.

He found her self-consciousness fascinating. 'No.'

'I'm glad you behaved the way you did. About Charley, too.'

'What do you mean "behaved"?'

'Oh – you never really lost control, and yet they both knew you didn't like them and wished they'd disappear. Maybe Tony did just disappear. Go to another town, I mean.' She waited.

'Well, I'm glad you realize that,' he said gently, after a moment. 'You may hear from him some day – a note of apology. He's got a conscience.'

'A conscience? Do you think so?'

'More than De Lisle had, anyway.'

'We'll never hear from him, will we?'

'Not bloody likely. Poor guy.'

'They're both poor guys – compared to you.' She was standing by her night table lamp now, working at one nail with an emery board.

'What makes you suddenly think that?'

'You think so, don't you?'

'Yes. But you've never thought so, even when we were first married.'

'Oh, Vic, that's not true!'

'I can remember right after we were married. You were happy and yet you weren't. You couldn't make up your mind if you'd made a mistake or if you couldn't do any better. So your eye started roving – long before you did.'

'I just stare at people,' she said, with a shy smile.

He smiled in return.

'Aren't I staring at you lately?'

'Yes. Why?'

'I have my reasons.'

'I'll bet you have!' He laughed.

She went wide-eyed, off balance. 'Don't kid me, Vic.'

'Did Trixie tell you the joke she heard today? Two turtles were walking—'

'And don't change the subject. For Christ's sake, I'm trying to be nice!' she yelled.

He smiled, appreciatively. She sounded like herself again.

'I just meant – I was trying to tell you that I admire you and that I like you. I like everything you do. Even your keeping snails. And I'm sorry for the way I've acted in the past.'

'That speech sounds as difficult as a grade school valediction.'

'Well, it isn't difficult. I made it – because I think I have quite a lot to make up for.'

'Melinda, what're you up to?'

She came towards him. 'Can't we try again, Vic?'

'Of course,' he said, smiling. 'I've been trying all along.'

'I know.' She touched his hair.

He barely kept from flinching. He stared at the edge of the rug on the other side of the room. He loathed her touch. It was insulting, he felt, simply insulting, considering all that had happened. He was glad when she took her hand away.

'Tomorrow's Saturday,' she said. 'Shall we make a picnic lunch and go out somewhere with Trixie?'

'I'd like to, but I promised Horace to go to Wesley with him to pick out some building materials. He's building a shed. Isn't it getting a little cold for picnics?'

'I don't think so.'

'What's the matter with Sunday?'

'I think Trixie's doing something Sunday.'

'Oh. Well, maybe you and I can go on a picnic Sunday,' he said pleasantly. 'Good night, Melinda. Sleep well.' He went out.

26

Trixie was doing something on Sunday. A little boy named Georgie Tripp was having a party and Trixie was invited and wanted to go. Vic had to drive her there at one in the afternoon. Trixie had thought she knew how to get to where the Tripps lived – it was out of town on a country road, and she had been there before – but she got lost, and Vic had to go back to the house for the directions that Mrs Tripp had given to Melinda by telephone that morning. When Vic got back to the house he found Melinda on the telephone talking to Don Wilson. Her back was to him as she stood at the telephone in her room, and for some reason, perhaps because he hadn't closed the car door, she hadn't heard him come back. He knew that from her intense voice as she said, 'I don't know, Don. I can't tell you anything ... No.' And then Vic's steps made a sound on the hall floor – he was not trying to walk quietly, was simply approaching slowly, though he was wearing his rubber-soled sports shoes – and Melinda turned and looked startled. Then she smiled into the telephone and said, 'Well, that's all for now. Got to go. Good-bye.'

'I think I'd better take that paper with the directions, after all,' Vic said. 'Trixie got lost.'

Melinda picked up the paper from her night table and handed

it to him. The frightened surprise was still on her face, and it reminded Vic a little of her expression when he fed her scrambled eggs late at night, except that now she was not drunk.

'How's Don?' Vic asked, already turning to go out of the house.

'Oh, all right, I suppose.'

'Well, see you in about half an hour,' Vic said, smiling. 'Maybe a little more.'

Vic was back from the Tripps' in thirty-five minutes and they started off almost at once.

'Do you mind if we go to the quarry?' Melinda asked. 'Why not, since we haven't got Trixie?'

'That's right, why not?' he said agreeably. He spent the next few seconds reviewing the tones of her voice, trying to decide if she suspected anything about the quarry or not, got tired of it, and tired of the piddling mentality – his own, after all – that had prompted him to wonder if she suspected anything. What if she did? It wasn't going to ruffle him. He could see himself and Melinda in a few minutes, huddled by a wind-blown fire chewing chicken bones, cave men without a roof. He chuckled.

'What's the matter?' she asked.

'Oh, nothing. I'm just happy, I guess.'

'Sometimes I think you're losing your mind. Did you ever think that?'

'I probably lost it years ago. Nothing to worry about.' As he approached the overgrown lane that went off the dirt road to the quarry, he asked, 'Is this about the place?'

'Don't you know?'

'We haven't been here in so long.'

No reaction.

The twigs, harsh and more leafless now, scratched at the sides of his car as it lumbered through the lane. Then they came out on the familiar flat in front of the excavation and stopped. Vic remarked that it was a fine clear day, and Melinda murmured some reply. She looked as if she were pondering a tack again. But it wouldn't be a tack about the quarry, Vic thought. He began to whistle as he gathered kindling for a fire. He let his search for kindling take him to the edge of the quarry, within six feet of the spot where Cameron had gone over. The little inlet where Cameron had sunk was half in shadow, but nothing seemed to be floating there. Any stains, of course, would probably be invisible from this height, but he squatted on his heels, rested his chin on his thumb, and peered for them, anyway. Nothing that he could see. When he stood up, turning at the same time, Melinda was not five feet away. She was approaching him with a solemn, set expression, and instinctively he braced his feet and smiled.

'Well, I've got this much,' he said, holding up some wood he had gathered. 'Shall we try it?' He walked towards the rock they had selected as a shelter for the fire, but Melinda did not follow him. Vic looked back when he got to the rock, and saw her staring down at the quarry. He wondered if she was going to propose a walk down the path to the bottom, and he decided that under no circumstances would he go down. Not that the place made him uneasy, he thought, but that there might be bloodstains and she might notice them. They might not look like rust stains. But at this moment she had no plans. He could tell that from her relaxed, purposeless stance at the rim of the quarry. After a moment she came back towards him and proposed having a drink.

They poured two glasses of iced Scotch and water from the thermos and ate a devilled egg as a canapé. The fire was doing nicely after a stubborn start. It was certainly not warm, but Melinda stoically took off her polo coat, spread it to lie on, and stretched out on the rock facing the fire. She was wearing her old buff-coloured corduroy slacks and her old brown sweater that had holes at the elbows. They had forgotten to bring the lap rug, Vic realized. Vic sat down, rather uncomfortably, on the rock to one side of Melinda.

'What did Tony really say to you that day he took a ride with you?' Melinda asked suddenly.

'I told you what he said.'

'I don't believe it.'

'Why not?'

She was still staring into the fire. 'Didn't you take him for a little ride and just dump him somewhere – dead?'

'Dead how?'

'Maybe strangled,' she said with surprising calm. 'Didn't you dump him somewhere in the woods?'

Vic gave a short laugh. 'Good lord, Melinda.' He was waiting for the quarry, perhaps, to cross her mind. She might have been going over, now, all the places in the woods where he might have dropped a body. Melinda knew these roads so well. Hadn't she thought of the quarry? Or would she think that he couldn't possibly have caught a big fellow like Cameron enough off his guard to have pushed him over? That was Vic's only explanation of her not thinking of the quarry. 'Aren't you getting hungry?' Vic asked. 'I'm ready for a piece of chicken.'

Melinda dragged herself up to help Vic unload the picnic basket. Roger was very interested in the chicken, but he was not allowed to have any. Vic sent him off chasing a stick. Then he and Melinda – just as he had foreseen – huddled near the fire and chewed their chicken, but Vic wondered if even in primitive times a man and woman whose relationship was more or less marital had ever known such mistrust of each other. The conversation of a few minutes before had not dulled Melinda's appetite for lunch. Vic smiled, watching her concentration on a chicken breast. They talked of buying Trixie a bicycle for Christmas. It was Vic's idea.

Then Melinda said, 'You know, Vic, I think you killed Charley and Tony, too – so why not admit it to me? I can take it.'

Vic smiled a little, his suspicions confirmed. The purpose of her sweetness and light lately had been to make him believe she was on his side. 'And then have you go to the police and tell them I've made a confession?'

'A wife can't testify against her husband, I've heard.'

'I've heard that she doesn't have to. She can.'

'But I just meant – as long as I know it—'

'Is this all you and Wilson can dream up between you?' he asked. 'It isn't good enough.'

'You admit it, then?' She looked at him, her eyes full of triumph.

'No, I do not,' he said quietly, though he felt angry. Or perhaps it was only embarrassment that he felt, for her. He remembered her embarrassing pretence of affection for him the night he had sat in her room. His anger drove him up. He wandered to the edge of the quarry again and looked down.

And there now in the twinkling water, he saw it. It was next to the step where he had pushed Cameron off, parallel with the edge of the step, just where one might have expected the corpse to rise, if it rose. It had risen.

'Coffee, Vic?' Melinda's voice called.

He peered harder, not bending his body because he did not want to arouse Melinda's curiosity, but tensing himself to concentrate all the power of his eyes. One end was lower than the other. It looked rather beige, but that could be caused by the damnable twinkling of the water lightening Cameron's brown tweed jacket. The weight at one end might be the rock in his trousers. At any rate, the chain had come off.

'Don't you want your coffee, Vic?'

He took a last staring look, trying to estimate how conspicuous the form would be to an ordinary person standing where he was, an ordinary unsuspecting person. Anyone seeing it would look twice, however, might even go down to investigate, especially if the Cameron story crossed his mind.

Vic turned slowly. 'Coming,' he said, and began to walk back.

Though Vic might have proposed leaving almost immediately,

in order to hear the radio concert he usually listened to on Sunday afternoons, he felt this would have been a small concession to his anxiety, so he waited until Melinda had had her coffee and a cigarette and suggested leaving herself. They packed the basket together.

They were home by three-twenty-five, and Vic at once turned on the radio in the living-room. He heard the throbbing, urgent beat of the fourth movement of Shostakovich's Fifth Symphony. At least he thought it was the fourth movement. He was in no mood to care whether he was right or not. He found the music somewhat disturbing, but he kept it on.

Before the concert was over, Melinda came out of her room, went out to his car and came in again. 'Vic, I left my scarf. I put it under a rock and I guess I forgot it.'

'Would you like me to go back for it?' he asked.

'Oh, not now, you're listening to the concert. Maybe you can get it tomorrow on your way to or from work, if you don't mind. Or I will. I kind of like that scarf. I folded it and put it under a rock pretty close to the fire, on the left facing the fire.'

'All right, honey. I'll bring it home at lunch.' Vic remembered it with the stone weighing it down. It showed how upset he was, he thought, that he had not noticed it when they were packing up everything else.

After dinner that evening, when Vic was reading in the living-room, Melinda came in from her room and asked Vic if he wanted a nightcap. Vic said he didn't think he did. Melinda went into the kitchen to fix herself one. On her way back through the living-room she said, 'You don't have to get that scarf at noon tomorrow, if you don't want to, because I have a lunch date and I won't be in at noon, anyway.'

'All right,' he said. He wasn't going to ask any questions. She had made at least two telephone calls from her room that evening, he thought.

27

The next day, Vic left the printing plant about a quarter of an hour earlier than usual to go home for lunch, though his times for leaving at noon and in the evening were so irregular that no one would have remarked a fifteen-minute difference one way or the other. He drove to the quarry between Wesley and East Lyme. This time he had taken a length of strong rope – clothesline – with him from the garage, and he intended to use one end of it to secure a good-sized rock and the other end to circle Cameron's body under the arms. It was a bright sunshiny day, and Vic did not tarry to have another look at the corpse in the water before he descended the path. He was careful going down, not wanting to tear his trousers on the brush or to scuff his shoes.

Once on the flat, he approached the place slowly, avoiding looking at the corpse until he was almost at the edge of the step.

It was a roll of paper – water-soaked pulp paper frayed at the end and tied in two places that he could see with twine. The surprise, the absurdity of it made him almost angry for a moment. Then he sighed, and the ache that went through his body made him realize how tense he had been.

He looked up at the blue sky and over at the rugged crest of the opposite side of the quarry. Nothing looked down at him but a few trees. He looked back at the roll of paper. One end was lower than the other, and it was about four-fifths submerged. Vic wondered idly what kept it afloat, wondered if it had a wooden spool of some sort in its centre. If he had been able to reach it with his foot, he would have shoved it out of the corner, but it was just beyond his reach. It had probably been in the quarry for months, drifting here and there with the wind. He moved closer to the edge, and stared straight down at the spot where Cameron had gone off. He could faintly see the horrible-looking step, yards below in the water, and it looked quite pale, as if nothing rested on it.

He turned around and looked for the bloodstains. There weren't any. It was as if another trick had been played on him. Then he saw the slight reddish discoloration between some little stones. What had happened, he realized, was that the rain or the wind had spread quite a bit of limestone dust and little fragments of stone over the stains. Pushing the stones aside with his shoe, he could see the stain now, a streak about four inches long and an inch wide, this one. But it was so pale by this time. Not worth bothering about. He looked around his feet critically. Not a single stain showed except the one he had deliberately exposed. He really might have saved himself a trip down here, he thought. Carefully, using his hand, he brushed the stones and the dust back over the stain that he had uncovered.

'Hi, there!' called a voice, and the other side of the quarry echoed it.

Vic looked straight up and saw a man's head and shoulders above the edge of the cliff, and recognized him almost instantly as Don Wilson. 'Hi!' Vic called back. He had stood up. Now he began to walk casually back towards the path that led up, stiff with terror and shame suddenly, because he remembered hearing – less than two minutes ago – a small, very distant-sounding impact which he had decided to ignore, and which he now realized must have been Wilson's car door closing. He might have been prepared if he had paid attention to it, but he had thought it came from farther away than the flat above where his own car was.

Wilson was moving towards Vic along the top, obviously looking for a path. He found it and plunged down. Vic, already on the path at a place too narrow to pass anyone, went back down the distance he had climbed. Wilson was down quickly, skidding and clutching.

'What're you doing?' Wilson asked.

'Oh, taking a walk. Melinda left her scarf somewhere.'

'I know. I've got it,' Wilson said, holding it up. 'What's the rope for?'

'I just happened to find it,' Vic said. 'Looks practically new.'

Wilson nodded, looked around him, and Vic saw his eyes fix suddenly on the roll of paper in the water.

'How've you been, Don? How's June?'

Wilson went down on the flat, apparently for a better look. He stopped short as if he, too, were surprised to find it merely a roll of brown paper. Then Vic saw Wilson look down at his feet, trying to see what he had been interested in on the rock. Vic started up the path again. Wilson was Melinda's luncheon companion, Vic supposed, and she had probably asked him to pick up the scarf on the way to Little Wesley. As simple as that. Simple and ghastly.

'Hey!' Wilson called.

Vic stopped and looked back. They had a clear view of each other. Wilson was stooped at the place where Vic had uncovered the stain.

'Is this what you were looking at? These look like bloodstains! I'm pretty sure they're bloodstains!'

Vic hesitated, deliberately. 'I thought so, too, but I think they're rust,' he said, and started to climb again.

Wilson was trying to trace the stains to the water, Vic saw. 'Hey, wait a minute!' Wilson called and walked towards him, his hands in his trench-coat pockets, his upturned face scowling. He stubbed his toe on a rock and came on. 'What do you know about those stains? Why were you trying to cover them up?'

'I wasn't trying to cover them up,' Vic said, and went on climbing.

'Listen, Vic, is this where you killed Cameron? I'm going to have the police take a look at this, you know. I'm going to ask them to take a look in the water. How does that make you feel?'

It made him feel naked and vulnerable. He hated presenting his backside to Wilson as he climbed the path. When he got to the top, he saw that Wilson's car was deep among the trees, standing in the lane. Wilson must have recognized his car and deliberately stopped out of earshot to spy on him. 'If your car's blocking the lane,' Vic said to Wilson as he came up the path, 'would you please back it up? Or come on through?'

Wilson looked confused and angry for a moment, then lurched off in the direction of the lane. It was a minute or so before Vic heard his car start, and he waited a few moments longer to find out what Wilson was going to do, and heard the motor approaching. Vic got into his own car and started it. He was thinking that if he got rid of the other snow chain in the back of his car, the one on Cameron wouldn't be very definitely identifiable. But there was, of course, Melinda, who would be glad to identify it, and who would probably say she could identify it when she really couldn't. Vic moved his car as soon as he could, and gave Don a wave as he went by him.

His one chance, Vic thought, was that Wilson might not be able to persuade the police to dredge the quarry. But if the police were convinced that the stains were blood – and, unfortunately, they would be convinced – they wouldn't need any prodding to look in the water. Vic glanced in the mirror for Don's car. He turned off the dirt road into the highway to Little Wesley without seeing it. Don was probably having a hard time getting through the lane.

Wilson would go to the police now, Vic supposed, just as soon as he got to Little Wesley. Vic pictured the police arriving at the house while he was calmly preparing his lunch, perhaps even eating it. He'd try bluffing Wilson again. The police already knew that Wilson was a troublemaker. The police were, after all, on his side. He might be able to discourage the police from going to look at the bloodstains, Vic thought. All it would take would be coolness.

But he knew it wouldn't go like that. The police would take a look at the bloodstains. If they wouldn't Wilson would inform Cameron's company, or inform Havermal.

Vic did not quite know what to do.

He thought of Trixie. The Petersons would take her, he thought, if anything happened to him. He stopped thinking about that. That was defeatism. Melinda would get her, anyway. That was worse to think about.

But still he did not know quite what to do.

He would go on about his business. That was the only way he could see it.

He had expected Melinda to be gone when he got to the house. Her car was in the garage. Vic got out of his car quietly, without shutting the door, and went into the living-room. Melinda was on the telephone in her room, and he heard her trying to end the conversation quickly, because she knew he had come in.

She came into the room, and he knew from her face that she had been talking to Don. Her face was a confusion of surprise, triumph, and terror. Then, as he kept walking towards her, she took a step back. He smiled at her. She was dressed to go out, probably to meet Don at the Lord Chesterfield.

'I've just talked to Don,' she said unnecessarily.

'Oh, you've just talked to Don! What would you do without the telephone?' He walked past her into her room, wrapped the wire of her telephone around his wrist and yanked it from the wall box. 'Well, now you haven't got one!' Then he crossed the living-room to the telephone in the hall and yanked its wire out in the same manner, so hard that the box came off the wall.

Melinda was standing by the phonograph, really cringing against it in an attitude of exaggerated terror, it seemed to Vic, her mouth open and drawn down at the corners like a mask of tragedy. Medea. Mangler of children and castrator of husbands. Fate had overtaken her at last. He almost smiled. What was he doing after all? Walking towards her.

'Vic!'

'What, darling?'

'Don's coming!' she gasped. 'Don't do anything to me, Vic!'

He struck her on the side of the head. 'So Don's coming and who else and who else? Cameron and Charley and all the rest?' He struck her again.

She reached for the cloisonné vase on the top of the phono-graph, and knocked it off. Then he struck her again, and she was on her hands and knees on the floor.

'Vic! – *Help!*'

Always that cry to other people! His hands closed around her throat and he shook her. The stupid terror in her open eyes made his hands tighten all the more. Then suddenly he released her. 'Get up,' he said. After all, he did not want to kill her. She was coughing. 'Melinda—'

Then he heard a car outside and the last barrier of his anger broke and he threw himself on her. He imagined he saw Wilson's lank figure and scowling face coming in the door, and he put all the pressure he could on her throat, furious because she had made him furious. He could have won, he thought, without her. He could have won without the telephone that had brought Jo-Jo and Larry and Ralph and De Lisle and Cameron to the house: Ralph the mamma's boy, Cameron the pachyderm . . .

There was a shout at the front door, and then Wilson, self-righteous, unsmiling, meddling, was bending over Melinda, talking to her. Her lips had parted. There was a bluish look about her eyelids, or was it mascara? Or an illusion? Vic heard Wilson mutter to the empty air that she was dead, and then following the direction in which Wilson had looked, Vic saw a policeman standing.

'What're you smiling at?' the policeman demanded, unsmiling.

Vic was about to tell him – 'At faith, hope, and charity' – when the policeman took him by the arm. Vic stood up, enduring the loathsome touch, which after a moment became comical, like Melinda's panic, with his usual amenableness. Wilson was babbling behind him, and Vic heard the words 'quarry' and 'De Lisle' and 'Cameron's blood', and he kept on walking with the men who were not fit to black his boots. He saw Trixie romping up the lawn and stopping in surprise as she saw him with the policeman; but frowning at the lawn, Vic could see that she wasn't really there. The sun was shining and Trixie was alive, somewhere.

But Melinda is dead and so am I, he thought. Then he knew why he felt empty: because he had left his life in the house behind him, his guilt and his shame, his achievements and failures, the failure of his experiment, and his final, brutal gesture of petulant revenge.

He began to walk with a spring in his step (the walk to the policeman's car at the bottom of the driveway seemed endless), and he began to feel free and buoyant, and guiltless, too. He looked at Wilson, walking beside him, still intoning his tedious information, and, feeling very calm and happy, Vic kept looking at Wilson's wagging jaw and thinking of the multitude of people like him on the earth, perhaps half the people on earth were of his type, or potentially his type, and thinking that it was not bad at all to be leaving them. The ugly birds without wings. The mediocre who perpetuated mediocrity, who really fought and died for it. He smiled at Wilson's grim, resentful, the-world-owes-me-a-living face, which was the reflection of the small, dull mind behind it, and Vic cursed it and all it stood for. Silently, and with a smile, and with all that was left of him, he cursed it.

Gillian Flynn on Patricia Highsmith:
The author of *Gone Girl* on how the suspense-fiction master influenced her own creation of charming psychopaths

No one writes sympathetic sociopaths as well as Patricia Highsmith. Except, perhaps, Highsmith's literary heir, Gillian Flynn, author of the chilling, twisty psychological thriller *Gone Girl*.

So maybe it's not so surprising that when Ms. Flynn was invited to host the *Wall Street Journal*'s book club, which brings in prominent authors to analyze their favorite books, she chose Ms. Highsmith's 1957 novel, *Deep Water*, a thriller about a suburban couple bent on mutual destruction.

Set in a sleepy, affluent suburb, *Deep Water* unfolds with a drumbeat of quiet dread as Vic Van Allen, an outwardly affable, well respected husband and father, broods over his wife Melinda's flagrant infidelity. Vic and Melinda's marriage implodes in front of all their friends and neighbors as Vic's patience evaporates and bad things start happening to Melinda's lovers.

The authors share an apparent affinity for charming psychopaths. (Highsmith, who died in 1995 and is best known for her series about the murderous impersonator Tom Ripley, called her protagonists 'my psychopath heroes.')

'It's a little on the nose that I love her so much,' said Ms. Flynn. 'I read *Ripley* first, back in the day, and what a revelation her writing was. There was this sense of impending dread. She's a very spare writer. I remember having my body temperature physically altered, becoming physically chilled at some point.'

*

When did you first read *Deep Water* and what struck you about it? It's not one of Highsmith's better-known works.

About ten or fifteen years ago, I came across it in a used-book store. I remember thinking, 'Why has no one told me about it?' People know her for Ripley *or* Strangers on a Train *but don't know a lot of her other stuff. And, it being a marital thriller where all the phobias and fears and darkness are based mostly inside of a couple's home, that has always interested me, that in-your-face warfare between a husband and wife.*

Both *Deep Water* and *Gone Girl* provide glimpses inside loveless, antagonistic marriages. You've previously said that in *Gone Girl*, the real mystery isn't the disappearance so much as the marriage itself and the question of why the characters stay together. The same could be said of *Deep Water*. Why do you think domestic life is such a ripe setting for suspense writing?

When you decide to pair yourself off with someone for life, it's supposed to be this psychologically and emotionally safe place you can retreat to. And often it doesn't turn out like that, and there's something very frightening about revealing not just your emotions, but your day-to-day existence to someone. It only takes a small step forward to get to the idea that wow, if anyone could really do me in, it would be this person. They've got all the goods on me.

What makes Highsmith such a masterful suspense writer?

She doesn't give anything away. She does not do your work for you. She gives you all the information. She's a very precise writer. You picture her using an eye dropper to put each word on the page. Everything is very specifically put in place, but she makes you do a lot of wonderful homework in having to think about her characters and put yourself in

*their positions and try to figure them out a little bit. She has a strange
ability to make completely unreasonable emotions and actions seem
extremely reasonable, where you find yourself completely empathizing
with a sociopath and murderer. There's something incredibly chilling
about that, looking up from a book and finding that you've been root-
ing for an average person's murder.*

The structure of this book is interesting because it's not a mystery
at all – a murder occurs almost right away and we witness it
directly, and the identity of the killer is never in question. Why
do you think this structure works, and how was she able to build
so much suspense into the story without resorting to any mystery
tropes?

*I think it's because from the second Vic commits that first murder you
realize that there's no good resolution here. Melinda's not controllable
in the way he thought she was. He's definitely not controllable in the way
she thought he was. And they're both stubborn and psychologically
entwined enough that they're not going to part, so you just know that it's
going to lead to something very bad for one or both of them. And it's that
delicious feeling of trying to figure out where it's going to go, but because
they've both become so unpredictable, in a way that's very true to their
characters. It doesn't feel cheap, it feels like two people going off the rails
together.*

You and Highsmith both achieve something quite remarkable in
your novels by making us root for the villain. How do you walk
the line between leading the reader along and delivering a really
shocking twist, but also making the revelation feel perfectly
believable in retrospect, like we should have seen it coming?

*To me, you're always playing fair when you're inside another person's
head. You're giving voice to the character's thoughts. You're not*

manipulating the reader if they find the person empathetic. Anytime you get that close inside a person's personality and thought process you're going to feel empathy toward them, which is exactly what a sociopath depends upon. I love that sense of feeling lured in and knowing against all better judgment that you should not be in communion with them, but finding yourself continually aligned with them. It adds this delicious uneasy feeling to it.

For anyone who's read your work and Highsmith's, the influence is obvious. Are there any specific techniques that you learned from her?

She does a great job of trusting her characters. She puts a lot of faith in building her characters and knowing her characters and letting them do the heavy lifting. Her stuff isn't overly plotted. It has this sense of wonderful inevitability about it. To me, the things that are suspenseful, that I find frightening, aren't someone jumping out of a closet or those kind of big scares, but instead that slow build of dread, and she does that really well. She kind of takes you by the hand and walks you toward the cliff. I like that sensation, and that's what I try to do in my books. You're kind of being pulled along, but the sense of inevitability is drawn not necessarily out of circumstance, but by these personalities that have been brought together.

LITTLE TALES OF MISOGYNY

Patricia Highsmith

'Extraordinary stories ... etched in acid and unforgettable. Let the reader beware' *Financial Times*

The title says it all. Long out of print, this cult classic resurfaced with a vengeance – from the man who makes the mistake of asking his prospective father-in-law for his daughter's hand in marriage, to Oona the alluring cave-woman. In these provocative, often hilarious, sketches, Highsmith turns our next-door neighbours into sadistic psychopaths lying in wait among white picket fences and manicured lawns.

'Splendidly repulsive' *Observer*

'Vicious black humour' *Guardian*

'For eliciting the menace that lurks in familiar surroundings, there's no one like Patricia Highsmith' *Time*

PATRICIA HIGHSMITH